THE RUMOR GAME

THE RUMOR GAME

BY SONA CHARAIPOTRA &
DHONIELLE CLAYTON

HYPERION

Los Angeles   New York

First Edition, March 2022

10 9 8 7 6 5 4 3 2 1

FAC-021131-22070

Printed in the United States of America

This book is set in Adobe Garamond Pro/Adobe

Designed by Torborg Davern

Library of Congress Cataloging-in-Publication Data

Clayton, Dhonielle, author. • Charaipotra, Sona, author.
Title: The rumor game / by Dhonielle Clayton & Sona Charaipotra.
Description: First edition. • Los Angeles ; New York : Hyperion, 2022.
Audience: Ages 14–18. • Audience: Grades 10–12. • Summary: At Foxham Prep, a posh private school for Washington, D.C.'s elite, a rumor gains momentum as it collects followers on social media, pulling three girls into its path—Bryn, who wants to erase all memories of the mistake she made last summer; cheer captain Cora, who desperately wants to believe in her boyfriend's faithfulness; and shy Georgie, newly hot after a summer at fat camp and ready to reinvent herself—but who can stop a dangerous rumor once it takes on a life of its own?

Identifiers: LCCN 2021029603 • ISBN 9781368014144 (hardcover) • ISBN 9781368044394 (ebook)

Subjects: CYAC: Rumor—Fiction. • Social media—Fiction. • Popularity—Fiction. • Dating (Social customs)—Fiction. • Bullying—Fiction. • African Americans—Fiction. • East Indians—United States—Fiction. • Private schools—Fiction. • Schools—Fiction. • Washington (D.C.)—Fiction. • LCGFT: Novels.

Classification: LCC PZ7.1.C59472S Ru 2022 • DDC [Fic]—dc23

LC record available at https://lccn.loc.gov/2021029603

ISBN 978-1-368-01414-4

Reinforced binding

Visit www.hyperionteens.com

To all the girls who have had things whispered about them.

And to all the girls whose truths remain unheard.

PART ONE

THE RUMOR

rumor [ˈrü-mər]: *noun*

1) a story or statement in general circulation without confirmation of certainty as to facts
2) gossip; hearsay
3) *archaic.* a continuous, confused noise; clamor; din
4) can destroy your life

From: Online Petition
Attn: Bryn Colburn
Sent: Thursday, October 10, 7:29 A.M.
Subject: Stand with the Student Body, Move Up Special Election!

Attn: Principal Rollins of Foxham Preparatory Academy
REMOVE BRYN COLBURN IMMEDIATELY

By signing this petition, the students of Foxham Preparatory Academy stand in solidarity and implore you and the school faculty to remove senior Bryn Colburn as student body president in order to keep our academic environment safe. She doesn't represent good morals and doesn't have the wherewithal to represent our community. She is unfit to lead us. The special election on November 8 is too far away, and the students deserve to have their voices heard immediately. Remove her and appoint Cora Davidson as interim president until the students cast their ballots.

Click here to sign our petition

BRYN

FRIDAY, OCTOBER 11
9:00 P.M.

THE THING ABOUT THIS YEAR IS THAT I MIGHT DO ANYTHING to get my old life back.

Mom would use her rehab checklist to flag this new attitude as . . . headed for trouble. Maybe. Potentially.

But I think it finally makes me feel like myself again. Determined. Focused. Razor-sharp.

"You sure we should be doing this?" Georgie asks, obsessively flipping down my car's vanity mirror. Her thick black hair is everywhere: across the car seat headrest, on her shoulders, some of it piled in a loose bun. I don't understand how she has so much, how it grew out so fast from the kiddie bowl cut she still had at the end of eighth grade when we stopped carpooling. Mine barely grows, and my side ponytail sits on my shoulder like the sad, wet tail of a dog.

When I stop at a red light, I pet my hair, trying not to think about how the doctor said stress has thinned it out around my temples, and how at some point it might actually turn into an accidental mullet. All on its own. Then everyone will think I'm a trashy white girl from

Hicksville, Virginia, while Georgie's a reincarnated Indian goddess.

I should get hair vitamins or something.

"Shouldn't your hands be on the wheel?" she says, her nose crinkling up. I notice she's gotten freckles on her face. I didn't know people with brown skin could get freckles, and I feel stupid at the thought. I've known her so long. Well, not really. She's been my next-door neighbor, forced-carpool-person-type thing forever. I don't actually *know her* know her. But since our fathers started working together this summer, it's been all "Can you hang out with Georgie and make a good impression?" blah, blah. If I'm honest with myself—like the Colburn family therapist wants me to be—then I'd admit I don't have any real friends left and she's the only person I have to hang out with. It's been five terrible, lonely weeks since school started.

I wave my hands higher in the air. "It's fine."

The light turns green. I rev the engine a little just to make her jump. I laugh. She laughs, too, but it's forced.

"This is a bad idea, don't you think?" she asks.

"I can still go places," I remind her, but I catch her eye, her message clear: *But for how much longer?* The whole school has turned against me because of what happened at the end of the summer.

But I have a plan to turn it all around. I have the whole thing mapped out in my notebook. My get-my-life-back-on-track plan.

"I need to talk to him. If I can just get him to hear me out . . ."

"*Him* him?"

"Yeah."

"You could text him."

"I've been doing that for weeks. He leaves me on read." I don't want to say my ex-boyfriend's name out loud yet. "And I'm not a girl who will be ignored." I try to summon the old courage I always had to speak my mind.

5

She shrugs. "We just shouldn't be going."

"Why not? Those are just your fears talking. Have faith." When your dad is a politician, you get good at convincing people to do things.

I turn right, then left, like my car's on autopilot. I could drive the whole way to my ex-friend Cora's house with my eyes closed. I need to talk to her, too, but one person at a time. First, Jase. Second, Cora. Third, Mom.

Georgie winces. "I can think of a hundred different reasons why. Number one: We're *not* invited."

I steal another glimpse of her. She's so beautiful now. A summer away and she doesn't even feel like that nerd anymore.

"What?" she asks, catching me looking at her.

"Nothing," I reply.

I wonder if she pities me because I've lost all my friends. Or if her dad also pushed her to hang out with me. If it's mutually beneficial at all.

"We're almost there, so . . ." I start.

"So we could still turn back."

She looks at me. Her eyes are bigger and brighter now that she's learned to line them, now that she's paying attention to the way she looks, now that she's become a new version of herself. She's lost at least forty pounds.

"How did it feel . . . to, like, lose all that weight?" It just comes out all hard, and I wish I'd softened it.

"Fine. The program was mostly running and gymnastics." She zips the words up in her mouth and volleys between watching my speed on the dashboard and texting on her phone.

I turn onto Cora's street. "We're here."

Cora's circular driveway is packed with luxury cars, even some Secret Service vehicles, as if it were a black-tie soiree instead of a high

school party. Her house is impressive. Better than the ones in my neighborhood. It's really old-school, a miniature—but not by much—of a
traditional plantation home, with pristine white shutters and a manicured lawn, the tulips color-coded like a scene out of one of those old
racist Southern movies. Except the family that lives here is Black. Cora's
dad is a Harvard-bred lawyer who works for the president. Cora's twin
sister, Millie, is a genius, and already at Harvard, even though she's only
seventeen and should be a senior like the rest of us.

I screech the car to a stop.

"Careful," Georgie says, and I can feel the anxiety creeping up her
spine and settling onto her shoulders.

"I thought I saw a cat."

"Where? I didn't see anything."

"It's fine, Georgie. Chill. Still getting used to the brakes on the new
car, okay?" I turn the engine off and glare at the Nigerian flag plastered
on the back window of the SUV in front of us. Abaeze Onyekachi's
car. An angry knot hardens in me at the sight of it. Wonder if anyone's
slashed his tires before. Wonder if I should be the first to do it.

"Do I look all right?" Georgie asks, flipping down the car's vanity
mirror to check her hair and makeup for the seventh time. She's wearing an expensive V-neck tee and strategically ripped-up skinny jeans,
and the whole outfit hugs her a little, but in all the right places. I picked
it out for her, modeled how to wear it correctly. We spent hours in my
pool-house-turned-bedroom going through it all earlier tonight.

"Why are you stressing?" I ask. "I thought you didn't want to come?"

"This is, like, a big deal for me," she whispers. "It's my first real
party."

I guess it is. I used to see her watching me and my friends from her
window as we'd sneak out or have parties in my bedroom. Never once
did I think to invite her over. She was that kind of acquaintance you

couldn't take with you anywhere. Someone might say something. But she was perfectly nice. And boring.

"You look great," I say, and mean it.

"You picked everything out," she replies.

"But you're wearing it. Take credit." Always know how to sell yourself. A good politician gets that, too.

We walk around to the back, and bodies are everywhere—all the popular people from Foxham Prep and even some of their personal bodyguards. Our school is a place where kids with important parents go: diplomats, politicians, people who work for the government, celebrities, etc.

Some groups circle a fire pit on an elaborate patio, while others lounge around the heated pool. Heat lamps reach above the water like red-hot fingers. In the distance, a huge bonfire rages. Tiny sparks flicker in the air like fireflies. It's that weird blend of too warm for October during the day, but cool during the night. That's DC for you. Mid-Atlantic weather chaos.

I tug at my hair, braiding and unbraiding it, ignoring the split ends, and thinking about how different fall break was for me at this time last year. I was with Christine, Bian, Cora, Baez, Rico, and the rest of the crew in Ocean City. We laughed. We tanned. We fell asleep outside.

People stop and look up at Georgie and me. Some giggle. Others whisper to each other. Boys from the lacrosse team—some friends with Jase—nudge and point.

Heat gathers in my cheeks. I know I have an ugly batch of hives dotted all over my neck.

Calm down, I tell myself, willing my fear response to chill the hell out.

A few people call out at us. At me, really. Taunts.

Georgie bristles and yanks me forward.

There are three kegs set up in the outdoor kitchen, along with chips, salsa, guacamole, fruit salad, and platters of finger foods. Uninspired fare. Lackluster. That was my role. Cora hasn't found anyone else to help menu plan. Clearly.

I wave at all my hecklers, bowing.

"Why'd you do that?" Georgie whispers hard.

"What was I supposed to do?"

"Ignore them."

"I can't *ignore them*," I say.

If only she knew how true that was. I keep a file on my computer full of screenshots of social media comments and articles written about me after the incident happened. I recorded every word of every comment people made about me. I tracked all the lies, all the rumors. I watched it spiral. I had to know. I had to be prepared.

"Yes, you can. Pretend they aren't talking to you."

"Uh, thanks for the brilliant advice," I snap, then feel a pinch of regret when I see surprise flicker across her face.

"I know plenty about ignoring people, and about being ignored," she says. "Or did you forget?" Her eyes burn into mine.

"I know." I touch her arm. I can't do this alone. "I'm sorry. I just . . . Let's get beers. I need a little liquid courage." I walk out of view of Jase's idiot friends.

"Too many calories. I'm going to go mix something"—she points over past the pool—"at that bar thing over there. Maybe seltzer or a diet soda. Be right back."

"Okay." I push away a twinge of fear as she walks away. I used to be afraid of nothing. I'd march into a party like this one and announce I had arrived, that the most stimulating conversation of the night could begin. But now my nerves feel like I've swallowed an earthquake.

I stare into the house through the windows. Couples find dark corners to curl up in. A group sits around a table, playing cards. People zip through the back door, wrapped in towels and headed for the pool. Last year, I was the first one over at Cora's house to set up, and the last one to leave the next day. I used to be somebody: someone you wanted to sit with at lunch or hang with in my pool-house bedroom, someone you hoped followed you back on social media.

Now no one talks to me. It's weird how one bad decision can change your entire high school status, your entire family, your entire life. And I need it to go away.

Focus on your list, I tell myself. *Jase first.*

I guzzle the beer in my cup and fill it again. I'm driving, so I know this will be the last one. But right now I need to soften the edges a little.

"Did you forget that no one likes you anymore?" Chance Olivieri points his camera at me, zooming in and out. It's old, clunky, vintage. "Have anything to say about it? Give me an exclusive and I *might* let you be part of my documentary."

My rival since the third grade. His greasy too-long hair flops over the camera, and his pale cheeks are permanently flushed. Everyone used to call him a clown and make fun of his rosacea.

"You wish. I won't be part of your trash, *and* I won't let you take student body president from me. You'll lose that special election."

"I won't . . . and we both know it. Nobody likes the scorned ex who bullies *and* almost kills the *other* woman. Not a good look. Never gets sympathy. Prepare yourself, sweetie." Chance pushes his camera closer to my face. "Plus, this documentary is going to win a prize one day. I'll be famous. It'll expose the bullshit social hierarchy of high school."

Yes, he's for real.

Chance Olivieri was the one who had the most to say after everything happened, like he reveled in sharing every newspaper headline and TV clip. Even made daily video recaps of what I did and all the bad press and comments swarming me and my family. My dad says he'll end up as a sleazy tabloid reporter or something one day. Doesn't have the vision to be a real journalist or filmmaker.

I put my hand up to block him. "You've been doing this stupid crap since ninth grade, and you've still got *nothing*. Maybe it's time to give it up and get a life," I spit back. "Or a girlfriend."

"Maybe you should get a boyfriend. Oh, wait, you almost killed the last one."

He blows a kiss at me.

I sneer and turn to walk away. I go past the pool. Everyone stares. Someone splashes at me. The back of my jeans get soaked. I bite my bottom lip. I refuse to cry. There have been too many tears.

Never cry when the cameras are on.

I spot Jase and some friends in the gazebo. The boys all dangle out of it, laughing and roughhousing.

My heart drops into my stomach. I need him to forgive me. I need him to tell people to stop attacking me online over what happened. I need to get all my friends back. He's the one who can make it all go away. I clench my fists and take a deep breath, then walk up.

The guys stop laughing and stare. Jase looks up, surprised. His cold blue gaze still sends a tingle through me. He has blond stubble, an almost beard now, and looks like the South Carolina beach boy he was meant to be. God, he's hot. No wonder I was so *into* him. Too into him.

"Can I talk to you for a second?"

They ooh and aah.

I keep my eyes squarely on him, not breaking contact, bracing for him to say no.

"Sure." He flashes a perfect smile, and his friends slap his arm and back.

But I don't care. That tiny word is an unexpected firework. One step forward.

He gets up and walks toward me. But not far enough away from the gazebo. Everyone snickers and listens, eager for a show. My heart beats so hard, I feel like I'm going to vomit it up.

"What's up?" His Southern accent slips out between slurred words.

"I just . . . just wanted to talk to you about what happened. I didn't get a chance to explain."

"Sure."

That word again. For some reason, it unsettles me. I'd been expecting a no, expecting to have to convince him. It knocks me off what I'd practiced when I imagined this moment. "It's . . . It was . . . my parents. That night. I'd found out something big . . . really bad. I wasn't thinking. I was super upset. It all got into my head, so when you didn't answer . . . I thought—I thought—"

Jase put his hand in the air. "It's okay."

My mouth drops open. "Really?" A weight starts to lift from my shoulders, and I'm not sure if it's the beer.

"I know where you're going with all this, and I get it," he replies.

"You do?" My heart lifts for the first time in weeks.

"Of course I do." He takes my hand. The heat of it sends a familiar surge through me. I want his touch back so much. "I know how crazy you are. Like your mom. Isn't she still in rehab? Shouldn't you be, too?" His charming smile darkens. "Like mother, like daughter. You're both nuts."

I stiffen and yank my hand back. Since the end of August, I've been called *crazy* 3,797 times and *nuts* 1,890 on all social media platforms. And who knows how many more times in group chats and private DMs—the ones I've been kicked out of.

Crazy is a terrible word.

Jase laughs, and it creates a ripple. The smirks, the chuckles, the pity, the hate. The guys break into raucous laughter.

"You don't know the whole story," I say. "If you would just let me—"

My pulse races, its beat flooding my ears. The pitch and crescendo of the laughter stretch and warp as if I'm trapped in a messed-up fun house where everything bounces back at me. The bodies blur. Party sounds become a nauseous hum. Like everything is underwater.

"I don't want to talk to you!" he yells. "Don't give a shit about what you have to say. I'm done with you. Sasha has better tits, anyways."

All the guys cheer. A knot hardens in my stomach. I clench my teeth.

I hold back rage tears as he fumbles toward the gazebo with his friends. I square my shoulders and walk away. *This was so stupid. It was too soon. I didn't think it through enough.* The rehearsal in my head, in my bedroom, in my notebook, jumbled. I'd even kept my distance the first several weeks of school to prepare. It all went wrong.

I have to find Georgie. We have to get out of here. I wipe my face.

Chance saunters past again with his camera. "*Tsk, tsk.* Show didn't go as planned, huh? No one buying your lies? Everyone knows what a bitch you are." He holds out a piece of paper and shakes it at me. "Want to sign this petition? I'm trying to get you removed as student body president a little early, you see. I've already got over fifty signatures."

"Shut up. Shut up. SHUT UP!"

"Wouldn't you like that? But nope, I'm good."

"I'm just looking for Georgie—and then trust me—I'll be out of here."

"She went in the house with Baez," he reported. "Even *she's* done with you."

My anger flashes hot. I shove him into the pool with his camera. He makes a huge splash.

That shuts him up good.

Bryn Colburn

Net loss of followers:
−3,528
Group chats:
0

Friday 9:34 PM

Bryn:

Where are you?

You said you were just getting seltzer.

Are you ignoring me?
Things went bad. I tried to talk to him.

I feel weird. I wanna go.

Friday 9:45 PM

Georgie:

I'm in line for the bathroom.
Spilled my drink.

Gimme a minute.

Friday 9:46 PM

Bryn:

I'll be in the car. Hurry up.

GEORGIE

FRIDAY, OCTOBER 11
9:43 P.M.

I CAN'T BELIEVE I'M HERE. IN CORA'S HOUSE. NEARLY IN Cora's bedroom. With Cora's boyfriend.

"There's a bathroom at the end of the hall. In Cora's room." A shirtless Abaeze Onyekachi leads me down a long hallway. Abaeze Onyekachi, the most popular boy in school, is helping me. Abaeze Onyekachi is breathing within a three-foot radius of me.

Baez, the guy everyone wants.

I'm sweating despite the AC blasting, and I'm shivering despite the sweat. My stomach is a mess of knots, and my brain is going like ten thousand miles a minute. Does not compute. About to explode. I've never been to an actual high school party—except for one with all Desi kids, but those don't really count, right? All the Indian kids get dragged to these family things with their parents. That's not a real party in my book, anyway.

My mum would be freaking out if she knew I was here. *I'm* sort of freaking out that I am here.

But brand-new me goes to parties. With Bryn's help. And it feels

16

really good. At least I look like I've got it together. Like I've done this a million times.

Except, you know, for all the sticky pink punch that's soaking through my new designer T-shirt, pooling right around where my belly used to be.

"You should be able to get cleaned up," he says with a smile. A very bright one.

Like every other person in school, I've always had a crush. Sort of. But he and Cora are practically married. The high school type of married. Been together forever. And even if I thought I had a shot, which I decidedly don't, you never go after someone's boyfriend. That's the rule for people who get to date. Or so I've heard.

His cologne leaves a trail, all musky and warm.

We've had at least two classes together every year since I moved here, and that's the thing about Baez. While everyone else just dismissed me as the big brown girl, he was always nice. Even when he didn't have to be. He understood what it was like to come to this country and start school not knowing anyone. His dad is a Nigerian diplomat, appointed here when Baez was twelve. Just before I got here. So he gets it. Not that we were, like, friends or anything. But still. He was assigned to be my student ambassador during my first month of school.

He glances back at me a few times, staring like I'm a stranger and not the girl who he's been in school with since seventh grade. It kind of makes me wonder if he thinks I'm a fangirl or something. I guess I am sort of a stranger now. I'm definitely not the old Georgie anymore.

OLD GEORGIE:

Height: 5'4"

Weight: Blocked out the numbers. Trust me. You would, too, if you had a mum who made you weigh in three times a day.

Pimpled, round face made even more attractive by a proper bowl cut.

Signature scent: sweat and baby powder, butter naan, and a top note of peanut M&M's from my secret lockbox.

Binge-eater.

T-shirts three sizes too large.

Straight-A student.

Nice to everyone.

Never been kissed.

From a famous family in India. And a total nobody here.

An immigrant.

Social media followers: ZERO.

Sometimes it still shocks me how much of me I lost this year. Feels like I lost a whole other person with the weight.

NEW GEORGIE:

Height: 5' 6"

Weight: The number Mum always wanted.

Smooth brown skin, thanks to the dermatologist. (But still too brown, according to Dadi.)

Long dark hair that flows past the strap of my new, smaller bra.

Cheekbones!

New signature scent: peaches and mint shampoo.

V-neck T-shirts, dangling jewelry.

Gym four times a week with Mum's trainer. New love of gymnastics. I can do a split!

No more binge-eating.

Straight-A student.

Princeton-bound.

A real first kiss.

Future girlfriend to somebody.

I almost stumble as I follow Baez down the hall.

Focus. Get out of your head.

The only conversation between Baez and me is the squishy noise our shoes make. Feels weird wearing them through the house, especially upstairs. And I wish I had the courage to make small talk. I've never been good at that. It comes out all tangled and "unintelligible," Mum says. She always reminds me that there's an art to gupshup, and I don't have the proper chitchat skills. Yet. I have a new body. Now I need the new personality to match.

Relax, I instruct myself. *Breathe.*

I have to say something. I *need* to say something. So I can be normal. "Too bad there's no wet T-shirt contest tonight," I say, like this is a teen movie and someone like me could ever be the star.

My stomach flips. I probably said the exact wrong thing, judging from the shocked look on Baez's face. But now he's taking in the way the wet pink splotches make my already-maybe-a-little-too-snug shirt stick to me. Heat crawls up my throat, settles in my cheeks. I've never had attention like this. I sort of like it. "Maybe I would have won."

I can't seem to keep my mouth from saying things my head hates me for.

Old Georgie would never have said anything to him at all. Let alone flirt. Let alone end up at this party in the first place, wearing a shirt this tight.

"Uh, yeah." He starts walking again. *What was I thinking?*

"Here it is." He opens a door for me and quickly follows me inside.

The massive bathroom has three entrances. One leads to the hallway, and the others to bedrooms. A marble-topped vanity with double sinks, ornate silver-framed mirrors. Casual, expensive, and elegant, but lived-in. Totally Cora. Totally the perfect Davidson family.

But it feels like the same old Georgie looks back at me: skin the color of chai boiled over, eyes tired but alert, those formerly bushy eyebrows worked into an impossibly fine arch by Mum's stylist.

We don't fit. Baez and I. Not like him and Cora.

Sometimes I wish I could find someone like him. Someone who matches me, inside and out. Someone who knows what I'm thinking before I say it and believes that roaming around the bookstore for an hour and then sharing a pizza is the perfect date, too. Someone who wants to kiss me. Maybe.

What if I was with him? I almost laugh at the thought. Guys like him don't date girls like me. Even if my parents magically decided to let me date, they'd never approve of Baez. Desi people aren't supposed to be with non-Desi people, according to Auntie rules. Closed-minded. And yeah, racist.

"You look different from last year," Baez says, the words slurring together.

"Yeah, I lost a small person," I joke, and it unexpectedly stings a little. He doesn't laugh.

I'm failing at this new-personality thing. And making myself feel shitty at the same time. Dr. Cat said it's internalized fatphobia to think about myself like that, but it's hard to turn it off in my head. Especially when it swarms all around me.

"I went to weight loss camp." Heat climbs up my back. I haven't really talked to anyone about it much. Or at all.

"My sister went to one two summers ago." His eyes are on me in the mirror.

"Did she lose what she wanted to?"

"Yeah. But I didn't want her to go. I've heard bad things about those places."

He's not wrong. Weight loss camps are definitely controversial. And definitely terrible if you think about it. But it's not like I had a choice. To my parents, appearances are everything. So they decided it was time I "do something" about my weight. And . . . other things. When you're a Desi kid—Desi girl, specifically—you do what you're told. You act right, dress right, get good grades. Go to an Ivy, marry someone *appropriate*. Whether you want to or not. "My mum made me go. Plus, Indian food isn't exactly diet-friendly. But always binge-worthy, which was my problem."

"Nigerian isn't diet-friendly either." He laughs. "But it's good."

My cheeks flush again. "I've been to your family's restaurant a few times with my mom and dad. It's great."

"Eh, too much of anything and you can get sick of it."

Don't I know it. Ever since I came back, my mother's been making me eat the same three "healthful" meals on rotation. "What I wouldn't do for a samosa," I say, grinning.

He smiles back, eyes crinkling. "Yeah, I get to go in on game days, but otherwise, no samosas for me either." Baez heads toward the linen closet and hands me a small towel. "I'll wait for you outside so you don't get lost getting back to the party."

"Uh, okay," I stammer, then close the door. I feel stupid. I didn't even say thank you.

I quickly take off my shirt and wash out the pink streak, watching the color run in the sink. I'll need bleach. I look around at all the expensive soaps and products. This bathroom is straight out of all the magazines I devoured when I first got to the United States. The ones I thought would teach me how to be American. The right clothes, the right hair, the right products, the right way to decorate your bedroom, the right energy.

A soft knock on the door startles me. "You okay in there?"

"Yeah, almost done," I call out too loud, terrified he might come in, even though he's given me no reason to be scared.

I yank the damp shirt back over my head and try to tousle my hair so it looks better.

He knocks again.

I pout my lips like the girls in magazines, then open the door.

"You good?" His eyes wander to my shirt, still damp.

"I tried, but couldn't get the stain out," I say, following his gaze.

"Lemme get Cora's hair dryer." He pushes past me into the bathroom and rummages in a cabinet under one of the sinks.

"Here it is," he says, pointing it at me like a gun. Then he hands it over. "Wanna try this? I can wait outside."

"Sure." I close the door behind me.

I plug in the dryer and blast the air onto the wet spot. After a minute, it's almost invisible. I take one last look at myself and open the door again. "That's better," I say to Baez, who's peering down at his phone.

"Good food photos!" he says, flashing my own sad social media feed back at me. "Especially that bucket of crabs at Larry's in Ocean City. Did you manage the whole thing?" His grin goes even wider when I nod. "That's how it's done."

My phone pings with a follow notification.

That makes me smile, too. And it makes me realize with a pang: *If I do kiss someone, I want to be the kind of girl who gets to kiss a guy like him.*

From: Dr. Catherine Hopkins
Attn: Jashan "Georgie" Khalra
Sent: Friday, October 11, 10:12 P.M.
Subject: Check-in/Hello!

Dear Georgie,

    I hope this email finds you well. It's been six weeks since your Greensprings Weight-Loss Program ended, and this email signals the start of our outpatient services. The support of Greensprings is available to you long after you've left us and is part of the package selected by your parents. The endeavor of readjusting to life at home brings new challenges, and we have resources set up to help you.

    I'll be introducing you to my colleague Dr. Divya Malhotra. She will schedule in-person sessions with you, picking up where we left off. In the meantime, please be sure to use your food and exercise diary daily. I've sent you three gymnastic programs in your area to look into, since you took such a liking to it. I'd also like you to work with Dr. Malhotra on exploring your family's emigration to this country and to refocus your attention on why you left India. Please try to spend some time journaling on this particular topic, as we at Greensprings believe that addressing the root cause of your behaviors will significantly improve your progress.

    Best wishes for the rest of the weekend.

Sincerely,
Dr. Cat
Dr. Catherine Hopkins, MD, LPC
Greensprings Wellness Camp and Fitness Center
"Not a Fat Camp, a Change-Your-Life Camp!"

Georgie Khalra

Followers:

35

Group chats:

0

CORA

FRIDAY, OCTOBER 11
9:55 P.M.

A GOOD PARTY IS ALMOST AS GOOD AS A PERFECT KISS. It should have a lot of smiles and laughter. The energy of it overwhelming, leaving a buzz through you. And most of all, it should make you feel like you'll never be alone ever again.

Those are the only kind of parties I throw, and everyone wants an invitation. But not everyone will get one.

I'm the type of girl that gets to choose you.

I walk from room to room, then do a loop outside, watching how much fun everyone is having. I add more sliced peaches and vodka to the punch. I look around, basking in this. I need to take it in. A habit I picked up from my momma, that pride. The only thing we have in common.

Senior year.

This is it.

I need to make every moment, every party, count.

Everyone will remember me.

I check the hashtag I made everyone use—#CovetingCoraFOX, my signature, of course—and it's filled with only the best photos. Everyone who's stuck at home—or better yet, not invited—will be ridiculously jealous.

Shouting pulls me outside. Chance Olivieri is almost naked, sitting on a pool chair, wringing his wet clothes out and cursing about his camera.

"What happened?" I hand him a towel.

"Bryn."

Rage shoots through me as I scan the yard. "Where?"

How dare she show up here—at my house—after everything? She wasn't always this dumb. Used to be one of the smartest people I knew. Anger bubbles up in my stomach. We had big plans and she ruined it, and I don't even understand what happened. Over the summer, she changed—went from driven and compassionate to suddenly obsessed with her boyfriend, Jase. From my wickedly smart best friend to a lovesick stalker who couldn't do anything but run after him. Now the cheerleading team is down two people, Baez still gets killer headaches from the concussion, and there's a messy special election, which means I may not get to keep my spot as student body vice president. Another thing Momma will hold against me if I don't get into Harvard and join my genius twin sister.

All because of her.

"Cora! Cora!" Adele stumbles up to the pool. She's small and blond and pixie-haired, with these big green eyes that always make me think she's a fairy or something. The opposite of me. Her freckly white cheeks are bright red, like she's been scalded.

"What?" I touch her shoulder. She's definitely had a lot to drink.

She grabs my hand and yanks me back into the house. "I—I . . . have to tell you something." The words sputter out, her eyes bulging.

"What is it? You okay?" My heart does a tiny flip.

"It's bad."

"Out with it."

"Your boyfriend . . ."

"What?"

"Baez is . . ."

"Baez is what?" I search her face for the answer.

"He's hooking up with Georgie right now. Upstairs."

"Puh-lease!" I roll my eyes. "He would never. We're, like, super good. And I don't know any Georgies."

"Jashan. Khalra. Or whatever. You know that Indian girl? She's in AP Calc with us. Sits up front. Super nerd. Quiet. She used to be really fat but isn't anymore. I heard her mom made her go to a camp or something."

"Don't say *fat*," I correct her.

"It's been reclaimed," she argues.

"But not by your skinny ass."

"Whatever, just listen." Adele takes my hand and leads me to the back staircase. "Everyone's talking about it. I even saw them go upstairs." Her eyes cut up to the ceiling.

"Impossible. Everyone knows—especially Baez—that *nobody* is allowed upstairs." I kiss her cheek. "Relax! It's cool. People are ridiculous." But as I make my way up the staircase, I feel her eyes on my back, heavy like a weight.

As I reach the top, I hear voices, then drunken laughter. "Who's up here?"

Baez steps out of my room. "Ahhh, babe."

I smile as he closes the distance between us in three big strides, spins me in a circle, and starts to nuzzle my neck.

I can't help it; a peal of laughter bubbles out of me. "What's going on?" I ask, and give him a little kiss. "No one's supposed to be up here."

Then I see her. A girl standing awkwardly outside my room. Jashan.

Georgie, I guess. She looks different. Not the shy, overweight Indian girl who always needed her eyebrows plucked and her mustache waxed. I feel like a terrible person because that's the first thing I remember about her.

"She needed to use the bathroom," he says, pulling my hips toward his even as I lean away to look at Georgie. "Spilled a drink on her shirt."

I want to say: *And I should care why?*

If my sister, Millie, was here, she would've blocked anyone from coming upstairs. She doesn't "do" parties, but never snitches, and always enforces my rules if anyone wanders. Because she and her boyfriend, Graham, usually hide out up here. But she's busy. At Harvard.

"Um, I'm sorry, the downstairs line was endless," Georgie says, trying not to stare as Baez nibbles at my ear. "And I needed a hair dryer."

I look her up and down. She could be a model. Hourglass figure. The kind guys like. Which no one should care about, but they do. People might just think she's hotter than me. Exotic, or whatever. Which explains why people are gossiping downstairs. People love it when pretty girls tear each other down.

"Nice shirt." I don't ask her where she got it. That would be too friendly.

"Thanks," she replies, too confident. Much more than I remember.

"I hate people being upstairs," I say. "That's one of my party rules. On every invite."

"Oh, okay, sorry. I didn't know." She blushes, and stumbles down the stairs.

I want to say: *That's because I didn't invite you. . . .*

But Baez is being so sweet, I bite my tongue. "Bye-bye." I wave her away, watching her disappear back into the party. "People said y'all were upstairs hooking up because *everyone* knows my rules. No one's allowed up here. You know that, Baez."

He pulls me closer. "I know, babe. But some drunk guy from another school was being gross in the bathroom line, so I thought you'd be okay with it. Brought her up here to clean up. She's really shy."

I decide to give him a little attitude. "And how would you know?"

He kisses me. "You're really beautiful."

His compliment sends goose bumps over my skin. I bite his bare shoulder. His skin reminds me of the dark crust on Momma's corn bread. Deep brown. He looks back at me with big eyes.

I pull Baez to the nearest room. Millie's. The walls are still papered in stripes, the telescope pointing out the window. I wonder if I could see all the way to Cambridge, Massachusetts, from here. Check on her. On her vanity is a picture of the two of us. There's a red lipstick stain on it, and I know Momma has been in here, kissing the photograph like she does when she's missing Millie. Momma had us in matching dresses—mine peach and hers pink—and no one could tell us apart. Two little brown faces. Two button chins. A smattering of freckles on our noses. Identical twins born less than an hour apart, and now one is a genius who skipped grades and went to Harvard a whole year early. And the other is left behind. Our lives couldn't be more different.

She'd be pissed if she knew I was in her room. Especially with Baez.

I plop onto her bed and stare up. She still has our little-girl canopies draped above hers. She's taped words onto the fabric—*Harvard, Lawyer, United Nations*. Her goals.

My life as a six-word memoir (my new obsession, courtesy of Mrs. Perkovich, my English teacher): *I'm a badass, too, basically Beyoncé.*

"She's gonna be pissed that we're in here." Baez points up at her goals and smiles.

I roll my eyes. She might be smarter, but I'm captain of the cheer squad for the second year in a row. Student body vice president, voted in by a sweeping margin. I throw the best parties and have a house full of people who both adore me and are terrified not to be my friend. My boyfriend is the hottest guy at Foxham Prep. I'm good with people. That It factor, my ex JuJu calls it.

I kiss Baez again, and he pauses. "You okay?" I ask.

"Headache," he replies, rubbing his temple.

"You had beer, didn't you?"

He shrugs.

"It triggers migraines, love," I remind him. "All that gluten."

"I know, I know."

They've gotten worse since the car accident and the concussion.

"Lay here for a while. I'll grab some aspirin."

I head back downstairs. The party is growing by the minute, swelling from just the senior class to what feels like half the whole school. I don't even know some of the people. Juniors. A few sophomores. Some from other DC and Maryland private schools. Some with important parents I've met at all the galas and fundraisers I've been dragged to my whole life. Some I don't want in my house.

My heart thuds along with the music.

Second six-word memoir: *This party was a terrible idea.*

"All right, guys, party's over," I shout.

I smile as people respond to me. Their eyes brighten, and they follow my directions. I'm like the song everybody knows the melody to, the one whose chorus no one can un-remember.

Everyone loves me.

They start leaving.

I start cleaning up. The crowd thins out in the backyard and inside the house.

Adele stumbles down the stairs, drunk and happy. Her new

girlfriend, Leilani, is by her side, and she's got this dumb, shit-eating grin on her face.

"Your place is so amazing, Cora," Leilani says, words running into one another like a train wreck. "I am so totally obsessed with your bedroom. I love that your mom still uses wallpaper. It's, like, so old-school and charm—"

"Adele, no one was supposed to be upstairs," I tell her again, but it's still not sinking in. It never sinks in. I should've locked the bedroom doors.

"Oh, relax, Cor. It was just me and Lei up there. I looked in all the rooms like you asked, and I was checking on that thing. You know."

"You cuss him out?" Leilani asks.

"Nothing happened," I say. "People say dumb shit. He's drunk and snoring. Migraine."

"You're hotter than her," Adele says.

"Oh, I *know*," I reply.

"So bring your hot ass with us. After-party at Jase's. You gonna wake Baez?" Adele asks. "Or staying here?"

"I've got to clean up before my parents get back tomorrow," I say, hoping, praying, that they'll offer to stick around and help. Knowing they won't. Only Bryn used to do that. I ignore the pinch. It's the first party I've thrown without her. And moments like this, when I feel alone in the crowd, when I feel abandoned even among friends, make me miss her the most. But I guess I didn't know her that well after all. "My mom—"

"Yeah, yeah, we know," Adele says. "I'll text you if anything interesting happens." She grabs Leilani's hand, and they're out the door.

Millie's boyfriend, Graham Williams, strides up. He's light brown, tall, and lanky. Should play basketball, but he's a clumsy mess. "You good?" he asks, pushing his glasses up on his nose. "I could stay and help you clean."

I smile at him. He started dating my sister last year when she finally realized it was okay to have a boyfriend. That it didn't have to derail your focus. He's been coming around a lot lately—for dinners or to just hang out in the den, like soaking up her presence. Anything to be close to Millie with her so far away now.

"I'm okay. Baez's going to help."

"Where is he?"

"Headache."

"Oh, those still?"

"Yeah."

Jase grabs Graham, locking an arm around his neck. "Yo, yoooo." His words are all slurred and his white face red. "Where's our boy?"

"Asleep."

"Wake him up." Jase grins. "He can rally. More beer. After-party at my house."

"That's what triggered the migraine in the first place," I snap, rolling my eyes.

"Let's go." Graham tugs Jase. "Tell him I'll text him."

"Awesome party, Cora," a stranger says on their way out. Most people are setting down their cups and heading out. Some wait in a line to get to the powder room. I cringe, thinking about how I'll have to clean the bathroom, too. Maybe Baez will do it.

"Thanks," I say.

Then the house is empty. I spend hours fishing cups from the pool and hot tub, taking the trash out to the curb, vacuuming.

My head's a mess of should-haves, would-haves. Why did I even throw this party?

A whisper in my head answers me: *Because you were mad about how quickly your parents run to Millie's rescue.*

I stand up straight. *I'm fine.*

I have to be.

The thing is . . . you can't ever let yourself lose control. Because then you could really lose everything.

Bryn:

Sorry I was quiet on the way home. It was just . . . a lot.

Georgie:

You want to talk about it?

Bryn:

No. You can probably imagine how bad it was . . .

Saturday 12:23 AM

Bryn:

I saw someone online say you guys were hooking up. You and Baez. That true?

Georgie:

No. He's just super nice. Which is still so surprising. Like, he doesn't have to be.

Saturday 12:32 AM

Bryn:

He hates me. Always has. 😑

Georgie:

Why?

Bryn:

So did you love it?

Georgie:

What?

Bryn:

My old life.

Georgie:

The party was fine.

Bryn:

It was great, and you know it.

Georgie:

Okay, yeah, it was amazing.
I still don't know if I belong or whatever.

Bryn:

You have to make people believe you belong.

FilmmakerChance

Saturday, October 12, 1:54 a.m.

♡ 300   ⚲ 53

Look at what we have here! Who's that sneaking up the off-limits stairs with none other than All-Star Baez? Why, it's former fatty turned beauty GEORGIE K. Get you some, GIRL! Rock that Bollywood bod. You earned that shit!

Hit me with your theories. What happened here?

KatNotKateLee: WHAT NOW?
52 mins   ♡ 13

BrynChildDC: Get it, G!
48 mins

> **SykeWard:** Did you guys see Bryn Colburn make an appearance?
> 2 mins   ♡ 62

ABadassMelody: I saw it all go down, if you know what I mean. She went upstairs with him. She was so hype about it. Why would he take her upstairs where no one's allowed unless there was some action?
40 mins   ♡ 137

AhMADManKhan: Whatchu saying, ABadassMelody? My boy's rep is at stake here.
32 mins   ♡ 117

FilmmakerChance: Shut the fuck up, BrynChildDC, and go away. Nobody wants you around.
31 mins   ♡ 450

ABadassMelody: You calling me a liar, Ahmad?

28 mins ♡ 150

JaseThaGod202: New babe alert.

26 mins ♡ 62

MerBear426: Watch out, Georgie. They'll do the same to you that they did to me last year.

26 mins ♡ 62

> **JaseThaGod202:** You deserved that shit, MerBear426.
>
> 16 mins ♡ 362

AdeleBelleParis1231: Take this shit down, Chance.

26 mins ♡ 120

PrincessChristine4578: That girl is NOTHING compared to Cora.

24 mins ♡ 160

SykeWard: Leilani said that when she went upstairs after Georgie left, she totally saw Kleenex in the bathroom wastebasket with lipstick all over it, and it wasn't Cora's.

24 mins ♡ 60

> **KayBae215:** I heard that, too. SykeWard.
>
> 2 mins ♡ 160

CallMeYourDaddyDavid: Girl fight! Girl fight!

20 mins ♡ 200

JessiBessyBoo: I thought BrynChildDC got sent to rehab?

14 mins ♡ 122

AJRiveriaTodelo301: Who's Georgie?

3 mins ♡ 10

Comments Loading

Georgie:

Can I come over?
There's weird shit about me online.

Bryn:

Oh, yeah. I saw. Am tracking it.
You've tripled your followers.

Georgie:

What do you mean you're tracking it?
B, this is bad, right?

Bryn:

I keep my eyes on everything. Ever
since Jase. I mean, it's just gossip.

Like, nothing happened, right?

Georgie:

Of course not. He literally showed me the
bathroom and stood outside waiting for me.

Why are they saying all this stuff?

Bryn:

Why does anyone say anything about
anybody? Cause they're jealous.

You got hot over the summer, Georgie.

39

Bryn:

It'll blow over. Not like with me.

Chance made a video of Jase reaming me at the party. So that's fun. 😵

So who's obsessed with who?

Georgie:

Whom.

Bryn:

At least people know who you are now. 🙁

Sunday 6:02 PM

Georgie:

BAEZ AND GEORGIE
WERE COZYING UP
SOLO AT CORA'S
PARTY.

BAEZ AND GEORGIE
DEFINITELY MADE OUT
UPSTAIRS IN CORA'S
BEDROOM.

BRYN

TUESDAY, OCTOBER 15
7:03 A.M.

"YOU HAVE TO START TALKING TO ME AGAIN," MY DAD SAYS, like he's just telling me I have to sit up straight. "I'm glad to see you in the house. It's been days since I laid eyes on you, Duckie."

I cringe at my childhood nickname. "I was out of milk." I open the fridge and rifle through it. Mental note: *Go to the grocery store and stock the pool-house fridge so you don't have to come in here.*

"I miss you." He sets down his morning paper. "I'm so proud you're following in my footsteps."

Ah yes. Congressman father, and his aspiring-politician daughter. The only thing he cares about. Part of me wants to tell him everything. How they're trying to box me out of meetings and stall projects until the special election. How they've been writing letters to Principal Rollins to get me ousted. How they're using whatever means necessary to take this from me.

"And how goes the presidency?"

I used to tell him all the details. He even helped me and Cora run our campaign. She sat at this table, all three of us poring over strategy documents and campaign posters and debating slogans. It used to be our thing. When I was a child, he and my mom always played a game, wagering on which I'd choose—food or politics. I'd wanted to be just like him.

I wish I could tell him the truth. I wish things could go back to normal. But I laugh hysterically instead, like one of those evil hyenas from *The Lion King*.

I don't even look up at him, knowing his uber-white skin is all flushed, like he has a tacky sunburn. No matter how much he tries, he can't push away the red when he's upset. A clear tell. Breaking his own rules. I wish I looked more like Mom. "How's Lenora? Maybe ask her how *she's* doing?"

"That's over. I told you—and your mother—that I'm committed to fixing my mistake. If you would just talk to me, maybe we could heal this?" He fishes for eye contact, his bright blue gaze burning into me.

If this were the movie version of my life, I would've let my parents send me overseas to a boarding school in Switzerland where I could hide, start over, and ride out the storm of their relationship. Put some distance between me and what happened. Then all this would've gone away. Everyone would believe I've always looked like I had it *together*. Because if my records ever get unsealed, I'll have explaining to do. I'll have to face what I did.

"You're not even on my list of people to talk to." I tap my notebook, which holds all my plans.

"Well, you're the first on mine," he replies. He pats the seat beside him, but I move the chair to the opposite side of the table and focus on my cereal. "We have to put this family back together again. Things have been tough since the accident and Mom needing to get help."

Help. Rehab. Mom. As if it weren't his fault. The memory of the night I found her all loopy from pills and wine makes my skin prickle.

That glassy look in her eyes. The wailing. Because of him. She went to rehab, and then I went "off the rails." Put this family back together again? Unlikely, sir.

I swallow my anger and squeeze my eyes shut, willing away memories of that night.

"Bryn." Dad stares at me.

"What?" I snap back.

"Have you spoken to your mother?"

"Have you?"

"She's not talking to me this week, and I can't go see her because the press has already had a field day with all of this. The center won't allow it right now."

They had to hire a PR firm to deal with Mom landing in rehab. He doesn't want anyone to find out the reason why. Or following him if he goes to visit. Like he's protecting us by sparing us all the tacky tabloid photos when he shouldn't have had the affair in the first place.

I'm too mad to fix things.

That August night plays on repeat in my head. I can still hear him saying, "I can't possibly understand why you did what you did," after the cops left the house. Then he called my mom at her fancy rehab and yelled. "We need to move her to a new school. Maybe in a different city. Move to Virginia, or perhaps even a boarding school in Massachusetts or Switzerland. *Something.*" They still argue about it at least once a week (if she's in the mood to talk to him) during their "check-in" calls. He doesn't think I can hear them from my pool-house bedroom, but he shouts at her on speakerphone. All the barking drifts out and down and into my windows like thick, heavy raindrops.

But he doesn't want to deal with all my questions about what he did to this family. Just wants to put a Band-Aid on it, out of sight, politics as usual.

"I need you to talk to me. We used to talk about everything."

The only person I want to talk to me is Cora . . . and maybe Mom.

I clench my teeth and shove away from the table.

"I can't." I storm out of the kitchen.

Georgie's waiting outside next to my car. "Finally," she says when she spots me. "I need to talk to you."

She's all twitchy and panicked.

"What's up?" We get in the car to drive to school.

"Everyone's talking about me."

"Relax, it's hardly everybody." I turn on the car.

"I've got, like, a hundred new followers since Monday, and people talking shit in my comments."

She fidgets in the passenger seat, tugging at her dress. It's too short. I picked out all her outfits for the week. But she still has to learn how to wear them. Can't teach her that. "No one has ever talked about me before." Her expression is awkward, like she doesn't know whether to smile or frown. "Not like this. And the truth is, nothing happened. I didn't do anything. I mean . . . Baez and I. Nothing happened. I told you every detail."

Ah, but that's where she's wrong. Georgie told me her version of the story, her version of the truth. But, as my mom is always reminding me, even the smallest action can have major consequences. And there are always multiple truths. Georgie left out the tiny, critical details, like when she put her palm on his shoulder, and that someone photographed it, videoed her going upstairs.

People believe a lot of things if presented with the right evidence. They did about me. "It won't matter."

"Remember what happened to Meredith Richmond last year? Josh lied about her. Posted those videos. Everyone was talking about her.

They hated her. The school kicked her out. I can't . . ." There's a panic rising in her voice. "Everyone is saying Baez and I kissed." Her eyes open super wide, flickering with fear. "They're all talking about me. Maybe I should tell Principal Rollins?"

"What is he gonna do? Call their mommies?"

"But—"

"Never snitch. That's a high school rule."

"I just hate it and—"

"Josh posted revenge porn of Meredith. The school didn't want a lawsuit. They paid for her to go away."

"*Really?* How do you know?" Her eyebrows lift with surprise.

"My dad."

"Right. Right." She bites her bottom lip, destroying her perfectly applied lip gloss. "Josh still graduated."

"The boys never suffer. Look what happened with me and J—" I swallow his name.

"I can't—"

"Wait!" That's when I get the idea. A messed-up, terrifying idea. The kind that's big enough to maybe help fix my life. The kind that's big enough, maybe, to help me fix things once and for all. The kind that might erase that one out-of-control moment, get them to really see how terrible it all is, and get me my old life back. "Listen! What if this could help . . . like, in a way?"

"Help?"

"What if I, as student body president, launch an anti-cyberbullying campaign? What if I use what's happening to you, these rumors, to raise awareness about how bad this shit is? Shine a light on slut-shaming."

"I'm not a slut."

"That's the point."

"Baez and I didn't do anything."

"You can keep telling everyone that. But it doesn't matter. People believe what they want to believe. Especially if given enough facts to support their already-made-up minds. A rule of politics. Like what happened with Meredith. Like with my accident. Everyone lied about stuff—and it didn't matter what I said. It went from the fact that I ran a red light and caused an accident to I rammed the other car off the road, then crashed into a tree. Spun out of control."

"They also said you egged Sasha's car and slashed her tires that night."

"Well, that part *might* be true, but that's beside the point." My hands squeeze the steering wheel, the memory rushing through me.

"I just don't know what to do."

"Do this campaign with me."

Georgie's shoulders jump.

"Hear me out! If everyone sees me fix it, then maybe the special election won't even happen. Everyone will see that I *am* the right person. Chance will have to stop trying to re-open the election, and Principal Rollins will cancel the whole thing. Maybe they'll all stop talking about my mistake."

"I don't know. It sounds . . ." Her phone pings. "More new followers. Over two hundred last night."

"Only popular people get gossiped about." I bite my bottom lip, hoping she'll do this for me. I need to launch something BIG to fix what I messed up.

"I always wanted that. Wanted to be more like you when we got to Foxham."

Popular. She doesn't say the word.

"This will help you. You'll also get more confidence, make more friends. A whole new person. That's what you wanted, right? What do you think?"

"I'm nervous. I don't like what people are saying about me."

"It's only a few."

"I know . . . but I still hate it." She shrugs.

"Which is why you should do this. Talk about that. Tell them how you feel. We can do it together," I say, like we're little girls gearing up to make rainbow-colored slime in her kitchen. "If the campaign works, they'll stop talking about you. But you'd still have all those followers. Make an impression. People will know who you are."

Her eyes lock with mine, hopeful. "And maybe we'll make a real difference. An anti-bullying campaign. It *would* look great on college applications. I know a lot of people were saying things about me. Even before this. Like, about my weight. It's hard being called fat every day," she says. "And not in the white feminist, we've-reclaimed-that-word way."

My heart lifts with excitement. "It'll be different this time. Everything will be different."

She gets quiet. The kind where you know someone has something to say, a question to ask. "What?" I press. "Spit it out."

"What's it like to have a boyfriend?" She looks out the window, watching our world go by.

"You mean what *was* it like to have one." I close my eyes for a long moment, picturing Jase. His long legs draped over the couch in my pool house. How he'd tickle me just to get us all tangled up, how he'd leave tiny love notes all over my body in ink and marker. I used to love how my space would fill with his scent, how long it'd linger after he left.

"Bryn?" Georgie's staring, and my cheeks burn, her voice slicing through the memory.

"Yeah, sorry. It was fine. I mean, it was great for a while. Like, really, great. Sort of like you're in this snow globe with only that person, your own little world. The only place you want to be."

She takes a deep breath. "I want that."

Jase's beautiful blue eyes disappear, replaced with rage. We're back in this car. We're back in this place where there's no snow and Jase hates me. We're back to reality.

I turn to her. "Maybe it's time for your first selfie. Let's give people something good to talk about." I pause at a light and grab her phone, scrolling. "You have, like, three photos up, and they're of your damn dog."

"Hey, Billi is adorable."

"*You're* adorable."

"I'm still getting used to . . ." She motions at her body, like it's a foreign object she's not quite sure she likes. "Everything."

"You're hot." And I'm coming to realize that if I'd really looked closely at her, I'd have seen that, even last year when she was bigger. But we're programmed not to see those things when someone doesn't fit the mold. "But you need to learn to embrace it. Keep all those new followers."

Her cheeks flush, and she smiles sheepishly. "Maybe I should."

I swipe to the camera on her phone. "Lean forward. Lift your chin. Push your arms in."

She clumsily follows directions, flailing and making faces.

"More cleavage. I wish I had what you have." The words hit me hard. I really do want what she has—a real chance at a fresh start.

Georgie giggles and twists awkwardly, posing for a thousand pictures before we settle on the one she has the fewest complaints about. She sucks in a deep breath and lets it out as she posts the photo, then looks at me. "I want people to see me," she says, a new glint in her eye. One I've caught so many times in my own when I look in the mirror.

Alert.

Ready.

Determined.

AhMADMachine: Hey brynchild don't think we forgot what u did!

LucyGoosy: brynchild Saw that clip of u again. The 1 from the news. U so crazy!

JasesGrl: brynchild you should b thrown outta school! You almost murdered people.

AhMADMachine: Did y'all see that video Chance posted from the party? JASE LET HER HAVE IT.

AdeleBelleParis1231: Exactly what the Big B deserves. brynchild

JasesGrl: Why haven't they arrested brynchild yet? TOTAL STALKER.

AdeleBelleParis1231: I heard her dad tried to get her out of all of it. Tried to get the red light camera footage erased. Almost got people killed. She should be in jail.

JasesGrl: Desperate.

AhMADMachine: Guess GeorgieGrl's learning from the expert, then, huh?

LucyGoosy: You know Baezinator denies EVERYTHING. **#hatetheplaya #lovethegame**

AhMADMachine: Nah, my boy don't mess. Especially not with That Mess. GeorgieGrl

LucyGoosy: That's not what I heard . . . **#trashbag**

REFRESH POST

GeorgieKhalra723

Tuesday, October 15, 7:45 a.m.

♡ 127   ◯ 13

First Selfie

VibsterMD: OMG, CUTEST!
20 mins   ♡ 14

SykeWard: You look hot. Man stealing hot.
20 mins   ♡ 8

RajLikeKing: You look beautiful, beta.
19 mins   ♡ 1

AllTheLoveleen213: Looking so pretty now, Jashan darling. Glad you dropped the weight finally.
17 mins   ♡ 3

BryanK619: HAWT
16 mins   ♡ 12

MauradelCampoInTheHouse: Little piggy in there somewhere.
15 mins   ♡ 27

NicoMuyRico020304: Hey hey. When you free?
14 mins   ♡ 4

AmirNotKhan007: 🔥 🔥 🔥
14 mins   ♡ 2

OoooNishantN: G! Barely recognized you! Come visit Seattle.
14 mins   ♡ 1

KatNotKateLee: Wow, Georgie, guess "summer camp" was a HUGE success, huh?

12 mins ♡ 12

AhMADMachine: Better chill, girl.

12 mins ♡ 34

> **WinnieWildWake:** Wait, AhMADMachine, who that? Isn't that G girl friends with her?
>
> **10 mins** ♡ 2

Hugh67898: Oink, oink. Never forget.

9 mins ♡ 17

Bryn Colburn
College Personal Statement
Draft 1

No one really knows what happened that night. ~~Except me~~. Not even me. One minute I was driving the car, the next minute I was running a red light. And ~~my love~~ my ex Jase's car had spun out of control in Georgetown. Airbags busted, the girls in the car with him screaming~~, like I tried to kill them. Or something~~.

~~Here's one thing I know is true: It was an accident. All of it. Even though you might hear different. See, that's the thing about high school and rumors. The truth underneath it all hardly matters. Because what people say shapes what people think happened—and in the end, that's all that matters. No matter what really happened~~.

It wasn't a big deal, really. Only the single moment that changed everything. And if they say the crime should fit the punishment, well, I think I've more than paid off my debt. Because in the end, the only life lost was my own. I told my parents that it was an accident. I don't know if they believe me. I don't know if I believe me, to be honest.

But one thing is true . . . the things that happen to us make us stronger. There's always a story behind them that will help you connect with others. This year has been really hard. But I've learned a lot. It'll help me understand other people and be a good political leader.

Georgie Khalra:
Followers:
1,423
Group chats:
0

GEORGIE

TUESDAY, OCTOBER 15
12:16 P.M.

"DID YOU HOOK UP WITH BAEZ?" RUTHIE ASKS. LIKE, straight out. No nonsense. Her foot tapping as she waits for an answer. Her face saying she might just kill me if I say yes. Her girls stand behind her, glaring.

My butt presses into Bryn's car door in the senior class parking lot. I'm frozen in place.

"Uh . . . no. We went upstairs together at a party," I stammer. "Like, he showed me to the bathroom. Why do you care?" In what world would anyone actually believe that *I* hooked up with Baez Onyekachi?

Ruthie coils a bleached-blond strand around a finger, then looks up. "Then why are people saying you did?"

I roll my eyes, but I'm shaking. "I don't know. Why don't you ask them?"

"Hmmm . . ." Her blue eyes scan over me, cold, calculating. In her head, things don't quite add up. I don't quite add up. "Don't lie to us. I'll make you pay. Trust me."

My hands are all clammy, and my hair clings to the back of my neck.

I swear my heart might give out. All I want is a bag of peanut M&M's. But at 250 calories per bag, they're so not worth it, and I'd have to give up the single piece of jalebi I'm allowed after dinner to make it work. They'd definitely take the edge off this situation, though.

I stammer another no, but Ruthie laughs hysterically. "He's hardly that desperate. He has a gorgeous girlfriend. You know? Cora." Then she turns and strides off to join her waiting pack.

I duck down beside Bryn's car, pretending to rummage through my bag. All I smell is grease and gas and pavement. I can't get my heart to slow down. Or my stomach to stop bubbling. I might throw up all over myself.

"Hiding, are we?" a sharp voice says from behind me.

I look up. It's Vibha. She's wearing a pleated herringbone skirt and a teal cashmere cardigan set. Knee socks, and not the sexy kind. Her cat-eye glasses slip down her nose. She looks like a conservative little copy of her mum, all pretty and prim. She's been a part of my life since the day I moved to America. We used to fit together like a pair of shoes. Smartest two Indian girls at Foxham Prep. We should be friends forever, but ever since school started, I've been avoiding her phone calls. And, well, *her*.

She sets her violin case on the ground just so she can cross her arms over her chest. "I heard about what happened at that party." She even sounds like her mum, the disapproval dripping.

Her gaze combs over my outfit as I rise, judgment flashing in her eyes. Disgust. Disappointment. And something else.

She could be much hotter if she tried. But her mum runs the show with her, too. I've just gotten better at dodging mine these days. Vibha's cute and safe and well-groomed. It's fitting that she's the president of the Model UN. And that she's already planning to apply for early acceptance to Yale. She's the perfect representation of what good Indian girls should be. It's why my mum likes her so much. She does "our country" proud, even though she was born in America.

I used to want to be just like her: great metabolism, slender frame, naturally milky golden skin. Like a Bollywood starlet. At weight loss camp, when they asked about the body we wanted, I always thought of her. Because, most importantly, she has this ability to eat her fill of samosas or jalebis without gaining an ounce. Or the wrath of my mum.

She taps her foot at me. "I didn't even know you went to parties like those," she says, and I frown. It's like she's been waiting for this moment, and now she's relishing it. That it just proves her superiority. "Your mom said you were in your room doing homework that night. And not taking any calls."

"I was. Until Bryn came over."

Vibs bristles. "She should've been removed as student body president on the first day of school, really. Principal Rollins has let this go on way too long. Because of who her father is. It's an embarrassment to Foxham."

I don't exactly know the details of "everything"—and neither does she, probably. She knows just enough to judge me for hanging out with Bryn.

"You really shouldn't associate with her. She's crazy. Like, certifiable. Ran Jase right off the road. Sasha's still suffering." She shudders. "Aren't you afraid to get in a car with her? To be around someone like that? You want that rubbing off on you?"

Since when does Vibs get to dictate what I get to do? "You shouldn't call people crazy," I correct. "It's offensive."

She huffs. "Whatever. That white girl has problems. Always has. Apparently her mom is in rehab."

Guess she's been reading the papers. Vibs generally sticks to hanging out with other Indian kids, or the occasional really smart Black or

Latinx girl from her APs. The ones who might be her competition for valedictorian. She likes to play it safe. Guess I do, too. Or used to. I don't know when that changed, really.

"You haven't been texting me back," she says. "I'm worried about you, Jashan." She hates my nickname, Georgie. But, like, "Vibs" isn't really working for her either.

I shrug. I don't have the answers she's looking for. I haven't really thought much about what happened with Bryn in August. Mum shipped me off to camp on the last day of school, and I didn't get back until Labor Day. Missed the whole thing. I've only heard bits and pieces, none of them from Bryn. Not that I've asked. Not that she's offered. So I've got nothing to say. But since school started, Chance keeps cornering me, trying to get me to talk to him on camera about Bryn and the accident. Like I have a clue. Like she tells me all her secrets.

"Did you really hook up with Abaeze Onyekachi?" Oh my god, not her, too. Vibs sucks her teeth, like she's somebody's old-school nani, *tsk*-ing as usual about brown people dating *outside of the community*. "Like, seriously? *Hook up* hook up?"

There's a tiny energy beneath her words. Disgust. Curiosity. Anger tucked in between them. The way she talks about me makes me *that* girl. The interesting one. The one *everyone* is talking about.

I've never been talked about this way. *Seen.*

It sends a little shiver down my spine. I can't figure out if it's all bad or maybe a little good. In a twisted way.

I don't answer, letting her stew in the lie.

"Not smart, Jash." Like she's reading my mind. Like she ever really could. "How could you? What if your mother finds out? He's . . . I'm not even going to say it. Plus, he has a girlfriend. Do you have a death wish?"

"Look, Vibs." I step closer, trying to slip into the old me. The one who looked up to her, who wouldn't do anything without asking her advice. "Honestly, I didn't *do* anything with him. It's just a stupid rumor. He helped me find the bathroom at Cora's house."

Her nose crinkles.

A few boys from the lacrosse team rush through the parking lot to their cars.

"Hey, Georgie," one says.

I blush. I have no idea who they are.

"Yeah, what's up, Georgie?" another one adds. They slap each other playfully, not waiting for me to respond before jumping in their cars and peeling out of the parking lot.

Then Jase and Baez walk by.

"What's up, Georgie?" Jase shouts. "Looking hot."

And I swear, my whole body stiffens. Like I actually did something wrong. Weird.

Baez shoves him in the back and flashes me a sheepish, apologetic grin.

Vibha studies me, picking at her cuticles. Her one bad habit. Her mum hates it.

The silence stretches out for an eternity, judgment sitting heavy and thick on my shoulders.

"I can't believe you! When did you start talking to lacrosse players? When did you start *knowing* lacrosse players?" She throws her hands in the air. "Remember our plan?"

I do remember.

Rethinking it now, it seems like something our moms dreamed up: We'd get into Yale—her first choice, of course—and room together. We'd have a blush-velvet couch, and sari-inspired curtains. Vibs would make a little mandir in one corner, and maybe I'd join her for some pujas. She'd force me to eat cardamom seeds each night as she tried to stick to her Ayurveda diet. On Sundays—cheat days—we'd venture to the gurdwara, and eat all the Punjabi home cooking we'd been craving. She'd stash idlis in the freezer, and we'd get a hot plate to heat samosas, wishing for our mums (or Nita Masi, in my case) to visit because they'd turn out soggy and gross. During finals week, she'd be in charge of making the Madrasi coffee, strong like her mother's, and I'd write up a schedule. We'd date twin Indian boys (or brothers, at least), future doctors or engineers like us, and would graduate with honors.

Now I don't know if I want that. If I ever did.

"It never included, like, you and lacrosse players and rumors," Vibha says. "I feel like I don't know who you are anymore."

That makes two of us. I just want to enjoy this moment for what it is—fifteen seconds where people, the ones who matter, might know my name. It'll be gone in a minute, this chance. I know it's a terrible, horrible, god-awful thing to want. But I do. And it scares me a little.

Like a miracle, Bryn appears then, walking toward us from the center of the parking lot. I've never been so happy to see her.

"There you are! Gotta go, Vibs. My ride's here. Talk to you later, okay?" I aim for casual. Like nothing's wrong.

"Hey, Vibs," Bryn calls out.

Vibs snatches up her violin case and stomps off. I make a mental note to call her later, make plans or something. I don't want to lose her. I just want to try something else for a while. What's wrong with doing something new? Being someone different?

We slide into Bryn's car.

"What's her deal?' she asks, starting the car engine. "She's always so intense."

"She heard the rumors." I shrug. "And if I'm honest, she only likes the old me."

"The new Georgie is a lot more fun." Bryn pulls out of the senior parking lot, letting the windows down and blasting music. She zips in and out of Washington, DC, traffic as we make it from the northwestern quadrant of the city to our neighborhood right across the Maryland line. Men honk at us and Bryn blows kisses, so I do, too. One flicks his tongue out like he wants to lick us, and we burst with laughter. So gross.

Crowded city blocks give way to pristine planned suburban subdivisions. Once this area was all sprawling plots of green and mirrored mini-mansions. Now it's bustling communities and big outdoor shopping centers.

"I need you to draw and paint posters for the anti-bullying campaign," Bryn says.

"Really?" I say, my heart lifting with excitement. I've always loved painting, though Mum considers it an impractical hobby she sometimes lets me entertain.

"Really," she repeats, looking straight ahead. "You're so good at it."

My phone erupts with pings and chimes.

"What's up?" she asks, peering over.

"Like a zillion comments on that picture you took." My heart races.

"Good ones?"

"Yeah," I say with surprise, scanning the messages. "A hundred more followers, too. But there's some stuff about that rumor."

She winks at me. "Don't worry. We'll get 'em."

And then maybe people will know who I really am, once all the bad stuff goes away.

I'm starving by the time I get home. I take off my shoes, drop my bag on the floor in the foyer, and head straight to my room to change my clothes before my mum can see them.

"Jashan!" Mum shouts. Like Vibha, she never calls me Georgie. She hates that I've let the teachers call me that instead of forcing them to learn how to pronounce my "beautiful," proper Indian name correctly—Jah-shun Khal-rah—or telling them that it means "celebration" in Punjabi. That it's an old family name to be proud of. She doesn't care that it's hard to pronounce.

The proper Indian name for a Good Indian Girl. Exactly what I'm meant to be.

GOOD INDIAN GIRL JASHAN:

1. Straight-A student with respectable Ivy aspirations.

2. Serves on the student government and as president of at least one résumé-building extracurricular group.

3. Trim, fit, healthy, and "lovely," with straight, silky hair and a creamy complexion.

4. Auntie-approved wardrobe. Preppy, BORING.

5. Takes small, delicate bites. Knows when to stop and what to decline.

6. Is a Model UN captain and champ.

7. Attends gurdwara services regularly and volunteers to do seva at least once a month.

8. Is known in the Auntie Network as a good catch for their Future Leaders of America sons.

9. Can't be bothered with social media. Except for cute family pics.

10. Supports a worthy cause, something that gives back to the Desi community.

11. Keeps her mouth shut, no matter what.

BAD INDIAN GIRL GEORGIE:

1. Got a 78 on her Calc test last week.

2. Didn't read the play for AP Lit, so that test tomorrow's gonna be a bitch.

3. Keeps hanging out with "weird white girl" Bryn.

4. Would rather go to NYU. And maybe study art.

5. In a fight with her Good Indian Girl BFF of six years.

6. Guzzled the punch (140 calories a cup) at a party she crashed instead of diet soda and spilled it all over her shirt.

7. Wants to kiss Baez (even though he has a girlfriend) because he seems like a nice guy to share a first kiss with.

8. Never meets the Good Indian Girl standards.

9. Maybe likes the attention the gossip brings.

10. Can't forgive her dadi for banishing her from India when it wasn't her fault. (It wasn't her fault, right?)

"JASHAN!" Mum calls again, and I dart back downstairs.
My mother is not one to be ignored. By anyone.

I slip into the kitchen to grab a snack before having to deal with her. I rummage through the cabinet, looking for something to tide me over till dinner. Popcorn? No. Chickpea chips? No. Mathi. Yes. Fried spicy, savory, crunchy biscuits—perfection. Like, a thousand calories, but I'm feeling so good, I'll even skip that jalebi tonight.

"Jashan!" Mum's practically on top of me now, glaring. "What do you think you're doing?" She snatches the bag of mathi right from my greedy hands, shoving it back into the cabinet. "You worked so hard all summer. Don't ruin it now. I'm so proud of you."

Her eyes are dismantling me, taking in the unruly waves in my hair. Mum is the perfect DC society wife, Desi edition. Think Padma Lakshmi in a pantsuit. Her hair is a sleek dark bob, her afternoon casual-wear is couture, her home socks are cashmere. She is a lady who lunches and knows how to serve a proper high tea with subtle Indian flourishes. Her curried-chicken-and-cucumber sandwiches are to die for, according to the Aunties. I wouldn't know, because she won't let me have any.

"Nita made you some salad—with avocado," she says, as if that's supposed to be so enticing. "And I froze grapes, if you want something sweet. We're having tandoori chicken and daal for dinner, so you'll want to balance appropriately." She pulls the salad out of the fridge.

I tower over it, admiring the neat circles of veggies, avocado in the middle, spiraling out into bright red peppers, cucumbers, tomatoes, and pickled red onions. Like a colorful, crunchy flower. Almost too beautiful to eat. And to be honest, I'm pretty sick of them. It feels like a diet of grass after a while, and I've been on it since the end of June. "Nita Masi made it look so pretty."

"Don't call her that. It's inappropriate. She's not your aunt. She's a housekeeper," Mum scolds while pulling the plastic wrap off the top and sprinkling the whole thing with chaat masala, lemon juice, and a touch of vinegar.

I roll my eyes. Works every time.

"Chal, bhet." She pats the barstool next to her at the endless gray-marble island nestled in the center of her flawless white kitchen. "Did you have Model UN today?" She pulls over a stack of envelopes. More college guides. I pretend to peruse them, even though she's already decided on the seven schools that I'll apply to.

"I think I'm going to skip it this year," I say, careful. "Vibs already paired with Amir, and I don't want to find a new partner. Besides, I thought I might try something new."

"Model UN looks great on your college applications. You've done it for three years already. Schools look for commitment and continuity—it shows you're capable of making smart, grown-up choices, no?"

I shrug and dig into the salad, imagining the salty crunch of the mathi in my mouth instead. I pick at it until I've made a satisfying-enough dent to make her happy. Everything I've ever done is to make her happy. Take the right classes. Lose the weight. Be friends with the right sort of people. All for her.

"Don't forget, we have a meeting with Dr. Malhotra to make sure you maintain your progress." She pats my hand, then starts rattling off all the things I'm going to have to do to make sure I achieve my goals. Her goals.

"Are you happy, Mum?" I interrupt her fussing.

A wrinkle of confusion creases her brow. "Why would you ask such a thing, beta? Of course. We are a very good family. We are blessed. Yes, yes, I am happy. We are a happy family."

She almost sounds convinced. Guess I'll get the hang of faking it, too. Eventually.

An hour later, I'm sitting in a stranger's office, telling her everything that's wrong with my life, trying to pinpoint the root of my "binge-eating problem." Dr. Cat promised this woman, a Desi psychotherapist named Divya, would be the solution to making sure I keep the weight off.

Her office is strategically warm and inviting. A gray velvet couch, a cream-colored throw, Indian mirror-worked pillows in bright colors. Magazines on the glass-topped table, a small fridge with juice, water, and tea, but no coffee. The windows overlook a busy DC city block, the Washington Monument waving from far off in the distance. I always wondered what they were thinking when they designed that. It's like the ultimate phallic symbol. Or a giant pencil. Although it's always reminded me more of tillewali kulfi melting in your mouth, the sugary-sweet ice cream dripping down your chin on a hot Delhi day.

"Georgie," the woman repeats in her carefully soothing tone. "Seems like there's a lot on your mind. What are you thinking about? Care to share?"

I shrug. "I'm not really thinking about anything." Lies. I'm thinking about *everything*.

"Okay, what would you like to talk about?"

Nothing. I can't figure it out for myself. How am I supposed to explain it to her?

"Dr. Cat told me you did exceptionally well at camp, but she's been very concerned at your lack of responsiveness since you returned to Foxham. Senior year is tough. Can you tell me about camp? How was it?"

I blink. Her questions open up a wave of memories: the intervention with Mum and Papa, loud "discussions" about my binge eating and weight, that first awkward conversation about Greensprings, the pamphlet sitting on the table between us. Then that endless drive to the middle-of-nowhere Virginia. The constant tug-of-war between hating myself for wanting to be there, to be thin, and wanting to be okay with my body just as it is. Was. And most of all, that weight I'll never shed—the looming desire to make my parents happy. "It was fine. I did it and it worked." I lift my arm, as if to show her.

"But how do you feel about it?"

"How am I supposed to feel?" I don't know what she wants from me.

"Do you think there's a way you're supposed to feel?"

I stare at the pictures on her desk. "I was okay for a while. When we moved here, everything felt different. I mean, new country. Puberty. Lots of new things to try. Lots of new pressures."

She's scribbling on her clipboard, and it's like she's doing math, trying to make the numbers add up.

"When I got my period—" I sigh. "Maybe that was it? I mean, I got hips. And boobs. And a belly. Then Mum put me on a million diets. Keto. Whole 30. Even Weight Watchers with all the Aunties, which was super fun. But nothing stuck. And it— It caused a lot of tension. My weight. For everyone. So it was pretty much Greensprings or surgery."

She makes notes, trying to keep her face composed. But the wince when I said the word *surgery* cracked the mask. "And how do you feel now that you've lost the weight? 'Made the goal,' so to speak?" She frowns. "There's no right or wrong answer here."

I take a sip of water, playing with the straw. Steel. Figures. "I don't know."

"I understand you don't want to talk about it, and that is okay. Talking about it can be uncomfortable or awkward." Dr. Divya's perfectly arched eyebrow lifts. "Your mother told me you're in Model UN—"

I shake my head. "I don't care about Model UN."

"What do you care about now?" The woman leans forward, drumming her fingers—neatly trimmed nails, pale pink polish, a lot of chunky rings and bangles—on the table in a soft, subtle rhythm, a tic she doesn't notice she has. I'm sure this gets old. The questions.

I'm probably her third patient today. I wonder where she falls on the Auntie spectrum, if she still group texts and gossips and judges people like Mum and her friends, even though she knows how brains work and why people make the mistakes that they do. Supposedly. "What's important to you?"

"Being beautiful."

The truth slips out, landing on the table between us, heavy and misshapen.

"What does that mean?" Her mask is up again, notepad poised.

"People wanting you." I tug at my skirt, thumbing the hem, ignoring her gaze.

"Do you crave that? Attention? To be desired?" Her voice is flat, careful, not implying that it's a good or bad thing. Just a thing. A way to be.

"I don't know. Maybe." I nibble my bottom lip, then stop, trying not to mess up my gloss. "I was ignored before. No one even saw me." I sigh. "So it's kind of . . . refreshing."

"Do you feel like they see you now? Does it feel good?" Her eyes burn into mine.

"Sometimes." But there's this other part . . . I shrug. "I'm sure it will blow over soon."

She looks up. "What will?"

"Huh?" The way she's looking at me now, it's like when Mum finds me swiping sweets. "I mean, just the interest." I look down, tugging my skirt again. "New school year or whatever. People are . . . friendlier. Like, on social and stuff. And in real life, too, I guess. It's . . . fun. Sort of. Before, it was just . . . silence. Or cruelty. Fat jokes. Whatever." I got used to letting them fall away, like I didn't hear them. "No one had anything good to say. Now—"

"So it's good?"

"Mostly." So far.

"How does that make you feel?"

My stomach rumbles. "I'm used to Mum and all the Aunties always weighing in." I let out a short, sharp giggle. "But it's nice to be noticed—" *By people who matter.*

"That does sound nice. Why do you think things have changed this year?"

"I'm a new me." I look her right in the eyes now. The old Georgie would've never.

"And who is the new you?"

I motion at my body.

"You don't think the old you could've gotten all of this? The attention. The comments."

"Of course not."

She plucks a picture from her clipboard. "Is this the old you?"

I nod.

"She seems pretty great. Beautiful smile."

"Old me carried baggage. Literally." I'm cracking myself up tonight.

The woman doesn't laugh, just stares, and it stresses me out, the way she's looking at me, like she can see inside my head. Like she's unraveling all the parts I've been trying to unknot for days, months, years, my whole life. And like she'll actually be able to do it.

"Listen to me, Georgie," Dr. Divya says. "And I want you to really hear me. You are not your weight. You are not your body. Your body is a part of you. Your body is good and strong and capable. You are good and strong and capable. You've *always* been good and strong and capable. Gaining weight didn't change that. Losing weight didn't change that. The Georgie in this picture is a kind, generous person. The Georgie sitting in the chair is the same person. A good artist. A supportive friend. An accomplished student with a bright future. It does not matter whether you are big or small in size. You are and were those things. You can be whatever you want. You can do whatever you want. Your size doesn't change that. I want you to say that back to me."

An evil laugh laugh escapes my mouth.

She frowns.

I'm laughing so hard now, the tears slip down my cheeks, hot and salty.

There's a small hand on my shoulder. I didn't even notice her getting up. "I want you to be gentle with yourself, Georgie." She says it so softly, at first I think it's just in my head. "You've been through a lot, and people are—have always been—very hard on you. I can tell. People who are meant to love you. People who are meant to protect you. That means, and this is unfortunate, that you never really learned to protect yourself either. How could you? You're only a child. But if you're willing, and open, I can teach you some ways to figure things out, to help you protect yourself. Okay?"

It takes me a minute, but I nod. That would be good, maybe.

"Say it, please."

"I can be whatever I want," I say through the sobs that rock my body. "My size doesn't change that."

I am not my size.

Tuesday 10:13 PM

Georgie:

I'm sorry, okay?

Vibs:

Whatever.

Tuesday 11:17 PM

Georgie:

Movie night this wknd?

Vibs:

You've changed.

Georgie:

I'm still here. Just trying out some new things, okay?

Country club? Indoor pool?

Vibs:

Maybe.

Adele:

Guess who I caught talking about you today?

Cora:

Who?

Adele:

Rude ass Jessica Griffin.

Cora:

She wouldn't dare.

Adele:

Oh, she tried it. Caught her at swim practice spreading lies about you and Baez.

Don't worry. I shut her up. Shoved her ass right in that pool. Reminded her.

Cora:

Good.

CORA

FRIDAY, OCTOBER 18
8:57 P.M.

I PEER THROUGH THE OLD-FASHIONED KEYHOLE ON THE bathroom door that leads to my sister's room. I see Momma running her hands over my sister's pillows and sniffing them, hoping she can still catch Millie's scent despite having Vero change the sheets every week. Her happy laughter pushes under the bathroom door. My knees jam into the cold tiles under me as I sink deeper into watching her.

"I ordered new sheets for you, thousand count, little Bird," she coos into the phone, like Millie is eight years old and coming home from camp, and not just coming down on a long weekend from her first year at Harvard. "Where's the train at now? What station did you just leave?" There's a pause. "I'm going to make biscuits from scratch for breakfast tomorrow, so you can have them first thing."

I hear Momma leave and head downstairs.

Excitement over seeing my sister flutters in my stomach. We'll do what we always do—lock our bedroom doors, watch a rom-com, and sleep snuggled in her bed. Maybe I can tell her about everything going on at school. The special election. The last-minute cheerleading tryouts.

All the to-dos for my college applications. She'll figure it out. She can figure almost anything out with her super-logical brain. And she's always on my side. No matter what.

"Cora!" Vero calls out from the hall.

I crack open the bathroom door, like she's disturbing me and I'm too busy and undressed to possibly open it all the way. But Vero's freckly brown face is the one that's frowning, and she's wearing that old-fashioned hair net that I hate. It makes her look like a lunch lady. She doesn't care how many times I tell her this. "Keeps the hair pins out of the food, mi abeja," she always says.

"Baez just pulled up." Her small frame is swallowed by a laundry basket. "His music is too loud. Tell him to turn down before Mommy gets mad." She shakes her head. "Doesn't like it. She told me." I want to tell Vero that Mama doesn't like anything. But neither of us wants her mad.

"Okay," I say, closing the door.

My stomach squeezes. My whole body hums with weirdness. There have been more and more strange things about Baez posted online. Still. Since the party. That he and Georgie hooked up. That he seems like the kind of guy who could wander, who would. I can hardly go on social media without being tagged in it.

It's all nonsense, of course. Mostly I'm just stressed that this talk is still going. Like, I thought Baez and I were above this rumor shit, but apparently I was wrong. Or maybe we're not as powerful as we used to be. He definitely didn't do it, though.

Unless that's why everyone's still talking? Maybe there's something I missed?

I shake my head. I twist half of my newly straightened hair up and let the rest wave out on my shoulders. I spritz myself with expensive perfume, slip into ripped-front skinny jeans, a magenta bra, and a sheer sweater that Daddy would call see-through and tell me to change out of.

I look at Georgie's social media. She barely has any pictures up. Stupid pet photos. Food. And one new selfie. I zoom in on her face and body. My stomach squeezes.

I'm prettier, I tell myself. Even though her hair looks effortless and gorgeous. Boys are calling her exotic. I'm definitely not that. Black girls like me don't get called that.

I glance out my window. I hear Baez shut his car door.

I rush down the front staircase and through the foyer just as he rings the doorbell.

"Vero!" I hear Momma call out from the dining room.

"Got it," I yell back. "It's just Baez."

"You're grounded from that little party you had—remember?" Momma calls out. "No visitors." They found out, despite my best efforts—a stray red Solo cup in the guest bath. Been on lockdown aside from school-sanctioned activities ever since. But I need to see Baez.

So I ignore her, rushing to the door. I open it, peeking out like I don't want to let him inside. The motion detector beams on. It makes it seem like he's glowing.

"Hi," I whisper. His eyes stare back, taking me in like it's the first time and not the thousandth.

"Hey." He leans in to kiss me. I move my head to the side and point up.

"Cameras," I remind him. "Daddy."

"Coooraaa," Daddy calls out. His thick Mississippi accent lengthens the syllables in my name. "We're not paying to air-condition the outdoors. Tell your guest that you're grounded and can't have company."

"He hates me. Still," Baez whispers. Even after all these years, Daddy's not thrilled about Baez. He'd be thrilled if I studied more. He'd be thrilled if I was more like Millie and less like me. Baez is always "the guest" in our house. Daddy never uses his name.

"But I don't," I say back. I try to pretend everything is normal, like I didn't look at any of the stupid posts online today.

"It's 'cause I'm Nigerian." He smiles. It's crooked and sly, and I love the tiny gap between his front teeth that his parents never bothered to get fixed. "'Cause he loves Graham."

"Maybe. But your mom hates me, too. 'Cause I'm *not* Nigerian."

"She'd prefer me with a Nigerian girl, yeah, but I sort of like this other girl. She's got super-long legs and these big eyes that only ever see me, even if there are a million people in the room. Do you know her?"

The way he describes me feels like it's not me right now. I stick my tongue out and tug Baez's shirt, dragging him forward into the foyer. I pull off his sunglasses and rub my hands along his hair, the tight coils he's thinking of growing out and allowing to lock. He needs a haircut. That's what Daddy would say. But sometimes I like it when it grows too long, so I can play in it and make my fingers smell like him.

He holds up a paper bag. "From the restaurant. Puff puff for your parents."

"The balls?" I tease. "Are they big?"

"Oh, shut up." He kisses my cheek.

"Suck-up," I whisper.

"You know it," he says back.

I march him to the dining room doors. I remember how my sister and I used to press our little-girl faces against the glass panels, wondering how long Momma and Daddy would have dinner, and if we'd ever grow big enough to join them at the nice table, instead of having to eat in the kitchen with Vero. Now I wish I could skip dinners with them altogether. I knock on the door.

"Come in," Momma says.

I slide them open. My parents sit across from each other at the table.

Candles are lit. Vero places fine china in front of them and fills their wineglasses. They have dinner like this almost every night, like they're out at one of the fancy restaurants in DC, near Capitol Hill, where Daddy works as White House counsel to the president. Or like they're on their very first date. Daddy brings her magnolias and lilies and red roses every week, and those sit on the table in between them. I used to think it was cute. I don't anymore.

"Baez's here," I say, stating the obvious.

"Evening, Mr. and Mrs. Davidson," Baez says. He's learned that manners get you everywhere with my parents.

Daddy clears his throat. "Evening." He looks up over his glasses.

Momma chews carefully, not smearing her deep-red lipstick, swallowing before she speaks. "How are you, Baez?"

"Just fine, ma'am," he says. "I brought you some dessert. From the restaurant."

"How thoughtful. Send our gratitude to your parents. How are they?"

Vero takes the paper bag and disappears into the kitchen.

"Mom is stressed, but great. Our second restaurant is keeping her busy. You'll have to come for the grand opening. My father is tied up with diplomatic things as usual." Now that his hands are empty, his fingers fuss with pockets, keys jingling.

Momma raises an eyebrow and runs her ballet-pink nails across her grandmother's pearls on her chest. "Somewhere to be, Baez?"

"Oh, no, ma'am. I—"

"Coraline, you're grounded," Daddy interrupts. "So I don't even know why you invited guests over."

I sigh. "I know. He came for—"

"I let her borrow my calc book. I popped by to scoop it."

"Scoop?" Daddy glares now.

"I mean . . . uh, I came to pick it up."

"Hmm. Turtle, you have thirty minutes to retrieve whatever *book* he's come to get." Momma loves to use that terrible nickname in front of Baez, no matter how many times I've asked her not to. Most people think it's cute. But it's really just another way for her to call me slow. Born one hour after Millie. Started reading two years after Millie. Left behind when Millie placed out of high school early. I might've won the sixth-grade spelling bee or gotten a B-plus in AP Chem, but I'll never catch up, never be extraordinary like Millie, no matter how I try.

Am I Millie-level genius? No. But I have more grace under pressure than she could ever manage. Not that anyone notices.

"Your sister's train gets in at ten thirty-five p.m.," she says. "We leave at ten."

"But that doesn't give us enough time," I say, trying to keep the whine out of my voice. I feel dumb for my wishful thinking. And I can see Baez's face fall, like he was hoping for more time, too. "We were going to study. Can't I see Millie when you all get back?"

"Big calc test." Baez adds his lie at the exact wrong moment.

A pocket of silence stretches out into every possible corner of the room. It sucks out the air and leaves behind pressure and heat. Baez cringes. Momma cuts another piece of her steak slowly, the blood a pool on the plate, then chews it, before responding. "Be in the car at nine fifty-five," she says. "Thank you."

"Okay, but—"

"Now, don't get embarrassed in front of your company." Her eyes meet mine, and her mouth is pursed tight.

Baez grabs my hand. I retreat with him to the basement den. He dives onto the big couch and clicks the remote like he's done a thousand times. "At least she gave us a half hour. I mean, you are grounded."

I close the door a little too hard, and it makes a loud bang. I'll pay for that later. Daddy doesn't like slammed doors.

"Do you need to—" Baez always wants to talk, but I can't. Not right now.

I snuggle close to him. I just need his arms around me and the sense that he loves me. I feel like I'm losing my touch. I used to be able to get Daddy to let me off the hook. I used to be able to get all the things I wanted. I used to be able to control what people said and thought about me. Everyone too afraid, too eager to be my friend, too adamant to stay on my good side. Everyone loves me and Baez.

He starts asking me a bunch of questions as we sink into our normal routine—arms and legs and hands tangled with one another—but I can't focus. My phone screen fills with more messages and more social media tags. There's no place to hide from those stupid rumors.

"I was hoping I could sneak you out. I hate going to parties without you." He says something else, but my mind is too full. "Did you hear me?"

"Huh?" I reply.

"I asked if you wanted to come to my momma's new restaurant tomorrow afternoon. It's not open yet, but I want to show you something."

"Oh."

He sees my eyes glance at my phone. He shoves it under a pillow. "My phone's a mess, too. I hate this shit. It's so dumb. I muted it."

I look away. He takes my face in his hands and forces me to look at him. He kisses me. "We're good, right?"

I kiss him back, pressing my answer into his lips.

It doesn't matter what they say. It's just him and me, and our little universe. No one else even exists.

• • •

Daddy pulls his car around the front of Union Station. I've always loved the ride into the city at night. When he takes the parkway in, it all looks beautiful and twinkling and enchanted. It felt sort of magical when Millie and I were little. Like we were headed to some faraway kingdom.

We're ten minutes early. Daddy says if you're only on time, you're already late. Jazz melodies pour in through the speakers as he takes hold of Momma's hand and kisses it. She lets him do it two or three times before she rubs her hand across his salt 'n' pepper beard, cupping her palm under his chin. They've always been very affectionate. No matter how much Millie and I groaned and complained and threatened to vomit.

"How'd she sound on the phone?" he asks Momma.

"Good," she says. "A little homesick. But good."

"Cora," Daddy says, looking back at me. "You excited to see Millie?"

If I say no, it'll be a huge issue. And I really do want to see her. It feels weird to have her gone so far away. Like there's a place inside me that's missing. But I'm not excited to share her with him and Momma, honestly. They're always so . . . intense about her. Daddy stares at me with expectation, waiting for an answer. He's not a man who deals well with being ignored.

"Yes, I'm excited to see her," I say, finally getting him to turn back around and focus on Momma. I don't say: *I'd rather be with my boy-friend at a party, making sure everyone can see how good we are together.* Millie would get it.

"There's nothing more important than family." Daddy launches into a familiar sermon about how our family was able to remain successful because we stuck together and never forgot our roots. His words blend into the melody of the notes coming through the car speakers. Horns, pianos, guitars erase all the pressure he piles on with stories of the past struggles of his grandparents in the South, his voice a droning backbeat to the rhythm that pulses through the car and into my brain. "Maybe

Graham will come over for brunch tomorrow."

He loves Graham. Perfect Graham. Millie never really had a *real* boyfriend before him. She'd never just had fun, like in one of those teen movies. The ones I lived in all along. Never a person meets a person and they fall in love, eat together in the high school cafeteria, hang out after school, make out in the basement, and sneak out on weekends.

Nothing about her life has resembled anything close to normal. Sometimes I wonder if she liked it or wished for something else.

"Can Baez come, too?" I ask.

"Maybe," Daddy says. Which means no.

I look at my phone. Baez sent me a ridiculous picture of him and his boys with beer caps up their noses. I want to laugh and be happy that he's thinking of me while at Jase's. But he's there without me, and there was no way I could've said, *No, don't go because I can't.* It would've made me sound ridiculous. I text him that he and his friends are idiots, then immediately regret it. I should've said something funny or, like, sent a smiley face. I quickly add one, but don't get a response.

Already there are pictures online: Adele, Christine, Leilani, and Ruthie doing Jell-O shots, then dancing on Ruthie's parents' bar. Ahmad making out with some white girl from Arlington. Jase and Baez smiling into the camera for a sloppy selfie, already wasted, half of Jase's face cut right out of the shot. There's other people around them, but I can't quite figure out who.

I hate missing these parties. I know we're all, like, living the same night over and over again. But I also know, somewhere deep inside, that the ones I miss are the ones where something big is going to happen.

I text Adele for an update. Nothing so far. I scroll through the feed, the jealousy bubbling in my stomach. Millie picked the worst night for her meltdown and emergency trip home. Always does.

My phone buzzes again. A photo from Adele. It's an over-the-shoulder shot of Baez. Talking to Georgie. She's got a wide grin on her pretty face, and her striped maxi dress leaves nothing to the imagination.

I text Adele back: What is she doing there? Who invited her?

Last I checked, that girl Georgie was nothing. And now she's, like, everywhere.

Adele sends video next. I can't click on it because my parents start cheering, spotting Millie, finally.

Adele texts back: Don't worry, I went over and broke the little sitch up. She's not talking to him anymore.

"There she is. Our college girl," Momma says, opening the car door. "Little Bird!" Daddy gets out, too, and makes his way over to Millie.

No one cares that I'm left in the car. I sink down into the plush leather seats and stream the video. My eyes cut between my parents' overjoyed embrace of Millie and the phone screen. I hear Baez's laughter mixed with Georgie's. He touches her hair. What is he doing? He should know everyone's going to see that and think the wrong thing. A Paranoia creeps inside me. *Does he think she's pretty?* I watch Adele try to playfully break it up, like the greatest best friend in the world. But it doesn't stop my heart from plummeting straight into my stomach, burning a hole right through my insides.

Millie taps on the window. She doesn't walk around to the empty side of the car. No, she opens my door, and I have to slide over to the seat behind Daddy's. I guess I don't *have* to. But it's so routine that muscle memory does it for me.

"Hey," she says.

"Hey," I say back.

She still looks the same.

We still look the same.

Always identical on the surface. Round brown face. A few freckles on our noses. Shoulder-length dark hair, pinned half up. She's even wearing lip gloss like mine. Ballet-slipper pink with a touch of glitter.

"Missed you." She leans over to hug me. My body freezes a little, and I pat her back, like she's one of the creepy old men at church who try to give all the women too-tight hugs. My skin is all clammy, and my pulse races. I need to be in two places at once, my mind a storm of worries and anger and upset.

"Umm-hmm. Yeah, me too." The pressure of her arms around me makes me feel like I'm going to suffocate. "Ugh, get off me." I shove her away, wiping at my eyes. There's shock on her face. Or maybe devastation. "I didn't . . . I mean . . . I just can't right now." The words are messy and hiccupping, nonsensical. But something in her face cracks with understanding. And that's the worst part, because it sends me sobbing. Her hand rests gently on my back. It could be my own. I hadn't realized how much I missed her. But now I can't stop.

"Are you okay, Turtle?" she asks.

"What's going on?" Daddy asks.

Momma's mouth is a stern, straight line as she glances back at me, like she's disappointed.

But Millie doesn't miss a beat and comes straight to my rescue. "You don't think you're the only one who missed me?" she says to our parents. "We're twins, after all. We've never been this far apart. And for so long."

I bury my face in her lap, and she traces her fingers along my neck until I calm down.

Aside from my occasional heaving sniffle, the car is dead silent the entire twenty-minute ride back. So I wipe away my tears, and text Baez a dozen messages until the emotion fades.

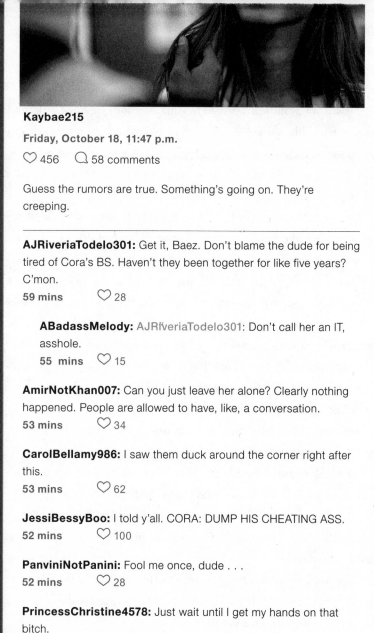

Kaybae215

Friday, October 18, 11:47 p.m.

♡ 456　　♡ 58 comments

Guess the rumors are true. Something's going on. They're creeping.

AJRiveriaTodelo301: Get it, Baez. Don't blame the dude for being tired of Cora's BS. Haven't they been together for like five years? C'mon.
59 mins　　♡ 28

> **ABadassMelody:** AJRiveriaTodelo301: Don't call her an IT, asshole.
> **55 mins**　　♡ 15

AmirNotKhan007: Can you just leave her alone? Clearly nothing happened. People are allowed to have, like, a conversation.
53 mins　　♡ 34

CarolBellamy986: I saw them duck around the corner right after this.
53 mins　　♡ 62

JessiBessyBoo: I told y'all. CORA: DUMP HIS CHEATING ASS.
52 mins　　♡ 100

PanviniNotPanini: Fool me once, dude . . .
52 mins　　♡ 28

PrincessChristine4578: Just wait until I get my hands on that bitch.
42 mins　　♡ 138

FilmmakerChance: So many lies. Something is going on.
41 mins ♡ 123

EstradaNada: I heard there was way more than just making out last night. They were in the downstairs bedroom.
39 mins ♡ 205

SykeWard: Wait . . . at like 10? I totally saw two people all over each other in the garden. Like dry-humping near the hydrangeas.
37 mins ♡ 215

DeeSquared228Squad: Girl, Dump His Ass. You deserve better. Come and get it. Wait what did you see, SykeWard?
36 mins ♡ 140

ZachWei876: Me too. FULL ON CONSUMMATION.
35 mins ♡ 92

PartyPartyPalak: You guys are making shit up. Jashan is a good girl.
32 mins ♡ 38

SykeWard: Is Baez as sweet as everyone thinks he is? No guy is. They're all assholes.
30 mins ♡ 25

AdeleBelleParis1231: Take this down. Baez is a good dude.
21 mins ♡ 13

TateNotTotBro1289: Someone def owes me $100. Jase, got my $?
12 mins ♡ 16

Comments Loading

Millie:

Hey, where are you?

Cora:

At Baez's. We're headed to his family's restaurant. I'm going to help.

Millie:

You, manual labor? Lol . . .
Can Momma and I come for lunch?

Cora:

It's not open yet. She knows that.
Shopping later?

Millie:

Ugh, Momma has me on the teen committee for that White House Halloween thing.

Saturday 9:22 PM

Cora:

Ugh, ok.
Tomorrow, movie marathon?

Millie:

Yep, perfect.

Cora
&
Millie's
Movie Marathon List

1. Love Jones

2. Love & Basketball

3. Blackout

4. If Beale Street Could Talk

5. The Wood

BAEZ AND GEORGIE WERE COZYING UP SOLO AT CORA'S PARTY.

BAEZ AND GEORGIE DEFINITELY MADE OUT UPSTAIRS IN CORA'S BEDROOM.

COMPLETE AND TOTAL YOU-KNOW-WHAT AT JASE'S PARTY.

BRYN

MONDAY, OCTOBER 21
2:23 P.M.

I MARCH INTO MRS. GRATTON'S CLASSROOM AFTER school for the weekly student government meeting. Head high. Shoulders pulled back. Focused. I clutch my polka-dotted notebook to my chest, like armor, and have my secret weapon at my side.

Georgie.

Cora stops talking mid-sentence.

I don't even flinch as I walk to the front of the classroom and stand right next to her. Where I belong. I miss being close to her and have to will my arms not to just reach out and hug her.

Everyone glares. They've been running me out of meetings since school started. Locking the door or blocking my path or threatening to have me removed from the room. So far I've retreated. But not today.

"What are *you* doing here?" Chance says. He's wearing a topknot today, and his camera sits on his shoulder, ready.

"I could ask you the same thing," I shoot back. "Didn't you *lose* to me? I don't remember selecting you for *my* cabinet."

"I run the news channel. These meetings are in my weekly report now."

Someone threatens to go get the student government adviser, Mrs. Córdova, from the teachers' lounge. Let them. Heck, they can call Principal Rollins, too. I won the election with Cora in sweeping numbers, and until there's a new election, I'm in charge. There's nothing they can do about it.

"You shouldn't be here." Lee Feldman, the secretary *I* selected, stands.

He doesn't even come up to my chin.

"You going to throw me out?" I challenge him. "With your bare little hands?"

His pale white face flushes.

"I am student body president. I was elected. I will govern. You've blocked me for weeks. But I'm done. Today, I kick off my first initiative of the year."

Georgie fidgets at my side.

"We should've just asked Principal Rollins if Cora could take over!" Lee shouts.

"How can you even show your face?" Cora says. There's acid in her voice.

"Like this." I put my hands on my cheeks and flash her my best smile. I wore red lipstick to show them all I mean business. My mom always wears this crimson shade when she's proudly presenting a new dish.

"You don't represent Foxham," Lee says.

"*Why?*" I challenge. "Because I made a mistake? Remember when you, *Lee*, accidentally turned in your older sister's World Civ paper in tenth grade—*oops!*—and your daddy had to rescue you from the student ethics board?"

He gulps and his cheeks turn red.

"All of you have made mistakes." I stand tall and proud, Georgie sort of hiding behind me.

"Hmm . . . let's compare." Cora points her fingers in the air, ticking off my mistakes. "You egged Sasha's car. Covered it with threats and slurs."

"Since when is the word *bitch* a slur?"

Cora's eyes narrow. "You also slashed her tires. Harassed her online. Oh, and . . . you almost *killed* four people, including my boyfriend."

Her words cut. I clench my jaw, trying not to let them break through.

Chance stands. "You should just resign, Bryn. Give it up already."

"I should do a lot of things—and so should everyone else." I look from face to face, welcoming a challenge. "I hereby call this meeting to order. Lee, please let the minutes show that Georgie Khalra is joining us today to help me announce and prepare for my first initiative as student body president."

Georgie's breath is rough, choppy. I take her hand and pull her forward, ready for my big speech. I find a point at the back of the classroom, and my practiced words flow effortlessly: "Many of you don't realize what a terrible few weeks these have been for me. To have the worst decision you've ever made thrown in your face over and over again on a sick loop. Bitten and chewed up. I've been mercilessly bullied online about what happened at the end of the summer. I can't sign into my email or social media accounts without finding thousands upon thousands of comments . . . even death threats." I walk back and forth, all eyes on me.

"It all spilled into the papers because of my father. When the right-wing media picked it up, the threats got worse. Rape threats and Holocaust pictures once they discovered my mother is Jewish. It was endless. It didn't matter what I said. How many times I apologized. No one wanted to hear my side of the story. No one would even give me a chance. Including most of you in this room." I take a deep breath, letting my gaze linger on each of them for maximum emotional impact.

"No one listens to each other anymore. When did we stop?" I go in for the big, rehearsed line: "We've run out of grace for each other."

Something my dad always says on TV.

Lee groans. I let my eyes burn into his. He fusses with his terrible, unruly curls, way too thick for that stupid bowl cut, and readjusts his yarmulke.

"Are you done?" Cora says.

"Actually, no." I clear my throat and take Georgie's hand again, unsticking her feet and pulling her beside me. "Given what's happening online right *now* with the rumors about Georgie Khalra and Baez Onyekachi . . ." His name is like grit in my mouth. "It's time to say something, to do something. To stand up and expose how social media has polluted everything, how we have to be the generation that changes how it's used."

Georgie's hand stiffens. I squeeze it tighter. Cora sits up straighter, and I can almost see the electricity shooting up her spine at the strength of my words.

"So I'm proud to announce my first project as student body president—a school-wide anti-cyberbullying campaign." I flip open my folder and pass around the handouts that I stayed up making with Georgie until 3:00 a.m. "We'll make videos and have the school news channel share." I glare at Chance, making sure he's *specifically* heard my request. My *command*. "And host workshops, build safe spaces, and—"

"What makes you think we want to do all of that?" Cora interrupts. "Or any of it?"

"Everyone is bullying poor Georgie right now—and in *your* name," I say. "Do you condone that?"

"I didn't tell anybody to do it," Cora hisses.

Georgie tries to say something, but her words sputter out, unintelligible.

"You didn't tell anyone not to." My words hold a challenge.

"Don't try to make me into the villain, Bryn," Cora says, her pretty eyes narrowing to sharp points. "You'll lose."

"Then be part of the solution."

"*I* haven't bullied anyone." Cora starts putting her things in her bag.

My heart squeezes, the regret a tiny vise. I pivot to face everyone with a smug smile. "Questions?"

"Screw you, Bryn," Cora huffs, sweeping out of the room.

I wait a beat, hoping no one will follow.

Everyone else starts reading the plan I distributed.

This will work. It has to.

After the meeting is over and everyone has signed up for their roles in the campaign, I try to find Cora. There's still time before cheer practice. And that's part two of my plan. The most critical part. Reconcile with my best friend. I take a deep breath. Now is the perfect time to talk to her.

"Wait for me at the car?" I tell Georgie, giving her my keys, and she nods.

I know Cora *too* well. She's hiding so no one can see her upset. She has to pull it together before facing her squad. No puffy eyes. No bloody streaks in the whites of her eyes. No stuffy nose.

I walk quickly, heading to the library to her spot—*our* old spot. The research stacks. There are window nooks where most seniors sneak off to make out in, but she's always hiding out here when she needs a break.

I rehearse what I'll say. I need her to forgive me. I need her to understand.

I dart down the hallway but freeze right before I make it to the library.

Jase is standing at a bank of lockers with Ahmad. They look up. His blue eyes narrow.

I take a deep breath, avoiding his glare. My heart rattles in my chest. Anger crashes in my stomach. Ahmad starts laughing. Jase waits until I'm nearly gone before saying, "Crazy bitch!"

I flinch, and hate myself for it. I almost run into the library.

Jase isn't shit, I tell myself. *Pull yourself together.*

I brace myself as I climb to the very top floor and head toward the back. I miss these places that were just ours—the ones at school, the ones in the city. Our little secret spaces.

The floor creaks. Cora spots me and startles. "Are you stalking me?"

"No." The lie almost coats my tongue. "I know this is where you come when you're upset."

"What do you want?" Her eyes are still bloodshot. She's been crying this whole hour.

"To apologize." My words tumble out in a whoosh, toppling over one another as if they too know this might be the only chance I get to tell her my side. To make her understand. "I just really got in my feelings, Cor. Like, he spent all summer telling me that we were the real thing, we were true love. And then he just, like, ghosted me. Called me crazy every time I asked him what was going on with the girls in his timeline, and wouldn't see me. Kept telling me he wasn't going to parties. But then he'd post all these photos and videos. Made me feel like I was ridiculous for questioning him. The gaslighting, the lies. I couldn't handle it. And after everything that happened with my parents, it made me paranoid. I didn't know what to think when I saw him with Keisha and Sasha. It all came out of nowhere. I . . . I . . ." I pause, swallowing the hiccup in my voice, not wanting it to turn into tears. "I didn't mean to run the red light. I didn't know Baez was in the car, too. You know I'd never hurt you guys."

"Stop." She puts her hand in the air. "Stop." Tears well in her eyes, dissolving quickly into sobs.

My feet are frozen in place as her shoulders bounce up and down, the rattle of sadness ripping through her. Cora never cries in front of people. Not even when she fell from the top of the cheer pyramid at the beginning of sophomore year and broke her arm. Not even when her grandma Rose died two years ago.

I don't know quite what to do. I take a few tortured steps forward, then sit beside her in the nook and wrap my arms around her. From there, it's muscle memory. I fail at holding in my own tears, the true weight of the gaping hole she left behind in my life. We've fallen back into a bubble, safe and familiar, one where we get to be best friends again.

The floor squeaks, popping the bubble. Cora scrambles away.

A freshman goes to grab a book from a nearby shelf.

We wipe our splotchy faces and blow our noses. She avoids my gaze.

"I really am sorry. I didn't mean to ruin everything. I didn't mean to hurt Baez. I didn't mean to hurt you."

She nods. "But it wasn't just the accident, Bryn. You were, like, *obsessed* all summer. We never saw you. When we did, you were like a hummingbird around Jase. There's a reason Baez didn't invite you that night . . . and when you showed up, you seemed unhinged." The tears appear again, her eyes red and puffy. "But weirdly, I sort of get it now."

It hurts to hear her say all that, and at first, I want to argue. I swallow that instinct and say instead, "You okay?"

"No, actually. There's a lot going on." She takes a deep breath. "And Millie's here." She lets out a small laugh, and I giggle, too. She loves and hates Millie in equal measure. It's something I'm starting to understand.

"I figured." My heart thuds at the possibility of her needing me. I know this is all about Baez and Georgie and the rumors. "I'm still here if you want to talk. Like, I know you, Cora."

She bites her bottom lip. "I do have a question."

"Anything," I reply, hope tentatively surging through me. Just let me be your friend again. Let me have my old life back.

"You've known Georgie, like, forever, right? She's your neighbor."

"I don't really *know her* know her. Carpool mostly. But we've been hanging out a little."

"What's her deal? Like, she came out of nowhere."

"After summer break, she's ready to do anything for a fresh start. *Anything*." Which isn't a lie.

"With other people's boyfriends? It's all so ridiculous." She hiccups, rubs her eyes. "I don't even believe the rumors. But then I saw those photos from the other night and . . . it's just hard not to feel jealous when everyone's talking like that. I don't think he did anything. But I'd die if he likes her."

Her phone screen fills with tags and texts and notifications. That used to be me. That used to be us. Now my phone screen is blank. No one wants to message me. No one wants me around. No one wishes they were me.

Everything gone. Because of one wrong move.

I shrug.

"Do you know . . . like . . . ?" She fusses with her hair, twirling the silky strands.

"Cora," a voice calls. We turn around. It's Baez.

"Been looking for you everywhere." His eyes narrow when he finds me standing there. They burn, the humiliation hot, my efforts shattered. We used to get along *fine* before everything happened. He'd even laugh at my corny jokes. But I always got the sense he was putting up with me for Cora. Like he'd try extra hard when I was around, like he was jealous of the time she spent with me. But now it's worse. When he looks at me, his eyes hold only disgust and judgment. He got a severe concussion in the accident. No matter how many apology bottles of wine my parents sent to his, no matter how many handwritten *I'm sorry* letters I wrote, I couldn't fix it. I didn't even get to explain. And he finally got what he wanted: Cora all to himself.

"See you later." She stands, ready to bolt. The shift is abrupt, and she's cold and unfamiliar again, a stranger. Not the Cora who was here again, just for a moment. She wipes her face, then walks away without another word, as if nothing happened at all.

I don't want her to leave. I can't let her. I bite my bottom lip. "Wait! I have an idea. . . ."

She pauses. "Gimme a second," she says to Baez.

"Cora," he starts.

"One minute." She turns back toward me.

"If I were you, I'd keep her close, you know? Control her, control the narrative," I say, too quiet for him to hear. "Make sure she knows not to cross you—if she doesn't already. I heard she was going to try out for one of the open cheer squad spots tomorrow."

It's a lie, the plan quickly unfolding in my head. "Maybe this is a keep-your-friends-close-and-enemies-closer situation. Whatever that cliché is. Plus, it's hardly drama anymore if you guys look like friends."

Her eyes find mine again. "Hmm . . ."

"I can help, if you want." She looks skeptical, but there's something there. Like we might just be up to our old tricks again. The look I've been waiting for forever.

"You know, you might be right about that," she says, slow and deliberate.

Baez rolls his eyes and pulls her out of the library. But me? I just smile.

Bryn:

So cheer tryouts Wednesday??????

Georgie:

Yeah. You gonna?

Bryn:

😁 Umm, I can't jump lol. I can argue and make speeches. And being photographed in those short skirts will come back to haunt me on my campaign trail.

Georgie:

All roads lead to the White House.

Bryn:

You know it. First female president.

But you've been talking about gymnastics . . . and everything.

Georgie:

Yeah right. Like Cora would EVER let that happen. And my mom . . .

Bryn:

Cora doesn't run the universe.

Georgie:

But she def runs the cheer squad.

Besides, I need to focus. My grades are a mess, and I need to start on early decision stuff and my mom is full speed ahead on Model UN.

Bryn:

Do YOU want to do Model UN? 😖

Georgie:

Does anyone ever actually want to do Model UN?

Well, maybe Vibha. 😊

Bryn:

You said you wanted this year to be different. This would be different.

Just saying. New you and all. Would help your confidence.

Monday 9:23 PM

Georgie:

Maybe you're right. Maybe I should. Might show some variety on college apps.

Georgie:

Maybe I can keep being a whole new Georgie.

Bryn:

That's the spirit. Yesssss. Don't forget to make more campaign posters though.

Georgie:

Working on it tonight. After watching a thousand cheerleading videos, I guess.

Washington, DC, Police Department

Washington, DC

Incident Report #9004679

Report Entered: Sunday, August 21, 02:24:34 A.M

CASE TITLE: Bryn Colburn	
Location	Date/Time Reported
1469 Wisconsin Avenue Washington, DC 20016	Clocked: 01:44:00

A.M. INCIDENT TYPE/OFFENSE: RUNNING RED LIGHT, FLEEING SCENE OF ACCIDENT

Reporting Officer: Crowley, Malcolm

Approving Officer: Williams, James

PERSONS	
Role:	Witness
Name:	Lucas, Sasha
Sex:	F
Race:	W
DOB:	1/6/05
Phone:	703-555-3128
Address:	3609 Porter Street NW

OFFENDERS	
Status:	Defendant
Name:	Colburn, Bryn
Sex:	F
Race:	W
DOB:	12/27/04
Phone:	703-555-2376
Address:	3456 River Road

VEHICLES	
Class:	Automobile
Description:	Red Convertible
Make:	Mustang
Model:	2012
Serial #:	K142839

NARRATIVE

Traffic cameras caught Bryn Colburn running a red light at the intersection of Wisconsin Avenue and P Street NW in Georgetown, causing a head-on collision. Plaintiff and four passengers—Jase Cunningham, Keisha Jackson, Abaeze Onyekachi, and Sasha Lucas claim that the defendant Bryn Colburn purposefully followed them and caused the accident. Defendant chose not to deny or confirm without a lawyer present, underage, not intoxicated as far as we can tell. Did a toxicology lab to check. Jase Cunningham claims that the incident was premeditated, the defendant was his girlfriend this summer, but they are now estranged. No previous history of violence in the relationship, according to both parties.

DON'T BE MEAN
BEHIND THE SCREEN

GEORGIE

WEDNESDAY, OCTOBER 23
2:48 P.M.

THE GYM SMELLS LIKE SWEAT. A BUNCH OF GIRLS HOVER, waiting for the cheerleading tryouts to begin. Including me, which still feels surreal.

Jase's girlfriend, Sasha, and her best friend, Keisha, sit in chairs, still decked out in their cheer outfits—clinging to those last hopes that maybe, just maybe, they'll be back. But Keisha wears a mechanical knee brace and Sasha's arm is in a sling and her leg is in a thigh-high cast that will definitely keep her from climbing up any cheer pyramids before she graduates. Still, they belong here. And I might never.

A girl zips past. She's bigger than me—I mean bigger than I ever was—and plows through like she owns the place. Monica Gates. Looking at her, you'd think she had it worse than me. The bullying. But she's super-confident, with a quick wit and a quicker laugh. She's not an outcast, like I was. *Am?* She actually does more than okay. Even dated Ahmad for a minute last year. And he definitely has a type. Monica isn't it.

But somehow, she always knows how to work it. Today, she wears a tank and skin-hugging shorts, her dark skin radiant, her usual Afro pulled into a massive high bun. Like this open spot was made for her.

If she can do it, I can, too, I remind myself. I took gymnastics all summer and loved it.

Everyone gets ready for the tryout. Some girls pull their hair into ponytails, others chat endlessly, and a few stretch out their naturally flexible bodies. I sit on the very edge of the first row, watching Monica, surrounded by some of the others, completely comfortable in her skin, acting like a fat girl trying out for cheer squad is no big deal. Like people won't post nasty comments about her later. Or if they do, she won't even care.

I wish I could not care. Sometimes I feel like maybe that could be me. And sometimes I feel like the old Georgie, like I never lost the weight in the first place.

Model UN is starting now, too. I could just get up and go now, do exactly what's expected of me.

But then I hear Dr. Divya's voice in my head: "You can be whatever you want. You can do whatever you want. Your size doesn't change that."

I inch closer to the group. "This is the varsity cheer audition, right?" I ask no one in particular, even though it obviously is. There's a box of pom-poms, and this is where the email said to meet for tryouts.

"Yes," someone answers, and her tone makes me immediately feel stupid. "But you know there are only two spots?"

Another girl smirks and adds: "And that Cora's one of the cheer captains."

I nod, feeling the flush climb up my throat to my cheeks. I'm so nervous that I can't connect the dots. "Sorry," I say. "Silly question."

One of the girls looks at me. "You going to try out in that?" She stares at my new dress like it's a trash bag. "You've got, like, five minutes until we start."

"No, of course not." I actually forgot to change. This is clearly a bad idea. I'm not cut out for this. I should come up with a different plan. *Get it together, Georgie.*

I scoot to the locker room and quickly slip into the black sports bra, a loose tank, and little burgundy cheerleading shorts I bought just for this audition. Nanima always says that deep henna red is a lucky color.

I head back out, claim a spot. But I can feel the others staring, their whispers making my skin itch. Talking in circles about me and Baez and Cora and what did or did not happen.

"G, you look good. Heard you went to Greensprings." Monica's words make me startle. "My mom's never tried that with me, thank god."

"Sometimes I wish mine handn't," I confess, surprising myself, and she straight-out laughs.

"I'm gonna go do a few laps before we start." Her eyebrows ask if I want to come.

"I still hate running," I say, and she laughs again.

"All right, then, G. May the best girl win." With that, she's off. And my nerves are back.

I lean down deep into a stretch the way Coach Lawrence taught us at Greensprings, grabbing my ankles and holding the position to increase my flexibility—and to hide from the girls talking about me.

Monica runs by again, her breath controlled, her speed respectable, and I realize how different she and I are. Now, but always. She doesn't let them dictate her thoughts, her moods, the way she views herself or the world. I still do. I need to be done with that. I wish I knew how.

Monica winks at me, and I smile back.

"What are you smiling about?" Cora walks along the first bleacher. "You won't be smiling when we're done with you."

The other cheerleaders burst with laughter, spouting off about how cheerleading is a sport and not some extracurricular activity to make you look cute or get boys.

Cora grins. She's got this confidence, kind of like Monica's. Claims the room as if she's made of a million bucks. Like she can't be touched.

"All right, ladies. You all should feel lucky that we're holding these tryouts. We had a full, top-notch squad until *crazy town* hit at the end of the summer." Cora nods toward Sasha and Keisha, who pat their broken bodies. "And as of an hour ago, we've only got one slot open," Cora adds. "The other one is already filled by Christine Vaccaro."

Christine waves and curtsies, clearly pleased with herself. Everyone claps and whistles. I try not to groan, plastering a smile on my face. I can be perky. I can be cool. I can be the best damn cheerleader anyone's ever seen. I've studied them at every pep rally, watched every teen movie, know it all by heart. I make myself believe it.

"We're sad that our girls are still recovering," Cora continues, commanding attention. "But if we want to place into nationals, we need a full squad." She introduces the cheer coach, Ms. Bailey, who gives a little speech about the team and how far they've come. Then Bailey turns the practice back over to Cora and retreats to a chair with her whistle.

"Jumps first," Cora says, and the other cheerleaders circle her, making a show of tossing her easily in the air, light as a feather. Which might be pretty close to the truth.

I line up with the other wannabes and try to follow along. Though my limbs are lighter, they still feel heavy, weighing me down.

"All right, start with the warm-up rotation." Ruthie divides us into lines of four, assessing our performance.

We do kicks and jumps and splits in the air. Sweat drips down my nose. My hair sticks to the back of my neck. Pit stains soak my bra and tank. I feel old Georgie creeping in, taking over, bringing me down. Monica catches my eye a few times, winks, trying to boost my confidence, but this isn't nearly as easy or effortless as the team makes it look.

Just as we're all a sweaty, frenzied mess, the gym doors snap open, and a few of the lacrosse players trample in from practice. Baez Onyekachi enters last. The boys settle onto the bleachers, ready for a show.

I want to curl up and die.

"Yo, man, look at your girl," I hear, and they all watch Cora as she soars and lands, soars and lands. Baez's proud as the guys whoop it up in the bleachers.

Stomach acid travels up into my throat. I don't want them to see me. Not like this. But I can't quit now.

Cora makes us do a thousand more warm-ups, learning a basic routine. We do it a hundred times—kick, bend, twirl, leap, split, kick, bend, twirl, leap, split, kick, bend, twirl, leap, split.

Baez doesn't budge, so neither do any of the other boys. He mostly watches Cora. But every so often, I swear, his eyes land on me. Which is the worst. Because I'm totally a wreck.

Cora claps her hands three times above her head, calling the team and the wannabes to attention. "All right, all right! Time for the real deal. One-on-ones. Each girl will do her routine for one of the players! After all, we'll be cheering for them." She starts assigning numbers, but before she gets to me, there's a commotion from the far end of the gym.

"Cora," Bailey calls from near the doors, waving her over. "We've got a situation. Ruthie, take over."

They disappear through the double doors, and Ruthie blows her whistle, delighted to be in charge. "You heard them," Ruthie says. "Each girl will do her cheer for the assigned player. Think fast, ladies. And be aggressive. Be-ee aggressive."

A few of the taller girls go first, cheering for Jase and Ahmad and

Reggie. Monica, cheering for Frankie, puts on a strong show, calling him a *hawt dawg*, which gets some hoots.

Then Ruthie turns to me, a glint in her eye. "You're up, Georgie girl," she says, her laughter laced with something sinister. "And you've got Baez."

Why would she do this?

Ruthie and a few of the other girls make eye contact and high-five each other.

But the whole gym goes silent. I can hear my heart thudding in my ears, the blood rushing to all the parts of me that feel dead right now.

And then there's a whoop that shatters it. "Give us a show, Georgie!" Jase shouts.

"Show your man how it's done," Ahmad chimes in.

Laughter echoes, and I stand there like an idiot. *Why won't people stop talking about those rumors?*

I may look completely different, but everything, everyone here, is completely the same.

I'm about to walk off when Monica catches my eye again. There's concern and something else in her gaze, rage maybe, and I know that if I walk away now, I'll be letting them win.

All the eyes in the room bore into me.

I paste on my best I'm-awesome-you're-awesome grin and pick up the pom-poms. I shout out Baez's name and twirl and jump and spin and do a series of back-handspring cartwheels. My kicks aim for the sky, my jumps send me soaring, my round-off is precise, and my split is so flawless, I think I might have hurt myself.

But I leap back to my feet and add a backflip not in the routine. My best move back at Greensprings.

The smile stays glued on, as perfect and perky as any of the ones on those white girls' faces in the movies. I can do this. There are roars and shouts and endless applause, and when I land in place, standing and smiling, Baez is up on his feet, cheering me on. Some of the guys are slapping him on the shoulder, shouting "Your girl, your girl," like we really are a pair or something. So I do a little curtsy, take a bow, and do another high kick.

Then the gym goes quiet again, and I realize that they're all looking beyond me, behind me now. I pivot and find Cora standing there. Eyes livid. Hands on her hips.

Ruthie skulks past me and whispers, "Seems like *someone* has a fucked-up crush. Told ya so."

Cora blows her whistle, loud and fast and mad. She claps her hands above her head again. "We really enjoyed meeting all of you, but as you know, only one girl will claim a spot today. It's not going to be an easy decision." She looks right at me, her tone dripping with hate, as she adds, "We've seen some really stellar work today, and some shitty work, too. Cheerleading isn't easy. We want someone who can make it look and feel effortless. One last huddle, ladies, before we break."

We gather up close, and she stares right through me like I don't even exist. "Next week. One name. Good luck."

The girls around me do Coach Bailey's cooldown stretches, complaining about the wait, the suspense. I try to hold on to hope. I bend over and let my hair out of its tight bun. It explodes, gleeful to be free, and I massage my scalp the way it said to in one of Bryn's magazines. Something about using the natural oils to nourish my hair after a workout—gross, but a guaranteed glow. When I stretch back up, the boys are watching me. Again.

"Who's the hot new girl?" Anthony says, loud enough for me to hear. Like he's never seen me before. Like I haven't been on two group projects with him in the last year. And done all the actual work.

Baez looks down at me. We make eye contact for the longest second ever. Well, at least that's how it feels.

I don't know what to do. Smile? Wave? Smirk? Wink? I don't know what my face looks like: if I'm all sweaty and gross or if he can tell that I need to get my eyebrows threaded this weekend with Mum or if I have something in my teeth—or worse, my nose.

Before I can say anything, they all stomp down the bleachers, some of them waving and whistling, then walk off, as if they were never here in the first place.

Around midnight, I hear Papa sneak in, long after Mum's gone up to her bedroom. He always slips in late after his evening "meetings," which we all know are when he goes to visit Asha, the lady he's been seeing on and off for the past five years. When he shuts the door to his study, I screep out of my room down to the kitchen. Nita Masi wrapped up the leftover naan and hid it in the fridge, but she never does a good job at putting it completely out of sight. Her gift to me.

"Thank you, Nita Masi," I whisper.

I break a piece of the bread in half, sprinkle it with a little water, and heat it up in the microwave. I only zap it for ten seconds. Mum could hear a flea jump off our dog Billi's back, if she ever had them. But she's impeccably groomed, as is expected of everyone in the Khalra household.

The old Georgie would've dipped all three leftover pieces of naan in the entire bowl of rogan josh, sopping up every morsel of the spicy lamb. The new Georgie is only claiming half a piece, no butter, no lamb.

The sneaking around got really bad when we first moved to America. I used to hide Dairy Milks and crisp, salty mathi under my little-girl bed, and sneak sweet, juicy rasgulle from the fridge late at night, the ice-cold syrup dribbling down my chin. I'd stay up watching old American sitcoms, trying to reshape my accent. Trying to forget why we left India in the first place.

I take my naan to Nanima's room, a suite at the back of the house. Papa had it added when Nanima got too ill to go back and forth between here and Delhi. Her door is always unlocked. I can hear the whisper of the bhajans she plays in her little apartment.

I tiptoe through her small living room, and past the mandir, where tiny fake candles blaze day and night, carrying Nanima's prayers to the gods. I pass her statue of Ganesha. The god of new beginnings, remover of obstacles. When I was little, she told me the story of how he got the elephant head in the first place, and I was upset for days, thinking about how a father failed to protect his child. I can almost feel Ganesha's eyes on me as I nibble my naan, pleading for it not to ruin my new beginning. Then again, he has a proud old belly and a sweet tooth, too.

On the mantel across from the mandir is a big arrangement of frames—family pictures. And there, tucked among them, is where I see it.

My heart leaps into my throat, and I swear it would jump right out of my mouth if I didn't close it. I lean over and gently lift the picture up out of its hiding spot, trying not to topple the other frames. It's me, my cousins, and him. From right before my family left India.

Vivek.

He towers over me. Seven years older. My heart drums. A disgusting sweat creeps down my back, light as fingers. I haven't seen his face since we left. I want to burn the picture with one of the candles on Nani's altar, but they're fake flames. I swallow down the angry sob that's crawling up my throat and steady myself against the wall.

I turn the frame backward, out of sight, and I stuff the last bit of naan into my mouth. I close my eyes, willing myself not to look into the mirror on Nani's wall. I fight the choking sensation of too much food in my mouth. I take a deep breath, try to swallow, trying to banish his face—but it's branded into my mind again, an old scar torn open. Those memories of India, once buried, sit like stones in my stomach.

Nanima's fallen asleep in her armchair again. The TV blasts an old Bollywood movie. I wrap one of her old shawls around her and sit at her feet. I lay my head in her lap, like I used to when I was younger. She pats my cheek but doesn't open her eyes. She doesn't speak anymore. Hasn't said a word in two years. But I know she's still in there. The warm wrinkles of her palm make me forget the guilt I feel, for stealing the bread and everything else.

"Nani," I whisper into the folds of her soft woolen wrap, which smells of jasmine and sandalwood, the same twin scents that filled her house. I only miss my life in India during quiet moments like this. It's my fault we had to leave. But the worst of it is the silence. Nani still spoke then. Her mind was sharp, and we spent our days dancing, eating, shopping in the markets. "I'm trying to fix it, Nani," I tell her. "Trying new things. Working on being happy, like you always wanted me to be." I remember one of the last conversations we had. We were sitting right here in her bedroom, one of her Desi soaps droning on the TV. Outside, neighborhood kids shouted and laughed as they kicked around a soccer ball. Nani squeezed down next to me on her couch.

"Jaan." She patted my cheek. "Your face is so long. Why?"

I shrugged. "So fat, you mean?"

She lifted my chin and made me look at her. Tiny lines branched out from the corners of her eyes, which are exactly the same shade of molten caramel as mine.

"Khush raho," she said. "Be happy. Time is too short."

She sighs, and I can almost hear the words in my head now.

Today, maybe, I took the first steps—leaps really—into trying to claim my own happiness. There may be a lot of obstacles in my path, but I refuse to stand in my own way anymore.

Wednesday 11:26 PM

Bryn:

How'd the cheer tryouts go?

Wednesday 11:33 PM

Bryn:

Are you alive?

Wednesday 11:42 PM

Bryn:

Hello?

Wednesday 11:44 PM

Georgie:

I don't wanna talk about it.

Bryn:

That good, huh?

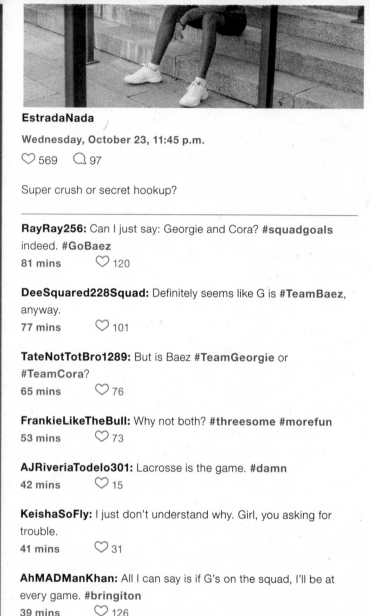

EstradaNada

Wednesday, October 23, 11:45 p.m.

♡ 569   ◌ 97

Super crush or secret hookup?

RayRay256: Can I just say: Georgie and Cora? **#squadgoals** indeed. **#GoBaez**

81 mins   ♡ 120

DeeSquared228Squad: Definitely seems like G is **#TeamBaez**, anyway.

77 mins   ♡ 101

TateNotTotBro1289: But is Baez **#TeamGeorgie** or **#TeamCora**?

65 mins   ♡ 76

FrankieLikeTheBull: Why not both? **#threesome #morefun**

53 mins   ♡ 73

AJRiveriaTodelo301: Lacrosse is the game. **#damn**

42 mins   ♡ 15

KeishaSoFly: I just don't understand why. Girl, you asking for trouble.

41 mins   ♡ 31

AhMADManKhan: All I can say is if G's on the squad, I'll be at every game. **#bringiton**

39 mins   ♡ 126

DeeSquared228Squad: If Cora lets that happen, I'll eat my track shorts.

34 mins   ♡ 19

BabeRuthieSweet1206: My girl doesn't bring her personal shit to the team. This is Business.
32 mins ♡ 82

BecksForDays: They did seem pretty cozy, though, right?
30 mins ♡ 35

SykeWard: I heard they started hooking up this summer, way before anyone saw anything at that party. New couple alert!
23 mins ♡ 215

FilmmakerChance: Couple name: **#Baergie**? I heard that, too, SykeWard.
21 mins ♡ 76

PrincessChristine4578: Cora and Baez are rock solid. Y'all need to STFU.
20 mins ♡ 24

> **SykeWard:** Okay, PrincessChristine4578. Prove it isn't true. Bet you can't, Christine!!
> **19 mins** ♡ 215

DunkCanCarter000: All of this is ridiculous. Who cares?
15 mins ♡ 59

Maisie7680: Slut!
15 mins ♡ 59

Comments Loading

Dear Georgie Khalra,

As co-captains of the team, Ruthie and I are so pleased to inform you that you've been chosen to fill the vacant spot on the Foxham Prep Cheer Squad! Welcome!!!

As you know, taking on a role as a cheerleader is a full-time commitment—we put in long hours practicing, performing, and serving our community, on and off the field. If you're as dedicated to the mission as we are, we'd love to have you join us.

Please let us know ASAP if you will accept the open spot—as you know, there were a lot of contenders, and this is a very coveted offer. Looking forward to having you on the team!

GO, FALCONS!
Cora and Ruthie

Baez:

You busy after practice?

Cora:

Why?

Baez:

I have a surprise.

Cora:

I don't like surprises.

Baez:

You always doing them for me.

Cora:

😮

Baez:

Get excited. Be ready at 8 tonight.

C'mon.

Cora:

Fine!

HAVE YOU EVER BEEN CYBER-BULLIED BEFORE?

DON'T BE MEAN BEHIND THE SCREEN

---

53 mins ☺ 79

Lluvy Rivera: My mom died sophomore year and people said I looked like shit in my photos.

---

41 mins ☺ 31

Courtney McPherson: I have two dads. My photos of us would get swarmed on social.

---

40 mins ☺ 25

Taryn Mbalia: I have had bad acne since 8th grade.

---

32 mins ☺ 175

Michael Cauman: I fell down the stairs in front of the entire junior class. Someone videoed it.

32 mins ☺ 82

Trey Williams: When Gus outed my business all over the place.

30 mins ☺ 12

Dee Dee Matthis: Suck it up! Life's hard.

30 mins ☺ 35

Whitney Corcoran: No one cares about this campaign, Bryn. Stop trying to make yourself relevant. Step down!

23 mins ☺ 215

Astrid Schwann: Everyone had so much to say about me being ace. So many jokes.

21 mins ☺ 260

Nell Peaks: Two words: Revenge porn.

20 mins ☺ 24

Aman Parekh: After my seizure in math class last fall.

18 mins ☺ 10

Mohammed Diallo: When my dad cut all my hair off and someone took a photo last year.

15 mins ☺ 59

Collin Lee: Who cares?

14 mins ☺ 45

Richie Winters: Yeah, after my mom lost her bid for Maryland governor.

3mins ☺ 100

Nafi Jordan: After my breakup with Mags last year.

CORA

THURSDAY, OCTOBER 24
8:23 P.M.

"LEAVE IT ON," BAEZ SAYS AS HE LEADS ME THROUGH some sort of doorway, blindfolded.

"Where are we?" I ask, holding tight to his hands around my waist.

"You'll see," he whispers in my ear. "Sheesh, let me surprise you."

I try to perk up. My boyfriend has planned date night. We're still an amazing couple, and these idiotic rumors dogging us can't change that. He still loves me, and I still love him. There's nothing wrong. Nothing can change any of this. I try not to be sour, as Momma likes to put it: "Always be pleasant and grateful no matter what, Turtle." But it feels like I've worked so hard only to have it all deflate in the middle.

The scent of candles fills the air, and Baez makes me take off my shoes. Softness tickles the bottoms of my feet. "Baez, c'mon."

"Fine. Fine. You're the worst." He removes the blindfold. "But keep them closed until I say *when*."

"Okay." I take a deep breath and pull fake excitement up from somewhere deep down.

"You can look now."

My eyes snap open. Baez's parents' new restaurant spreads out around me, dimly lit and lovely, even half-done. The walls are papered in beautiful rich golds and hunter greens and creamy whites. The start of a quilt-like mosaic art piece sits to the left, made of fragments of the Nigerian flag. Buckets, drapes, covered tables, and construction gear are scattered throughout. Big windows look out into the city, and the sounds of sitar music filter in from the Indian restaurant next door. Here, though, it's just the two of us, and the quiet of our heartbeats, maybe aligning for the first time in what feels like days, weeks, months.

The place is still mostly empty, but one table sits in the middle of the dining room. Candles glow, scattered between still-steaming platters of food. A vase holding dozens of roses is the centerpiece, petals fluttering down occasionally as the breeze blows through the giant windows.

"It's still a work in progress," he says. "But I wanted to cook you a little something from the new menu."

"You cooked?" I ask, eyebrow cocked with suspicion.

"Why you acting so surprised? I've made stuff for you before." He leads me forward to the table, pulls out my seat, and invites me to sit.

I ease into it like it's a bathtub full of scalding water. Why can't I just enjoy this? *Snap out of it*, I tell myself.

Six-word memoir: *Learn to let it go already.*

But I don't know how. People don't usually talk about stuff as long as they've talked about Baez and Georgie. Not unless it's true, like with Bryn and Jase.

He unveils each dish he made: a glistening mound of jollof rice, steaming egusi soup with thick white garra, skewers of suya, pounded yams, and more. The plates are nice. They're not as pretty as the ones his momma makes, but they look decent and smell so good my stomach grumbles. While he launches into how hard it was to try to make these family recipes, I remember the first time I met him.

Baez used to always say, "Don't worry, we're bonded by blood. No one will ever replace you."

The summer he moved here from Nigeria, our mothers met at a party and Momma invited them over for tea.

"Go and play," his mother told us, like we were six years old, and not twelve.

"Show him the playroom," Momma insisted.

But Millie hid in our room, so it was left up to me to entertain him.

The minute I saw him I knew I wanted to be his friend forever. There was something about the way his eyes crinkled when he flashed that grin, even then, like his soul was smiling. Like he really saw you. And he saw me as me. Not one half of Millie and Cora. Not Momma's little Turtle.

I darted to the little playhouse I had in the room and dug in one of my hiding spots. I rubbed my thumb across an old-fashioned razor I'd stolen from Daddy's shaving kit. Sharp and silvery, it hooked like a crescent, almost the exact shape of the ten-dollar croissants Momma always made Vero get from La Petite Bakery. The blade could've peeled our fingers, lifting the thumbprints right off, easy as taking the skin from an apple.

I showed it to him, along with my box of Disney Princess Band-Aids.

He pressed his back against the door, ready to scream.

"What's wrong with you?" I said, unaware how frightening I probably looked with a razor in my small hands.

"What are you doing?" He put his palms out so I couldn't come any closer.

"We're doing a blood pact." He always says I'd smiled like I'd just asked him to play tea party or something.

"Why?"

"Why not? It'll be like a blood marriage."

The only thing I knew about marriages back then was that people dressed up and they kissed at an altar and had children and fought late into the night and then made up. Still might be about all I know about it, to be honest.

"Hold out your hand," I'd ordered.

"Is this safe?"

"We're going to be best friends forever. Husband and wife. Married by blood."

His eyelashes fluttered, curling up like half-moons. He pulled his hand back and forth until I grabbed it and dug the razor into his thumb. "Will you be my blood friend and husband? And promise to keep all of our secrets?"

"Yes."

"Should've said 'I do,'" I corrected.

"I do."

"Now, you cut me," I commanded.

He reached for one of the Band-Aids to stop the bleeding, but I pulled my hand away.

"No, wait, we have to rub our blood together for this whole thing to work. Quick. Do it." I handed him the razor and presented my thumb.

"I can't do it," he said. "I can't hurt you."

"It's fine. Don't you want to be friends forever? Like, even when we're all wrinkly?"

He stumbled over the word yes, probably because he didn't know me at all. But I liked the idea of having a friend forever. A friend with his eyes. A friend I chose, not like Millie, who stole all my space and all my air.

I pushed the razor into his hands again. "C'mon, it's fine."

For the first time in my whole life up to that point, I did something without thinking it through, without making a worry list, without sleeping on it. It only took a quick poke at my skin and a small movement to draw the tiniest line of blood from the fleshy pad of my thumb. I didn't make a noise, and smiled at the sight of the redness. He grabbed my bleeding finger and smashed it hard against his, moving them in tiny circles against each other to mix up the blood, and something shifted in the world, locked in place, never to be undone. Our thumbs, both dripping red and hot and sweaty and swollen.

"Do you want Jasmine, Pocahontas, Snow White, or Ariel?" I'd asked, looking through the box of Band-Aids.

"Fish for a Tiana one," he said. And I laughed.

I wrapped the mint-green Band-Aid around his thumb. "She will remind you of me and keep my blood in you. We're married now. We'll keep each other's secrets."

Because that's what a blood pact is.

"Cora . . . *Cora.*"

Baez gawks at me.

"Oh, sorry." The room resharpens around me.

"What's wrong?"

I want to say *Nothing.*

But the weight of all those online words sits heavy on my shoulders, and no matter what, I can't shake it off.

"Just remembering," I say.

"Remembering what?"

"When we did our blood pact."

He smiles. "Oh, you mean when you stabbed me?"

I want to laugh.

"What is it?"

My phone starts pinging on the table. All the comments filling in once again, almost like they could pop out of my phone and stretch between us. The flow of it hasn't even *slowed down.* "Are you attracted to her?"

"Who?" His eyes narrow.

"You know who."

"I'm into *you*. I'm attracted to you." He reaches for my hand, but I pull away.

"Just answer the question." I cross my arms over my chest.

"She's pretty. She's, like, okay." He pushes food around on his plate. His forehead crinkles, reminds me of the grooves in a molasses cookie.

"She's all exotic and I'm not."

"What does that even mean?"

"You know."

"I don't." He purses his lips.

My stomach twists, and I hate myself in this moment. I'm Cora Davidson. I'm not worried about anyone or anything. I'm on top. "Black girls aren't seen as, like, *exotic* exotic . . . not like her. I'm beautiful, yeah. But regular. Guys love biracial girls or, like, girls from other countries."

"What are you even talking about?"

I glare at him, my eyes wanting to bore a hole into his forehead. "Stop pretending you don't get it. We talk about celebrity couples all the time, and I always complain about the Black guys and what they say about us. And the women they date and marry."

"Yeah, but that isn't me," he says, reaching for my hand again, but I don't let him take it. "Nothing happened. All that shit is stupid lies and rumors. You know that. I was nice to her. That's all."

An unwelcome tear rolls down my cheek. "There's a video. You're touching her hair."

"What?"

I click open my phone and show him what Adele sent me.

"Jase busted out that Silly String shit, and it was everywhere. She had a piece left in her hair. People were teasing her about it looking like cum. I plucked it out. No biggie."

"But it is a big deal. People saw you. They're already thinking things. And then at tryouts, you were cheering for that girl—for Georgie—knowing full well how I would feel. What everyone else would say."

"I told you, nothing happened. And at tryouts, well, your *friend* Ruthie fully set that one up. And dickhead Chance was in the gym filming it. I didn't know that. What did you want me to do? This shit sucks for me, too. They're saying I'm a dog, some sort of asshole. You think I like the shit they're saying about me? Or the stuff they're saying about you?" He balls his hand into a fist. "I don't like it either. When you search my name, this stuff comes up. I don't want coaches seeing this. I barely know the girl. But I'm not gonna be an asshole to her—like everyone else is being, like you're being—because you mad. Because you're jealous."

His hand is heavy on the table. I want to take it in mine, press our thumbs together like we did when we were little, make the whole world and all those endless words they say, the lies they tell, go away. But I can't.

"I wanted to tell you something tonight. That's why I brought you here. I wanted to talk about *us*, and next steps, and our plans for the future. Go through my college list with you. But I need to get one thing clear first, Cora. Okay?"

I nod. Trying not to crack again. But paranoia swirls inside me.

"Do you think we have a future? You and me?" Baez asks.

I nod again, steadier this time. "That's what I want more than anything."

"Then we should do it. Our plans. Apply to the same school. Get a place. It doesn't have to be here." He smiles. And I know how much that will take from him, leaving his family behind. "Anywhere you want. Boston, up by Millie. Maybe New York. Even California."

I nod again, the tears rolling hard and fast. "I'd like that." My voice shakes as I say it. I don't know if it's because I'm finally getting what I want. Or because the words feel hollow now, too little, too late. Maybe a bit of both.

We eat in silence, and it's so different than we've ever been that I can't take it. I stand and walk to his side of the table, climbing onto his lap as I pull off my sweater. Right now I just need his arms around me and his mouth on mine, and the feeling that he loves me to erase what everyone's saying online about him and Georgie, and all the worries swirling around in my head. "Hey," he whispers. "Easy. There are cameras in—"

"I don't care," I say, my hands moving too quickly, a button flying loose off his button-down. I'm kissing him, but he's holding my shoulders back, trying to look at my face, trying to be the caring boyfriend he is. That's not what I want right now.

He tries to say something else. I kiss him again to shut him up, but he's still talking. "You always get what you want, don't you?" he says between kisses, not quite giving up.

He's finally kissing me back, hard, fast, urgent. "Yes . . . yes, I do." I'm back in control.

Before I can get in the door, Momma is already calling my name from the living room.

"Turtle, guess who dropped by?" Her voice is all syrupy.

I cringe, wanting to creep upstairs and dive headfirst into bed and maybe video chat Millie. I'm not even curious about who they're fawning over.

"Baby girl," Daddy says.

That one means that I can't just pretend I don't hear them. I don't want to get grounded again. I sigh, take a deep breath, square my shoulders, and walk to the living room.

I peek my head in before committing.

My parents sit on the couch with Graham. Millie's boyfriend. He spots me and grins. "Hey, Cora!" His cheeks are sweaty, probably from the interrogation my father has given him tonight. Even though they love him. Much more than Baez. Graham's mom builds cybersecurity software for the DC government, and his dad is a famous jazz musician who Daddy grew up with.

"Graham was missing Millie, even though she was just here. Isn't it sweet?" Momma beams at straight-A, uber-polite, super-sweet, perfect-boyfriend Graham.

"Awesome," I grumble.

Then I feel bad. I actually love Graham. He and Baez are close, too. I just can't deal tonight.

"Hey," I say.

Momma pats the seat beside her on the couch.

"I can't. Got a paper," I lie.

"I'm about to go, too. My parents hit me with a curfew until college acceptances come in."

Daddy laughs and pats him on the shoulder. "Good plan. What's your top choice?"

"Yale," he replies. "Maybe Harvard, to join Millie."

Daddy nods his head in approval.

"Hey, C, I left my hoodie and graphing calculator here," Graham says to me. "You seen it? Millie said it's in her room. Mind grabbing for me?"

"Sure. Meet me in the foyer."

"Cool."

I dart upstairs and into Millie's room. It's right on her desk with a note and Graham's name scrawled on the envelope. I sneak and read the handwriting.

Wear it for me, then send to my dorm. I want it to smell like you. Also, programmed your calculator. Your formulas were all messed up.

Love you,

Millie

My heart pinches with jealousy. I think of Baez. Graham is never the guy you hear rumors about. He's cool and everyone likes him, but no one is checking for him. Would she even believe them if people started shit?

My phone buzzes, and my skin gets hot again. Everything is fine. I'm okay. Baez is okay. I just wish they'd stop it already. Tears prick my eyes, and I quickly swipe them away.

"You find it, Cora?" Graham calls out.

I rush back downstairs, where he waits for me.

"You good?" His eyes scan mine.

"No," I reply. Tired of pretending.

"What's up?"

"Senior year just isn't turning out to be what I thought it was gonna be. Millie's not here. Things are weird with Baez. I've got to get it together."

"I know." He shrugs.

"And the shit online . . . ugh!" I admit.

"It's not true." He puts a warm hand on my shoulder. "That's my boy. I know him. You know him. He wouldn't do that."

"People do a lot of things they *say* they wouldn't do." Weirdly, Bryn's face pops into my head. The night she slept over after finding out about her father's affair. She never thought her dad could do something like that. "But I'll take your word and his word for it."

"I've been at all those parties. He's not into anyone but you. He's never been," he says, taking the hoodie, calculator, and note from my hands. "Call Millie. Like, figure it out. I promise you, this shit is a whole lie. Maybe people are just jealous because you two are the best couple in the school, but it's weird. I don't know why this has stuck around so long. Almost seems like somebody's messing with y'all. 'Cause I've never seen Baez do a thing."

Cora:

Everything's a mess.

Millie:

Turtle, you okay?

Cora:

I keep fighting with Baez over dumb shit.

Millie:

I saw what they're saying. About Baez.
Online.

Cora:

It's all bullshit. You know him.
So not true. But . . .

Millie:

Still. Hard to read that. I'd be pissed if people
were talking about Graham like that.

Cora:

Yeah. It's been rough.

Millie:

You know I'm here if you need me.
No matter what.

Cora:

I know.

Love you. I miss you.

Millie:

Ditto. 😎

Cora:

Hey.

Bryn:

Hey hey. How's it going.

I heard Georgie made the team. 😜

Cora:

Yeah. So I gotta do something about this G situation.

And I think I'm gonna need your help.

BAEZ AND GEORGIE WERE COZYING UP SOLO AT CORA'S PARTY.

BAEZ AND GEORGIE DEFINITELY MADE OUT UPSTAIRS IN CORA'S BEDROOM.

COMPLETE AND TOTAL YOU-KNOW-WHAT AT JASE'S PARTY.

GEORGIE AND BAEZ HAVE BEEN FOOLING AROUND FOR MONTHS BEHIND CORA'S BACK.

PART TWO

THE LIES

lie [lī]: *noun*

1) an intentionally false statement
2) a falsehood
3) from the Old English *lyge*
4) we all do it

BRYN

FRIDAY, OCTOBER 25
3:45 P.M.

THE CAMPAIGN HEADQUARTERS LOOKS GREAT. BETTER THAN great. Spectacular. I circle the table I set up in the cafeteria. Georgie's poster tripod almost glitters. Cora and I spent months in the spring picking out the right power colors for our campaign. We drove to a weirdo occult shop outside of Baltimore and asked a fortune-teller to help us make sure we won. We burned peacock-blue and magenta candles for weeks.

I run my fingers over the tablecloth, wishing she was here with me. Hoping my plan to get her back works. Hoping that she might still be my VP. I inspect the photo booth I set up in the far corner. One of my volunteers, my cousin Anabelle, gives directions for the camera to be installed. This is it. Today, the campaign launches.

It'll be Foxham Prep's very own confessional. A place for students to record their take on online bullying.

I wave at people who pass by. "Want to sign my petition?"

Most roll their eyes at me or laugh in passing. It just hardens my resolve. I'll get tons of this when I run for president. I'll be ready. This is just a test.

"Take a photo, share your story, and get a button," I call to another group of students passing by. "Support the cause!"

"Only if you tell us how you landed four people in the hospital," one says, getting a laugh from everyone else.

Their voices grate across my skin.

"What's the real story?"

"You still a psycho?"

"What you gonna go off about this time?"

"You wanted them all dead, didn't you? Admit it."

"You gonna try to murder people again?"

Like some sick and twisted joke of fate, Jase walks through the cafeteria at that exact moment. Everyone whispers, staring back and forth between us.

I turn around, a knot of anger swirling in my stomach. I used to love the feeling of his eyes on me. The warmth of it was like his hands all over me.

I ruffle the photo booth's curtains, making sure it looks perfect, giving my brain something to do until he leaves. I squeeze my eyes shut and push away the laughter and Jase's face and the sound of his voice. He's just grabbing a sports drink and an energy bar before the lacrosse game. Who cares what he thinks? What any of them think?

One day he loved me—deep, wet kisses and fingers and hands all over me, lost in my hair, presents for no reason, endless online chats and texts, the light buzz of headaches from all-night phone calls—and the next day, he didn't. Done. Gone.

I remember the jingle of my keys as I walked to my car that night.

I remember hating the way they sounded, holding them so tight I couldn't hear them anymore.

I remember the deep red pattern the metal left in my palm.

My car sputtered alive when I'd cranked it, like it didn't want to go anywhere, like it was perfectly happy to sit in the garage, completely uninvited to Baez's end-of-the-summer party. I'd been a little off. My parents' mess made me anxious, had me second-guessing everything. Christine and Ruthie said they felt weird when they were around Jase and me. I was too possessive. Too all-about-him. They needed a break. Even Cora.

Jase was being strange. Too quiet. Too busy to hang out. Then I saw a picture of him at Baez's house, and I drove there anyway. Down Wisconsin Avenue into Georgetown. People poured out Baez's front door like ants. Hip-hop beats escaped the house windows and vibrated my car.

I texted Jase one line after another.

No answer.

Then question mark after question mark.

Left on read.

Hours went by, and I sat there, alone.

Then Jase stumbled out of the door with two girls by his side, his arms thrown across their slender shoulders. *My* boyfriend. He turned his head right and left, whispering in their ears, saying things that made them giggle. He unlocked his car, tossed his beer can onto Baez's lawn, and pulled his phone out. Full of my texts. But he shoved it back into his pocket as if the screen was blank, and the girls jumped inside his car. I didn't find out until later that Baez was in the car too, passed out in the back seat.

I remember following them.

I remember taking a shortcut around the block so I could pull up beside them, so I could make sure he saw me.

I remember how the light turned and how I had to run the red light to keep up.

I remember the bright flash of the street camera.

I remember the noise of the crash.

I remember the crunching and glass shattering and the hot burn of the airbags.

I remember the sound of sirens and the salty taste of blood.

I remember fleeing the scene.

Chance's laughter yanks me out of the memory. I whip around to glare at him.

"He's gone," he shouts. "You can relax now."

"Why, were you stressed? 'Cause I'm not." My hands are shaking though.

"He's a dick, anyways. I don't know why anyone would be into him."

"You just wouldn't get it."

"Guess not. But I know I wouldn't let him get to me."

I glare at him. "Thanks," I mumble.

His table holds a flat screen playing a campaign video. Different scenes from the school campus. Interviews with students and faculty. Famous alumni clips. Very clever. Very presidential. He has full access to the school news channel. Could be effective. Easily shareable. But my photo booth will be like a retro throwback kind of thing. Fun. Inspiring. I hope. I need it to be.

His eyes follow every move I make, so I take one of his pamphlets from a nearby table and rip it to shreds, relishing the way his mouth drops open with shock, how the deep red climbs up his white neck to the top of his pasty forehead. Then I blow him a kiss.

"Just give up," Chance says.

"Why should I?" I spit back.

"You don't have what it takes anymore. You never really did in the first place." He cleans the mini flat screen on his table, shining it with a rag. "High school rules dictate that this amorphous thing called popularity allows you to win an election. It has nothing to do with substance. Everything to do with the silly social rules we all buy into." He reaches for his camera. "My documentary will expose it all. Reveal the truth."

"Whatever, Chance. You don't even want this." I jam my hands onto my hips. "You just want me to *not* have it."

We've always been at odds. Ever since elementary school, when the teacher said to go right, he was the kid who had to go left and get us all in trouble. Couldn't just follow, always the one who opted out and ruined the unanimous vote. But when his mom lost her job on the Hill and they moved, he turned sour. Set his sights on me. I became the villain in his story. And then in everyone's, I guess.

I glare at him, and he laughs.

"I think I'd do a better job. It's as simple as that. I'd challenge people to do things differently. Not maintain the status quo." He sets his camera down and pulls his too-long hair into a dark topknot. "And you . . ." His eyes scan me. "You embody the status quo. Tiny version of your parents. From your boat shoes to your polo shirt to the pearl earrings you inherited. You love it, everything being the same. That's not change, Bryn. It's the opposite."

He stutters on the word *opposite*. I tell myself not to be an asshole. Not to dredge up one of the many reasons we hate each other. In eighth grade, I had a period accident, the blood staining my uniform, and he took a picture and started the nickname "Bloody Bryn." Which followed me the whole school year. I retaliated with a video parody of my own—of his stutter. My parents grounded me for three months after the principal brought us in for mediation. It was a shitty thing to do, yeah. But he started it.

I need to blast him, but my phone buzzes.

A notification from Cora.

My heart does a backflip.

I fumble as I tap her message. Four small words make my heart race: Can you meet me?

I look up at Chance. "I have much bigger things to deal with. I'm actually important. People need me."

I write back: Yes, on my way.

I speed down U Street to meet Cora at Southern Sweet Jubilee Ice Cream Parlor, where we used to always hang out. I can almost see her waiting for me. Already in *our* booth, playing with her hair and combing through the menu, even though we order the same thing every time. Deluxe waffle split drenched in caramel sauce with extra cherries.

My heart drums as I circle the block looking for parking. My phone is a melody of dings and pings as more comments appear on social media about the rumor. A pit burns in my stomach. I remember all the things people said about me, and how I woke up dreading my phone, how I blocked my social media apps for weeks to avoid tags, how I thought it might never go away. Guilt and anxiety shoot through me.

Calm down, I tell myself. *You're sweating. Get it together.*

I ignore texts from Georgie. She'll have to find her own ride home today. I have to take this chance to fix things with Cora. Before going in, I open my notebook and flip to her page. Cora's picture stares back up at me from the collage of pictures of us together, pasted next to a list of all our favorite things to do. I review my plan over and over again. The words almost pulse on the page as my eyes scan them for the hundredth time. My practiced speech. Fully thought out. Fully realized. I just have to deliver it right.

Make her remember how good a friend you are.

Make her remember all the great things you did together.

Make her remember that she *needs* you.

I send her a text to tell her I'm walking up. *Breathe, Bryn, stay calm.*

Walk at a normal pace.

But I'm so excited, I nearly run.

You got this, I tell myself as I push open the door and hear the familiar little chime.

I spot her in the far corner booth. Our booth. She's drinking a glass-bottle cola, drumming her fingers on the menu. Sometimes I miss her so much it's like a punch to the gut.

This is supposed to be our year.

Bryn and Cora.

President and VP.

Best friends.

I'll make those words true again. Things will settle back into place. Like nothing—no one—ever derailed them at all.

I ease up to the table. "Hey."

She looks up. "Hey."

I slide into the booth, my speech bubbling up inside my head. I open and shut my mouth a few times. Ugh. *C'mon*, I scream inside. But a silence stretches between us, only broken by the waitress stopping by to take our order. "Should we get our usual?" I ask.

"I'm, like, not trying to have all those calories. I ordered a soy milkshake before you got here." She nibbles her bottom lip, picks at the menu edge. Cora isn't the kind of girl who calorie counts or watches her weight. Her energy is all off.

"You okay?" I let the question ease out carefully.

"I'm fine."

The response is too small to hold all the things happening with us. With her. With everything. She waits while I order something new since she didn't order our usual.

"I wanted to meet up to, like, clear the air, you know," she says. "Or whatever."

"Really?" My heart flips again. "Can you forgive me?"

She purses her lips, considering my question.

My pulse races. The same way it did the night of the accident, when I told her it was me. She'd called me from the hospital, and I went to meet her. I couldn't stop shaking after what happened. I didn't know what to tell her, especially after she told me Baez was badly injured. He could have been killed because he didn't have his seat belt on. I didn't know how to tell her that I messed up. I didn't know how to say that running that red light caused it all.

"What you did was dumb."

"I know, I know. I didn't mean for the accident to happen. I just wanted to know deep down that Jase was doing what I thought he was. After everything that happened with my parents . . . I was just . . . a mess." The words sputter out. "Like, everything got messed up. I couldn't trust the things he was saying." I leave out the part about how Baez put a wedge between us. I leave out the part where he poisoned her against me. I leave out the part where I feel like he never liked me to begin with.

"I finally, like, *get it* get it. How you could be pushed to the edge like that." She doesn't look at me, instead staring at a point on the wall behind my head. "And I'm not loving Jase these days. He's had a lot of things to say online. A real asshole."

"He doesn't have *real* friends," I say, each word feeling like grit in my teeth. "He has people he can use. I found that out the hard way." The regret of it all tastes bitter. "I don't know what I saw in him."

"Muscles." Cora snorts.

We both laugh, and the waitress sets our desserts between us. It feels like old times again.

"It was just such a bad decision," she adds.

"The worst one I've ever made." The memory of it still makes my skin hot. "I'm sorry. About Sasha and Keisha, and so sorry Baez got hurt. I've been apologizing to him and his family since. Everyone hates me . . . and maybe I deserve it."

"I know," she replies. "He told me."

"I hurt people, and I let you down. Now you hate me, too." I swallow the tears.

She reaches her hand across the table and squeezes mine until the shaking subsides. "I don't hate you. It's okay. I understand now."

"Can I ask you something?"

Her eyebrow lifts. "You're going to do it regardless of what I say."

"Are you and Baez okay?" I soften my voice, trying to be nice about him.

"Well, today we're fine. But tomorrow, I don't know. I can't seem to get a grip on my feelings about it. Like, in my heart . . . I know he didn't do it. But there's that little whisper, you know? Talk doesn't last this long when there's nothing to substantiate it."

"Yeah, rumors can do that. It's like, they start because people are jealous and want something to happen, like for you guys to break up . . . and then they just turn into the truth, somehow, like they are self-fulfilling. Like what happened with me," I say. But I don't add how she's better off without him.

"Baez says the same thing."

I try not to grit my teeth.

"That people are being ridiculous. They want to see a show. They want to mess with us."

"I can offer a distraction. We *could* work together again—as president and vice president? I really need you."

"The campaign is actually working. Super brilliant. I'm getting a lot of online hate, too. People wondering why I'm still with Baez. People judging me. Someone even made a meme about it all. It's gone viral."

"So what do you say?" I let the question ease between us. Not too aggressive. Not too pleading. Not too eager. She's easy to run off.

She looks skeptical, but there's something there. A glimmer of something familiar. Like we might slide back in place again. The look I've been waiting for forever.

"I'll think about it."

ONLINE POLL

Who's Hotter?
Beyoncé wannabe or
new Bollywood babe

CORA	GEORGIE

GEORGIE

SATURDAY, OCTOBER 26
1:35 P.M.

VIBS STARES AT ME, WAITING FOR ME TO ANSWER HER question, to confess how lost I am without her and her Auntie-like guidance. We're sitting at our father's golf club at the heated indoor pool. While our dads play a round, we watch her cousin Roo splash. I don't know whether to be honest. It's been a week from hell. Or narak, as my mum and other Hindus call it. Sometimes I wake up and it's all good comments on my photos. And other times? It's terrible. People calling me a homewrecker, a bitch, a slut.

I settle on "It's been fine. All the extra training sessions Mum has me in are kicking my ass." And toning my thighs. They'll definitely help once my cheer practices start. But I'm sure she doesn't want to hear that.

Her eyes hold suspicion.

"Well, I'm grounded," I add. Apparently I missed a few therapy sessions with Dr. Divya. Oops. "Lucky my mum let me out of the house at all."

"Your mum loves me."

Vibs is right about that.

It's nearly Halloween, but the leaves have barely turned orange and the atrium's glass enclosure reflects a bright, cloudless sky more reminiscent of summer than fall. We soak up the sun even though our mums would cringe at the idea of us getting any browner. "Too much chai and too much sun will make you dark. So only have a little bit of each," Mum always says jokingly. But it's not really a joke. Or funny. It's racist.

I take off my cover-up to reveal the high-waist two-piece suit Bryn made me order online. The diagonal stripes make me look skinnier. Or at least that's what one of the magazines said. I like the way the bottoms hide the tiny looseness I have left on my stomach from dropping all the weight. And the retro vibe makes me feel like a pinup girl. A little brown Marilyn Monroe, a bit of old-school Zeenat.

Vibs sits up, her glasses sliding down her nose. "Whoa," she says, her eyes combing over me. "Leaving anything to the imagination these days, Jash?" She runs her hand along her plain blue one-piece suit, the barometer of modesty. "Guess I shouldn't be surprised."

It's an easy hit, but it still stings. I feel good. Why's she trying to make me feel bad? I decide to ignore it, to focus on lying out. I need to be mindless and motionless for a minute, to just forget about everyone and everything.

I spray on sunscreen, sending some straight into Vibha's open mouth. Serves her right. She hasn't shut up since we got here, yammering on and on about her class schedule, mid-semester exams, and the fourth paper she has to write. I start to laugh as she sputters. This all feels normal, familiar. Hanging out with her. A glimmer of my old life. A part of it that wasn't so bad.

I lean back on the lounger, perching my sunglasses on my head. A few male servers gawk at me as they pass by with trays of iced tea and mint juleps, and one older man—who could be about Papa's age—stops to stare.

I ignore Vibs's prodding to cover up, and when she throws me a towel, I tuck it behind my head. I shouldn't let them look. And later I'll probably hate myself for letting these assholes think they deserve a show. But right now it just feels good to be *seen*. Appreciated. Wanted. For, like, the first time in my life. Like Dr. Divya said, I can be whoever I want.

And I am so not the old Georgie anymore.

"Really, Jash," Vibs says. "I barely recognize you. And, like, it's not about your body. Your personality is different."

I fight the heat climbing my throat. "I am different, Vibs. And I worked hard to get here." She doesn't say anything. "I spent a long time being ignored," I snap, like Bryn or the other white girls at school, who just say anything and everything that comes to mind. Or at least that's how it seems. "I spent a lot of time feeling hideous."

Vibha sits up, frowning for a long moment, then says, "You were never hideous."

And I can't help but laugh.

"I'm serious, Jash," she says, staring down at her hands. "You're beautiful. But you were always beautiful. I wish you knew that, like, deep down."

"I finally *feel* beautiful," I say to her.

A cute, younger waiter swings by to drop off free mango smoothies. "For the lovely ladies," he says with a wink. "On the house."

I smile and say thank you.

Roo climbs out of the pool and scoots onto a lounger, sloshing water all over. She reaches eagerly for a glass, grinning at the guy.

"Rohi," Vibs says, using her given name, like she's Roo's mum. "We should send them back. That's weird."

Roo retreats, a small child who's been scolded.

I hand her the glass. "Take it, Roo."

She reluctantly sucks the thick mango liquid through the straw, staring at Vibs the entire time. I hand one to Vibs, too. She makes me hold it for a while before she finally caves.

I can feel Roo staring in awe. At fourteen, she barely fills out her one-piece, even though she's coveting mine, like I'm one of the girls I always admired, always wanted to be. "I'll send you the link," I tell her, and she grins, taking another sip of her smoothie.

Vibs scoffs. "Seriously, Jashan, life isn't just about what you look like. And honestly, you've made a big mess of things. Have you even started your applications yet?" I can see her to-do list in my head. "The early-decision deadline is soon."

"I don't know if I want to go to Yale anymore." The thought slips out by accident, half-baked. Did I really just say that? Did I really mean that? Everything has changed this year. Or at least I want it to. I'm not quite sure I know what I want anymore.

Vibs chokes on her smoothie. "What?"

Roo cowers in her lounge chair.

"Of course you want to go to Yale. We've been planning it—"

"*You've* been planning it." I shrug. "I'm planning to explore my options."

"What options? Art school?" She snickers. "You don't have it in you."

And just like that, she kills the vibe again. She's almost as bad as Mum. Suddenly, it feels heavy, the knowledge that we haven't fit together for a long time now. Maybe it is time to let her go, to stash her away in the back of the closet with all the old clothes I can't wear anymore.

"At least I'm willing to try to step outside the pretty, pretty box with a bow on top that my mommy put me in." I don't even sound like me. I sound like Bryn. Mean.

Roo's jaw drops, though I have to give Vibha credit—she doesn't even flinch.

The whistle makes both of us turn.

Jase Cunningham. Bryn's ex. He's headed in our direction. He's got no shirt on, and his swim trunks drip chlorinated water.

"Oh god. Him, too?" Vibs asks, but I don't get to answer before he's towering over us.

"Hey, hey, pretty lady," he says to me, all smooth and slick. He's a white-boy stereotype: blond, tanned, muscular, smug. His face is all red and splotchy, and his hair slicked down. I've pretty much never talked to him, but he hangs out with Baez and Ahmad and the lacrosse team. I used to see his car parked outside my house, watch him tiptoe through Bryn's lawn to her pool house in the middle of the night. I used to wonder what it was like to have a boyfriend, to just sneak him in at 3:00 a.m. like that.

"Um, hey," I stammer.

Oh god, oh god, oh god. Why are you talking to us? What am I supposed to do? What should I say? Am I even allowed to talk to him? Bryn would freak.

"What's up?" he asks.

"Nothing." I never know how to answer that question. Like ever.

"Catching some sun?"

"Yeah." I flinch as he sits beside my legs, his hand landing on my calf, his eyes working their way up my entire body. The heat of his gaze burns hot as the sun overhead. It makes my stomach flip, like the smoothie's gonna come right back up.

Roo focuses on finishing her drink. But Vibs gawks at him. For once, I'm grateful. "Aren't we in Precalc together?"

She slides her sunglasses down her nose. "I'm in AP Calc."

"Oh, there's someone who looks just like you in my class." He flashes a big white grin, and I cringe. He's totally mixing her up with another Indian girl.

I laugh. "Could be any one of us, just swap out a name, all the same." Who am I, even?

"We don't all look alike," Vibha snaps.

He grins. "Clearly," he shoots back, the tone of it making her mad. He turns to me again. "Because you—I would definitely remember you."

Vibs sucks her teeth, slipping her sunglasses and headphones on, tuning us out.

Roo props up her book, watching the live show over it like a respectable freshman.

His palm moves up my calf, and it takes all my strength not to pull my leg away. "You coming to my party?" he says with a grin.

My heart thumps so loud I'm afraid everyone can hear it. "What party?"

"My birthday. Not until November but . . . you heard it here first. Eighteen. I'll be texting it out. Gimme your number." He doesn't wait for me to say yes, instead takes my phone and puts his number in it. "Gonna hit me back, right?"

My stomach twists. "Yeah, I guess." My words trip over themselves.

Vibs's eyes burn into me from behind her glasses.

"I'm only inviting beautiful girls," he adds, too loud. Then he leans in, like we're sharing a secret. "So you'll come, right?"

He's talking about me.

I'm one of *those* girls now.

I look at Vibs, her mouth hanging open in shock and disgust, like she's some Auntie about to hit the group text.

I'll give her something to share. "Guess I have to, huh?"

"Bet." He starts to get up but sits back down. "And come on, final answer: You hooking up with my boy Baez?"

Vibha flinches.

I force a smile. "Nope. Sorry to disappoint you."

"I have a girlfriend and all, but you got to know that I'm the best lacrosse player. So if you were going to hook up with one of us, it should be me." He stands, dripping water again, and saunters off, but turns back to look. The heat in his gaze lingers, my heartbeat thrumming in my ears, incessant.

Vibs yanks out her headphones. "What's wrong with you?"

"What?" I reply.

"You were flirting with him."

I shrug. "So?"

"So?" Her arms are crossed over her chest in signature fashion. Roo peeks out from behind her book. "Truly unbelievable, how much you've changed."

"You said as much. Guess I've changed too much for you to hang out with me, then." I snatch up my stuff. I'm so tired of her judgment. All I did was chat with him for a minute. I storm out, but she's right behind me, her hands tugging my arm.

I turn and push her away, hard, and she nearly topples backward, grabbing at an empty chair, which clatters to the concrete. Even after everything, I'm still bigger than her. I always will be.

"What the hell is wrong with you, Jashan?" she shouts, rubbing her leg where it hit the chair. "That *hurt*!" There's a bruise blooming there already, but the hurt splashed across her face is worse. I try to feel something—sympathy, guilt, remorse—for pushing her away like that, for causing physical pain. But all I can feel is the rage.

"What do you think is wrong with me?" I'm shouting now. "All I wanted is to try something a little different. To be someone different. And here I am, and it's all exactly the same." Then it hits me. "No, actually it's worse. I can't do anything right, I can't get anything right, I can't even breathe, and all you do is remind me of every single stupid thing that's wrong with me. That's why you've always loved having me there, a sidekick who makes you look perfect in every way."

I take a deep breath, trying to calm myself down, but the tears are rolling hot and furious now. I can't even be embarrassed by them; all I can see is red. The red of Vibha's face, the red of my fury. "Well, I'm done. Once and for all. If I've changed so much, you are no longer required to be my friend."

Rohi rushes over, the shock on both their faces making me laugh out loud.

"I'm no longer thinking about what I should or shouldn't be doing according to you!" I shout. "I'm *done*."

Ursula:

Did you guys hear what happened at the country club this afternoon?

Nicki:

Hanji, han. That Khalra girl has lost her damned mind along with all that weight.

Neelam:

Well, she must be pretty hangry, the way Suleika controls her diet.

Nicki:

Vinod:

I think she needs to see a psychiatrist.
Do you think Suleika would react badly to a recommendation?

Nicki:

She's seeing Divya, no? But she needs a complete inpatient intervention. Pagal. Fully. The whole family, henna?

Ursula:

You heard what happened in India, nah?
What prompted their move in the first place?

Neelam:

Oh, they don't speak of that. I made the
mistake of bringing it up once.
Suleika was LIVID. That poor girl.
And now all these rumors. Shameful.

Ursula:

Rumors always come from truth, though.
Everybody knows that.

Ruthie:

Georgie!! Monica!!
Welcome to the Foxham Cheers!

Cora:

Yes, welcome! It's a lot of work and
commitment, but we know you can do it!

Monica:

Bring it.

Georgie:

OMG THANK YOU GUYS SO MUCH FOR
YOUR CONFIDENCE IN ME! I WON'T LET
YOU DOWN! I'M SO HONORED TO BE
A PART OF THE TEAM!

Ruthie:

Down girl! Why you yellin'?

Sasha:

Gotta say: I like the enthusiasm!

Cora:

Me too! More to come soon but
get ready to have your ass kicked.

Ruthie:

And she's not even joking.

Georgie:

CORA

MONDAY, OCTOBER 28
3:46 P.M.

I WATCH MY GIRLS GET READY FOR CHEER PRACTICE. They're beautiful, athletic, wearing perfectly ironed uniforms and flawless makeup. Just how I like them. Mini representations of me.

Even Georgie. She's started wearing her hair like mine and the other girls, and you'd never know she's new to the squad, that she didn't always belong. That she couldn't be just like me. Or even replace me. I shake that thought away.

I try not to grimace, wondering if Bryn's idea was actually a good one. Before the accident, Bryn was the one to make things fun, the one to amp things up, the one with all the drive. But I added Monica as an alternate, just in case I have to get rid of Georgie.

Ruthie steps up beside me. "I still think we should kick Indian oink-oink off. I don't trust her."

"Don't call her that. Either of them. None of that shit on my squad, okay?"

Ruthie snorts and rolls her eyes.

"Gotta keep her close and watch her, right?" The thought has crossed my mind a million times since we let Georgie join—I mean, what kind of idiot am I, inviting this kind of drama into the one good part of my life? Cheerleading is my place away from everything. But if I do kick her off now, I won't be able to keep her loyal. To make sure that she doesn't think my boyfriend is someone available to her.

Ruthie cackles. "Yeah, I guess. I'd rather just destroy her."

She bumps her hip into mine in solidarity, then turns back to the group, preparing to check each girl off on her sheet.

"I see you, slacking, G. Get that ass UP," Sasha says from her seat. There's a mean gleam in her eyes, and it gives me the *in* I need.

I cross my arms over my chest. "Georgie! You heard Sasha! GEORGIE."

Her head perks upright.

"Fifteen suicides," I say. I can't quite keep the glee out of my voice.

"What?" she replies, getting to her feet.

"Punishment for being . . . new."

She gawks at me like she can't believe the words coming out of my mouth. "Did you hear me?" I jam my hand to my hip. "I'm speaking English."

Monica catches my eye and she looks disappointed.

"What?" I challenge.

Her eyebrows lift. "Nothing."

I swallow guilt. I shouldn't have said that. It was too mean. Rude. Bigoted. Ugh. What's happening to me?

Georgie's cheeks flame. Glistening with sweat, she's kind of even more beautiful than she was. Perfect full lips, high cheekbones, and that golden skin. You can't take your eyes off her; she's that universal kind of beautiful. The kind that makes every boy want to be with her. The kind that makes her exotic and everyone's type. She winks at me like she's got all the confidence in the world.

But I can't bring myself to walk it back. "Do we have a problem here?" I tap my shoe. I can feel the low grumble in my belly. Hate.

"I heard you," she says. "It's just . . ."

"Just what?"

Everyone is watching now. No more stretching or warming up. All eyes on me and Georgie. And whatever this war is between us.

"Nothing," she mutters, and turns to run up and down the gym.

"Good," I say. "Keep it that way. Follow instructions."

She runs back and forth, ducking at each cone we set up. Other students watch her with confusion as the rest of my girls just holler. The other girls chuckle at Georgie struggling, and it feels good. I know it's because they also think she's super pretty now and want her to suffer a little for it. I do, too. Before her, people didn't think they could talk about me and Baez.

Sweat drips down her legs and arms, leaving a splotchy wet trail on the gym floor. I try to focus on our new routine. My body goes through the motions, but my brain is far away. Thinking about Baez. Thinking about why people think they can talk about us. Thinking about how to turn senior year around and go out with a bang.

The boys' locker room doors open, and the lacrosse team pours out, headed for the fields. They whistle and hoot and holler at us. Some of the girls wave. Baez and Jase are last to walk past our practice.

Baez winks at me. I blow him a kiss.

But when I turn around, Georgie is staring right at him.

"What are you looking at?" I say to her.

She panics and starts stuttering.

The boys exit.

I scowl at her, then clap my hands and bring everyone into a circle.

"So, Georgie, Christine, and Monica," I say. "You are about to embark on phase one of our initiation process. Inside the activity room, you will face certain obstacles that will test you. Cheerleading is a sport. Cheerleading is a sisterhood. We must all be close. This is part of that transformation. The captains and I set this obstacle course up all day yesterday to make sure we all bond together and have the best squad this year."

There are more whoops and hollers.

"You ready?" I lead everyone to the activity room doors. I point at Christine. She rushes forward to open the doors.

It's pitch-black inside, aside from little dot lights on the floor. The other girls start giggling and screaming from the excitement of it all.

I shove the girls near me into the maze of moon bounces and ropes courses.

"Move your asses!" Ruthie shouts.

I watch Georgie out of the corner of my eye. She lingers along the edges but works hard, trying to keep up. I try to pull my attention away from her and to the rest of the girls.

Ignore Georgie.

Ignore the rumors.

Ignore all the whispers.

The rage boils over.

Suddenly, an image of Baez and her leaps to mind: him nuzzling under her jaw.

"Move it!" I bark at her. But none of that happened. None of that is real. Why is my brain betraying me? Still, I double down: "Move your ASS."

Then one of the other cheerleaders slaps her back and butt.

"Ow! Stop hitting me!" Georgie shouts.

"We'll hit you harder if you don't move," I say.

Her body smacks the ground, falling flat on a ropes course on the floor. Other girls scramble up, quickly working their way through by putting one foot in each section. Christine's wiry and quick. Monica strategic and methodical. Georgie? A mess. She's got strength, but gets flustered, letting her anxiety throw her off. Her shoes get all tangled up, two seconds too slow as she tries to get her knees up and her feet through each opening between the ropes. Her legs are like putty from all those suicides.

I watch smugly from behind, following all the girls through the obstacle course. They tumble out of the last bounce house and are led outside. We shove them into a mud pit we made. They have to duck and climb under a rope maze. They claw their way forward. The mud gets all over their legs and down their shorts.

I want them to think: *Why did I sign up for this again?*

And to know it's hard work being part of a squad. You have to earn this.

I watch Georgie struggle. Ruthie glances at me and smiles. She kicks Georgie in the back of the leg.

Georgie flies, tumbling face-first into the mud.

"That's for messing with Baez," I hear her say.

I can't wipe the grin from my face, as hard as I try. I know I shouldn't like the way everyone, both online and off, has come to my rescue— even though I don't need saving. But it feels good to be loved like that. Protected.

I watch Monica help Georgie to her feet, and the worry piles up in my stomach. I need allegiance. From all of them. That's the point of a team, right? And the captain is queen.

"Welcome to the squad," I say once everyone is finally through. "If you can get dirty with your sisters, then you can spot your sisters. We don't shit on each other. We have each other's backs."

Georgie laughs, unexpectedly. An awkward, high-pitched sound. She clasps her hand over her lips. She's flustered, mud caked all over her.

"Something funny, Georgie?" I snap, and feel my eyes narrow like Momma's when she's angry.

She shakes her head. "I laugh sometimes when I'm nervous. Silly habit, sorry!"

The other girls roll their eyes.

"Maybe it's better if you aren't on the squad if you can't take this seriously." My tone is ice.

"I know some things that she takes seriously," says Ruthie. "Like hooking up with other people's boyfriends."

Georgie's face reddens.

"Cheerleading is about sisterhood, Georgie." She flinches when I say the words. "So far, you haven't been very sisterly. Do you think you're cut out for this, to be one of us?"

She swallows hard.

"This is just the beginning," Ruthie says. "If you can't take the heat . . ."

"Only the strong survive this. But some people aren't made for sisterhood. Some people have other priorities. If you don't think you can handle it, then . . ."

"I can," Georgie says, her voice breathless, her face determined. "I want this."

"Then you'll need to prove yourself," I say. "To all of us. But especially to me."

She smiles, and I grin back, but it's a mean thing, vindictive, angry.

"Go, then. A hundred suicides. Now."

As she stumbles off, eager to please, desperate to be a part of this, of us, my girls rally around me, watching my every movement. I should feel like I've won, right? But in that moment, I feel like I might have just lost everything.

I throw my duffel bag in the trunk of my car and slam it. My head's a mess of guilt and worry and impending party plans—Baez's eighteenth birthday is on Halloween.

"Angry?"

I look over my shoulder and find Chance waiting. He plays with his too-long hair and grins smugly at me.

"What do you want?" I cross my arms over my chest. "More for your little documentary?"

His cheeks turn red. We used to be friends at the start of high school. Back before Baez and I got really serious. Back when I was hooking up with his cousin JuJu. Back before I broke her heart. Back when I didn't have the courage to let everyone know we were dating. Sometimes the sight of him makes me remember that time, and I avoid him because of it. She transferred schools because of me.

"Why is everyone so worried about my documentary?" he says with a smile.

"Because you're an asshole and get off on this shit."

"If you don't have anything to hide—"

"Haven't you done enough? I've seen the stuff you post online. I see *everything*."

He shrugs, and it's infuriating.

"Cut the crap, Chance. What do you want? Is this about JuJu? That why you're doing this?" I close my eyes and see her beautiful brown face, that pink bow of a mouth. I shake my head. I regret who I was then. A fucking coward.

He smiles. "I see someone still feels guilty. But no, I have a proposition for you." He steps closer to me.

"No." I unlock the car, ready to dismiss him.

"You haven't even heard what it is."

"I don't care." I open the car door.

"Be *my* VP instead of hers," he says as I start to climb in.

"Why the hell would I do that?"

"Why not?" He rushes to the car door, holding it open.

I give him a long look, not even bothering to waste breath on our history, how annoying he is, how much I *don't* want to work with the likes of him.

"We both know I'm the better pick."

"You lost to us. Fair and square, last spring. What's your issue with her?"

He balls his hand into a fist. "You're always choosing the *wrong* people, Cora. That's your problem. It'll catch up with you one day."

There's something on the edge of his words. Something he isn't saying. Not just about JuJu.

"Fuck off, Chance." I speed away and just miss hitting him in the process.

I'm in total control.

Monday 6:34 PM

Cora:

Got your flowers, babe.
All thousand of them in the back seat.

Baez:

Hehehe 😊

Cora:

You're cute.

Baez:

I know.

Cora:

Baez:

So . . . can I sneak over tonight?

Monday 8:47 PM

Cora:

Yeah. After midnight.
We have to talk about your bday party.

Baez:

Cool.

Georgie Khalra
Followers:
3,273
Group chats:
10

Monday 5:57 PM

Bryn:

How'd practice go? Everyone loves your poster. I've gotten twelve new videos edited today. People have a lot to say about this whole thing— and cyberbullying.

Can you make me like a series of posters based on what people say? Can be abstract. Like a crime scene tape of comments . . . or like a chalk outline of a body and the chalk is the comments. Really, you can do anything.

You're the artist. You probably have better ideas than me.

Monday 8:33 PM

Bryn:

You okay?

RIP Georgie.

Georgie:

It was great, actually. I think it's gonna be awesome. And I'll make you something.

Bryn:

🙂

Okay, good. You can do this.

GeorgieKhalra723

Monday, October 28, 10:12 p.m.

♡ 765   ◌ 125

New cheerleading outfit!

KeishaSoFly: Looking good, G! Work it!
42 mins   ♡ 30

SykeWard: You're trying to steal Cora's life. Watch out for this bitch.
40 mins   ♡ 40

TateNotTotBro1289: GIRL, DO YOU EVEN KNOW?
35 mins   ♡ 26

DeeSquared228Squad: Guess that uniform looks good on everyone. Even hoes. Hos? How do you spell slut?
28 mins   ♡ 134

FrankieLikeTheBull: Forget Baez. Date ME.
26 mins   ♡ 21

AhMADManKhan: I just don't understand WHY.
23 mins   ♡ 24

AhMADManKhan: Like, is it a Halloween costume, or what?
22 mins   ♡ 88

AJRiveriaTodelo301: DAMN. Who knew?
20 mins   ♡ 23

RayRay256: You can cheer me on ANYTIME.
19 mins   ♡ 121

JaseThaGod202: Looking good, G.

18 mins   ♡ 128

WongsterArt: You look awesome.

16 mins   ♡ 23

DialloNotDiablo: Miss you at Model UN!

13 mins   ♡ 3

Comments Loading

BAEZ AND GEORGIE WERE COZYING UP SOLO AT CORA'S PARTY.

BAEZ AND GEORGIE DEFINITELY MADE OUT UPSTAIRS IN CORA'S BEDROOM.

COMPLETE AND TOTAL YOU-KNOW-WHAT AT JASE'S PARTY.

GEORGIE AND BAEZ HAVE BEEN FOOLING AROUND FOR MONTHS BEHIND CORA'S BACK.

CORA PUT GEORGIE ON THE CHEERLEADING TEAM TO KEEP AN EYE ON HER.

BRYN

TUESDAY, OCTOBER 29
6:00 P.M.

MY DAD'S DRIVER TAKES THE LONG WAY TO HIS OFFICE tonight. I fuss with my power suit. I'm dressed for the job I want—the first female president—and I'll be in a room full of the people who could make it happen. It's another Democratic fundraiser, but this time, it's my favorite of the year. Halloween on the Hill. Even though I'm not talking to my dad, I couldn't pass up going as his date while Mom is away. Plus, Mom called me today and convinced me to go. She's got an uncanny sense for when Dad needs me, *and* she's got, like, a compulsion superpower or something. Always gets me to do the thing I don't want to do.

His tuxedo hangs in a garment bag, almost blocking my view of the city. I got him a mask that he will refuse to wear. But at least he'll have some sort of costume. That's the nicest thing I can do for him right now.

The downtown buildings whiz past in shades of stark white, their columns feeling like pillars on the houses of giants. It still feels weird to live in this city—four tiny quadrants, eight wards that control the entire country.

The car pulls into a checkpoint at one of the entrances to the Capitol Complex. Three Capitol police officers stand near their cars, checking IDs.

"I'll wait nearby until you're ready to go to the event," the driver, Mr. Kofi, says.

"Thanks," I tell him, and climb out of the car with Dad's tuxedo. I walk to the glass-walled checkpoint. A guard sits inside with a computer.

"Identification."

I give him my driver's license and he goes through all his checks: metal detectors, bag screenings, the works. He asks me if I love visiting my dad at work, as if I'm headed into a regular office building for a bring-your-daughter-to-work-type situation versus heading into the United States Capitol, where very few civilians get to go.

An escort waits to take me to my dad's office. My heart always flutters as I walk these halls. So many important people who have done so many important things have worked here. I want to be like them. Do things that change people's lives . . . for the better. One day.

The escort greets my dad's secretary. Her name is Candy.

Sort of ridiculous.

I told Mom he should get a new secretary because no one with a name like that should be taken seriously. "She's basically a peppermint stick," I'd said during my first visit to his office. Mom called my statement sexist and claimed I'd swallowed the same misogynistic poison that permeates our culture. She added it to the list of things I need to work on. It's a very long list. But she has her own list, too.

"Hey, Bryn." Candy fusses with her blond old-lady mushroom haircut before going to knock on my dad's door. "He's finishing up a call but should be ready for you shortly."

I wander around his office glancing up at other portraits of former

Speakers of the House. Second in line for the presidency. I think about how many times my dad thought about running for president when I was younger. My mom's problems were unable to withstand the spotlight the campaign would put on everyone. The wood creaks beneath my feet, and I think about all the important feet that have walked on this very same wood.

"Duckie," Dad calls out from the office.

I cringe at the pet name but try to lose my frown as I enter his office. The big window behind his desk looks down at the green lawn of the complex and all those beautiful stark-white buildings.

"What kind of mask did you bring me?" he asks.

"One you won't wear. An Italian carnival mask."

"Sounds refined." His furrowed eyebrows meet in the middle of his forehead. "We'll go in just a little bit. Waiting on an email. How's school?"

Candy appears in the doorway with a tea cart. For a while, Dad used to insist on us having tea together at 5:00 p.m., "like a civilized family." It went from little tea parties in my little-girl bedroom upstairs to official teatime. Like we're actually British or something.

But we haven't done this in a long time. I don't think either of my parents want to spend time with me anymore. And the feeling is mutual. With Mom in rehab, Dad stays in this office until late anyway.

"How's governing the student body?" he asks, handing me a gold-rimmed teacup. "Given everything that happened?"

"Fine," I say.

Ugh, my words are coming out all clipped despite the promise I made to Mom on the phone about being warmer to him. But I can't seem to forgive him for cheating. I can't seem to let things thaw.

He purses his lips.

"Better, actually," I try. "I launched my first campaign of the year."

"Oh." His eyebrow lifts with surprise.

"An anti-cyberbullying initiative."

"It's getting traction?"

"Yep. I'm having people share videos about times they were bullied online, using a dedicated hashtag and even a photo booth that records the videos and populates them onto the school's social media accounts."

A smile creeps into the corner of his mouth. "I taught you well."

I don't tell him that he's right. That would give him too much credit. But he *did* help me win my campaign for student body president.

"Turn the sour into the sweet. Spin something bad and damaging that's happened to you into sugar."

I nod.

Dad adds milk to my cup. "Well done."

"I won't let anyone take this away from me. I worked hard." I remember sitting at our kitchen table, him poring over all my campaign slogans and promises, his signature red pen in his hand, making notes in the margins, tweaking my message, making me a blueprint for victory. If he had gotten a chance to run for president of the United States, he would've won. If it weren't for Mom.

"Mom will be happy to hear that."

My shoulders jump, like I've been hit in the back. My teacup freezes right before my mouth.

"You need to go see her," he says.

I sigh. "Have you seen her?"

"That's not what we're talking about. You know I haven't gone to see her. We don't want the media knowing what center she's at. They'd swarm again."

I wish she was here. I wish she didn't need to go away. I wish everything wasn't so broken. She's the third person on my list. I take a breath to yell about it, but he puts his hand up, like he knows what I'm going to say.

"We've all made mistakes. She's not a social pariah," he says. "And neither are you."

I don't know what that word means, and I don't have the courage to ask him for a definition. I make a note to look it up.

"Judgment is not what we need right now." He gets up and takes his suit bag to the bathroom in the back of his office. "No one in this family is perfect."

He said the same thing the night of the accident, when the police came to the house. I'd peeked out of the pool-house window, the red-and-blue beams of light cutting through the blinds. I held my breath until I heard footsteps coming along the path and the knock at the door. They'd caught me running the red light. They'd caught me fleeing the scene of an accident I caused.

"Bryn. *Bryn.*"

My eyes startle open to find Dad all dressed—even with his mask on—ready to go. His Secret Service agent stands in the doorway ready to escort us.

"You okay?" Dad asks.

"Yes," I say, and whisper to myself: *I will be once I get my old life fully back.*

The banquet halls at these things always smell like perfume. Syrupy sweet. Cloying, like a competition between old ladies to see who can try on the most of those free testers at the mall. It's as if everyone in this room is trying their best to outtalk, outdress, and outsmell their opponents. Anything for donations. Anything for votes. Anything to be important and on top.

The masked Halloween on the Hill fundraiser ball is an annual thing for our family. We always come to see and be seen. If Mom were here, she'd probably dress up like a First Lady from the past, as she's done every year that she wasn't in rehab. At the last ball, I was a hipster Alice in Wonderland in a blue-and-white pinafore.

I look around and spot other kids from school. Their important parents mingling and milling about. If this were last year, I would've been hanging with them, spiking our punch, and running around until our parents made us sit at the banquet tables for dinner.

I sigh. Usually, I'd be a chatterbox talking to the important senators and representatives or chiefs of staff or lobbyists or journalists at my dad's table, or flitting about the hall, trying to introduce myself to as many of the new cabinet members as possible. Making sure everything I knew about all these folks in the room was accurate.

But tonight, I sit in silence, surrounded by old people, picking at my rubber chicken and overdone green beans. The accident hangs over me like my very own rain cloud, making me wish I had an umbrella to hide me from the thunderous whispers and lightning-shock stares. I wish I could erase him, erase the entire relationship.

Dad's on edge. There have been questions about Mom cropping up all night, and his fake smile and the "she's doing great and is on holiday" lie is wearing thin. I pick at the edge of the tablecloth and can't even distract myself with social media, because the invitation forbade unauthorized photos or videos. Like any teen dragged to this fundraising banquet would ever want pictures of the people here anyway. Well, okay. Maybe me. I'm the only teen who knows who all these people are.

Dad thumps my hand and leans close to my ear. "Try joining the conversation. Women's rights in Iran or the water situation in Flint, or something you learned in school. The climate crisis. It's landing in your generation's lap. You'll need to be ready to discuss topics like these on the fly."

Dad thinks everything is good for me now. With Mom gone again. Now that I've made a mess of my life and he can't see how hard I am trying to put it all back together again. Maybe he doesn't believe a word I told him about the campaign. Maybe he thinks I can't turn it around. "People just don't come out to support like they used to," some old lady says haughtily, then laughs. "Well, unless, of course, they're Republicans."

"It all comes down to money," a man adds, slamming his arm down on the table to make his point.

The woman leans over and whispers, "I heard his wife just got a new SUV." She says scandalously, "And it's definitely not a hybrid."

Dad nods politely. "We're on the wait list for an electric. But it's still two years long!"

The woman smiles. "Yes, but you're on the right side of humanity, and that's the important thing."

Dad sits up straight and looks at the room's entrance. "The Davidsons just arrived. I need to talk to Edward." He darts from the table, trying to beat the rush of reporters.

The thought of Cora being here sends a shiver of excitement down my spine. Dad navigates the crowds headed for Cora's very important father. Their entrance commands attention, and although Millie's missing this year, they still make a perfect picture of elegance.

Cora's mom wears a graceful black dress with a flowered jacket. Not in costume. She's beautiful and striking and so much prettier than every other woman in the room. Mom would say she's a portrait of perfection, able to be photographed from any angle. Cora's like a miniature of her, also in black, but with a tulle skirt that makes her look like a ballerina. Her hair falls sleek around her shoulders, and she wears a bejeweled silver mask. The effect is breathtaking, and all eyes are on her.

When Cora and I used to be dragged to these, we'd sneak away and find a spot to gossip in. We'd point to all the women who have had plastic surgery and things injected in their faces or laugh at the wives who drank too much and said dumb things. We entertained each other while our parents did their business, sucking up and blowing hot air up each other's asses.

I text her, and she looks up and smiles.

It's *almost* the same one from before the accident. Only a little hesitation left. My heart hopes that soon I'll be close to her again.

The woman beside me pats my hand. "Did you hear me?"

I startle back to the conversation at the table. "No, ma'am, I'm sorry."

"I asked you when your poor mother was going to return."

My heart starts to hammer. "Oh, uh . . ."

"I read all about it in the papers, dearie. It's hard being a politician's wife," she replies with a wink. "They can't keep from chasing skirts."

My stomach turns sour. I text Cora and tell her to save me from this small talk. She tells me to meet her in the hall.

"If you'll excuse me." I step out of the banquet room into the nearly empty lobby of the fancy hotel. A fireplace roars, and tall bookshelves hold a weird assortment of books. I run my fingers over them as I wait for Cora.

"I would've thought you'd still be in hiding," a voice says.

His voice.

I brace myself and turn around to face Jase.

He's wearing an offensive Egyptian pharaoh costume.

"Nice costume," I say, heart drumming.

"My dad's the pharaoh, and I'm the prince. Clever, right?" He grins, white teeth flashing. "Did you come here tonight knowing you'd see me? Still obsessed?"

"Hardly," I say. "What I am obsessed with is making sure everyone knows the truth about you."

"And what is that?" He bites his bottom lip. It used to charm me. But now I feel ill.

"That you played me . . . You play every girl you're with. A sick game. Girls are like ice cream, there to be enjoyed, devoured." Sometimes I don't understand how we ever got together, how I ever loved him. But when I was with him, I felt safe. When I think about all that's happened over the last few months, I feel like an idiot.

"Too bad Chance isn't here with his little camera to catch you when you start crying again," he taunts. "What did I ever see in you?"

Anger rises inside me. "You stole all my friends."

The accusation hangs there between us. We stand in silence for a while, the crackle of the fire keeping us company.

"They're my friends now." He smooths the front of his costume.

"Not for long."

He laughs. "You tried to *kill* me. You think people will forget that? Forgive that?"

"Wait till they find out the truth about you. What you told me. The night of your mother's garden party? When that subpoena came?" Everything bubbles up. All the rage from the night of the accident and every day in between. All the lies. All the ways he found to belittle me online.

"Who would *ever* believe you?"

"About what?" Cora walks up. Her eyes volley between us.

"Nothing," Jase says. "Nice costume."

"Can't say the same about yours," she replies, cringing.

"Lighten up, Cora," he says before rushing off.

My eyes follow him, burning into his back.

"What was that about?" she asks.

A bitter taste lingers in my mouth. "Nothing I can share." Yet.

GEORGIE

FRIDAY, NOVEMBER 1
2:46 P.M.

"HEY, G, LOOKING GOOD," FRANKIE EPSTEIN SAYS, LETTING out a slow, low wolf whistle, like he's going to devour me. "You doing Halloween tonight? Cuz I'd like to dress you up."

"I'm playing painter," I say with a smile, pulling out my smock and art bag. "It's been too long."

"I didn't know you were an artist," Riley Wong says, leaning close to my locker. He's had the one right next to me for three years now, but this is, like, the third time in my entire high school career that he's actually spoken to me. "What kind?"

"I'm not really an artist. I mess around with mostly acrylics, but it's just a hobby, according to my mom."

His eyes light up. They're a deep brown and super shiny. He's tall and muscley and has this buzz cut, so the guys keep calling him an Asian Mr. Clean to piss him off. "That's what I started with," he says, peering into my art bag. "Now I'm on to oils, and I've been doing a lot of comic-art stuff, trying my hand at a graphic novel. I'll show you sometime." He smiles. "Or you could show me yours."

My heart does this weird little drop, then jumps. Did he just—

"I mean, like if you have a portfolio or something," he stammers, staring at his feet. "Anyway, I'm going to art school in New York. What about you?"

I shrug. "I don't know. My parents definitely have Ivy ambitions for me." I gather my stuff. "But New York sounds cool. I've been reading up on the different schools. And there are so many amazing kinds of art to explore."

Riley takes my phone and puts his number in it, all casual, like it happens every day. "Well, if you want to talk about it or whatever, I'm around." He grins, rubbing the back of his head. "And I'll see you at Baez's tonight, right?" He's looking at me intently, and I can't tell if it's because he's hoping I'll be there, or, more likely, if he's trying to unravel all the things he's heard, figure out if it's true what they say.

"Don't think so," I say. It's Baez's birthday party. Pretty much anyone who's anyone is going. The whole cheer team will definitely be there. I should be there. But I'm grounded after the incident with Vibha at the pool. Mum heard all about it.

"Oh, I was thinking we could maybe hang out." He's standing really close, his eyes reading my face, hopeful.

A warm sensation creeps up my neck to my ears. Is he saying he might like me? Like the real me? Artist Georgie. Fumbling Georgie. Silly Georgie. The one no one notices? The one no one ever actually likes? Nah.

He probably likes the girl everyone keeps talking about online.

"Maybe." I turn back to my locker, digging through my stuff, and soon I can't feel Riley's gaze on me anymore. I stand back up, muscles sore and tired from cheerleading, and make my way down the hall and into the cafeteria. A shortcut to the senior parking lot. No practice tonight due to Baez's Halloween birthday party, and I'm not complaining.

The cafeteria empties out, students yapping about their costumes and big Halloween plans as they scatter like marbles.

I feel eyes boring into my back—an all-too-familiar sensation lately—and turn to face it head-on.

Mistake.

It's Vibha and Amir. She scowls at me, tugging him forward.

He whispers something in her ear as I pass. She blushes like she does when she likes something. I bet they're secretly dating. Which would be a super scandal with the Aunties, I'm sure, because she's Hindu and he's Muslim.

I honestly thought I'd miss Vibha more.

"I mean, look at the length of that skirt. No wonder my mom forbid me from hanging out with her," Vibha says really loudly. "And I heard she's failing AP Calc."

Amir shrugs. "It's a hard class," he says, and I can tell Vibha is disappointed as I grin at him. I feel a sudden surge of spite.

"I actually got a B-plus on the last exam," I say, deciding to egg her on. "Cheer has an eighty percent rule. You can't drop below that in any class or you have to sit out practices. So Christine gave me her notes, if you want to borrow them. They made it so much easier—"

The rage explodes out of Vibha like a rocket. "Do you think I EFFING care, Jashan?" she practically spits, even more annoyed when I start laughing. Effing! "No one cares about your grades. Not when they can all just stare at your ass hanging out." She shoves Amir hard.

"Your jealousy is showing!" I yell back.

"You've changed." It's like she can't come up with anything better.

"Or maybe you have." I step forward, challenging her, raising a brow. I'm not the only one with secrets, apparently.

"Stop looking at her like that." Vibha slaps Amir's arm.

"Like what?" He gapes.

"You're drooling," she says, and then stomps right up to me. I think she might actually hit me, but a body steps between us.

Jase. He's, like, a full foot taller than me, and towers over both Vibha and Amir, who's grabbed her arm, trying to hold her back.

"Hey, hey," he says. "Chill. Why are you always so uptight?" he asks Vibha. Flames literally shoot out of her ears as she storms off, Amir running to keep up.

"Uh, thanks." My voice is a big whoosh of air, deflating all the stress I've been holding in. "I thought she was gonna slap me or something."

"Looked like it," Jase says, gazing down at me. He's got a dimple in his left cheek. And his eyes are like the ocean on a stormy day. "But you seem like you could hold your own. Right?"

I nod. "It's been a day. A week. Like, a year."

"Yeah, I feel that," he says. "But look at you. You're doing okay."

Am I?

Maybe I am.

I smile to myself and shift my bag from one arm to the other.

"What are you grinning about?" He's smirking at me. "All right, then, let's put that grin to good use." He grabs my hand and leads me over to Bryn's anti-cyberbullying photo booth.

I wonder if he knows it's all her doing.

"You coming? There's room for two."

Part of me wants to be that chill, carefree girl who can go into a booth with a random guy I've barely talked to and pose and make kissy faces for the camera. But my stomach's doing that weird warning flip again, like this is a bad idea. I mean, he's Bryn's ex. Aside from Baez, he's, like, the next most popular kid in school. And he's taken, too. Sasha's still on the squad, despite her leg, and she never lets us forget it. So this is wrong for so many reasons.

"C'mon, it's for a good cause."

I don't know how to say no. So I don't say anything at all. Next thing I know, he's got my hand and he's leading me forward, and Dee Dee Mattis is shooting fire glares from the student council table.

There's barely any room in the booth. He sits, and it's a tight squeeze, and suddenly there are hands on my hips, and I'm perched on his lap. I freeze. If this were last year, both of us wouldn't have been able to fit in here at all. Because of how big I was. But I try not to think about that. Or being touched by a boy. Which is weird and uncomfortable and my brain is slightly screaming now, but I need to shut it off. He isn't Vivek, or even one of those creeps leaving comments. He's actually kind of hot. So why am I freaking out?

"You ready?" He reaches over me and starts pressing buttons on the screen, his arms grazing my hips, my waist, my breasts. It's, like, the literal closest I've been to a guy, ever. Except for Vivek. And he doesn't count. "Let's do photos instead of a video." He presses another button on the screen, changing the booth's mode.

"No, wait. Let me check my hair." I fuss with myself in the mirror beside the big camera screen and catch him staring back at me.

"You're beautiful. You know that, right?" he says. "I can't believe we haven't hung out before. Are you new?"

I want to say: *You didn't see me because you were dating Bryn.*

I want to say: *You didn't see me because you didn't want to see me.*

I want to say: *You didn't see me because you're fatphobic, like almost all the boys at school.*

"No, I've been here since seventh grade. But I was sort of a different person," I admit, puckering my lips and adding more tinted lip gloss to them.

He watches me, his eyes on my lips, and my cheeks burn. I'm still getting used to this whole being-seen thing, being seen like *this*.

I see him, too. The way Bryn and others do. But in a different way, too. Most people don't study others like I did. Do. That's what happens when you're invisible. You notice the small details. Like how he has tiny freckles across his nose, the perfect family of little ants. Or how his skin is almost perfectly smooth, aside from a few blond whiskers.

"Okay, let's do this, beautiful." Part of me loves that he calls me that.

He pushes the button before I say yes, pulling me back onto his lap. Light flashes in bursts, the bright beams blinding me.

"You look so serious. Funny faces."

"I'm not funny," I say with a shrug. I don't know if I know how to just let myself be carefree like that. The old Georgie bubbles up, all nerves.

He pokes at my side.

I cringe. Always hate that.

He does it again.

I squirm, but he doesn't let go. "Hey."

He tickles me.

I burst with laughter. The big belly kind. Unexpected and uncontrolled.

He catches my face, holding it in his hand. "You're stunning." He tries to kiss me.

I yank myself back. "What are you doing?"

"Kissing you."

His hands disappear in my hair, his tongue trying to push its way into my mouth as he tugs at the strands.

Shame seeps through me as I pull away. "No."

The light flashes again. The bright beams pulse through my eyelids.

"Why?" he asks, leaning back in. He connects this time, and his legs tangle with mine, and the camera flashes again. It's weird and gross and doesn't even feel like a real kiss because I'm trying to squirm away. I know the pictures will show how we're a mess of parts. Ones that should've never touched in the first place.

"I can't," I repeat.

"But why?" His eyes get all sheepish, like a puppy who's been told he can't have a treat.

"For one, I don't know you."

"You could get to know me." He fishes the developed film from the tiny slot under the camera screen. A long strip of four snapshots. He inspects them, then shows me. The first one is me all serious. The old Georgie still there. The second is my big goofy grin, because Jase is tickling me. The third is the kiss. The kiss that shouldn't have happened. The last one is me in shock.

I reach for them. "We should probably get rid of those."

"What if I want to keep them?" he says, lifting them above his head, out of my reach. I stand on my tiptoes, trying to grab them, but he pulls me close, trying to kiss me again, pressing me into the back of the booth. This time I dodge him, but he buries his face in my neck. "Your hair smells so sweet, like jasmine."

Ew. I wrench out of his grip, reaching for the photos again, and he dodges my hands.

"Do you like old books? Because I have this great copy of the *Kama Sutra*."

I roll my eyes. "Racist much?"

He laughs. "Lighten up. I'm into Indian girls. I'm really into you."

"Well, I'm not into white boys," I say back, trying to bolt.

He grabs my arm, blocking me in. "We both know that's a lie. And you're into Baez, too. I saw the way you looked at him . . . and I *love* my boy. But trust me, you can do better."

"I didn't hook up with him."

"I heard all about it." He winks and holds up the picture strip. "Promise, for my eyes only."

"There's a line," Dee Dee says into the booth, too loud, tugging at the curtain. "Y'all done?"

He starts to pull back the curtain. "Our little secret." He slips out of the photo booth, like he was never there at all, leaving me alone inside.

I feel almost drunk.

The light buzz of a headache.

Heart ready to burst from beating so hard.

But then the guilt rushes through me. *Do I tell Bryn?* My ears flood with the noise of the camera resetting and the pattern of my heavy breaths and the beat of my nervous heart alongside it, all my fears swirling into one terrible storm.

Dee Dee Matthis pulls the curtain back. Dying to be let in on the secret. Dying to share it with the world. Her dark brown face twists with horror.

The camera flashes again.

"I don't always like Bryn, but she doesn't deserve this, Georgie. Especially after all she's been through," she says, taking off before I can even unravel what happened.

FilmmakerChance

Friday, November 1, 4:10 p.m.

♡ 1278   ◯ 86

Has Georgie moved on from Baez to Jase?

FrankieLikeTheBull: Riley wants a piece of that. Jase better not be moving in.
58 mins   ♡ 520

HeidiGrattonSunshine: Girls should be able to hook up with whomever they want. Stop shaming people.
49 mins   ♡ 130

DeeSquared228Squad: I saw them in the anti-cyberbullying photo booth.
45 mins   ♡ 189

SykeWard: I know we hate Bryn but liiiiiiike how could Georgie? After what he did to her. Jase is trash
44 mins   ♡ 215

SantiagoRodriguez84: I saw Jase with red lipstick on in the lunchroom.
42 mins   ♡ 210

BBeaumont213: What about Sasha? They've been together since August.
38 mins   ♡ 1000

KeishaSoFly: Don't start shit, SykeWard. We don't know what happened.
30 mins   ♡ 120

RayRay256: Jase gets 'em all.
29 mins   ♡ 22

LiLiKim512: That booth is getting mad action. Heard Suz and Tucker hooked up in there yesterday.
24 mins   ♡ 1310

PettyMar: Man, Bryn set up this whole anti-bullying thing all for Georgie, and she goes and hooks up with her ex in that booth? She's really out here. Foul. Cold.
23 mins   ♡ 298

WinterIsComing789: RIP Georgie. You about to die. Cora's mad. Now, wait to see what Sasha is about to do to you. We'll see if Bryn gets to you first tho. That girl still isn't right.
23 mins   ♡ 21

DialloNotDiablo: She's OUT there doing the most.
21 mins   ♡ 13

MistyMaura: Bryn is gonna go off on her, too. Watch her burn Georgie's house down. She's crazy, AND they're neighbors.
20 mins   ♡ 327

ShahKing87: You gonna hook up with any Indian guys, Jashan? Or just the ones that are *not*.
14 mins   ♡ 34

WongsterArt: Uh, G, I thought we were gonna meet up and make art and shit?
10 mins   ♡ 180

Comments Loading

AEZ AND GEORGIE WERE COZYING UP SOLO AT CORA'S PARTY.

BAEZ AND GEORGIE DEFINITELY MADE OUT UPSTAIRS IN CORA'S BEDROOM.

COMPLETE AND TOTAL YOU-KNOW-WHAT AT JASE'S PARTY.

GEORGIE AND BAEZ HAVE BEEN FOOLING AROUND FOR MONTHS BEHIND CORA'S BACK.

CORA PUT GEORGIE ON THE CHEERLEADING TEAM TO KEEP AN EYE ON HER.

GEORGIE AND JASE HOOKED UP IN THE PHOTO BOOTH AT SCHOOL.

CORA

FRIDAY, NOVEMBER 1
6:24 P.M.

"DON'T HATE ME, BUT I THINK THE RUMORS ARE ALL TRUE." Adele's sprawled across my bed, her pale-white legs tangled in my comforter, while Bryn is on my beanbag trying to fix the brim of her Mad Hatter hat. We're supposed to be getting ready for the big Halloween scavenger hunt I planned for Baez's birthday—before all this mess started. But we've just been lounging for the past hour. It almost feels like old times, when no one was mad about Bryn and we all hung out.

I sigh. I was waiting for Adele to say something about it all. But I was hoping it wouldn't be this. "That could, like, never happen." My eyes focus on my phone, scrolling through all my social media feeds. The tags have been multiplying every day. This *thing* just won't go away. "Baez said it didn't happen."

"Did you see what Chance Olivieri said, though?" Her pale eyebrow lifts. "Like she's messing around with Jase now, too? Come on."

"Chance is a liar," Bryn says. "Remember all the shit he said about me?"

Adele doesn't even acknowledge Bryn. She still can't believe I've "forgiven" her. I tried to explain, but she has to get over it. Bryn was gaslit by Jase. I need her right now. I finally understand why she was so anxious and erratic and obsessive before the accident, how she could've been pushed like that. Social media is making me feel ridiculous, too.

"He's an idiot," I reply without looking up. "Always stirs up trouble 'cause he doesn't have anything to do."

"But Dee Dee isn't, and she said it, too. I mean, the pics don't lie. They were definitely in there." Adele clicks through her phone. "See? She was standing right outside." She flicks her finger across her screen again. "And here."

She flashes supposedly a screenshot of pictures from Jase's social media—before they were deleted. Georgie and Jase kissing in the photo booth.

"Oof, actually . . ." I lean closer to Bryn. "C'mon, Bryn, you gotta admit that's rough?"

Bryn cranes to look, her cheeks flushed red. Then she gets up and plucks Adele's phone out of her hand. "That's my confessional booth."

"Hey," Adele protests, but I shoot her a look to relax.

"She wouldn't hook up with him," Bryn says confidently, handing the phone back to Adele.

"How do you know?" Adele eyes her.

"She's not into white boys." Bryn plops back onto the beanbag chair.

"Racist, much?" Adele replies.

"She doesn't have to be into white boys," I say.

Adele sits up straight. "But—"

"Do you know how many people tell me they're not into Black girls? They, like, volunteer that shit. Right to my face. Letting me know every girl like me isn't good enough." I scroll through my social media feeds and show her pictures. "Look! So many of them put comments on my photos like . . . *You're hot for a Black girl . . .* or *I'm not into Black girls but could be into you.* So Jase won't die from one girl not being into him."

"I . . . just meant —" Sweat appears on Adele's forehead, making the front of her pixie haircut all wet and stringy. "Leilani is Filipina and . . . we're together."

"You meant that everyone is supposed to like everyone . . . which, yeah, that's great and all," Bryn says. "But that's not always how it works. Georgie's family is *real* serious about marriage and dating and stuff. So I don't buy it. Not Baez. And not Jase."

"What Jase does is his business," I say. Even though he's with Sasha. And she's my friend. I know the hurt she's probably feeling right now, with everyone speculating about her and Jase. Because I'm living it, too. I start to text Sasha. A tiny part of me feels guilty at the tiny burst of relief that the rumors are shifting away from Baez and onto Jase now. And there are pictures. Hard to argue with that.

"I just don't trust her," Adele says. "She's messed with Baez, and now she's messing with Jase, her supposed best friend's ex." She throws her hands up in the air. "Can you blame me?"

"You don't trust *anyone,*" I say.

"It's a good policy," Adele proclaims, cutting her eyes at Bryn. She's been like this ever since the divorce between her mom and dad got super nasty this summer, so I can't really blame her. If she knew what happened with Bryn's parents, maybe she'd be a little nicer.

I clamp my eyes shut. "I don't want to hear any more, okay? Like no more about those stupid rumors. Tonight's supposed to be fun. I spent months planning this scavenger-hunt birthday party."

"But—"

"Seriously." I put my hand up.

"I'm just worried about you."

Six-word memoir: *I want this to go away.*

"I'm fine," I say.

"You keep saying that, but, like—"

"Adele, just chill," Bryn says, but that makes her flare up.

"Nobody asked you," Adele snaps at Bryn.

I ball my hands into fists beneath the comforter. "It's all good. Like, it's lies. So stupid. Georgie's on the cheer squad now, and if either of them is lying, Bryn is gonna help me figure it out. She's close to her." I suck my teeth. "You never liked Baez, anyways. You just want me to break up with him."

Adele purses her lips like she's sucking on a lemon. "That's not true. He's, like, okay. But—" Adele exhales. "You could do better." I see Bryn watching our exchange closely.

"What's better, Adele?" I challenge. And I know she means . . . JuJu.

"Nothing. Forget it, okay?" She focuses on flipping through her magazine.

"Don't be a bitch." My stomach clenches.

"Okay." Adele sits up quickly, her shoulders all tense. "Fine."

Ugh, she's mad. I'll have to deal with all those feelings later.

Sigh.

"It's complicated," Bryn says, taking my side about my relationship, which is surprising, because she and Baez never really got along either.

"Okay." Adele slides off the bed and to a tray table full of snacks that Vero brought in.

I shrug my shoulders. This is exhausting. Everything is exhausting. I want to curl up in my comforter and block out the world. Except I can't, because Bryn is all wrapped up in it. "It's all dumb and not a big deal." The words hold half-truths. I avoid her eyes. "Let's get ready. We need to be there early and set up the clues . . . and I need you . . . both right now."

An hour later, we're on the lacrosse field on our school's south campus. My girls are all huddled around me with bright eyes, eager for a good night, a night to talk about all week, all month, all year. Something that will make high school memorable. Their Halloween costumes sparkle and catch the field lights. Mermaids, sexy witches, zombie cheerleaders, and Disney Princesses.

I hold a flashlight beneath my chin, like we're all tiny again and at a sleepover and I'm about to tell the scariest story they've ever heard. "Watch for school security guards," I tell them as we prepare to plant clues for the scavenger hunt. "I photocopied their scheduled rounds while helping Principal Rollins today."

Christine gives out tiny slips of paper.

"The first clue we'll release online will lead everyone here for the first stop." I hand a plastic-wrapped object to Ruthie, then another to Christine, and a third to Bryn. "Those who find these treasures will get to the second location fastest."

"What's the big prize?" someone asks.

"His boys took care of that. I don't even know what it is." I clap my hands. "So, let's get it done. Ahmad and Jase will bring Baez in, like, fifteen minutes."

I post the first clue—a picture of Baez's lacrosse stick.

My girls scatter out in all directions. I watch them laugh and race around. Adele and Bryn even pair up. The iceberg between them starting to thaw. They'd do pretty much anything for me, and it reminds me just how good I have it. Their excited laughs are swallowed up by the large field, a cold fall breeze whipping around their hair and skirts. They're beautiful, but it's more than that. There's a unity here that feels rare. It's something Millie never had—a squad. All the excitement erases the tension from my conversation with Adele earlier.

Those rumors aren't true.

Everything is fine.

I'm fine.

Baez's fine.

We're fine.

Rumors don't mean anything.

Thirty minutes pass. Headlights stretch across the grass. The first cars arrive. The field starts to fill with bodies in a matter of minutes.

A smile erupts inside me when I spot the outline of Baez striding toward me. I hope to never not know the shape of him. He's carrying his excuse for a costume in his hands. A bowler hat to match my 1920s flapper look.

"Hey, pretty girl," he says, sliding his arms around my waist. I'm wrapped up in his scent and the warmth of his hands. Always so warm, I wonder what he does with them before he sees me.

His lips find the skin of my neck, sending prickles through me, and we slip into our own bubble. Everything evaporates—the crowd, the noise, the field. It's just us under the lights.

"And just who are you?" I tease. "I don't think my boyfriend would like you all up on me like this."

"You don't know me all of a sudden?"

"Stranger danger."

His mouth opens in mock upset.

"I'm not sure who you are. 'Cause *my* boyfriend forgot to text me back earlier. So—"

"You got rid of me that quick *and* it's my birthday, too?"

"It's your birthday?" I say.

"I think so."

"Are you sure?"

"Do I get something if it is?" He bites his bottom lip.

I kiss him. His mouth tastes like beer, and I wonder how many he had before getting here.

"You're going to get a migraine."

"Thanks for the reminder, Mom." He kisses my cheek.

"Look, your gluten-free ass will be mad in, like, two hours."

He grins at me, then nuzzles his face into my neck until I relent. "Eighteen, it's a big birthday," I say, my words rushing into his mouth as I pull away.

"Just means I can vote."

"Or go to jail."

He slaps my ass playfully, and I jump upright, then lean in and bite his neck. He kisses me again, his tongue heavy.

"Get a room," Ahmad shouts, and the bubble is popped.

I gaze around. A messy pile of cars are now parked alongside the field. The whole junior and senior class is here. Like almost three hundred people. "You're popular. All this for one boy," I say. "Everyone's here for you."

"More like for you," he replies. "No one would miss one of Cora Davidson's parties. And a scavenger hunt with prizes." He takes a little bow. "I do feel special."

Jase approaches with a megaphone. He flashes me his signature cocky grin, the one so many girls fall for. "You ready, Cor?"

I nod, my mind wandering, wondering if he did kiss Georgie, if he did all those things they're saying. Just like they did about Baez. "If you stay ready, you never have to get ready. Learn it."

Jase laughs, then rolls his eyes.

"What are you up to?" Baez asks us both.

"You'll see." I slip my hand in his.

"Party people!" Jase calls out through a megaphone. "Shut up!"

The crowd buzzes with laughter.

"It's my brother from another mother's birthday, and we're gonna turn up tonight and show him a good time."

Everyone hoots and hollers.

The lacrosse team darts from the crowd and surrounds Baez.

I step back as his teammates slap at his arm and rough him up, putting him in a headlock and punching at his sides. They threaten him with eighteen ass whuppings. Their infectious love and laughter makes the swirl of anxiety that's wrapped me up fall away.

"The mission tonight is to find the location of Baez's birthday party first. There, you will find your handsome reward. Clues are hidden at three different places—each one leads to another. If you're here, you've already successfully figured out the first part." Jase sends everyone out on the hunt. They scatter like ants all over the grass.

Free from his fans, Baez returns, wrapping his arms around me again. He nuzzles my neck and whispers, "Where does the first clue lead?"

"Your favorite burger place on U Street."

His entire face lights up when he smiles. "What are we supposed to do while we wait for everyone to complete the scavenger hunt?"

"You don't want to play along?"

He pokes his lips out. "I'd rather play with you."

"I have some ideas," I reply, and yank him in the direction of the cars. "And a plan. But wait, let me make sure everyone's got a ride to the party." I text the group chat, adding Bryn. Ruthie offers to drive the rest of the girls. "Okay, I'm all yours for a little bit."

"Or forever." He kisses me, then takes my hand.

I start driving him to Christine's house—the location of the last clue and the party. He holds my hand and kisses it as we drive and listen to his favorite playlist. We're almost as sappy as my momma and daddy. His phone is a firecracker, the screen exploding with thousands of social media posts and text messages.

A tiny whisper grows louder over the music: *Are any of those from another girl?*

I see Georgie's face in my head. I should trust Baez. Believe him. I love him. And I know he loves me. But some of the nonsense has settled deep inside me, finding all these new cracks and crevices I didn't know existed.

Baez ignores his phone. "Where are we going?" he says.

"Christine's house." I turn on her street. It's one of those newer neighborhoods that my mother hates. Houses built from boxes that all look the same. She complains about all the new little subdivisions every Sunday as we drive to church.

"Ugh, you know how much I *like* her," he says.

"Be nice."

"Only for you." He leans over the console and nuzzles his face in my neck.

I squeal, his stubble tickling and prickly. "Her parents are out of town, and she volunteered to host your party. Wait until you see all the stuff she's done."

I pull up to the gates and security booth. I roll down the window to punch in the code she texted me.

The guard leans out of his window, his white face grimacing. "Excuse me, what do you think you're doing?"

"Punching in the code," I reply. A spark of fear shoots up my spine.

"I haven't seen you before," he barks. "Do you live here?"

"No, but—"

"Then how do you have the code?"

My muscles tense.

Baez scooches closer from the passenger seat. "Dude. Chill out."

"What did you say?" the guard replies.

I put my hand on Baez's chest. I plaster the biggest grin on my face, the one I always use at Momma's charity functions with white folks. "I'm sorry, sir. I'm visiting my friend Christine Vaccaro and her family. She lives at 18 Maple, and she's one of my best friends, so I have the code. I've been coming here since they moved in at the beginning of last year. I'm like a sister to her. Please feel free to call the house to confirm."

I want to say: *Both my house and Baez's house are triple the size and worth of all the houses in this gated neighborhood, so no, we're not here to steal.*

His eyebrows lift with suspicion, and he leans back into his booth, snatching the phone.

"That guy's an asshole," Baez whispers. "A fake cop."

"But one that can call the *actual* police before the party has even started, so relax."

"How does he know that we don't live here?" Baez dissolves into a tirade.

"Probably because he's memorized the pictures of all the people who do live here." I don't want to talk about the fact that this hypervigilant security guard is harassing us because no Black people live in this neighborhood. Not tonight. I don't want to sour the mood even more. And I don't want any trouble, not when my very tall Black boyfriend is officially eighteen. Ripe to be charged as an adult. Ripe to be harassed.

The guard hangs up the phone. He doesn't open the window again; rather, the gates open for us.

I blow him a kiss and wave.

Asshole.

I drive to the very back of the complex, where Christine's house sits. The farthest one away from the others. The whole thing is decked out like a haunted house. Thumbnail-shaped tombstones dot the yard. Ghosts haunt the trees. Scary music and lights set the mood.

She delivered. And it's not even tacky.

I text her and let her know we're going to her pool house to hang out until people arrive. She sends back a smiley face.

"No one is here," Baez says.

"That's the point." I drag him into the tiny house beside her pool.

Navigating it feels familiar, I guess because I spent so much time in Bryn's pool house once they converted it into her bedroom. I think that was the beginning of the end for her—too much privacy, too much freedom. When no one's watching, that's when it's easiest to get in trouble. You don't have to go out of your way to stir things up, like I do with my parents.

Christine's pool house is like a miniature cottage version of the house, with a full living area and kitchenette, along with a bathroom and loft, which is more private than the rest of the space.

"I'm going to give you your birthday present before everyone else arrives," I tell Baez, leading him toward the stairs. I'm craving time with him alone before all the craziness of the night.

"This place is nice. I don't think I've ever been to Christine's spot before," he says, peering around, distracted. He veers toward the kitchen, and then the living area.

"You've been to her old place."

"I can't remember."

"'Cause you were always drinking and I drove."

He laughs. "Probably right."

He goes to sit down.

"Nope. Come with me." I take his hand and pull him toward the stairs again. He follows, but for a minute, it feels reluctant. "And leave your phone. It keeps lighting up."

"Yeah, all the dumb posts about—"

I kiss him, pressing the words back into his mouth, hoping that he realizes that I don't want to talk about *that*.

We take a breath.

"Question?" he asks.

"Answer," I reply.

"Did I see Bryn at the field?"

I bite my bottom lip. "Yeah."

"Why?" His eyes narrow.

"Ugh, long story. I'm, like . . . thinking about forgiving her."

"I don't think I ever can. She almost killed me and my lacrosse career, all because, what, she couldn't wait for Jase to text her back? Yeah, she's not getting my forgiveness anytime soon."

"I know," I say with a kiss. "You two have never gotten along. Different personalities."

"It's not that. She's just constantly bugging out," he replies. "Told you to watch out for that girl. Something's off with her."

"You just don't know. Like, some stuff was happening with her. Even that night."

"I know more than you think. Just be careful."

"And you should be careful with Jase," I press. "He's a dick."

"Here we go." He kisses my neck, startling me out of my anger. "Can we not argue? Especially on my birthday."

"Fine, fine." I take him to the loft. There's candles and a pack of wine coolers. I hit play on the stereo, and old-school hip-hop buzzes from unseen speakers. I lead Baez right to the bed, pushing him down onto it and straddling him as I start peeling off layers—his and mine.

"Remember this?" I ask.

"Is this our first time again?" He takes my hand.

"Maybe." I run my hands over the smooth brown of his chest. I plant kisses on his cheeks, his neck, his collarbone, running my hands all over him before reaching for his belt. I can feel him sighing as I let my mouth travel, his pulse racing and his breath catching as I make my way down.

We tumble around, kissing and touching and finding each other. Within a second, he's shifted us all together, his weight heavy on me as his body envelops mine. We move in unison for the first time in weeks, and it feels like maybe we're in sync again.

When we're finished, he tucks me into the sweet spot just under his arm, where I can hear his heartbeat start to steady, his mouth warm on my neck, my cheeks, my lips.

I try not to think too much as we lie there afterward. I trace my fingers down his forehead, tapping each one of his tiny moles. He tries to bite my fingers.

"Happy birthday," I whisper. "I've gotten to see six of them now."

"Have we been together that long?"

"You don't remember?" A flicker of heat rushes to my cheeks. I will it away. He's just been drinking. "Well, not *together* together. But you know. Our blood pact?"

"I do, but not after eight beers." He laughs.

I still remember the seventh-grade version of Baez—so bright, so full of light, he was almost blinding. This one is a little rough around the edges, his calloused hands running along my shoulders and stomach, reminding me of how much has changed, even if I want it to stay the same.

The sound of voices and cars and music push through the windows. My heart squeezes. I know it's time for the party to start, but I wish I had a little more time with him alone. Maybe this feeling would stay.

Knocks rattle the door.

"Do we have to go out now?" I say, trying to hide the whine in my voice.

"You planned this whole thing," he replies, and I can hear the smile on his face.

Knocks shake the windows. The shapes and shadows lurk outside, threatening to burst in, to ruin everything. Voices chant Baez's name, like he's a god and not just the star of Foxham Prep.

"I have to give the people what they want, right?" I say. "Release you to the masses."

Baez kisses me, then says yes. He jumps off the bed and grabs his clothes, pulling bits on as he heads downstairs. He puts on the bowler hat, and I put my flapper costume back on, far more reluctantly.

"Ready?" he says, but he doesn't wait to hear my answer.

I nod yes, but really want to say no.

He's barely got his pants back on when he opens the door.

The lacrosse team grabs Baez, still shirtless, and leads him away.

"Gotta borrow the birthday boy," Ahmad says.

"We'll bring him back," Jase whispers to me. "But maybe not in one piece."

I follow them out, watching them parade him up to a makeshift stage Christine set up beside her pool. They force him to chug beer. His chest is wet.

"Eighteen for eighteen!" Ahmad shouts.

The music crescendos as he guzzles.

I shake my head, knowing he'll vomit this up later and be all whiny and sick. His stomach is a hot mess.

Christine stumbles up to me with Baez's cake. "It's time. Otherwise, the ice cream will melt."

I catch her wobbly hands before she drops it.

Georgie stands next to her. I'm surprised to see her, although I shouldn't be. She's part of my squad now, right?

She's dressed like Marilyn Monroe, complete with the blond wig. The wig looks ridiculous. But there's something about the way she shimmers tonight—like she doused herself with pixie dust—that makes it hard to look away. The white wiggle dress emphasizes every curve, in a good way now, which feels different and just a little terrifying. And she seems transformed; her personality more confident, more adventurous.

My stomach twists. Even though it shouldn't. Those rumors are nonsense. She told me so herself. She promised to prove herself. But those pictures with Jase. If she could do that to Bryn . . .

"Thanks for getting cake," I say to Christine, and try to smile at Georgie.

"I have the candles . . . and the lighter," Georgie says, her words a jumble.

"You drunk?" I ask her. "Already?"

"Yeah," she says with a giggle. "I don't know what happened."

"Pumpkin punch happened," Christine adds. "I've had a lot, too."

I lift my eyebrow.

"We sort of initiated her while you were busy in the pool house," Christine reports, and I kind of hate her for it. I do all the initiating, and Georgie hasn't been on the squad longer than a second. Neither has Christine, for that matter.

I walk forward with Christine and Georgie following me. I spot Bryn, and she makes her way over, helping me hold up the cake.

The music pulses as Baez continues to drink. His friends punch their fists in the air and chant his name and slap his back.

I laugh at the stupidity of it all as I approach the stage with Baez's cake. Jase buzzes around me with his phone, videoing. The light blares at us. "We're making a video for Baez—and of course, you all need to show the birthday boy how much you care?"

"I guess you're all right," Christine replies, sticking out her tongue.

Anthony zips between us. He shouts into Jase's camera. "Wooohooo, number thirty-seven! You'll always be number one in my book. Happy birthday, man." He does a smirk, then points toward me. "Hope it's a good one."

"Anything to say, Cora?" Jase replies. He purposefully steps in front of Bryn, blocking her. She storms off.

I make a fart sound with my mouth. "I've loved him forever. He knows that. Now, get out of my face."

"What about you?" He turns to Georgie, handing her another cup of punch, and his eyes travel all over her.

She gulps it down.

"Hey, go easy," he says with a laugh, but doesn't stop recording. He leans in to touch her and I shiver. "That stuff's got a kick."

"Yeah, well, we Punjabis can handle our liquor," she replies, the slur in her words proving her wrong.

"Pun what?" he replies.

"Never mind." Georgie holds up the candles for Baez's birthday cake and shouts. "I have a song for the birthday boy, of course."

I shoot Christine a look. She's all grins. Is no one going to stop her?

Everyone turns to Georgie.

She saunters up, playing at Marilyn Monroe from one of those old classic movies, but a sloppy, drunk version. "Let me sing it to you, Baez." She's looking at Jase, seducing the camera, when she says it.

She winks and nods. People take out their phones.

She jumps and twirls and flips her dress in the air while singing a sexed-up rendition of "Happy Birthday." She leans forward, giving Jase a clear shot of her cleavage.

For a minute, I feel like I'm hallucinating. Did she really just do that? My heart races, and I can feel the vomit working its way up and out. I have to stop myself before I say or do something I'll regret. I'm about to leap forward, to put an end to this stupid act, but before I can make myself move, Georgie wobbles backward, the full weight of that punch hitting her, and crashes straight into me and the cake, taking us all down.

FilmmakerChance

Friday, November 1, 11:57 p.m.

Someone put on a show and it wasn't a good one.

KeishaSoFly: I don't know, y'all. That girl needs HELP.
68 mins   ♡ 3

AhMADManKhan: I've been saying is all I'm saying.
67 mins   ♡ 76

SykeWard: She did way more than just sing. Did y'all see what she did with Jase? Poor Bryn.
67 mins   ♡ 76

FrankieLikeTheBull: Riley wants a piece of that. Jase better not be moving in.
58 mins ·   ♡ 520

MarcusIsKing: Sloppy slut!
49 mins   ♡ 120

Chelsea432: Chill on the shaming. Chill on the bullying. Find something else to do.
49 mins   ♡ 130

RayRay256: I thought it was funny, tbh.
48 mins   ♡ 120

MerBear426: Lay off her. Y'all don't talk about every single sloppy thing white girls do.
45 mins   ♡ 189

DialloNotDiablo: I heard she hooked up with Baez for his birthday. Did Chance get footage? You know he gets everything.

42 mins ♡ 210

ABadassMelody: Cora ain't playing with this bitch anymore, I'll tell you that.

38 mins ♡ 192

RiRiLeeWashington120: This is why you have to learn to hold your liquor! Catch you slipping like this.

38 mins ♡ 1000

DeeSquared228Squad: I told you all. What a MESS. I saw her and Baez go into the pool house.

35 mins ♡ 150

SykeWard: Georgie's the kind of girl that doesn't just want attention . . . she wants it all. Including Baez. And Baez is the type of asshole that hides how fucked up he is. He wouldn't turn her down.

34 mins ♡ 764

PrincessChristine4578: Ooooh, you a mess, girl. Now stay away from Cora's man. SykeWard, are you Samantha Hawkins?

29 mins ♡ 22

ChaseTheGirls: Couldn't make this shit up if you tried. AMAZING NIGHT. Amazing.

26 mins ♡ 200

MikeSheppard129: Sloppy drunk girls do things they regret.

24 mins ♡ 1310

LaLaLeahJenkins42: Why is she thirsting for Baez like this? She could get anyone else. You don't know that, SykeWard.

23 mins ♡ 298

JessiBessyBoo: You make all girls look bad.
23 mins   ♡ 21

AdeleBelleParis1231: Hope somebody held up your hair before you puked.
21 mins   ♡ 13

NathanC986: She could be prettier if she wasn't so sloppy.
20 mins   ♡ 327

JaseThaGod202: I'm into curry.
14 mins   ♡ 34

BethBabe237: Lay off, y'all.
10 mins   ♡ 180

Comments Loading

BRYN

FRIDAY, NOVEMBER 1
11:59 P.M.

"WHAT ARE YOU DOING?" I TRY TO GET GEORGIE OFF THE ground. She's covered in cake and frosting, and she's a blubbering mess of a person.

Everyone is laughing and scooping cake from the grass, trying to salvage a piece or two. Some of the boys ask if they can lick it off both Georgie and Cora. Disgusting.

"I . . . messed up." Her voice breaks, and a tidal wave of tears explodes.

"Just get on your feet." I try to hold her up, but she's as slippery as a fish, covering me in frosting and glitter and sweat.

No one is helping. Everyone is laughing. Cora is trying to figure out how to get another cake while trying to get Christine to break out the hose to clean up the mess. Chance is recording the chaos. My stomach twists. What is happening to her? This isn't the Georgie I know.

The crowd hoots and hollers for Baez as he scoops some of the cake from the ground.

Cora threw me a Mad Hatter tea party last year for my seventeenth birthday. I try to remember what it was like to be so popular. To have so many people invested in my birthday. Or even know it's my birthday for that matter. I probably won't have a party at all this year.

People start to whisper about me.

"What's she doing here?"

"Guess Cora forgave her."

"Ugh, she's still the fucking worst."

"I dunno, I sort of feel bad for her. Jase messing with her new bestie. Sad. And now she has to clean up this mess? Shit."

I grit my teeth, my eyes fixed straight ahead. I just need to get her cleaned up and back to my house as quickly as possible. This'll ruin my sleepover at Cora's house tonight.

Ahmad is right behind me, nearly stepping on my heels. "You gonna go psycho on us tonight?" he says. "Or now that our boy Jase dumped you, you've got your marbles back?"

Ahmad makes an offensive cuckoo-for-Cocoa-Puffs sign, and Anthony laughs, drunk and dumb.

I want to punch them both. "Shut the hell up, Ahmad."

He flicks my ponytail from behind, and I dodge his touch.

"Get away from me," I shout back, drawing more attention I didn't want. My face burns. I'm still getting used to being around everyone again. When I'm near Cora, she's like a human force field. No one would dare say anything, but it's also like I'm not there. Cora may have forgiven me, but everyone else will take more work, because when she's not around, it's open season. I keep moving, trying to focus on my phone, trying to hold Georgie up.

Anthony laughs again. Some girl I don't recognize sees what's happening and, remarkably, distracts him. "Anthony! Shut up. It's old news."

I dart away, losing them in the crowd.

"Georgie," I say in her ear, "you gotta stand up. I can't drag you."

I'm about to walk into the pool house when a body blocks my path. Purposefully.

It's Sasha. She's got a decked-out, bejeweled crutch. "Cora might've invited you, but you should have sense enough not to show your face. Why are you even here?" Her voice is too high, like she's been sucking on a helium balloon. Is this what she's always sounded like? How can Jase even stand to listen to her?

Maybe they don't do much talking. The thought punches me in the stomach. Then I see those pictures in my head. Of Georgie kissing Jase.

"I'm trying to help," I say. "I'm going to take her home."

Christine and Ruthie come up.

"Indian Marilyn Monroe did the most tonight," Ruthie says with a snicker.

"I know you came just so you could see Jase," Sasha barks. "He's *over* you. So just stop, okay? It's so pathetic. We're together now."

"No shit, I didn't realize that," I snark.

Georgie groans, then vomits all over her dress. And me.

"Ugh, gross," Sasha says. "Get what you deserve. Both of you."

Georgie starts crying again. Christine and Ruthie help me carry her. We shove our way inside the pool house. I push through the bodies without apologizing, ignoring the dirty looks and whispers while Georgie sobs.

I get her into the bathroom. I try to clean her up. Georgie sits on the floor, her Marilyn Monroe costume covered in orange-colored vomit, her blond wig disheveled, and her makeup smudged with tears.

"I don't know what happened," she says, her words knocking into one another.

I help her stand. "You'll sleep it off."

"I sang to him."

I wrap her wobbly arm over my shoulder. "I know."

"Baez. It's his birthday, so I sang the song. But it was a mess."

"You're a mess right now." My heart squeezes. All these rumors have changed her, changed her life.

"I can't go home," she says between sobs, snot running down her nose.

"You can sleep it off at my house. Just get the rest of it in the toilet."

I see Christine hovering in the doorway. "You're a good friend, Bryn," she says before disappearing back to the party with Ruthie.

Georgie's head bobs over the bowl, heaving and spitting and sputtering. I search for towels in the cabinet and medicine to settle her stomach long enough to get her home. I can't have vomit in my car.

The sound of someone else vomiting comes from the bedroom. I ease open the other bathroom door and look. Baez is sprawled across the bed, now covered in cake, and vomiting into a bucket. *Yuck.*

"Let's go, Georgie." I get her to her feet and out of the bathroom. "It's fine. Just a few more stairs. You can do it."

We make it back downstairs. I help her stumble through the whispering crowds. All eyes are on us, and not in the way I used to crave.

We make our way through the house, and I try to force her to walk faster. Her legs are weak, her feet tripping in white stilettos.

"We're going to go out the front door," I tell her.

We pass the living room.

Jase walks out of it with Sasha tucked under his arm, her mouth swollen and lipstick smeared.

Did I use to look like that?

His blue eyes narrow. He's still the most perfect-looking boy I've ever seen. Sasha's leaning into him heavily, her leg brace a good excuse to snuggle close. In fact, knowing Jase, the accident is probably the only reason they're still together at all. She follows his gaze, and her eyes land on me, flashing with hate again.

Georgie almost falls out of my arms, I'm so frozen in place.

Memories hit me in waves, like Pandora's box opening. All the mess spewing out. It all started with her at the beginning of the summer. I saw a weird comment on Jase's social media from Sasha. And just couldn't let it go. I started an online war with her, back and forth, pages and pages and pages of insults. So many I can't remember what triggered it all. I couldn't stop until Jase did what I asked and blocked her. But by then everyone had already seen it. The start of my obsession with Jase, my need to have him all to myself.

I pull Georgie forward. We have to get to my car.

"Oh, look, babe," Sasha says, watching me. "Trash taking out trash."

"Hey, Bryn." His voice snaps me back into the moment, and I look up at him.

"Even covered in puke she's hotter than you," he says with a laugh.

Sasha cackles and points at Georgie, who has apparently vomited again.

It's like a punch to the gut, hearing the words out loud like that. Knowing that everyone else hears them, too. That he does it on purpose, to control me, to control us all. Knowing exactly which bruises to press down on. Which scars to rip open.

I hustle Georgie into my car. She's a crying mess again. I get her in my back seat. I wipe tears from her face. Guilt piles up inside me as I look at this different version of the person I knew. This new Georgie spiraling out of control.

I turn on the car and squeeze the steering wheel. All the things I wanted to say bubble up in my throat, and I want to vomit, too. My phone buzzes. The screen fills with social media tags. Taunts and threats. I'm used to it now.

Someone posted a picture of me looking lost and confused. A lamb headed to slaughter. The commenters are divided between loving me again and still hating me for what happened this summer.

Then there are posts of Georgie. And the video. I click on it. A drunk Georgie singing "Happy Birthday" to Baez Onyekachi like some sloppy stripper.

A new iteration of the rumor shows up in the comments: *Georgie gave the birthday boy her virginity. A private party in the pool house.*

EZ AND GEORGIE
ERE COZYING UP
OLO AT CORA'S
ARTY.

BAEZ AND GEORGIE
DEFINITELY MADE OUT
UPSTAIRS IN CORA'S
BEDROOM.

COMPLETE AND
TOTAL YOU-KNOW-
WHAT AT JASE'S
PARTY.

GEORGIE AND BAEZ
HAVE BEEN FOOLING
AROUND FOR MONTHS
BEHIND CORA'S BACK.

CORA PUT GEORGIE ON
THE CHEERLEADING
TEAM TO KEEP AN
EYE ON HER.

GEORGIE AND JASE
HOOKED UP IN THE
PHOTO BOOTH AT
SCHOOL.

BAEZ AND GEORGIE
HAD SEX AT HIS
BIRTHDAY PARTY.

DC Teen Lovers' Spat Claims Political Casualties!

The *DC Rag*—August 31

The son of South Carolina Congressman Jason Cunningham was involved in a car accident on Wisconsin Avenue that also injured three other underage passengers. Jason Alan Cunningham II, 17, was hospitalized at MedStar Georgetown University Hospital with severe injuries to the neck and shoulder when a car ran a red light. The *DC Rag* can exclusively name the person who caused the accident—Bryn Colburn, daughter of Speaker of the House Nigel Colburn and celebrity chef Melinda Colburn.

Cunningham II and Bryn Colburn had split as a couple months ago, and says a source close to both parties, the girl's jealousy was out of control before the incident. Her running the red light set off a chain of events that caused Cunningham's car crash—with three other passengers in the vehicle, including his new girlfriend, Sasha Lucas, and Abaeze Onyekachi, the son of a Nigerian diplomat to the United States. Lucas and the other passenger, also a teen, are in stable condition but suffered injuries. The ex-girlfriend, Colburn, did not suffer any injuries and fled the scene, which could trigger hit-and-run charges. Police have yet to press charges, but it seems likely that the teens' families will pursue the case. Congressman Cunningham's office as well as the Speaker's office declined to comment on the incident.

From: Georgie Khalra
Attn: Cora Davidson
Sent: Sunday, November 3, 11:23 AM
Subject: SO SORRY!

Hey Cora,

I just wanted to say I'm so so so very sorry for what happened at the party with the cake. I clearly had too much punch, and I've never actually been drunk before.

Anyway, I'm really sorry. I didn't mean for any of that—any of it—to happen. I hope you can find it in your heart to forgive. Again.

Sincerely,
Georgie

From: Dr. Divya Malhotra
Attn: Jashan "Georgie" Khalra
Sent: Sunday, November 3, 3:32 PM
Subject: Missed Chat

Dear Georgie,

I hope this email finds you well. I'm a bit concerned that you missed your scheduled bi-weekly check-in three times already—including the chat we scheduled for this morning. I've been trying to reach you, but have not received a response. I understand that things are beginning to get hectic with school and college applications, and Halloween, I'm sure, but the suggestion you made about joining the cheerleading squad in our last update has me worried. Your failure to turn in your food diaries for the past three weeks also concerns me.

I'm requesting that we schedule another meeting with your parents within two weeks to address these issues, since my attempts to reach out have been ignored. Please let me know immediately your earliest availability, otherwise I think it best that we begin to involve your parents in your aftercare.

Sincerely,
Dr. Divya Malhotra

GEORGIE

MONDAY, NOVEMBER 4
8:05 A.M.

I SIT IN DR. DIVYA'S OFFICE, STEWING. HER LAST EMAIL—AND the looming threat of her tattling to my parents—got me to haul my butt to her office downtown before heading to school.

"Can I ask why you thought Riley's interest might not be genuine?" she says, tapping the clipboard.

There's silence for a minute. Except, of course, for the rumble of my stomach. Which is *still* recovering from the nightmare that was Baez's party.

"I'm sorry," I say, reaching for one of the mini-muffins in the basket on the coffee table. Mum would not approve, but I think we've got doctor-patient confidentiality, or whatever. "I mean, it's just—never happened before." Except. Nope. That doesn't count. "So I wasn't quite sure how to handle it. I'm not allowed to date."

"And why do you think that?"

I nibble at the muffin. "I mean, you've met my parents. Like most Desi parents, they're total control freaks. Mum picks my clothes, picks my meals, will pick my college, pick my major, and eventually, I'm sure, pick my husband." I shrug. "Cultural expectations. Familial expectations. Societal expectations." I pop the rest of the muffin into my mouth. I'm dying to reach forward and pluck another one from the basket, but I lean back, controlling myself. I'll have to cut out a diet soda at lunch and dessert. "Gotta stay in line, follow the rules."

Dr. Divya taps on the clipboard. "I see that you're craving another muffin. But also stopping yourself. Can you tell me about your thought process there?"

I frown at my hands. "I can hear my mom's voice in my head, the warning. And, you know, like, the rest of them, too."

She scribbles and nods. "Who are 'the rest of them'?"

"The Aunties. It's like this coven where they gather to decide the rules: doctor, engineer, lawyer? Check. Lean, tall, fair. Check. Don't eat too much. Don't talk too loud. Stick close to the community. No dating, especially not non-Desi boys. They've got a whole list of dos and don'ts laid out, so there's no room to figure out who you actually are."

"Is that what you're doing with cheerleading? Figuring yourself out?"

Am I? I shrug. "I guess. But it's like another box. One I've picked for myself, climbed right in." Should I tell her about Friday? About the video? About the shitshow that awaits me once I leave her office?

She leans forward, fingers tapping the table. "Georgie, I'm concerned that some of the patterns that led you to the binge eating might be resurfacing. Some of this, of course, is the stuff you mentioned—the weight of expectations. Your mother's. Your community's. Your peers'. Your own." Boom. There it is. "And that's the big one."

"Or it was."

"I've noticed that you use humor—self-deprecation. Have you picked up on that?"

"I guess." I can feel myself inching closer to the muffin basket again, and lean back into the couch, creating distance. "This is a safe space, right? Please don't call my parents about this."

"This is always a safe space." She takes a deep breath, like she's using some kind of meditation or calming exercise on herself. And she's supposed to be the therapist. "You can talk to me about anything. I can only help you if you let me. So you need to help yourself. Because no one can make you feel something unless you let them. No one can put you in a box unless you allow it."

I stand, not really wanting to leave and go to school and face everything, but not really wanting to stay. "Okay."

The only thing anyone can talk about when I get to school is that video.

The video.

The video of me singing to Baez.

The video of drunk me making an ass out of myself.

The video of me coming on to someone else's boyfriend—the boyfriend everybody already thinks I hooked up with.

Ugh! Never drinking again.

Vibha's standing at my locker, phone in hand, ready to yell at me like some gassed-up Auntie. Her non-boyfriend, Amir, stands behind her, looking shocked and sorry. I wish I could snap a picture, send it to Dr. Divya. Explain some of the things rolling around in my head.

"Jashan, really?" Vibha says, hands on her hips.

"Really!" I reach to smooth down the Peter Pan collar on her shirt. "Looks like you've got a wrinkle there."

She scoffs. "What's gotten into you?"

"Everything," I say, just to make her face twist in horror.

"Do you know what they're saying about you?" she barks, then runs through every iteration of the rumor, like she has them all written down in her planner:

"Baez and Georgie hooked up in Cora's own house.

"Georgie and Baez have been fooling around for months behind Cora's back.

"Georgie and Jase kissed in the photo booth at school.

"Baez and Georgie had a Halloween hookup."

"Oh, alliteration! How fun." I rearrange things in my locker. "Why are you here? You made it clear. We aren't friends. You don't like me. Not the new me."

"I want my *old* friend back."

"The one who sat there and never said a word? Happy to play your sidekick? That one?"

"I don't like this one. It's almost like you *like* what everyone is saying." She storms off, Amir following like a lost puppy.

Her anger sort of makes me feel good. Strong. Weirdly.

I shove my locker closed and race off to find Bryn. I head into the lunchroom, where she's campaigning: handing out our campaign flyers, shouting out her slogans, and trying to welcome people to tell their stories in her photo booth. I'm almost out of breath when I reach her.

"Hey," she says. "Vibha just ran through here looking pissed and cursing your name, basically. What'd you do?"

"Apparently I have a new personality now."

Bryn laughs. "Yeah, you kind of do."

I scoff. "Well, she doesn't like it. Whatever." Once the anger fades, the panic returns. "I need your help."

Bryn's staring at me all strange.

"What?"

"I gotta know." She frowns. "But you were too drunk to ask. And I didn't know how to text about this."

"What?" I knew it was coming. The video—

"Did you hook up with Jase in the photo booth?"

"I didn't. I wouldn't."

She holds up her phone. Guess those pics are posted, too.

"He tried to kiss me. I mean, did. But I shut him down."

She deflates like a popped balloon. "Sounds like Jase."

"I don't know all the, you know, stuff that went on between you, but I'd never." I put a hand on her shoulder. "You get that, right?"

"It's just so many rumors. That one was weird, you know?"

"All of them are weird."

"You know what I mean."

I grab her. "So what do I do about this video?" Thinking about it makes my head hurt. "How bad is it? I tried watching it a hundred times but couldn't press play. Too scared."

Bryn scrambles for her phone and opens it. As it buffers, my heart beats to the pulse of the spinning wheel on the small screen. I hide my face in my hand, peering at it from behind my fingers, the way I'd sneak to watch horror movies with Papa when I was little.

Bryn pushes the play button. I see myself in front of Christine's pool. Trashed from that punch. My voice sings "Happy Birthday," shaky and slurred. The video camera zooms in on me smiling. I don't even recognize myself.

DRUNK GEORGIE:

1. A Marilyn Monroe costume hanging dangerously low.

2. Polka-dot bra peeking through, along with my cleavage.

3. Splotches from the punch stain.

4. Sweat pools on my top lip.

5. My red lipstick is smudged around my mouth, like Ronald McDonald's.

6. Blond wig.

The sound of record scratching interrupts my singing, a sampled beat replacing my voice. The camera zooms in and out on my boobs. A picture of Baez appears. It's from one of his games. He's excited after scoring a winning goal. The image dances back and forth near my chest. A ticker-tape scroll frames the whole thing. On repeat is the word *SLUT! SLUT! SLUT!*

My stomach clenches. "Turn it off," I say, anger erupting through me.

Bryn fumbles with the phone. "But there's more. Sounds of moaning and hooking up." And screaming. She doesn't mention the screaming. But that's definitely not me.

"Turn it off!" I put a hand on my forehead. I try to remember what Dr. Divya said this morning. *No one can make you feel something unless you let them.* But how do I stop it? "Someone made this. Took the time. Edited it. Who would do this?"

"This has Chance's name all over it." Bryn shuts the phone completely off. "Do you remember singing that night? That asshole Jase brought around a camera so people could wish Baez a happy birthday."

It all feels like a lifetime ago. Like a giant, cosmic joke. "Why would Chance give a shit about this? About *me*?"

"It's my fault," she says.

"What do you mean?"

"It's because you're in my cabinet. That's why he did this. You're on my team, so you're a target."

"It's not supposed to be like that," I say.

"I know. That idiot. I bet I can trace the IP address via the video—and catch him. Or flag it, at least." She mumbles some tech nonsense while my brain fills to the brim with a million more worries. So much for taking Dr. D's advice. "This is totally more about Baez than about you. Someone is trying to make him seem like an actual bad person. Which he is, sometimes. He, like, took Cora from me."

"What?" I can't track her connections. I can't really think logically at all right now. But this is about Jase, too. Now.

"I think you should make a video for the campaign." Her eyes shimmer. "That'll help you fix it. That's the answer. Tell your story. Take control of the narrative."

I consider her idea.

"You can't let them say that stuff about you."

"You're right." I take her phone. "I won't let them put me in a box." I'll make my own. "You good at shooting videos?"

"I'm decent," she says with a wink.

UNKNOWN:

You better back off, bitch.
You're gonna get yourself in trouble.

Heed my warning, slut.
I'm not messing around.

Georgie:

Who is this?

Millie:

Hey Turtle. Did you start the early decision paperwork? Deadline's looming.

Want me to look at it for you?

Want me to send you mine?
I still have it on my hard drive.

I miss you.

Cora:

Sorry. It's been busy.

Millie:

You really should get it done though.

Cora:

I will. You okay?

Millie:

I miss you guys. It's hard.
But I'll be home for Thanksgiving.

Cora:

I'm ready.

It's not the same without you here.

Baez:

Hey, love. Pick you up for dinner tonight?
Mom's making jollof rice and chicken.

Know it's your fave.

Or I can bring some for you and your parents.

Haven't seen them in a while.

Or you.

Miss you.

So . . . dinner?

Baez:

Stopped by. Vero said you weren't home.
Leftovers with her.

Maybe tomorrow?

CORA

FRIDAY, NOVEMBER 8
9:40 A.M.

EVERYONE'S STARING AT ME, BUT FOR ALL THE WRONG reasons.

I walk through the halls, hoping and wishing that all the mess with the video from Baez's birthday party would blow over. It's like every day I wake up with the same wish and it doesn't come true. That everything would go back to normal. That I could have the best senior year. That I could do everything I set out to do. The way I've always planned.

I only looked at my social media feeds three times yesterday—my new self-imposed limit. I feel like I'm losing it when I see that people are still talking about us instead of the thousands of other dramas that populate high school. The special election is today, even, and no one is talking about it. Last night, I binged TV shows and movies with Millie, who watched with me via video chat. Self-care and all that. Twin rituals.

People glance from their phones to me.

Obsessed.

Snippets of people's conversations find me as I walk to my locker. I sneer at them, sending a reminder of who I am. Cora Davidson. The most popular girl at school. And they shouldn't forget it.

One white girl, a stranger, probably a sophomore, says, "Oh my god, you see how red she got? Her face matched her lipstick. Didn't realize Black people could blush like that."

"You all can shut the whole hell up," I say loudly, and they scamper away. I can't shake the tension as people stare and stare and stare. The feeling is spiraling. Worse than before.

"I should probably feel bad for her, but I can't stop laughing at how dumb it all is," some guy I don't even know says.

"I know," his friend whispers back, like I can't hear them. "It's like, how many times has she embarrassed someone at school? Now she gets to see how it feels."

My heart starts beating faster, my jaw clenching. Have I really done that? My brain tries to comb through these past four years. All the small comments and reactions and interactions. But I don't remember being mean to anyone.

Six-word memoir: *But that doesn't mean you haven't.*

I get to my locker and find Adele leaning against it. "There you are," she says, holding up her phone. "I cannot believe—"

"I don't want to see it," I tell her, pushing her phone out of my face.

She steps to the side, and I open my locker so forcefully, the door bounces off the neighboring one with a loud crash.

"You can't ignore it forever," Adele says. "Maybe it'd be better if you said something about it. Or you could fill your feed with photos of you and Baez and let everyone know, like, y'all are pretty much married. No trouble in paradise. That's what I'd do."

"That's not happening," I say. "I don't want anyone to know that it's getting to me. I refuse to let it get to me."

"But it *is* getting to you."

"Thanks for the reminder. I thought you were supposed to be one of my best friends?"

"Fine, fine. All right," Adele says, though I know she'll push again. But then she leans closer to me and says, "What do you want to do? Confront Georgie?"

"I'm going to deal with Georgie and all of it," I say, even though I don't know exactly *what* I'm going to do. "Alone."

She frowns. "Cor, I feel like you're not telling me things. Like you don't want my help, and you're not letting me be there for you. Ever since you started talking to Bryn again, you've been changing."

Here we go. I'm not in the mood for Adele's dramatics. This isn't about her. It's about me. She isn't the one who's being talked about and dragged and tagged all day long. Bryn never pulled this shit. And she went through it. On her own. I need to find her. She'll help me figure out how to fix this. She is Queen of the Spin. Got it all from her dad.

"I'm sorry, okay?" I say, mostly to shut Adele up. "I need some time alone. I'm trying to figure it out."

Adele perks up. "Apology accepted. I'd do whatever you want. Even mess with her. Fuck her up a little. Let her know you shouldn't hook up with other people's boyfriends. Make her pay."

"Chill. We're not doing a takedown."

"Slumber party convergence, then?" She bats her big eyes at me.

"Yes," I say. "But you have to invite Bryn, too."

"Fiiiiiine."

The bell rings, and everyone scrambles. I loop my arm in hers—to make her feel better, to make myself feel better, too, maybe—and we walk through the crowd, forcing everyone to move for us. Like it used to be. There are more stares, more whispers, more laughter, more speculations.

But her support creates a bubble around me. I ignore it all. Let the words fill me up. Reminding them of who I am.

I'm Cora Davidson.

I'm important.

I sit through my morning classes with my notebook perched in front of me so it looks like I'm paying attention. But I can barely focus. When the teachers have their backs turned, the kids sitting closest to me keep shooting me smug looks, and I want to take a bow.

Are you not entertained?

All the whispering makes my skin itch during calculus class. All the whispering in psychology triggers a headache. But when they keep it up during my English lit class, I stare right back, smiling and waving.

That shuts it down.

Mr. Walsh turns around. "Miss Davidson, is there a problem?"

My face heats up, but I give him my sweetest smile. "No problem at all. Never a problem."

Great. Everyone will be able to see the panic oozing out of me, the emotional earthquake about to explode.

Mr. Walsh's sonnet reading is not enough to keep my mind off of it all, so I take a risk and slip my phone out of my bag, holding it on my lap so it's hidden. Someone has posted another Who's Hotter? poll, with pictures of me and Georgie in our Halloween costumes. Her Marilyn Monroe to my sexy flapper. Votes for her beat mine so far. The comments hit me one after another.

Cora isn't as hot as she used to be.

Georgie is more exotic.

Sorry, but G's got better hair. Saw it spill out of that terrible wig.

Cora's still got it—but she better watch out.

I'm more into Indian girls than Black ones.

Team Cora. Always.

Georgie is a freaking glow-up.

Baez would look cuter with Georgie. Mixed kids for the win.

My stomach drops, and my eyes burn with tears. Angry ones. I hate all of this, and it's been going on forever, just an eternity of random classmates talking about us. Whoever is behind all the polls. Whoever is stirring up this shit. Whoever keeps continuing to talk about this. My whole body tenses. The rage swirls inside me, ready to be let loose. I text Millie over and over, but she doesn't answer.

I ask for a bathroom pass and make Baez meet me in the senior parking lot. It's almost lunch, and people are getting in their cars, going to grab food and come back for the next period.

"You're being weird," Baez says, leaning against his car. Like no hello, no kiss, no nothing. "Bad mood? Let's grab samosas and butter chicken from Rasika. I can call it in."

"Do not mention Indian food to me," I say. Just the thought of it is enough to make me sick. "This shit online is way too much. I've had ENOUGH of it! We have to do something. Now."

"Cora, really? Not today, okay?" he says, tired. "It's all stupid."

His words are tinder sparking the argument.

"How can you just ignore it all? The stuff they're saying? You see those polls today? She's winning."

People are pausing, stopping to listen, like we're their favorite lunchtime show. And even Chance has his camera out. But it's too late to stop this now.

"Really?" Baez says, like a smug smart-ass.

"*Really*," I spit back. "I see the way everyone treats you. Like you're some goddamn sex god. High fives and fist bumps. Everyone thinks you're with both of us."

"I hate this shit, too. I told you that. I don't like anything about it."

He tries to take my hand.

"How can you be so relaxed about this?"

"Because it's not about me. Not really. It's bullshit, stuff people are making up." He shakes his head. "I won't let them get to me."

"Easy for you to say," I huff. He doesn't understand what it's like to be a girl. The way we're judged. I don't want to have a very public, very loud, and very impossible-not-to-watch fight in front of everyone. I just want it all to go away. I'm shaking, and I have to make it all stop. I have to go.

I make a break for it, trying to bust through the growing crowd. But he grabs my hand and pulls me back, arms wrapped around me, still, close. "Cora, chill." He has a way of talking that is unquestionably sexy but infuriating if you are trying to have a fight with him. "I don't know how many times I have to tell you. I love you. I want you. I don't want her. Or anybody else. And that girl's not even cute."

I stand for a second, staring at him, trying to wrap my head around what he just said. "I . . . okay, one: Does that mean you would cheat on me with a cute girl? And two: She has totally gotten hot. Like, under her clothes. Hot. Everyone's talking about it. And three: She's, like, got a whole different personality. Ready for anything."

I hate the words coming out of my mouth. I hate that I can't keep it all in. I hate that any of this bothers me. The paranoia is consuming me.

His face flickers with annoyance. "I didn't think you were this insecure. I'm not gonna defend myself every time someone says anything," Baez says, "I already told you: Nothing happened. I'm not gonna, like, send roses a million times because someone told you I did something wrong. And I've sent you plenty."

All of a sudden, he acts unbothered; his face relaxes, his answers smooth and seamless, like I've made this whole thing up. Like it's not something that has been buzzing for weeks now. It's the thing that finally triggers my tears. He's not acting like my boyfriend right now. Not the one I've loved my whole life. That Baez would understand. This one looks like he wishes he were a stranger.

"You think I'm fishing for more *roses*?"

"I just don't get why you're acting like this," he says.

"I could get other people. I could go back and be with JuJu." My ex's name is a firework between us. A bruise. "I don't have to be with you, you know?" I keep pushing him. Stoking his temper. Millie always said I was the kind of girl who gets mean when I'm scared. "JuJu would *never* do this to me." Out of the corner of my eye, I can see everyone in the parking lot shift, like they were pretending not to listen and now we've got their full attention.

His face twists.

"You want other people?" Baez says, throwing his hands up. "Get other people! Go back and fuck with JuJu. Go sleep with her. Get you a new guy, too."

He knows his lacrosse team is watching now.

He's a different person.

I can feel my whole body vibrating, shaking like I'm in an earthquake, but the rest of the world is still.

"You think this is fun for me?" Baez is finally raising his voice, and it makes me cry even harder.

"You've changed," I say.

"*You've* changed," he snaps back.

We stand in silence for a few very long, very awkward minutes. There's only my cries and Baez making random hand gestures accompanied by loud, aggravated sighs.

"All the questions, all the worrying, all the paranoid shit. You make me want to lie," Baez says. "I mean, look at you right now."

It's the cruelest thing he could have said in this moment. Mascara runs down my face and I can't get any part of my body to stop shaking, and my mouth is open, gaping. I feel ugly, for the first time in my life. And messy. And sort of unhinged.

"All these people can't be wrong," I say.

He sighs. "Then maybe they're right."

He walks away, leaving me a sobbing, heaving mess.

EZ AND GEORGIE
ERE COZYING UP
LO AT CORA'S
RTY.

BAEZ AND GEORGIE
DEFINITELY MADE OUT
UPSTAIRS IN CORA'S
BEDROOM.

COMPLETE AND
TOTAL YOU-KNOW-
WHAT AT JASE'S
PARTY.

GEORGIE AND BAEZ
HAVE BEEN FOOLING
AROUND FOR MONTHS
BEHIND CORA'S BACK.

CORA PUT GEORGIE ON
THE CHEERLEADING
TEAM TO KEEP AN
EYE ON HER.

GEORGIE AND JASE
HOOKED UP IN THE
PHOTO BOOTH AT
SCHOOL.

BAEZ AND GEORGIE
HAD SEX AT HIS
BIRTHDAY PARTY.

CORA AND BAEZ
HAD A MASSIVE
FIGHT. IT'S OVER.

RiRiLeeWashington120

Friday, November 8, 1:09 p.m.

♡ 2089   💬 987

It's over in paradise.

NicoMuyRico020304: Cora and Baez broke up. Damn!!! It's the apocalypse.
48 mins   ♡ 23

SykeWard: Told you he did it!
45 mins   ♡ 23

    ABadassMelody: Come on, we don't know that. Let's wait and see what they say.
    44 mins   ♡ 15

AmirNotKhan007: It was just a little fun. LOL!
39 mins   ♡ 54

ChaseTheGirls: Georgie went after Baez. That's her fault. Not his.
36 mins   ♡ 62

JessiBessyBoo: Georgie broke the girl code. AND she's on the cheer team, too. Not for long though.
32 mins   ♡ 128

PanviniNotPanini: Maybe Georgie will be the new Cora. She took her man and maybe her spot, too.
27 mins   ♡ 28

AJRiveriaTodelo301: Georgie went after him. Some girls just like boys that already HAVE girls.
22 mins   ♡ 160

AhMADManKhan: Yo, anyone else feel like all of this is messed up?

19 mins   ♡ 82

WongsterArt: Who the hell is SykeWard?

18 mins   ♡ 80

> **SykeWard:** I used to go to school with you, dickhead WongsterArt. I sat behlnd you in Trig.
>
> **4 mins**   ♡ 12

DeeSquared228Squad: Cora should've been broken up with Baez. More fish in the sea.

17 mins   ♡ 14

KatNotKateLee: Georgie is a bitch for doing this.

14 mins   ♡ 89

CallMeYourDaddyDavid: They were the longest running couple in the school.

10 mins   ♡ 75

ZachWei876: I'll date Cora now that she's done with Baez.

8 mins   ♡ 92

PrettyPalak: Georgie didn't do this.

5 mins   ♡ 32

TateNotTotBro1289: Georgie is a bitch.

1 mins   ♡ 34

Comments Loading

Baez:

I'm sorry for blowing up!

I shouldn't have yelled.

All of this stuff is stupid.

I'm sorry.

I just want you to believe me.

Saturday 3:35 AM

Baez:

Ugh, please. I'm sorry.

BRYN

I'M DRAPED ACROSS CORA'S BED. RUTHIE, CHRISTINE, and Adele are tucked into each corner of her room, taking out Korean face masks or scrolling through streaming apps or picking over all the snack trays her housekeeper brought in.

Operation Distract Cora Post-Breakup. And myself, if I'm being honest. Yesterday was the special election and I have to hope/pray that I got enough votes to get my whole life back.

"We could watch a rom-com?" Christine says, then swallows that thought, catching a nasty look from Adele. "Or no, like killing. Yeah, let's watch a murder mystery."

Cora stares at the ceiling. She hasn't said much. A few words here and there. Her phone lights up with unacknowledged messages and alerts. She looks at it every few seconds before chucking it in her covers. Her eyes are all bloodshot and the brown skin around them puffy from crying.

"Want to—" Adele starts, but Cora starts crying again.

The sound sends worry and guilt and sadness through me. "He's an asshole, okay?" I stroke her back, remembering how she did the same for me when Jase started getting all distant and weird. "It sucks. But you deserve bigger and better."

I mean, in the beginning it hurts and everything. I've done my fair share of crying and eating inappropriate foods, like chocolate chip cookies covered in whipped cream and caramel sauce, because all I wanted was ridiculous amounts of sugar to get rid of all the feelings. I was sad and angry and confused and all of those things. I know what it's like to be in her spot.

Christine, Ruthie, and Adele still don't know what to do with me, but they're softening. I called each one of them right before school started. Spent all of Labor Day practically on the phone. I left messages. Twelve per person. I thought if I left an even number of messages, it'd be lucky enough to erase what happened. Mom would say that this behavior falls in the bracket of obsessive-compulsive disorders. That I need to watch it. Maybe. But she's not here to watch me. No one returned my calls. I chew on my nails, ignoring all the things I know about this unfortunate habit.

Adele takes out a pack of gum, offering it to everyone.

"Chewing gum gives you flatulence," I say. "You know, gas. Major farts. Big-time."

She glares at me. "And chewing your nails is disgusting."

I make a fart noise with my mouth, thinking it will make them laugh. It doesn't, but they don't hate on me either. That's a win these days.

I try to tune out the gum smacking. It's depressing, truth be told. And compulsive. It's not just me who thinks that. Mom has always said things like gum chewing and hand washing and face picking are compulsive behaviors covering up latent anxieties. And I know a lot about anxiety now. It has crept inside, threatening to leave cracks in the confidence I've always had. But I tell myself that Cora wants me here, no matter how many times the girls give me dirty looks or whisper under their breath.

They bombard Cora with compliments, and insults about Baez.

"I never liked him," I say, adding to the chorus. And it's not a lie. I close my eyes remembering that night, right before the accident, how he'd caught me snooping around Jase's house. I'd just wanted to see if he was home like he'd said he was and popped by. Harmless, really, I thought at the time. Baez was sprawled on Jase's couch. He spotted me in the window. Bet he told Jase. Bet that's why Jase broke up with me. Bet he told Cora not to be my friend anymore.

"Let's liven this party up," I suggest. "A game, maybe?"

"Just . . . stop trying so hard, Bryn," Christine snaps.

"C'mon. Two truths and a lie." I climb off the bed. "You tell everyone three things. Two have to be real and one is a lie."

They stare back, skeptical.

"It'll be fun. If we guess wrong, we drink." I pull one of my mom's bottles of vodka from my overnight bag. "A good distraction."

"I'm in," Cora says, climbing out of bed. "I need a distraction."

I wink at her. I'll make her feel better.

We sit in a circle on the floor.

"Who's first?"

"I'll go," Christine volunteers. She twirls her long blond hair around her fingers. "I'm still a virgin. I never flashed Coach Forna, despite what the swim team said. I've been secretly hooking up with Maggie—from the track team."

Ruthie's eyes get all big. "Your slut ass is not a virgin. That's the lie."

Everyone laughs.

Christine squeals and kicks her feet in the air. "Fine. That was too easy."

"I thought you were with Rico?" I ask.

She rolls her eyes. "I am. So what?"

"That makes you a cheater."

"What are you, the police?" she replies. "You go next since you're such a pillar of virtue."

"Fine!" I stretch upright, accepting her challenge. "First, I didn't mean to run that red light."

They all snicker. "But, side note, I did mean to slash Sasha's tires." Wide, scandalized eyes stare back at me. "I regret it, though." Somehow, they lean a little closer, smile a little more warmly.

I hold up my index finger. "Second, I practice witchcraft. And third, Jase is a piece of shit who SWATted his girlfriend at his old school because she wouldn't sleep with him."

I watch as Jase's deepest, darkest secret settles into them. Their mouths drop open with shock.

"That can't be true," Cora says.

"What's that?" Ruthie asks. "Swatted?"

"When you make a false police report in the hopes that the SWAT team will show up at someone's house and swarm it," Christine says.

"I found out after we broke up. She DM'd me." I hold up my phone to signal that I have the evidence.

"What a dick," Adele says. "Like, I've always known he was trash."

"What! So you *meant* to run that red light?" Ruthie asks. "Girl, you've been denying those rumors for months."

"No, the game is two truths and a lie. The lie is that I'm a witch. I've been asking for people to listen to the whole story, to give me a chance and understand how I got to that point."

"Oooookayyyyy . . . so what is it?" Christine asks.

"I'd just found out that my dad was cheating on my mom the night before. Found her all messed up on wine and pills and laid out on the floor."

The girls' eyes get big. Only Cora knows the whole story.

"Jase had been telling me for months that he wanted to go to college with me, that we'd be together forever. Then he started saying that the person he was texting all the time was one of his teammates. That I definitely didn't see him checking out Sasha, I must have imagined it. He stopped texting me as often, but when I asked, he said I was being clingy. After everything with my mom, I got all suspicious and nervous. He wasn't answering me that night, so I went to see what he was doing. That's when I saw him." I try to keep the frog out of my throat as the anxiety of retelling it makes everything rush back. "That the little voice inside me telling me it was the truth . . . was indeed correct."

Cora looks down. A tear rushes down her face, and she quickly wipes it away.

"I didn't mean to hurt anyone," I say, pleading my case. "I just, like, finally knew for sure I wasn't crazy like he said, like my dad had said about my mom. And I just wanted him to know that I'd seen him. That I knew he was lying to me. So I ran the red to try to catch him. I wanted him to see me in the car, to know that he couldn't lie to me anymore."

"Whoa, didn't realize you had all that going on," Adele admits, pity filling her eyes.

Cora darts from the bed to her bathroom without a word.

"Shit," Christine says. "We shouldn't have talked about this." She looks around to the rest of us. "All right, who's on back-patting duty this time?"

"Let me talk to her." They look at me gratefully. A tingle zings up my spine. Determination. I slip into the hall and go to the other bathroom door, in Millie's room, and knock softly. "Cora . . ." I whisper before cracking the door.

She's on her bathroom rug, big tears rushing down her brown cheeks.

"You okay?" I ask, joining her.

"It's fine."

The words are too small to hold all the things happening with her.

"It's not fine." I wrap her in my arms and hold her for a long moment while she cries. I don't mind as her tears soak my shirt and skin. I'm happy to be needed. Her sobs quiet after a while, and I take a nearby towel and clean her up. Just like I did for Georgie at Baez's party. Just like I did for my mom the night she found out about Dad's affair.

"Can I ask you something?" I brush her hair off her shoulder.

Her eyebrow lifts. "You're going to do it regardless of what I say."

I smile. She knows me too well. I pull out a folded campaign flyer from my pocket and show it to her. "Will you just be my VP again? The election was yesterday and there's a good chance that it went in my favor. I feel really solid about it. You need the distraction, and I need you."

She bites her bottom lip, considering my question.

"Can you forgive me? Really, really forgive me this time? I didn't mean to hurt Baez. I didn't mean to hurt anyone," I say, trying to keep the whining sound out of my voice. My pulse races with the possibility that the plan is working. "It's not the same without you." I let the question ease between us. Not too aggressive. Not too pleading. Not too eager. She's in a vulnerable state.

She looks skeptical, but there's something there. A tiny thaw, a crack in the ice. Just enough to shatter it.

"Yeah, I'll still be your VP."

CoraBae526

Saturday, November 9, 9:16 p.m.

♡ 5698 ◯ 2765

Prez and VP back at it! Watch out!

KatNotKateLee: Well, well, well . . . back at it.
52 mins　　　♡ 13

AhMADManKhan: Ugh . . . now I have to deal with Bryn's crazy ass again.
44 mins　　　♡ 55

CoraBae526: Shut up AhMADManKhan.
43 mins　　　♡ 38

BrynChildDC: Bryn + Cora 4ever
40 mins　　　♡ 137

FilmmakerChance: Eyeroll. Vomit.
38 mins　　　♡ 120

ABadassMelody: Okay, okay, this might be interesting
35 mins　　　♡ 150

SykeWard: Two peas in a pod . . . or whatever. Maybe Bryn will help Cora kill those rumors?
32 mins　　　♡ 117

　　AdeleBelleParis1231: SykeWard, who the hell are you?
　　31 mins　　♡ 126

ChaseTheGirls: When did Cora get so dumb? Hello! Remember she almost killed your boyfriend and your friends?
26 mins　　　♡ 62

CoraBae526: ChaseTheGirls, ex-boyfriend. Fuck him. I do what I want.
25 mins ♡ 387

AdeleBelleParis1231: Well this is new.
26 mins ♡ 120

PrincessChristine4578: Hmmm.
24 mins ♡ 160

FilmmakerChance: Honestly, they don't stand a chance. I know all your secrets, Bryn.
23 mins ♡ 200

SykeWard: Stop being haters AdeleBelle and PrincessChristine4578.
23 mins ♡ 13

DeeSquared228Squad: Everyone forgives her.
9 mins ♡ 128

MollyMollMichaels: The bullies running the anti-bullying campaign. Now I've seen everything.
2 mins ♡ 12

Comments Loading

Bryn Colburn
Followers:
347
Group chats:
2

GEORGIE

SATURDAY, NOVEMBER 9
9:30 P.M.

"MAYBE I SHOULD CANCEL?" I TALK TO MYSELF WHILE standing in front of the mirror. "Ugh. This is a bad idea."

I stare down at my phone, a text from Riley Wong confirming our meetup tonight. A late movie. My first-ever date. "I should've never said yes. What was I thinking?"

New Georgie says yes to dates, a voice inside reminds me.

I storm into the walk-in closet, taking it all in. While I was gone this summer, Papa had the room next to mine renovated to look like a celebrity's closet: a lighted vanity, a floating island in the middle to store my jewelry and accessories, sections for all the new clothes Mum's stylist bought, and shoe racks for loafers, kitten heels, and ballet flats.

My eyes drift high above, where little matching baskets hide tiny mountains of old clothes. The big clothes. Mum wouldn't let the stylist throw them out, in case I fluctuate, and "waste all our money," as she likes to say. I circle the room, tracing my fingers over the fabrics. Seersucker. Khaki. Cashmere. Stripes. Gingham. All appropriate, modest, and tailored shapes for my new body type. All the right clothes for someone who wants to be invisible and blend into the preppy fold of Washington, DC. Mum-approved. And all boring as can be. Most of my secret clothes are at Bryn's pool house, but she's not home and not answering my calls. I'm going to have to do this all on my own.

If my life were a movie, I would have several effortless and perfect options. My hair and makeup would be flawless. Cheekbones and silky hair and soft lips. And a real friend, someone who knows exactly the right words to say, whispering in my ear, offering advice.

I take a deep breath, dig out a deep-V-neck sweater and pull it on. Slightly snug, a touch of cleavage. Just enough to annoy Mum. That'll do. I run a brush through my hair and touch up my lip gloss. Need one more thing. Earrings. I rifle through the meenakari jewel box Nanima gave me until I find the perfect pair. Pale pink, mirror-worked jhumke, dangling like little chandeliers from my ears.

I think I look pretty. Kissable. But my stomach churns, empty and angry. *You can do this. You can do this. You can do this.*

I take one last look.

I hear Dr. Divya's voice in my head: *You can be whatever you want. You can do whatever you want. Your size doesn't change that.*

"You do look pretty," I say to myself for the first time. "You deserve nice things."

Riley texts again. He's parked down the block.

I turn off app alerts on my phone. I grab shoes, take a deep breath, and sneak down the back staircase. Mum and Dad are at a charity function and Nita Masi is in Nani's suite, serving her dinner. No one will look for me. I slip out the side door and walk to Riley's car.

The window slides down. "Hey," he calls out.

I wish he would get out and open the door. But he doesn't. So I open it and slide in.

"Hey," I reply.

"You look gorgeous," he says, and I can't stop smiling.

"Thanks."

He drives down the block. The silence between us is thick and heavy with anticipation. Is this how it feels to be on a date? Am I supposed to be this nervous? Even though he's had the locker next to mine since ninth grade? But I don't really, *really* know much about him. Both of his dads work in the government, like mine, and he has three younger sisters. It's weird how you can be in the same class with someone for years and still be a stranger, kind of. But I guess people are saying the same thing about me now.

"Which theater are we going to?" I ask, wondering why he's not headed toward Georgetown or into Maryland.

"It's a surprise."

I squirm. Do I like surprises? I don't think I've ever had one outside of my dad bringing me carved elephants and bangles and sweets from his trips back to India. Mum definitely doesn't like surprises.

He turns down a nearby block and parks in front of a beautiful house.

"Where are we?"

"My house."

My heart hammers. He's already parking. Should I say something? "I thought we were going to the movies."

"We are. You'll see."

My brain fills with a thousand nightmare scenarios. What if his parents aren't home? What if he wants me to go in his room? What if—

"Maybe this was a bad—" But he's opened the door, offered a hand.

He leads me around to the back side gate, his palm resting on the small of my back. I try not to flinch, not to give away the panic that's swirling inside me. He doesn't seem like that kid. Not like Jase cornering me in the photo both. Or Vivek . . .

I hear Dr. Divya's voice in my head again: *Nobody can make you feel anything you don't want to feel.* That has to be true, right?

Just breathe, Georgie. People go on dates every day. You'll be okay.

Thousands of twinkling lights are strung up along the fence. Four chimineas cluster around two cozy seats, the clay ovens crackling with small fires. A huge screen stretches high above the chairs. My heart lifts at the sight of it.

"I thought this would be cool." I feel his eyes on me, waiting for my reaction. "You like it?"

"It's— You did this all for me?" I wander around the yard, the warmth of the ovens pulling me in. "Amazing."

He grins at me, handing me a steaming cup. "Hot cocoa."

I smile back at him. "This is so awesome. Thanks," I stammer out. "I can't— I just—" All the words zip out of me.

I try not to think about how many calories are in the hot chocolate or the whipped cream or the marshmallows. I will skip breakfast. Lunch, if I have to. I take small sips and let the liquid roll around on my tongue, savoring the sweetness of the chocolate and the moment.

"We could stream just about anything. Or I've got a lot of different movie picks. I stole these from my sister's room." He shows me two DVDs: *Pretty in Pink* and *Sixteen Candles*.

I pick *Sixteen Candles*. I love these old movies. Even though they're racist and sexist. I used to watch them back in India, imagining this was what life in America was like. We sit beside each other in the chairs. They're close enough that I can smell his cologne and see the tiny blush lurking beneath the pale brown of his skin. He pulls the cover off the table in front of us, and there's a variety of theater snacks—caramel corn and candy and diet soda and licorice. He's thought of everything. It makes my stomach flutter, to think about how much care he put into tonight. For *me*.

"If you need to use the bathroom, you can go through the back door to the basement. Just take your shoes off first."

I nod.

The movie starts.

He reaches for my hand, and that's when I realize I'm shaking.

"You okay?" His voice is soft.

Enjoy it. Don't ruin it. "It's nothing. It's just . . . everything is so different now."

I focus on the flames eating through the wood in the chiminea, avoiding his gaze. The fire turns his skin the blood orange of my favorite cake, a Nita Masi specialty.

"I can imagine," he says. "Not sure if you know, but Cora's officially trying to hook us up." He's grinning.

"Really?" I'm shocked. She's said nothing to me about it.

"It's her thing. To hook up all the girls on her squad."

"Oh" is all I can manage. Deflated. I thought this might be real.

"She didn't tell you?"

"No." I fiddle with my sweater, not sure what to think or what to do.

"Figures," he says. "She probably needs to focus on fixing her thing with Baez."

Would I be here if Cora didn't suggest it? Does he actually like me at all? What does he think about the rumors? Have he and Baez talked about them? I wonder how close they are. I wonder if he knows how Baez feels about the rumor. He's practically ignored it online. I wonder if Riley talked to Baez about Cora hooking us up.

Riley takes out a thermos and fills my cup with more hot chocolate. I sip slowly, happy for the distraction as the conversation lulls. Cora's name sort of ruined everything. It hangs there, in the air, like storm clouds looming.

"Their shit is a complete mess." He continues to talk about Baez and Cora.

"Are you and him close?" I ask.

"Yeah. All of us on the lacrosse team are," he says, reaching for my hair. I pull back. Too fast.

He clinks my earring, the mirrors throwing shadows. "These are pretty." He smiles, touching it again, grazing the skin above it.

"Thanks," I say, feeling like an idiot. Wishing I was carefree and casually elegant. Like Cora.

I try to pay attention, but I can feel Riley stealing glances at me. "What?"

"You're really beautiful."

I used to long for those words. And now they worry me. "Thanks, I guess."

"You guess?" He grins at me.

Beautiful.

I try to let the word sink in. I'm the *new Georgie.* That girl would own it. Papa used to call me beautiful when I was a little girl, and Mum used to make me stand in front of a mirror and wave to "the beautiful little girl." But I never felt it.

Riley tucks a strand of my hair behind my ear, like we're in some teen movie. I don't move this time. And before I can take another breath, he's taken my hot-chocolate cup and set it down, leaned in, and kissed me. His lips are warm and full, and he tastes like marshmallows. He parts my lips with his tongue and gently pushes it inside.

I flinch.

He pulls back. "You okay?"

My mind spins. I like him. I think he likes me. But this is normal. I should relax, just sink into the moment, let it happen. Stop overthinking everything. Stop ruining everything.

He's leaning back now, his face worried, like he did something wrong. Like it might be too late.

So I sit forward, taking his hands in mine, looking up at him through my lashes, the way they always do in the movies.

"It's okay," he whispers, his words hitting my mouth. I feel his hands on my waist, pulling me forward, out of my chair and into his.

It's going to be my first *real* kiss. I need a handbook. The only other kiss I've ever had was from Jase, which was awkward. And my cousin Vivek. Which was *not* what I asked for. It was the thing that made my family move across an ocean to avoid the scandal that happened. The worst thing to ever happen to me.

Not this time. This time I get to tell the story. *I'm okay.*

I push away the bubbling memories. I breathe slowly, stealing glances at the two freckles on Riley's brown eyelids, the tiny V-shaped crease in his forehead. I feel the panic starting, so I reach up, letting my hands graze the sides of his face, tracing the slight stubble along his jaw. I let his tongue slip deeper into my mouth. I let his hands wander up my sweater, roaming soft and gentle along my stomach.

I let my heart race and my mind wander, until all that I can see are stars.

Cora:

Hey. I'm coming up.

Millie:

Oh! That'll be fun.

When?

Cora:

Like, now? I'm already on the train. Gets in at 5:30.

Millie:

Wait, like in a few hours?
What about school? You okay?

You didn't write me back about Baez.

Cora:

I know. I'll tell you when I get there.

Millie:

Okay! Cool!

I can't wait to see you. I miss you so much.

Cora:

263

CORA

SUNDAY, NOVEMBER 10
1:10 P.M.

THE EXPRESS TRAIN TO BOSTON WILL GET ME INTO SOUTH Station right before dinner. Everyone's talking about the video of my fight with Baez, and my social media is on fire, and I can't deal. The spiral of rumors just keeps getting worse and worse, and it feels like nothing will stop it now, like the leaves falling off the trees as we barrel past. It all has to come down, bare now, before I can start fresh. Maybe that's what I really need. To go somewhere far, far away, to start over, where nobody knows me or expects a specific version of me.

Maybe that's what Millie wanted, too.

She's already waiting for me when the train pulls in, the worries that mark my face etched on hers like a mirror. "What's going on?" she says, that edge in her voice making her sound more like Momma than ever. But not scolding. Just careful, concerned. Like I'm the baby and she's the big sister, even though we're just minutes apart.

"Everything is awful."

She links her arm in mine, and we take a cab to the campus dorms. They're tucked away in Cambridge, all red brick and churches, the trees already quivering in the fall air. Very pretty, but cold, lonesome almost, and it occurs to me that *this* is why Millie misses us and home, the sunshine in November, the comforts Momma gives her. Here, clouds block the sun and the leaves are already gone, making me shiver.

She walks ahead and I follow, a few steps behind, like always. It hits me then that I may not be able to chase her—here, to Harvard, but anywhere, through life—forever. There are spaces she's at home in that I'm not, and the same goes for me. Home, DC, and Foxham in particular, was one of those places. She just never fit in. Didn't look the part. A lot like Georgie, I realize. Except that everyone forced her into that tight little box they made for her. Even me. Right from the start.

Millie's dorm room window overlooks the Charles River, just a small strip of it, then the city of Boston beyond it. Her little corner looks like home, with a bulletin board covered in the same gold-and-white-striped paper that covers Millie's bedroom, and a small, airy canopy above her bed. It looks like a child's room, even though Millie feels like a grown-up to me here. So beyond my reach, the small gap between us a gaping hole now, one we might never fill or cross.

Millie starts taking out snacks and raiding her mini-fridge, asking me what I want to eat and drink.

"Stop fussing over me." I grab her arm, determined to have a sliver of my old life back. We do what we always do: curl up in bed and start bingeing a TV show. She's always big spoon and I'm little spoon, like it's been from the day we were born, and even before that. Momma used to tell us that that was how we were positioned in her stomach. She thinks it's a cute story to tell, and I never let her know how much I sort of love it. We fit like puzzle pieces, Millie and me. But sometimes we're in different puzzles altogether.

I turn over and stare at her. Some of her freckles, *our* freckles, have faded. The acne scars that used to leave dark spots on her deep brown skin are getting better with the products I've sent her.

"What?" she says, unable to take my staring. "You're as bad as Momma."

"Ouch." I shove her shoulder. "I don't want to be like her."

"You are . . . sometimes." Her big eyes stretch wide.

"No, I'm not."

"You're good with people, throw the best parties, you know just what to say." She smiles back at me. "And you scrunch your nose just like her when you're mad."

"I do not."

She laughs and shakes her head. "You have her effortless grace, unlike me. I never know the right thing to say or how to make people like me."

"People *better* like you or they'll have hell to pay." I take her hand.

Her eyes water. "I don't have you here to rescue me. To make sure I always have friends or at least people who are nice to me."

"And I don't have you at home to remind me that everything is fine." My phone glows with a text from Vero. It's a picture of her holding a bouquet of roses, and the words: Cora, baby. You have a delivery.

Another picture comes. The message on the card.

C,

I miss you. I don't know what is going on. Text me back.

Love, Baez

"What is it?" Millie asks.

I show her the photo.

She kisses my cheek, her leg heavy on mine, her arm the soft spot I've been craving. "You ready to talk about it?"

The tears I've been holding in all day, all year, pour out. I tell her about the rumors and the parties and the fight I had with Baez.

"You done?" she asks. Straight to the point. Just like Daddy.

"I guess so?"

Millie pulls me up and wipes the tears from my face. "I've been watching this online. Sometimes people would tag me accidentally. We've got to think it through. Something isn't right. You know as well as I do that high school rumors don't stick around this long if no one is *doing* anything to fuel them."

"Which is why it feels like something's up, why Baez and I got in that fight."

"How long have you known Baez?"

"Since we were twelve."

"Has he ever messed up? Like ever? Can he even?" Her eyes narrow. "And nothing like this."

I don't say that answer out loud. "He was an asshole when I last asked him about it."

"I saw the video," she admits. "But I can't say I wouldn't have been, too."

"What?"

"Cora, when you get mad, when you fixate, you won't let anyone get a word in. You have your target and you go for it. Nothing that he said mattered that day. You had your mind made up. You were fishing. Looking for confirmation."

My stomach squeezes. Is that what happens when you have to swallow down the truth?

"Baez is like a brother, like family. He's always been around. He and Graham have gotten even tighter this year." She yanks me from her bed. "He can be dumb, but not this dumb."

"So? He must've done something if people are still talking."

"Do you know *anyone* who has ever seen him do anything? Like, one of your *friend* friends. Adele? Christine? Ruthie? Keisha?"

"Adele saw him touch her hair."

"Okay, that's one thing, but it's hardly evidence. Anything else?"

I think for a second, and it's like a sun rising above my anxiety and worry. "No. No one. Everyone in our group has been defending him. Graham even said Baez never left his sight the night that you came home and I missed Jase's party."

"The night Baez was supposed to have hooked up with her upstairs." She slips out of bed and paces the perimeter of the tiny room, holding her phone in her hand. "What if it isn't true, Turtle?" she asks, reading my mind the way she does sometimes. The way I can never read hers. "Did you think about that?"

My brain is a tangle of worst-case scenarios and stressors. She scrolls, the noise of her taking screenshots echoing like rapid fire.

"When did this whole thing start?

"Who was at that party?"

Her questions come one after the other, her brain too fast for me to keep up with. "I don't know." That's all I've got. "I just don't know."

It's dawning on me: Someone hates me. Enough to feed this monster. Someone cruel and vicious, who *wants* me and Baez to break up.

Who did I piss off? I've said shit, stirred stuff up, started rumors before. Definitely repeated them. But this is something else. Because a little touch on the shoulder doesn't spiral into all of this by itself. Nope. Someone's mad. I just need to figure out who.

I start to make a list of people I dislike or who might dislike me in my head.

But I can't think of a single person who would mess with me in this way.

Why would they do this to me . . . and Baez? How could it cause everything to fall apart, years and years of us in our little bubble, disintegrating just like that, in an instant?

She sits at her computer, pulling up all the screenshots. "Okay, come here."

I lean over her shoulder.

She starts sorting them into folders, marking them in some pattern, some language I just can't read. "Hmmm," she says, to herself, rubbing her chin the way she does when working on logic problems. "Maybe . . ." She shakes her head. "Wait!" She pulls a few more up, then stares at the screen for what feels like hours.

"Dee Dee is not a reliable source," she says, and the words feel familiar, like I've heard them before. Or know someone who'd say them, think them. She rubs her chin again, frowning at the screen.

She rattles off social media comments:

"SkyeWard: Leilani said that when she went upstairs after Georgie left, she totally saw Kleenex in the bathroom wastebasket with lipstick all over it, and it wasn't Cora's.

"SkyeWard: Wait . . . at like 10? I totally saw two people all over each other in the garden. Like dry-humping near the hydrangeas."

"Who's this person?" She points.

I blink at it, trying to unravel it, to remember. I shrug. "I don't know." SkyeWard. The name sounds familiar . . . but why? I've definitely seen it pop up on my feeds. "SkyeWard . . . I don't think I know them."

"They're here consistently. Like clockwork. Invested. An engine. Stirring the pot. Moving things forward." Then she takes a deep breath—a eureka moment. I've seen them so many times before, it all coming together in her head. "Making shit up." She nods. "People challenged them, though, and Adele asked them who they are. But they're saying wild stuff."

"SkyeWard . . . SkyeWard . . . hmmm."

"Cora, their name isn't *Skye*Ward. It's *Syke*."

"Oh," I say, thumbing through more pages and more comments from this person. They have no pictures up on their profile.

"That's the one. Maybe not the root—though I'm not dismissing that completely. But definitely a propeller. Pushing, shifting, changing. It's right there, the pattern. Your culprit. Syke is always taking annoying-ass gossip and pushing it further. It's weird. This person says they used to go to Foxham. Who didn't come back this year?"

My mind tries to think through the kids who transferred out. But I can't think. I'm stuck on the name.

SykeWard. But who is it? That's a weird name. And why would they do this? Do they hate me that much?

"It's not just you." She's reading my mind again. "Look at the players. She's—and I do think it's a she, based on her tone—moving you like chess pieces. You. Baez. Georgie. Strategically leading the commenters to new versions of the rumors. Or adding more theories. Like flooding the comments with misinformation." She scrolls through more photos and reads more comments aloud:

"SykeWard: She did way more than just sing.

"SykeWard: I heard they started hooking up this summer, way before anyone saw anything at that party. New couple alert!"

It all snaps together. Like math. Or magic. A little of both. "That's it. You solved it. This has to be it."

She shakes her head, unwilling, as always, to take credit, even when it's deserved. "The pieces are all there. You handed them right over. We just always need both our brains to figure out the puzzle." She takes a deep breath again, bracing herself. "You should talk to Georgie." She frowns when I do. "I know it will be hard. And I know you don't want to. But, C, you've got to. Whatever this person did to you, what they did to her was far worse. No one should deal with this alone."

I smile. It's something she used to say to me a lot when we were little, when she'd meet Momma's great expectations and I'd fall short in comparison, because how could anyone compare, compete, with the genius of Millie? It's hitting me now that only one of us thought it was a competition.

She pushes my hair off my face. "I've missed you. I've missed this. I forgot how much I needed it."

"Me too," I say, and mean it. Being alone in the house with Momma and Daddy has been tough. Her presence keeps their edges soft. Her presence probably would have prevented me from getting into this online mess in the first place. She would've told me from the start that it was all a big show. That I was missing something.

Millie stands, abrupt, familiar. "Now, you hungry? It's pasta night."

Cora:

Hey G!

Georgie:

Uh, hey!

Cora:

Can we talk?

Georgie:

👀 Sure, what's up?

Cora:

In person.

Georgie:

Of course.

VOTING BALLOT: **SPECIAL ELECTION**

INSTRUCTIONS: To vote for a ticket, fill in the bubble beside the name of the ticket you prefer.

PRESIDENT AND VICE PRESIDENT:

○   CHANCE OLIVIERI
ELANA CHEN

○   BRYN COLBURN
CORA DAVIDSON

Please return your ballot to Mrs. Gratton's office by the end of the school day on Friday, November 8. Results to be announced on Wednesday, November 13.

BAEZ AND GEORGIE WERE COZYING UP SOLO AT CORA'S PARTY.

BAEZ AND GEORGIE DEFINITELY MADE OUT UPSTAIRS IN CORA'S BEDROOM.

COMPLETE AND TOTAL YOU-KNOW-WHAT AT JASE'S PARTY.

GEORGIE AND BAEZ HAVE BEEN FOOLING AROUND FOR MONTHS BEHIND CORA'S BACK.

CORA PUT GEORGIE ON THE CHEERLEADING TEAM TO KEEP AN EYE ON HER.

GEORGIE AND JASE HOOKED UP IN THE PHOTO BOOTH AT SCHOOL.

BAEZ AND GEORGIE HAD SEX AT HIS BIRTHDAY PARTY.

CORA AND BAEZ HAD A MASSIVE FIGHT. IT'S OVER.

GEORGIE IS HOOKING UP WITH RILEY NOW TO MAKE BAEZ JEALOUS.

PART THREE

THE
GAME

game [gām] *noun*

1) a form of play
2) an activity
3) a manipulative scheme
4) a secret or clever plan
5) tricks

BRYN

MONDAY, NOVEMBER 11
6:46 P.M.

I LOOK AT MY FUTURE AS I GAZE INTO THE ENTRYWAY OF the Sky Ward Ranch Rehab Center. They say most people end up like their parents. So I guess I'm destined to be overly enthusiastic about all sorts of red wines—a good merlot in particular—and take detox "vacations," as my mom likes to call them. Or burn all the incense and get all the crystals, thinking it'll get rid of an addiction.

I walk slowly down the brightly lit halls, clutching my notebook to my chest as if it can protect me from this place. I don't *actually* want to see my mother, even though she's number three on my list. Even though it's the perfect distraction as I wait for the election results in just a few days.

I check in at the desk.

"Third door on the left." A woman points.

I take a deep breath. It's been hard to think about how to talk to her, how to revisit that night, how to figure out if my family is going to be put back together again.

My dad's driver sits in the parking lot, waiting to take me back home. I think about turning right back around. I could do this another time. But Dad's disappointed face fills my mind. Even when I'm mad at him, even when we're still barely on speaking terms, even when he caused all of this and flip-flopped our whole family, I still don't want to see that disapproving look in his eyes.

The scent of gourmet food drifts toward me from the dining room. Fresh flowers sit in beautiful vases outside every fancy room. A masseuse is dragging her equipment down the hall. Ridiculous amenities that Dad has been complaining about when he doesn't think I can hear.

"My beautiful girl. What a nice surprise," Mom says when I finally get to her room.

The sight of her reminds me that I do miss her. If I let myself actually feel.

She's wearing sweats and sitting up in bed. I'm still not used to her short blond hair. It used to be long, and she'd wear it in elegant updos for parties. But when I video-chatted with her last week, it was suddenly cut into a shapeless bob. She said she felt freer, like she could be her true self. Right now, her bed head is making it stick out in all directions.

She's an echo of herself. A light dimmed. Even her usually tanned skin is pale and translucent white now.

There's a mug of coffee on her nightstand and a tray holding a covered plate at the foot of her bed. Room service.

I bet the therapy sessions aren't so bad either. Better than our family one.

Mom motions for me to come join her in the king-sized bed, like I've done a million times since I was a little girl and she sent herself away to places like this. Being a chef isn't exactly good for people with addictions, but I think she likes her spa rehabs, too.

I plop down next to her, still holding my notebook. She brushes my hair out of my face, but her hands fidget and tremble, like there are tiny earthquakes going off inside her.

"Don't you have school stuff?" she asks. "Or is there a holiday or something?"

"It's almost seven p.m. And it's Veterans Day."

"Oh. Stupid me." She smacks her own forehead. "I lose track of the time in here. It's the energy. It's all weird. A fog, you get what I mean?" Her eyes get all intense. "How are things?"

"Fine, I guess," I say.

"Your father is a piece of shit." She reaches past me to her nightstand and picks up a pack of fancy cigarettes and lighter. "He hasn't visited once."

I don't remind her that he can't. That the press would make this whole thing into more of a clown show than it already is. "I don't want to talk about him," I say, even though he's definitely part of the problem.

Mom takes a long drag of her pitch-black cigarette. She blows the smoke away from me. The scent heady and sweet, reminding me of Christmas.

"Are you supposed to be smoking in here?"

"No," she says, and takes another long puff. "Your father's probably up all night making a mess and eating terrible food and so into his work that he's not looking after you."

Sometimes I look at them both and can't understand how they ever found each other.

"Mom, please." But I really want to say: *If you weren't in here, you could look after me, too.*

"What else is going on?" she asks. "I can tell something's up. I'm sensitive to energy, and you came in here like a little tornado. Out with it."

"I've been really, *really* lonely," I admit. "It's hard to be alone all the time when you're used to having people around."

"What's going on with your friends? With Cora?"

"Remember . . . I told you they wouldn't talk to me. Because of what happened?"

She takes another long drag of her cigarette. "Did they understand what happened?"

"A little."

"You should fight to get them back. The only people who have come to see me in this place are my female friends. The men always let you down."

She makes it sound simple, as if you can flip a light switch and have the things you want back.

"I've sort of got Cora back." A warmth settles over me. As soon as I win that election, the rest will fall into place. My whole little group. Christine, Ruthie, and Adele will lay off me, and the guys will stop acting like I'm the worst thing ever. Then I can get rid of Jase. Everyone will know the truth about him soon enough.

"That's good. That's good." She takes another drag. I hate the smell, but I don't move away from her.

"I've been hanging out with Georgie more."

"Mrs. Khalra's daughter? The one from next door?"

"Yes."

"She was away all summer, right?" Mom blows smoke rings.

"Weight loss camp." I finally relax into our old patterns, setting my notebook between us, and showing her pictures of Georgie's social media on my phone.

"Those places can be toxic and society should do away with them," she says. "She looks really good. Though I thought she looked fine beforehand. She's going to have an uphill battle mentally, though. It's really hard to lose that kind of weight and not have it affect your sense of self. Truly changes your spiritual energy." She continues to diagnose Georgie: low self-esteem, body dysmorphia, disordered eating. Like she's some TV psychologist and not a chef. "So, is that it? I know there's more. I have an alert set up with your name." Her eyebrow lifts. "There's a lot going on, my Duckie. Terrible energy right now. I can sense it in you, too."

"It's nothing." I lean back into the feathery down pillows.

"I thought you promised never to lie to me?" She turns my chin and forces me to look at her. "That was always your father's role."

Her words twist in my stomach, mixing with guilt and anxiety. I work up the nerve to tell her.

"It's that I've been, like, alone, you know? With you here and no one talking to me . . . I tried to fix it. I tried to get my life back."

"Okay," she says, putting out the cigarette. "What is it?"

"There's these rumors." I ease into telling her, explaining about stuff going on online and my anti-bullying campaign.

"People always talk. They're bored and make shit up. They think it will make this universe more exciting."

I squirm. "High school."

"Even after it." She points to a stack of newspapers on her desk. "Are people still talking about you and what happened?"

"Not since the rumors about Cora's boyfriend started."

"People are so fickle. On to the next controversy after they've chewed you up and discarded you. Always hunting for something to point at and make fun of. Something to make them feel better about themselves."

The truth of her words settle into me. They make my stomach turn. I start sweating. All the rumors about Georgie and Baez are a tornado in my head. The twists and turns of it. The darkness. I feel sick.

"Hmm," she says, scooping up my notebook. "You only start using notebooks when you're anxious or in too deep. What's going on, Bryn?"

I reach for it, but she's too quick. "Don't—"

The pages flutter open. All my scrapbooking of the rumors laid out. Pictures and social media screenshots and lists of rumors and possible rumors.

"What is this?" she asks.

"Nothing." I try to grab it. "Give it back, okay?"

"Doesn't look like *nothing* to me."

"Why are you being nosy?" I snap.

"Why are you hiding things again?" Her eyebrow lifts, her eyes intense.

I feel myself flush so red. "Oh, like you did with Dad's affair?"

The hurt blankets her face. "That's not fair. I didn't know. There were a few hints, but I brushed them away." Her eyes glare into mine. "His energy was off, but he did a hell of a job hiding it and covering his tracks."

We sit in silence for a while. I don't even know how to have a conversation with her anymore.

"This isn't about *me* or your dad. We will recover. *I* will recover. It's about you. All of this is affecting you in dangerous ways. I should've seen it before. The accident. The fact that you've been so distant." Tears fill her eyes, and then mine. "Why are you filling that notebook with all of that?"

She flips it open and scans through page after page of scribbled details, notes fished from trash cans, sad and blurry social photos, screenshots of comments. To me, the rumors feel alive, writhing along the paper, ready to explode with possibility. My pulse races. I feel like it's the accident night all over again. I'm out of control.

She jostles my shoulder, her cold fingers shocking me. "What is this obsession? You only act like this when you want something."

I feel a tingle in my fingers, and that small, dangerous itch crops up inside me. The one that causes me to make bad decisions. The one that has made me do all of this. I have to calm down. I have to breathe.

I start to lie. "I don't know, I just—"

"Wait, Bryn. Look at me." She stares deep into my eyes, touching her fingers to my cheek, then glances at the set of my shoulders, my mouth. "You did something," she says, realizing. "Did you do this?"

My heart hammers in my chest. The words tumble out of me: "I didn't mean to. I mean—I didn't mean for it to get so big. I just thought if people stopped talking about me and talked about something else— someone else—that I'd be okay again." The words feel like rocks in my mouth. Excuses. But I can't stop them from sputtering out.

She leaves the bed and goes to the window. "You thought you could control it."

I trace my fingers over the front of the notebook. "I thought if Cora and Baez broke up, she'd need me. I'd have my vice president back, my best friend back, and maybe it would erase what happened. Things could go back to normal. I could fix everything. The campaign was *real*. I *was* bullied. It was relentless. I just thought if everyone saw how bad it was, they'd forgive me." I almost vomit.

She walks back over to me.

I bite back tears.

"My darling, you've been through so much. I know all about being pushed to the edge." She traces her fingers up my shoulder to my chin. I lift it up so she can look me in the eye. "We don't let people make us act out of character. I didn't raise you to make a mess. To be a mess. You can't let people see you down—or force you into corners you have to manipulate or twist your way out of. That's not our way."

Mom's always been good at that part. After all that happened, she stood next to me at those press conferences, her back straight, head held high, looking polished and like nothing would ever get to her. Even if she was falling apart inside. She'd crumble later. Come here and hide.

I wish Mom was home now, instead of here. I need her. I don't want to go back to an empty house, one that doesn't even feel like home, with only Dad. He's out most of the time anyway, and I'm holed up in my pool house, alone. Since late August, my life has felt like a cyclone, everything I love blown away. I've been desperate to put it all back together again.

"When are you going to come home?" I ask.

She shrugs. "I don't know. I'm not even sure I want to."

Her words sting, and my eyes well up with tears. How can she not want to come home—to me?

"You have to fix it." Mom's eyes fill with seriousness.

I get up from the bed. The mattress is too soft. I would sleep terribly here. "I've got to head back."

"Did you hear me?" she presses.

"Yeah," I reply.

Mom gives me a quick hug. "Yeah, what?"

"I'll fix it. I'll make the rumors go away." I dart out of her room and back down the hallway. I don't want to end up like her, in a place like this, still hypocritically lecturing about integrity and strength. I've already done whatever it took to get my life back, to reset my world after it fell apart. I won't ever let that happen again.

From: Jashan "Georgie" Khalra
Attn: Dr. Divya Malhotra
Sent: Monday, November 11, 11:32 PM
Subject: Food Diary

Hi Dr. Divya,

    I took your advice. I also met someone nice. Can we talk about that next time? I don't want to blow it, and I've been messing up a lot.

Thanks,
Georgie

GEORGIE

TUESDAY, NOVEMBER 12
12:46 P.M.

I PUSH THROUGH THE GLASS DOORS OF THE CAFETERIA, heading into the senior courtyard to wait for Riley to have lunch. The sun is warm, but the air is crisp and cold. There are six magnolia trees out here, with big arms, perfect for crawling up into. They're the closest to the Indian banyan tree, the one thing I miss most from back home. In eighth grade, we walked over from the middle school campus building to take a tour of the upper school. From the first time I saw the trees, I wanted to climb up into them and hide. Their arms always seemed like they could support my weight. No matter what.

Despite the tightness of my jeans and the sign that says *Do Not Climb in the Trees*, I scale the trunk and sprawl across one, letting my legs dangle as I read *The Crucible* (yet again) for English class. I'm still getting used to this whole hanging-out-with-a-boy thing. All the questions. All the anxiety. Is he my boyfriend yet? We've only been hanging out for a few days. But we've done a lot of kissing. What does that mean? Does he have to ask me to be his girlfriend, like in the movies? Why is there no manual?

The wind tangles inside the thick leaves and helps me fall into the pages.

Then I hear my name.

"Georgie."

I look down, expecting Riley.

But it's Baez. I sit up too fast and my head thwacks against one of the branches.

I rub my forehead and cringe, feeling stupid.

"You okay?" he asks.

"Yeah," I say, a little too loud, like he's just called my name off some roll sheet at the beginning of class. At first, I don't know what to do. Get down? Talk to him from here? So if someone sees us, no one will think anything is happening. Or has happened.

I hesitate. We stare at each other for the longest minute ever. *Guinness World Records*-style. He looks so different now. He even feels different. Sadness seeps out of him. His eyes are all bloodshot.

"Can you get down? Can we talk for a second?" he says. "Do you think that would be okay?" There's worry in his voice, but it feels like it's more for me than for him.

I scoot out of the tree, avoiding any more potentially embarrassing hazards. I feel stupid that he had to ask me to get down. This close, I notice he has golden sunflowers in his eyes. One of Bryn's fashion magazines says the bursts of color around one's pupil are signs of luck. They make him look even more handsome. "What's up?" I say, trying to sound cool and relaxed and not like this guy who's watched his life unravel right beside mine is standing a couple inches away from me. How do we connect now?

I feel eyes on us through the courtyard's windows, watching every move.

"I'm guessing you heard." His voice is super formal, like he's talking to a stranger instead of someone who has been in school with him for six years.

"No. What?" I say, sort of knowing it's something bad.

"That Cora and I broke up. That everyone thinks you and I hooked up at my birthday party."

"Yeah, that. I don't know what that's about," I say. "Stupid, right?"

I should say more because it's *more* than stupid. It's become a whole thing. Like a Cora-breaking-up-with-him kind of thing.

The tension of it all swirls in my stomach. "I was a mess that night," I say. "Too much punch."

"I passed out early. I woke up in Christine's pool-house guest room. Wasted. And I get these migraines from the accident." He looks terrified. "I'm in love with Cora. I'd never do that to her. Drunk or not."

"I know," I say, feeling a little dizzy.

The memories of the night hit me in waves. The sound of his laughter. The smell of the punch. My Marilyn Monroe costume. The stupid birthday song. He shows me his phone and a new account—one that's not Chance Olivieri—tracking all the rumors. A picture of me and Baez, one I don't remember being taken. The caption: *Baez and Georgie had sex at his birthday party.*

Wait, how do I not know about this?

"Do you have any idea who started this?" He scratches his head.

The words and images just keep twisting the truth, pushing everything further and further away from reality. I catch a glimpse of myself in the glass behind Baez's head. The new Georgie. Perfectly styled. Makeup impeccable. The dictionary definition of a *glow-up*. But in this moment, I wish I could just be the old Georgie. With her stomach. That unibrow. All two of her friends. Old Georgie would've never ever gotten into a mess like this.

"Georgie."

"Georgie."

Baez's voice bursts through the chaos of my thoughts.

"I'm freaking out here. Cora's freaking out. She broke up with me."

"This is crazy."

Baez kicks at one of the loose rocks and jams his hands in his pockets. "I thought it would, like, go away."

Why can't I say anything else? Why can't I think? Words zip around in my head like unsettled bees, but none come out.

"But everyone's still talking about this. They're swarming Cora and calling me a player. Giving me all this attention. Dumb shit like that. It's fucked-up. Could you tell her nothing happened between us?"

"Sure. Of course. Nothing happened. I mean, I've *told* her that before." That's pretty much the only thing I can do. Tell the truth.

He kicks at the rocks again, and I find a spot on the tree's trunk to pick at. My stomach feels like it'll collapse in on itself.

"Yeah, okay. Thanks." He heads back inside the school without another look at me. A few students point and whisper at him as he closes the senior-courtyard door.

I will tell the truth. No matter what.

Monica pulls out a yoga mat and starts to stretch beside me. We're always the last ones after cheerleading practice. I'm not sure if she stays behind, like I do, mostly to avoid the locker room with all the girls, or if she actually likes to stretch for an hour after practice. I still don't know how to undress in front of all those eyes, all the questions and judgment lingering beneath each glance. Muscle memory sends me to the bathroom stalls or into the showers to fully wash and dress without being seen.

"How does it feel?" she asks.

"What?"

"To not be an alternate. To actually be on the team." She's flattened herself like a pancake, legs splayed in both directions, her deep brown skin glistening with sweat. I wasn't able to do that until camp. I learned so much about what my body could and couldn't do there. With gymnastics and Pilates and ballet, I found out it could do a lot. More than I ever thought. More than I allowed myself to do before.

"Cora hasn't exactly let me cheer at any of the games yet. So I'm still sort of sitting on the bench, too." I lift my arm over my head and stretch it. "And I'm not sure I want to."

"What do you mean?" Her eyebrow lifts and her eyes narrow.

"I'm scared. Of doing the routines in front of the whole school."

Her mouth purses into a frown. "Then what the heck are you doing here?"

A hot flash works its way up my neck. I've offended her. I try to speak, but the words are all garbled.

"So you joined the squad to sit on the sidelines?"

"No." But my voice shakes when I say it.

"Then what?" She sits up. "You earned that spot on the squad. You can jump your ass off. What else you waiting for?"

"I—"

"You losing that weight doesn't change who you are."

The words ring in my ears, echoing what Dr. Divya said. I thought I believed them. Yet here I am.

"But it did." I'm trying to be someone else, someone more interesting than who I was before.

"You didn't grow wings and learn to fly or something. It's just weight." She shrugs. "The sooner you figure that out the better."

Her words become the weight now. They make me feel silly and stupid for being so scared. But I don't know how else to be. "How do you not care?"

"I'm going to ask you like my momma asks me—did worrying about it make you lose any weight?"

I shake my head. "No."

"Will the worries help you jump better?"

"No."

"Or nail the choreography?"

"Oh." I gaze down at my shoes. "I get it now."

"Then prove it. 'Cause I'd switch places with you in a heartbeat. I'm ready to cheer and dance. But I won't get to. You will. Stop acting like you need to apologize for being fat once."

"Don't say *fat*."

"Why? Because some white girl told you not to? What's wrong with it? That's what I am. That's what you were. There's nothing wrong with it."

Shame swirls in my stomach. "I didn't mean—"

"Stop being so scared all the time. You're going to miss it all worrying about what everyone thinks about. When they're just worried about their own shit." She gets to her feet and rushes off to the locker room. "Live your life."

I'm left with her challenge. My mind races through all the things I could do. Should do. There's too much to process. I plop down flat on my yoga mat muttering to myself.

"You ready to talk?" a voice says from above.

I look up and find Cora.

"I can give you a ride home."

"Okay. That would be great." My heart drums in my ears; my brain spirals through all the things she might bring up. Baez. Bryn. Cheerleading. Most likely, the rumors. This is my chance to do what Baez asked me to. To fix the damage.

On our way to the senior-class parking lot, Cora says goodbye to a thousand people. And they wave and chat and make small talk with me, too, her starshine spilling over.

I slide into her sleek white car like I'm easing into a scalding bath, slow and deliberate. I'm still not used to being close to her. A tiny tremor of fear flickers through me.

"How's it going?" I ask in an almost whisper, not sure how to start the conversation we have to have. "I—I wanted to talk to you, too."

Cora doesn't turn on the car. Instead, she turns to face me and holds out her phone. "Do you know who this is? Like, any idea?"

She's zoomed in on a weird name in the comments of her last picture. SykeWard.

"No, I don't know who that is."

"She's been starting and hyping up so many of these rumors—my sister thinks this person is a girl. But I'm not sure."

"She's all over my feed, too." I open my phone and show her more comments from SykeWard under my pictures. There are a lot. Some random and harmless. Others outright mean.

Cora takes a deep breath and pulls out a piece of paper. "My sister made a document of all the things SykeWard has said over the past few weeks. Look at the pattern."

My eyes scan all the rumors laid bare in a curlicue font. "Why would she do this?" The rage inside me flares.

"I don't know."

"How could something so little grow so big?" I search her eyes, hoping to find a flicker of kindness, maybe the path to a truce. But I'm going to have to be the one to initiate it. "Nothing happened. I swear. Between me and Baez. Not on Halloween. Not ever."

"I believe you, actually. That's why we have to stop it. We have to find out who this is." She swallows. "This shit is messing me up. So who hates you?"

"Huh?"

She takes out a pen. "We need to make a list of enemies. They could be potentially behind all of this."

"No one knew who I was until this year," I say with a shrug.

"Well, we've both pissed off this SykeWard person. Enough for her to play with us both. Do you like the things people are saying about you?"

"No," I reply.

"Then let's fix it."

"How?"

A grin tucks itself into the corner of her mouth. "Play like they're true."

"What?" My heart starts to thud.

"We find a way to out this person. Set a trap. Let them get comfortable that whatever they're trying to do is working. Pretend. Then out them."

"How?"

"Let me do the planning. Step one, I just need you to act like these are true." She grins and turns the car on. "Then I'm going to throw you off the cheerleading squad."

I gulp. "Wait—" She shoots me a look. "Okay."

"I'll take care of the rest. Just trust me."

The reality of her words rushes into my body, and my head feels light for the first time in days, weeks, months. "Our turn to play a little rumor game," I say. "Because I'm done being messed with."

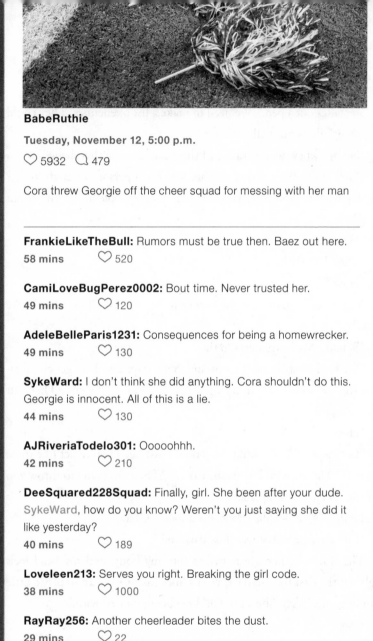

BabeRuthie

Tuesday, November 12, 5:00 p.m.

♡ 5932   💬 479

Cora threw Georgie off the cheer squad for messing with her man

---

FrankieLikeTheBull: Rumors must be true then. Baez out here.
58 mins   ♡ 520

CamiLoveBugPerez0002: Bout time. Never trusted her.
49 mins   ♡ 120

AdeleBelleParis1231: Consequences for being a homewrecker.
49 mins   ♡ 130

SykeWard: I don't think she did anything. Cora shouldn't do this.
Georgie is innocent. All of this is a lie.
44 mins   ♡ 130

AJRiveriaTodelo301: Ooooohhh.
42 mins   ♡ 210

DeeSquared228Squad: Finally, girl. She been after your dude.
SykeWard, how do you know? Weren't you just saying she did it
like yesterday?
40 mins   ♡ 189

Loveleen213: Serves you right. Breaking the girl code.
38 mins   ♡ 1000

RayRay256: Another cheerleader bites the dust.
29 mins   ♡ 22

PettyMar: Dumb girl shit.

23 mins   ♡ 298

RajLikeKing: This is wild.

23 mins   ♡ 21

DialloNotDiablo: This is what she gets.

21 mins   ♡ 13

WinnieWildWake: Bitch deserved it.

20 mins   ♡ 327

AmirNotKhan007: Back to U.N.

14 mins   ♡ 34

WongsterArt: Lay off, y'all.

10 mins   ♡ 180

Comments Loading

Tuesday 5:34 PM

Bryn:

You ok?

I saw the stuff online. About the squad.

What happened?

Tuesday 5:45 PM

Georgie:

I don't want to talk about it.

Tuesday 5:56 PM

Bryn:

Okay.

CORA

THE KITCHEN IS FILLED WITH BOUQUETS OF RED ROSES. Vero races around, trying to find space for all the arrangements.

"What's going on?" I drop my cheer bag in the mess room.

"For you, baby." Her face lights up. "They keep coming. So many."

"Me?" I pluck a card from one of the bundles and fumble with the tiny envelope.

Momma strides into the kitchen. "Turtle, what is all this?"

"I don't know yet." I flash the card at her, pretending they're not from Baez.

The doorbell rings again. Vero darts off to get it.

Momma starts complaining about this thing and that thing. But my eyes are fixed on the handwritten note:

> Cora,
> I'm sorry.
> Please forgive me.
> Love,
> Baez

My heart races. I open another card from another bouquet. It's filled with lines of poetry. Another has inside jokes. Some chronicle all the fun things we've done together.

Momma snaps her fingers. I look up. An angry wrinkle creases her brown forehead. "Did you hear me?"

"Yes, ma'am."

"What in the world is going on?" She puts a hand to her hip.

"Baez and I broke up. That probably makes you happy."

Her nose crinkles. "I'm sorry to hear that."

"Are you really?" The tears prick my eyes and my voice breaks. I hate myself for it. I try to clear my throat, push out the sadness.

"He's a nice boy."

I scoff. "You never really liked him. Not the way you like Graham."

"That's not true."

We stare at each other. My teeth clench and my pulse races. It's so weird how much Millie and I look like her. She's the third twin, everyone says. Sometimes I hate having to share a face with so many others.

"I just felt like he was a distraction from your studies." She fusses with her pearl necklace.

"And Graham isn't?"

"Millie—she's more focused than you. At least on school." She takes a step closer. "You got serious with that boy so quickly, Turtle."

My life as a six-word memoir: *I wish she'd stop with that.*

"His name is Baez. Abaeze Onyekachi, Mom."

She purses her lips. "The point still stands."

"I've maintained an almost-perfect GPA."

"Almost."

"I'm *not* Millie, Momma." My voice rises despite my trying to hold everything in. "When are you going to understand that?"

"I never said you were." She doesn't flinch or frown at the accusation.

"You are both my precious babies. I don't compare you."

"You just did," I mumble.

"What did you say?"

"Nothing." I take another card from a nearby bouquet, waiting for her to punish me for my tone or my attitude or my body language. But I can't hold anything in right now. I can't be the respectful and dutiful daughter. Everything is bubbling out of me.

I want to scream: *Someone hates me and is trying to ruin my life.*

Before I can move, she's right beside me, pulling me into a hug. "I'm sorry." At first, I'm so surprised, I don't move. And then, like a dam breaking, I crumple in her arms. The tears pour out, and I feel like I'm a tiny version of myself again. One that craved crawling into her lap or snuggling up beside her. The nape of her neck smells of honey and lavender, and her skin is still as soft as I remember.

"It's gonna be all right," she whispers.

I want to believe her.

I need to believe her.

I text Baez after dinner and tell him to come over after midnight so we can talk. I take a shower in the basement bathroom so Momma doesn't hear me. It's Daddy's man cave, where he shaves because Momma doesn't like his little hairs clogging up their upstairs sink. I go through Daddy's shaving kit. I rub my thumb across his old-fashioned razor. Like old times. When Millie and I first started high school and she got to skip a grade, I would steal it from this case. Sharp and silvery, it hooks like a crescent. The blade could peel my finger and lift the top layer right off, easy as taking the skin from an apple.

I used to touch the cool blade to the underside of my wrist after too-hot showers, when my skin would be still warm. I used to stare at my wrist for hours, wondering how deep the brown color went. If it'd disappear after the first layer, or the next, or if the pigment runs into the bone.

All those old feelings come back.

The tingle to feel the burn.

To feel anything other than what's been happening.

But the bracelet Baez gave me loops around my wrist, and Daddy's old grandfather clock chimes, knocking me out of my haze. I put the razor away. I promised myself and Millie and Baez and JuJu I wouldn't do that anymore. I'm okay. I will be okay. I slip into cute pj's, and wait for Baez's tiny knock on the basement door.

I hear Baez's footsteps. I open the door before he gets down the small flight of stairs. He stumbles a little.

"Hey," he says.

"Hey," I whisper. "You've got to be soooo quiet, okay?"

"Okay." He smiles. "Whatever you say."

We sit on the couch. I study him. His eyes are all bloodshot and he looks exhausted. The deep brown of his skin looks different. Like he hasn't been sleeping well or eating enough. That makes two of us.

"I got your flowers. Thanks."

A tiny smile breaks across his mouth. "I shouldn't have said what I did. I'm sorry. Everything got out of control."

"I'm sorry, too." I take his hand in mine, and they fit like my favorite pair of gloves. "I have to show you something."

I take my laptop from the table and show him a document Millie made of all the comments and their frequency, plus all the info she could find about SykeWard. I explain my theory—our theory—about what's happened. That we're being targeted.

His eyes grow big. "What is going on?"

"Someone is setting us up. Someone is making all this up. This person."

"Does that mean you believe me?"

"Yes," I say with a nod. "And I'm sorry I didn't. Georgie told me nothing happened. It's just—"

"People were so nasty," he says. "I tried to argue with them. I saw the things they were saying to you. How they weren't saying them to me."

"It was gross. Sexist. Disgusting."

"I don't think people calling me a player or congratulating me on having a bunch of women is cool. And it didn't even matter when I told the truth. It was like just because people were saying something made it true."

"I know," I whisper.

He leans forward. I meet him. Our foreheads kiss. "It's okay," he whispers.

"It's not, but it will be." I kiss his face a dozen times. I trace my finger over his slender nose, counting a few new moles that have lingered since his trip to Nigeria at the beginning of the summer, and circle his cheeks and the lines that edge his mouth. Dark hairs are starting to sprout along his chin, and it won't be long before he has that thick beard that all his brothers, his father, and his uncles have.

I kiss him.

"I want to keep you forever," I whisper. He's the first boy I ever kissed, the first boy to send me a love note in the sixth grade, the first boy to ever touch me.

"And I want to keep you," he says back.

"You love me." I smooth his eyebrows.

"I love you," he whispers. "We're meant to be."

I kiss his mouth.

"You love me, and only me."

"Always."

We kiss until we're both breathless. "What are we going to do about this SykeWard person?"

"I'm setting a trap," I tell him, that familiar energy zipping through me. Like I'm almost myself again. "I need your help."

He stares at me curiously. "Uh-oh, I know that look."

"We have to pretend that the rumors worked. Everyone has to believe that we broke up. That you actually did what everyone said you did."

"But—"

"I already talked to Georgie about it, too. That's why I said I threw her off the team, but it's fake. She's going to help. She's getting a lot of hate online. But only you, Georgie, Millie, and I can know. Has to stay our secret to make sure it all works." I stand up and explain my whole reasoning. Millie analyzed it from every angle. That's how I know it'll be perfect. "This person has to feel triumphant. Like their little game worked. That way they slip up. Say the wrong thing. Millie is working on trying to see if she can track their IP address, too."

"The two of you could take over the world." He grins. "But who hates us like this—who would do this shit?"

"I don't know. But we're going to find out."

BAEZ AND GEORGIE WERE COZYING UP SOLO AT CORA'S PARTY.

BAEZ AND GEORGIE DEFINITELY MADE OUT UPSTAIRS IN CORA'S BEDROOM.

COMPLETE AND TOTAL YOU-KNOW-WHAT AT JASE'S PARTY.

GEORGIE AND BAEZ HAVE BEEN FOOLING AROUND FOR MONTHS BEHIND CORA'S BACK.

CORA PUT GEORGIE ON THE CHEERLEADING TEAM TO KEEP AN EYE ON HER.

GEORGIE AND JASE HOOKED UP IN THE PHOTO BOOTH AT SCHOOL.

BAEZ AND GEORGIE HAD SEX AT HIS BIRTHDAY PARTY.

CORA AND BAEZ HAD A MASSIVE FIGHT. IT'S OVER.

GEORGIE IS HOOKING UP WITH RILEY NOW TO MAKE BAEZ JEALOUS.

CORA THREW GEORGIE OFF THE CHEERLEADING TEAM BECAUSE IT WAS CONFIRMED. GEORGIE AND BAEZ TOTALLY HOOKED UP BEHIND CORA'S BACK.

From: Principal Rollins
Attn: Bryn Colburn
Sent: Wednesday, November 13, 7:09 AM
Subject: Special Election Results!

Dear Bryn,

    Congratulations on being the winner of the special election for student body president. Your anti-bullying message resonated with the entire school, and you won once again, reclaiming your presidency. I was very impressed how your campaign turned a mistake you made into a learning opportunity for the whole community.

    Well done, Bryn. I look forward to continuing to work with you and your cabinet.

Best,
Principal Rollins

Georgie:

OMG OMG OMG OMG OMG!
CONGRATS! YOU DID IT.

Bryn:

I still sort of can't believe it.
Ready to be my secretary?

Georgie:

I don't know how. You sure?
I'm not going to do a good job.

Bryn:

Chill. You'll do fine. And I need you.

This is part of being popular.
People inviting you to do things.

Georgie:

Bryn:

You ready, VP?

Cora:

As I'll ever be. I really just need the distraction.

Bryn:

This'll do it. You ok?

Cora:

No, but whatever. It's all true. He's a cheater.

Bryn:

Wanna talk?

Bryn:

You ok?

What happened?

Cora:

The rumors are true.

Bryn:

Wait, what? How do you know?

Bryn:

??

Cora:

I don't wanna talk about it. I'm pissed.

Bryn:

You sure? I feel like people are just making up things.

Cora:

Georgie will pay.

BRYN

WEDNESDAY, NOVEMBER 13
8:52 A.M.

I STAND BEFORE THE ENTIRE SCHOOL DURING MORNING assembly. Cora is to my left. The stage lights warm my cheeks, and I squeeze the tiny rubber duck that my dad gave me in ninth grade to keep in my pockets for speeches. Big enough to feel the weight of comfort, but not too large to be a distraction. A speech talisman.

Principal Rollins reads all his boring announcements about this and that before introducing the results of the special election, announcing me and Cora as the winners. I push my shoulders back and prepare to give the speech of my lifetime. The first of many. One that will be shared on news outlets when I run for president in the future. One that will be pointed to when people have to rise from the ashes like phoenixes, triumphant once again.

I try not to yawn or rub my eyes. I stayed up until 5:00 a.m. perfecting this, knowing I'd win, and putting the final touches on the anti-cyberbullying video montage. I try not to panic about the fact that my VP and secretary now hate each other. I try not to think about how everyone has seen their very public, very dramatic fight online after

Cora kicked her off the team. I try to forget that I have to fix what's gone down between them, get rid of those rumors fast.

I stare out at the faces. Mostly a blur from the lights. But I catch a few eye rolls and deep sighs and slouches. When they should all sit up straight and prepare to listen. Principal Rollins invites me to the podium.

I glance back at Cora and she mouths: "You got this."

A surge radiates through me. With her by my side, I'm almost back to my old life. Now to show them all.

I clear my throat and motion at Georgie, who sits in the front row. She darts to the left and up to the stage.

The lights dim, and the massive projector screen descends behind me. There are snickers all around. Heat claws up my neck, and I ball my hands into fists before reaching to graze the head of the rubber duck in my pocket.

It's going to be fine.

I think about all the promises Chance made when he challenged my presidency. Bullshit promises, like study hall flex time, a lunch delivery option, internship credit. But he never talked about changing the culture of the school or making people feel safer or helping mobilize all of us to get things done.

Big mistake!

"Anyone can make silly promises about new lunch options or longer study hall periods," I tell my classmates proudly. "But what Foxham really needs is a big change. As your president, and with a stellar cabinet by my side, I'm making it my mission to be that change."

The video plays. The snickers and whispers cease. A dozen or more students tell their stories about being bullied online. The impact. The struggle. The aftermath. A few cry and several reveal how they tried to end their lives after the swarm of comments.

The video ends with me.

My words.

"There are three sides to every story. But when the world only thinks they know one, they decide to fill in the details of the others. Whether they're true or not."

The lights turn back on. I take a deep breath and speak into the microphone: "This year started off rocky for me."

Someone shouts, "No shit!"

I don't even stop to address it.

"I made a massive mistake. One that broke high school norms, broke actual laws, broke a few bones and bumpers. And even the lamp-post down on Wisconsin Avenue and P Street."

People chuckle.

Humor and self-deprecation for the win.

"What I learned was that people mess up. Even me. Someone who always wanted to be perfect. To do the right thing. Say the right thing. And always be on the right path. But I learned that even I can make a dumb decision. I won't stand up here and say what I did was right. Because it wasn't. I won't stand up here and tell you my version of the story. There were things that happened that you all don't know about. Even if you did, it might not change anything. There are pieces to the puzzle that are missing. But it didn't seem to matter. Everyone had made up their minds. Taken the evidence as presented to them and branded me *crazy* and a *psycho*, which are harmful words to call someone. Slurs. Like many of my fellow classmates, I was a victim of cyberbullying. Not just from other Foxham Prep students, but from the world. Everyone marched into my mentions on social media and said whatever they wanted to say. No matter how I felt about it, no matter how much I apologized."

I take a deep breath.

"What I want to do is use what happened to me, what happened to so many others here at Foxham, and try to make sure it doesn't happen again. No matter how perfect, how careful, how smart you are, we all find ourselves in the hot seat at some point. No one is immune. Right now, somewhere online, someone is talking about you. Someone has something to say. A critique of what you've said or done, what you're wearing or shouldn't have worn, what you should be doing or not doing. Our words travel."

I step from behind the podium and outstretch my arms for the finale. "I messed up. But let's work together to make sure our school is a place where everyone feels safe."

Cora starts a round of applause that ripples out. A few of the students who appeared in the video montage stand.

"I have big plans to continue to shed a light on this and other topics that our generation is facing, with Georgie Khalra as my new secretary." I motion for her to come closer and out of the stage-wing shadows.

Cora scowls at her.

Not now, Cora, please, I think, but I also feel terrible that I'm the one that started all this. I'll clean it up later.

Georgie strides out prouder than I've ever seen her.

"Together the three of us will change Foxham into the place it should really be."

Whistles and stomps and claps reverberate through me.

It's official. I'm back.

I head over to Georgie's house after having dinner alone in my pool house. I want to see if she'll make more posters for some of our initiatives. I probably should've called first, since it's almost seven, and she could be having dinner with her family, but she's just next door and what could it hurt?

I ring the doorbell, and a woman that isn't her mother answers. She works in the kitchen, or maybe throughout the house. I'm not sure. I've actually never been inside her house before.

"Is Georgie home?" I say, peeking around her.

She frowns, calls out something I don't understand, and motions me inside. I never took the time to notice how different her house is from mine. Rich sherbet orange–colored walls, thick rugs, and gilded mirrors. And it's warm and smells delicious, like I could eat everything inside it. Mine mostly feels like a hotel and has the scent of store-bought potpourri.

Georgie pops out of the kitchen with a mouth full of something. "Bryn," she garbles, her eyes wide with shock. And I realize that this is the first time I've been over here, even though we've lived next door to each other for, like, six years now.

Her mom comes out behind her, wearing a full purple sari. She asks me a thousand questions about my mom and dad. She stuffs me with those little fried things that my dad loves from Maharajah Palace restaurant before Georgie can get us upstairs to her bedroom.

"Your mom's intense," I say, throwing myself on her bed.

She frowns.

I correct myself. "Like in a ridiculous mom way. Like mine."

"Yeah," she says, quickly cleaning up magazines and nail polish from the floor. And what looks like used tissues. Gross.

"What's up?" she asks. "You didn't text."

I look around her room. She's got a few posters up of Indian movie stars, I guess, and an easel and paint and brushes stashed in a corner. A wall of bookshelves is filled with old, fancy editions of kids' books. Reminds me of my old bedroom inside my parents' house, before I moved into the pool house. I'm kind of jealous of her closet, though. It's a huge walk-in.

"My mum is obsessed with you now," she reports. "You made me your secretary. It'll look good on my college applications." She sits opposite from me and clicks on her TV. A weird Indian movie blares, and she quickly changes the channel.

"What happened between you and Cora?" I ask.

Georgie flinches and fidgets. "It's nothing."

"Uh, she hates you now. Wouldn't call that nothing." I fish for eye contact with her. I used to be able to predict her behavior. Now it feels like she doesn't really need me. Not with her clothes or makeup. Not for advice. Not even on how to deal with all of this. "You said nothing happened between you and Baez. Like, the night of his birthday? Did I miss something?"

Her phone buzzes, and I see Riley Wong's name pop up. She stashes it under a pillow. She's twitchy and weird. All the things I told myself about this being okay have been turned upside down after seeing my mom. I have to fix it now that I've almost gotten my life back. "Why is Riley Wong texting you?"

"We've been hanging out," she says, like she's drawn her name and his in a thousand hearts. "He's sweet."

"You dating him now?"

"Sort of. Like, nothing is official or anything." She blushes, which makes her brown skin look really pretty.

"You didn't tell me."

She flips through a magazine. "Well, you've been busy. The campaign and all."

"Right." The guilt sloshes around in my stomach. "I'll try to get Cora to put you back on the squad."

"It's fine. If she wants to be a bitch, then let her be a bitch."

I bristle. I've never heard her talk like this before, more like me and less like her. "Oh."

"But don't worry—I'll play nice when we have to do student government stuff. I need this for college apps."

Who is she right now?

"Okay." We sit and go through magazines in silence. I steal glances at her as she plays with her hair or puckers her lips like the models in the spreads. "You've changed."

She looks up at me and stops. "Isn't that what you wanted? Isn't that what everyone wanted?"

I shrug. I'm not quite sure what I want anymore. And that thought really scares me.

WongsterArt

Wednesday, November 13, 7:45 p.m.

♡ 3965   ◯ 3768

Georgie and me all cuddled up. #NewBoo

AhMADManKhan: Yoooo, make sure Baez ain't messing around with your girl behind your back, Wong.
45 mins   ♡ 76

FilmmakerChance: High school love never lasts.
38 mins   ♡ 23

AnthonyThaGreat3000: Me next.
32 mins   ♡ 217

PrincessChristine4578: Homewreckers don't deserve love.
30 mins   ♡ 32

SykeWard: Cute couple. That whole Baez thing wasn't real. You can tell. Look at how much they like each other.
28 mins   ♡ 210

> **FilmmakerChance:** How would you know, SykeWard? And who are you?
> **8 mins**   ♡ 82

AnthonyThaGreat3000: Bet she gonna make the rounds. I'll wait my turn.
22 mins   ♡ 21

KatNotKateLee: Cute couple alert. I'm here for love.
20 mins   ♡ 98

DeeSquared228Squad: Moving from one guy to the other. Slut much?
10 mins   ♡ 23

GEORGIE

FRIDAY, NOVEMBER 15
7:46 P.M.

PINK NEON LIGHTS WASH OVER ME AS I STAND NEAR THE Lucky Pins sign. The bowling-alley vibe is old-school kitsch meets nightclub chic—the music blaring, the lights flashing, the crowd mostly young. I've never done this before. Never done a lot of things, actually. Like been on an actual date. One-on-one. In a public place.

But here I am. Ready to bowl and make a fool of myself.

I'm excited, but not in a butterflies way. More like in a live-wire way. Because Riley keeps stealing glances at me, like he can't not look. And it's making my stomach flip-flop and slosh, like it's filled with those slippery orange fish from the tank in that Chinese restaurant Papa always used to take me to on Sunday afternoons.

I focus on tying my shoes. I didn't know bowling required special shoes, but here they are: super stiff, size six, one red, one blue. The problem is my skirt. It's short, too short, something Bryn made me order, and it keeps sliding up farther as I bend down on the bench to reach the shoes. Riley grins, his eyes grazing the length of my legs, then kneels down on the floor in front of me and ties them. His hands are warm on my ankles and then up my calf. Then he stands and offers one, tugging me up off the bench and right into his arms. I wrap mine around his neck, and he pulls me closer, leaning down to close the space between us. We don't stop kissing for what feels like a whole three minutes—my first PDA—and it hits me that I feel safe with him. Comfortable, even if he is looking down at me like I'm a slice of chocolate cake and he might just devour me. The difference is that I want to kiss him back.

As we head toward the lanes, I spot a few of the Desi kids that my mom always pushes me to hang out with—Sapna and Ronak and Akshay. Not kids from Foxham, but we see them at parties, the gurdwara, and other local stuff. I wave, casual, as Riley grabs a lane several aisles over, on the quieter side of the alley.

"Thought we could play a round, then grab food," he says as I make my way over carefully, nearly slipping in my shoes. He grabs me, steadying me, and pulls me close. I breathe in his now-familiar scent, my arms wrapping around his neck, my fingers fussing with the buzzed edges of his hair, which is growing in slightly. He plants a small kiss on my nose, then a light one on my mouth, the promise of more interrupted by the thunder of the bowling balls rolling forward, the lane lighting up, all set for action. He grins. "Ready?"

I nod. "You go first. Show me how it's done."

I watch him as he lifts up a few different bowling balls, testing their weight. He picks a larger orange one that looks like a sunburst in the flash of the disco lights, holding it in one hand, then the other. "Has to be just the right size," he says, demonstrating, "and your thumb and middle two fingers go in the holes right here." Then he heads toward the foot of the aisle and rolls the bowl straight down the lane in a single, smooth motion. It hits the pins, knocking over all but one of them.

I cheer and he smiles. "That was pretty good, right?" I ask as he walks back toward me.

"Not quite a strike, but yeah."

He leads me back toward the lane, and we look at all the bowling balls. I immediately settle on a blue tie-dyed one. It looks like a swirl of paint the color of the sky. I weigh it in my palms the way he did, and he frowns. "Might be too heavy," he says, then picks up another—purple one, slightly smaller. His arms slip around me as he takes the blue one and replaces it with the purple, adjusting my thumb and fingers into place. "Better?"

I nod, but all I can think about is his hip against mine, his breath on my neck. I love being here with him. Like we're in our own little bubble. I step away, nearly slipping in those stupid shoes again, and try my best to saunter to the aisle, feeling his eyes on me, watching every move. I lean forward, and my skirt hitches again. *Shit.* I drop the ball like a bomb, letting it roll, and it skitters off into the gutter. Not a single pin. I do a little curtsy, anyway, my laugh nervous.

"Guess I was wrong," he says, walking over with the tie-dyed ball in his palms. "Maybe you need a little more power."

I grin. "Definitely more power."

This time, I pick up the blue one, trying to find the right grip. He comes up close behind me again, adjusting my arms and my fingers. His arm grazes mine as we head toward the lane. "All the way back, then roll it forward, so it's smooth. We're gonna try for a straight path down." His hand is on mine as we pull back like a slingshot, then let go as the ball spins away from us, swirling like paint in a mixer. It's almost graceful, the way it swooshes forward, picking up speed, then clangs into the pins, knocking every last one over.

I leap with excitement. "Strike! I got a strike. It is called a strike, right?"

He laughs, and says, "A strike has to be the first roll, but I'll allow it, I guess. Only for you, though."

I run forward, slipping again, and wrap my arms around him, reaching up on my tiptoes for a kiss. The first time I've ever kissed him first. He leans down, smiling, and kisses me back. His arms are around my waist, his hands wandering lower. He kisses me again, his tongue pushing forward. My heart pounds, the blood thundering in my ears, faster and faster.

This is how it's supposed to feel.

"Thought that was you," a familiar voice says, breaking the spell, and I yank away, abrupt, caught. "Making more bad decisions, I see."

Vibha.

Sanjay, Amir, and a few of the other Indian kids from Foxham stand off to the side, waiting for her. My friends, or at least I thought they were, until she pretty much got them all to abandon me.

"Guess you've got a new toy this time, though, huh?" Vibha says.

Riley looks confused. "What's your problem, Vibha?"

"Clearly you're the one with the problem, Riley," she snaps. "Happy with your sloppy seconds. Or thirds, now, from what I've heard."

I say nothing. I won't give her the satisfaction of a response.

Riley steps forward, his face red, anger blazing, and I pull him back. But then Amir takes Vibha's hand, a small gesture, too comfortable, familiar, and she flinches for a second, yanking away. Exposing her secret.

And I could be mean. Out them. How would Vibha's mother feel when the rumors started swirling about her daughter? How would Vibha manage the damage done? Caused by just a little indiscretion, a tiny lapse in judgment, a secret revealed in the wrong time and place, to the wrong people.

I could give her a taste of what I've been going through. But no matter what's happened between us in the last few months, once upon a time, she was my friend.

And sometimes my only friend.

"Let it go," I whisper to Riley, taking his arm. "Not worth it."

Vibha's eyes flash; then confusion clouds them.

Amir steps forward this time, trying to defuse it. "Have fun, you guys," he says. "See you around, Georgie."

They shuffle away slowly, finding a bank of alleys on the far side of the space, until it's just her standing there, something like rage still simmering.

"They're waiting for you," I say, and my voice is soft, half hate, half grace. But she doesn't move. "I won't say anything. If that's what you're worried about. He's a good guy. And it's no one's business."

She nods, turns on her heel, and leaves without another word.

Riley looks confused for a second, then pulls me in close to him again, his face my hair, breathing it in. "You okay?" he whispers. "That was a lot."

"Yeah. We've known each other a long time," I say. "Maybe too long. So she feels like she can—" I take a deep breath, something shuddering through me. "You know how it is. Brown kids gotta stick together, right?"

"Well, how else are they going to report back to all the parents?" he says, laughing, looking down at me.

"The Aunties."

"You know Chinese ones are as bad as yours, right?"

I laugh into his chest. "There's no way. The Desi ladies don't mess around."

He lifts my chin, making me look up at him. "I love it when you laugh." He kisses me again, and his hands slip up under my shirt, his touch light, careful. I try to relax into it, to not pull away. It still feels strange, having someone else be that comfortable with your space, your body, familiar enough to just reach out and touch you, claim you, like they know you, like they get what you want. But he must, because he leans down and kisses me again, sweet, soft this time, his mouth on my lips, my throat, my ears, his hands making small circles on my back, slow and safe. Then he's grinning down at me again. "Was that your stomach roaring or mine? 'Cause I could eat, too."

I nod. "Chicken fingers and fries? And a diet orange soda." I calculate all the calories in my head. I'll have a salad for dinner and no dessert.

"Perfect." He walks off to get us the food, and I make the mistake of looking at my phone for a second. More notifications, more comments, more bullshit. I shove it back into my bag and push random buttons on the scoreboard, creating team names for me and Riley: KhongStrong, GeoRiley. Nothing quite works.

A shadow falls over me, and I nearly jump when I realize it's not Riley coming back with food.

I turn around.

"Hey, beautiful. What are you doing here by yourself?" It's Jase, too close as he pulls me up with one hand into a hug that feels too tight. There's a girl who's not Sasha standing right behind him, smiling brightly.

"Oh, hi," I say, trying to shove him off, and he grins, leering, as he takes a step back and grabs the girl's hand.

"I like your skirt," he says, his eyes scanning like an X-ray, making me feel naked. "This is Lee Ann, by the way."

"Li-Yan," the girl clarifies. She's small, Chinese, and stunning, with long black hair and dewy skin. She's wearing a strapless dress that's way too dressy for bowling. "Nice to meet you."

"Where's Sasha?" I make the mistake of asking, and Jase laughs out loud.

"Why you so worried about it?" he says, stepping too close again. "Jealous?"

"Hardly." I just feel bad for the girl.

Thankfully, Riley walks over with the food then, two trays full of way more than we need. Chicken fingers, little burgers, fries, nachos, the works. He always overdoes it, and I kind of love that about him.

"Hey, man," he says, surprised to see Jase. "Hey, Li-Yan, how've you been?"

He knows her? He turns to me. "She goes to my church," he explains. "Her dad is on Sunday BBQ duty with my dads."

"Is this Georgie?" she asks.

I grin. Does that mean he's been talking about me? "In the flesh."

Jase smiles, too. "Indeed, it is."

Riley shoots him a look, but Jase doesn't seem to notice.

"You guys want some food?" Riley says.

Mum would freak if she saw this spread. Luckily, what she doesn't know won't hurt her, or whatever.

We all sit on the benches near our aisle. Jase grabs a handful of fries, digging right in, as Riley passes me a basket with some chicken and fries. Li-Yan picks at one of the little burgers, taking small, delicate nibbles. Riley devours one in two bites, then grabs another. I eat a few fries, careful to take my time. The slower you eat, the quicker you realize you're full. That's what the camp counselors said.

Jase reaches for the sodas, but Riley intercepts him. "That one's G's," he says, grabbing the orange soda and handing it to me. Diet. He's been paying attention. I smile at him, and he squeezes in next to me. I squish in close, offering him a sip. He slurps, and I laugh.

"Aw, how sweet," Jase says, his voice mocking. "Little Riley Wong's got a girlfriend."

There's nothing *little* about Riley. They're the same height and size.

"I guess I do," Riley says, grinning at me. "Ain't she gorgeous?"

Li-Yan smiles, but Jase licks his lips. Gross. "Remember what I said, Georgie. White boys are better." He roars with laughter, and this weird shiver shoots up through me.

"You wish," Riley challenges.

Li-Yan laughs.

I push a nearby button, resetting the game to two teams. "You first," I say to Li-Yan and Jase.

He winks at me before leading her down to the alley so they can start a game.

Once out of earshot, I lean closer to Riley. "I don't get it," I say as we watch Jase all over the girl. "Why would *she* be interested in him? And what about Sasha?"

"Eh, guys like Jase always need extra," Riley says.

I grimace, and he laughs. "Oh, G, such an innocent."

"She seems so awesome." Too awesome for him.

"Yeah, it's weird. I mean, I guess he's got money. And status. And looks." He shrugs. "Jase technically only 'dates' white girls, but from what I've seen, he's got a pretty big Asian-fetish thing happening." He looks down, picking at the fries in the basket, and I know what he's thinking. "Like, I know you guys hooked up, or whatever."

I take his hand, and he looks up at me. "We didn't," I say. I pull him closer, because I want to make sure he gets it. "I didn't hook up with him. He cornered me, that day in the photo booth. Like, brought up the *Kama Sutra*. All that bullshit." I shudder. "He kissed me. I didn't want to kiss him." I think back, how wrong it felt, how freaked-out I was. "And I told him so." I take a deep breath. "Then he posted all those pictures. But they aren't the truth."

He looks surprised, then furious. And maybe a bit happy. "He's trash. I'm sorry that happened. Jase doesn't hear no a lot. And he doesn't take it well."

"Then why are you guys friends?" I don't mean to make it an accusation, and I get it, I guess. Proximity. Strategy. Alliances. All the reasons I thought Vibha was my best friend all those years. The things that come with being a part of a community, the things you don't have to keep explaining. The reasons I miss her even now.

"He's a lacrosse guy," he says, shrugging. "We're all friends, I guess. I mean, we all hang. All the athletes do. But I don't know if he's really my friend. Some of those guys are assholes, yeah. Not all of us, though. Promise."

I nod, wanting desperately to tell him about the whole plan with Cora.

Riley purses his lips, then smiles. "But it would be okay if you had. You're allowed. To do what you want. To kiss who you want." He fumbles the words. "I mean, maybe it's best not to go around, like, hooking up with other people's boyfriends or girlfriends or whatever. But I'm glad you're my girlfriend." The word still sends this little thrill shooting through me. "I'm glad you're mine."

I squish in even closer, so there's literally no space between us. "I know. And I will. Kiss who I want." Then I kiss him, just to prove my point.

Georgie:

This is harder than I thought.

Cora:

You have to. We have to.

Georgie:

I need to tell Riley at least. He's gonna get hurt.

Cora:

You can't. Not yet.

We have to stick to the plan. Can't tell anyone, okay? Not Bryn, not Riley.

Georgie:

You told Baez tho?

Cora:

He has to play along, too. Duh. Don't you want to figure this out?

Georgie:

Okay, okay. Yeah.

Cora:

It won't be much longer.

JASE'S 18TH BIRTHDAY

IT'S MY PARTY . . .

Come one, come all (and I do mean COME!) to the party
nobody wants to miss. Jase is celebrating his 18th in style. His
dad bought him the new Aston. Come take a look, be jealous.
He might even take you out in it. And you are amongst the
lucky few to make the cut. So be there, if you dare.

WHEN:

Saturday, November 16 @ 11:00 p.m.

WHERE:

My house
(if you don't already know the address then . . .
you aren't someone who I want there)

WHY:

Because who doesn't want to celebrate the day
Jase came into the world?

CORA

SATURDAY, NOVEMBER 16
9:46 A.M.

I SIT AT ONE OF THE ROUND TABLES AT MOMMA'S LATEST charity brunch, her sorority fundraising event for pediatric cancer. Beautiful Black women wear their Sunday best, even though it's Saturday, and twinkle like stars beneath thousands of tiny lanterns in the event room. Important Washington, DC, government people mill around exchanging gossip and small talk.

I'm all dressed up, and yet I can hardly begin to feel pretty. Not in this room with all these women.

I thumb the swan placard holders and plaster on a fake smile as people ask me the same questions over and over again:

"Where will you end up going to school?"

"Plans to follow your sister to Harvard?"

"What's it like to be a twin?"

"Is it weird being separated since Millie left to go to college early?"

"Will you study law like your father?"

I nod and pretend I can't hear them over the old Black music blasting through the speakers. A few others whisper about Foxham and all the reports on its toxic culture. They dredge up past scandals—when Josh Silverman released revenge porn of Meghan Lackey last year or how Rachel Beaumont's cheating ring got busted last year or the fact that Katerina Wilkerson was forced to leave after calling out a senator's son for homophobia—and the current rumors that have reached the parent circles.

But no one dares pull their kids out. Not when it's a place where all the former presidents' kids have gone. Not when the school will always cater to important parents and change the rules as needed.

Momma and Daddy exchange tense whispers about Millie, who sits sulking with her arms crossed against her chest. She's home early for Thanksgiving break. The stress of being away has been getting to her.

For once in my entire life, they aren't arguing about me. Daddy flashes Millie a stressed look, then whispers to her. I know exactly what he said without having to hear it: "Sit up straight and fix your face."

I try to get her to talk to me. Anything would be a great distraction right now. I'm missing Baez since we have to play this game. "Hey, you okay?" I ask Millie.

She's sulking, and definitely doesn't want to talk. I try again and promise her that we can watch rom-coms later. I need the distraction, and I know she does, too. "Where's Graham?" I ask.

"Volunteering or something. He said he'd see me later." She flashes me a sad smile. "I wish he was here. I already haven't gotten to see him, and his family's heading to Hawaii in the morning. Leaving a week early for Thanksgiving. I won't even get to hang out with him."

Waiters fill our water glasses. Warm bread baskets appear and disappear, and music drifts around us.

Muscle memory makes me look at my phone, and I instantly regret it. The social media tags continue to whirl with more nonsense about Baez and Georgie. I click off my notifications with a sigh. Keeping up the lie is hard. Seeing all the things everyone has to say wears on me. Even when I know they aren't true. I helped Baez craft some posts about hooking up with Georgie, but watching all the boys comment and brag on him makes my stomach sick. And Georgie's being swarmed with slut-shaming, which was inevitable, so I hope she's taking my advice to sign off completely. One day I'll write an essay or something about how girls are treated more shitty than guys online.

Jase and his pompous dad walk over. His dad is the number one kiss-ass, as Daddy calls him. He's all tanned and almost orange looking. He's always offering my father a rare and expensive cigar, no matter how many times Daddy tells him that he doesn't smoke.

"You coming to my party tonight?" Jase says, his blond eyebrows wiggling like he's some cartoon character.

"Yeah," I reply.

"It'll be even better than one of yours." He sticks his tongue out.

"Whatever."

"You too, Millie." He jostles her shoulder, and she flinches. "Lighten up."

She scowls at him, sending him back to schmooze with his dad. "I hate him."

"Everyone does," I admit.

Fingers graze the back of my neck, and I know who they belong to. I tip my head back and look up, and there's JuJu's beautiful, smiling face. She places her chin on my forehead in a backward hug, her skin soft and peach-scented and familiar, even though it's been forever. Her dark curls are pulled into a bun, and the lantern lights slice against the rich brown of her cheeks.

It's been four years since we've seen each other. She looks even brighter, a cloud of purple chiffon and laughter. She's so different now, off chasing her dreams of acting in LA.

"Hi," she says.

The word doesn't even form in my mouth correctly. Some mangled version of "hey" comes out. My heart knocks against my chest.

"Can we talk?" she asks.

My stomach squeezes. It's been forever since we've even *talked* talked, since everything happened at the start of high school.

I nod and stand.

"You okay?" I say to Millie.

She shrugs.

I take it as a yes.

Momma nods in my direction, giving me the green light to leave the table.

I follow JuJu out of the room and into the near-empty lobby of the fancy hotel. My heart knocks against my rib cage.

"It's been a long time," she says. "I thought about telling you I was coming today, but then lost my nerve. It's been forever."

"Yeah. But sometimes I see you in the pages of my favorite magazines, looking so beautiful."

We sit on a plush velvet sofa tucked close to the fireplace. We curl into it, our dresses swallowing us.

I steal glances at her. She's changed. Feels all grown-up. Like she's living this adult version of our lives. Just earlier than everyone else. Sort of like Millie. Her acting career has really taken off, and all this feels like a waste of her time. I felt like a waste of her time.

"I see Millie is miserable," she says, biting her bottom lip.

"Ugh," I reply. "Upset with a test she took, probably. That's what I suspect. I know her moods."

She smiles. "Twins."

We sit in silence for a while, the crackle of the fire keeping us company. The last time I saw her she said she never wanted to see me again.

Then Chance started treating me like shit at school because of what happened between us.

My words get all jammed up. I used to know word for word what I'd say to her if I saw her again.

"I've missed you," she says.

"I've missed you, too," I reply. Our friendship was always complicated. Something heavy has always floated between us, and most of the time it stays buried in the sand, like a rock at the bottom of the ocean. But sometimes it escapes its sand cage and bobs on the water's surface. Whenever *it* comes up for air, we both change. Usually for the worse.

"I thought you never wanted to see me again."

"I didn't," she admits. "I'm here with my mom. I signed on to do some charity photos, and I'm flying back to LA tomorrow to start shooting my next film."

"Good for you," I reply.

"But I saw you and thought we needed to talk. Chance said—"

"He still hates me."

JuJu smiles. "He's loyal. He loves me. He put me back together after—everything." She takes my hand.

I flinch.

"You okay?"

I nod. Her deep brown fingers entwine with mine. JuJu traces letters in my palm, and we sit in silence for a while. The comfort of her scent and skin slows my heart. I remember how close we were, how much simpler things were back then. "You look beautiful tonight."

"So do you," I reply.

"Chance said you were having a tough time."

"I'm sure he's delighted."

She smiles; one of her deep-set dimples appears. "I see the two of you still don't get along."

"He's always stirring shit up."

"Or he sees things you don't. He's got a keen eye. He's going to make a good filmmaker."

"You have to say that. You're his family. But, JuJu, he is always the drama. Always has something to say."

"Maybe what he's noticing and saying is true. Ever thought about that?"

"Well, he said my boyfriend cheated on me. Think that's true?"

Her eyes narrow—the hazel of them still impossibly beautiful. "Maybe."

"Well, it's not."

"Then why get so upset?" she presses. "Seems—"

"I can't talk to you about this." I scowl, but before I can say another word, she lifts my chin and kisses me softly. A simple brush of our lips that pulses with promise. A reminder of all there was between us.

"I can't, Ju," I whisper. But I let her kiss me once more, missing the way she tastes.

"I thought you and Baez broke up?"

"Uh . . ." *Shit*. "We did. It's just . . . everything's a mess," I say, trying to make my voice all half-formed and wobbly, so it's convincing. "But I'm fixing it."

The plan will work. Has to work.

A photographer wanders up. "Picture, please?"

JuJu scoots even closer to me. Her scent making the hairs on my arms stand up. She leans her head against my shoulder.

The lights blind us as he takes several shots before moving on to another pair in the hallway.

She turns back to me, and her perfect eyebrow lifts. "You sure it's worth it?"

"This has destroyed Baez's life. And, like—us." I want to tell her that it's all a lie. That we're going along with it to figure out who did this, but I can't. She might tell Chance. She isn't my JuJu anymore. She isn't the person who would hold all my secrets, my thoughts, my feelings.

"I still don't understand why," she says, and there's a new hard edge in her voice.

"Why what?"

"You chose him over me? And still do."

Sometimes I don't understand why either. Maybe deep down I didn't think Momma and Daddy would accept another thing that made me even more different than Millie. "You were about to go away. Chasing your dreams. Which you've done. I'm so proud of you. I knew you'd outgrow me."

"That's really selfish, Cora."

"I know," I whisper. "I'm sorry."

My life would be so different had we stayed together. There would be no rumors. I would have a famous Hollywood girlfriend. I wouldn't have to tell all these lies. I could've been happy with her.

"My JuJu," a voice calls out.

I look up. A white woman from inside a circle of other white women waves. "Who are those people?"

"My aunt. Chance's mom and the board of Sky Ward Ranch," JuJu says, waving back.

"Wait, what?" I sit up straight.

She looks at me strange. "It's my aunt. Chance's mom."

"Yeah, yeah, but where does she work?"

"At a fancy rehab center called Sky Ward Ranch. It's out in Virginia."

My heart plummets into my stomach.

It was Chance.

"What's wrong?"

"I have to go." I jump up.

"You always do," she grumbles.

I whip around. "You *left* me."

"Not before you broke my heart."

I rush away but glance back over my shoulder at her, wishing I had time to really tell her the truth.

Cora:

It's Chance.

Georgie:

Wait, what?

Cora:

He's the one making this up.

Georgie

But why? How do you know?

Cora:

Long story, but he hates me.
I should've known.

Georgie:

What are we going to do?

Cora:

Throw the biggest party ever.
Out his lies. On video—his favorite.

Cora:

Help me plan a costume party.

Bryn:

OMG, yes.

When?

Cora:

After Thanksgiving.

Bryn:

Theme?

Cora:

Gatsby. 1920s. Masks. What you think?

Bryn:

Yesss.

BAEZ AND GEORGIE WERE COZYING UP SOLO AT CORA'S PARTY.

BAEZ AND GEORGIE DEFINITELY MADE OUT UPSTAIRS IN CORA'S BEDROOM.

COMPLETE AND TOTAL YOU-KNOW-WHAT AT JASE'S PARTY.

GEORGIE AND BAEZ HAVE BEEN FOOLING AROUND FOR MONTHS BEHIND CORA'S BACK.

CORA PUT GEORGIE ON THE CHEERLEADING TEAM TO KEEP AN EYE ON HER.

GEORGIE AND JASE HOOKED UP IN THE PHOTO BOOTH AT SCHOOL.

BAEZ AND GEORGIE HAD SEX AT HIS BIRTHDAY PARTY.

CORA AND BAEZ HAD A MASSIVE FIGHT. IT'S OVER.

GEORGIE IS HOOKING UP WITH RILEY NOW TO MAKE BAEZ JEALOUS.

CORA THREW GEORGIE OFF THE CHEERLEADING TEAM BECAUSE IT WAS CONFIRMED. GEORGIE AND BAEZ TOTALLY HOOKED UP BEHIND CORA'S BACK.

CORA'S MOVED ON QUICK—HOOKING UP WITH EX-GIRLFRIEND JUJU OLIVIERI-ORTIZ, CHANCE'S FAMOUS COUSIN AND OLD FOXHAM STUDENT.

BRYN

SATURDAY, NOVEMBER 16
10:46 A.M.

"PUT THE BOXES FOR CANNED GOODS IN THE FAR CORNER," I direct volunteers. "And the one for dry goods to the left. Make sure to label them." It feels good to order people around again. I mean, for a good cause and all. The Saturday Turkey Drive is underway, and my second initiative of the year is sliding into place. We'll have enough food to feed at least three hundred needy families this Thanksgiving.

"Add Tofurky to the list," I tell my new treasurer, Isabel Hewitt. "Not everyone eats meat. Even the needy deserve to have choices. That's a human right."

She eagerly scribbles in her notebook, following closely behind me.

The sound of her pen scribbling down all the brilliant things I'm saying fills me up.

"Shouldn't Cora and Georgie be here?" she asks.

"Cora's at a brunch fundraiser for her mom, and I need to check on Georgie. I think she's sick." The last part's a lie because I don't know where the hell she is. She hasn't answered my texts. Weirdly. Probably hooking up with Riley. Vomit. But I guess that's how people felt about me once I started dating Jase.

Students flood the lunchroom with their donations.

"Hey, B!" Alexandra shouts. "Brought stuffing and cranberry sauce."

"Box to the right," I say.

"I've got reusable plastic containers."

"Box in the center."

It feels good to have people not sneer at you or grumble or make comments.

"Good work, Bryn," Mr. Oshiro, the physics professor, says in passing.

I nod and smile, then leave Isabel to oversee the sorting of the donated food while I head over to the photo booth. I want to check how many new videos have been recorded in the past week. Georgie's campaign poster looms overhead, and I swallow down all the frustration I feel about her. She's actually popular now. She got what she wanted. And so did I. Plus, she's gotten a taste of my ex, too. Though that wasn't part of the plan. But it all erases some of the guilt I feel about the rumors getting a little out of hand.

I open the back of the photo booth the way the technician showed me and send the downloaded videos to my file cloud. I'll stitch them together and feed them to the school's social media accounts later.

"You've really turned a corner, Bryn," a voice says.

I look up and find the senior-class guidance counselor, Mrs. Ramirez. She's all grins, admiring Georgie's poster and running her dainty fingers over the curtains to the photo booth.

"You've reestablished goodwill. Done something amazing for the school community. Turned it around. I'm proud."

I flash her a smile. Only slightly fake. The lie is getting easier to tell, shifting in place of the truth as if it was supposed to be that way all along.

"Maybe next semester you can help with another related campaign—body positivity."

I'm hoping she'll move along so I can take this smile off my face and get back to ordering people around. "Of course, Mrs. Ramirez. I would love to."

I turn around and flinch.

Chance Olivieri leans against the photo booth. "Isn't Bryn so helpful, Mrs. Ramirez? Exactly the person you'd want in charge of just about everything?"

Mrs. Ramirez nods in agreement, then saunters away, mildly confused.

"What do you want, Chance?" I say. "I'm very busy and important."

"It seems that way." He circles me like I'm his prey. "Like you've gotten exactly what you've wanted."

"I worked hard and won the special election. Your little plan didn't work," I challenge him. "You heard Mrs. Ramirez—I turned my life around." The words almost feel true.

"But at whose expense?" He smiles. "I know your secret."

"I don't have any secrets." The lie coats my tongue.

Chance laughs. "Everyone does. And I just couldn't figure out how you did it. Until yesterday."

My eyes narrow. I wish they were lasers that could turn him to dust.

He runs his hand over Georgie's poster. "It was clever, I'll admit. Didn't even think you had it in you."

"I don't have time for your games, Chance. Run along and go video something for your stupid documentary. Or better yet . . . do something good for a change and donate to Foxham Prep's Turkey Drive. We'll even take a donation from you. Despite your nastiness." I turn around and reset the photo booth, preparing it for more students to record their messages of hope or confessions about being bullied.

He *tsk-tsks* and lifts a cardboard box. It's full of dry goods. "Just for you, SykeWard."

I flinch. "What did you call me?"

"Isn't your mom checked into the Sky Ward Ranch Rehab Center? That's what my mom said. She's an administrator there."

A jolt makes my stomach flip.

"It took me a while to put it all together. Mom's complaints about the congressman's wife, the one who keeps smoking in her room. The one whose kid caused an accident." He pauses to smile. "I saw that name pop up on my social media. It kept stirring the pot. So familiar. SykeWard. Clever. Knew too much. So invested. Then I remembered Cora's party. How pissed you were. How you shoved me in the pool and ruined my four-thousand-dollar camera. The night it all started."

I whip around, trying to keep my anger in check. "I don't know what you're talking about."

A smile tucks itself into the corners of his mouth. "Oh, but you do. The whole school should still be talking about what *you* did. How you ran Jase off the road, straight out of some fucked-up soap opera. But you're smart. Very smart. You deflected. Shifted focus." He licks his lips like he's preparing to bite me even harder. "Changed the narrative. Super strategic. Gotta give you that. Must've learned that from your dad, Mr. Spin Doctor. Also, a liar according to my mom."

"That's not true." I ball my hands into fists. I try to stay calm.

"You're a good liar. Very much your father's daughter. I *almost* believed you."

"Why don't you spare me all the drama? Wrap up your accusations so I can get back to work."

"You always go too far. It'll blow up in your face. I won't even have to do a thing."

"What are you talking about?" My pulse races. "You're desperate. You're just mad you lost."

"Just you wait. It's going to be an even bigger scandal than your little accident." He takes out his camera and clicks it on.

"Get that out of my face."

"You'll have much worse to face once everyone finds out."

I gulp.

A weight crashes into my stomach.

The hours feel endless as I pace in my pool house, trying to figure out what to do. Chance's threat morphs and plays on repeat:

I know your secret.

I know you're SykeWard.

I know what you did.

A sick refrain. "What am I going to do?" I say aloud. *"Fuck!"*

I open my notebook, combing through each rumor page and all the printouts of the comments. I run my fingers over everything. All that I've done.

Maybe I should just tell them? Come clean. Explain.

"Cora, I broke you and Baez up so we could be friends again."

"Georgie, I added to the rumors about you so I could get *my* real best friend back. Get my life back."

"Baez, you never liked me and you made Cora hate me, so . . ."

Saying it out loud makes it sound even more monstrous. It felt so small, no big deal, when I did it. But now . . . Sweat coats my forehead. I have to erase everything. It'll be my word against his. People already hate him. I run to my computer and sign in to all of SykeWard's social media profiles. I delete them. I try to wipe everything clean from my browser history. I check all the profiles I commented on to make sure everything is gone.

Lastly, I check Chance's feed. My heart almost stops. He's got screenshots of SykeWard's posts and comments and tweets up with the promise of a big reveal interspersed with hundreds of photos of the party happening at Jase's house.

I have to tell Cora. At least.

Before I can think too hard about it, I'm in my car and driving to Jase's house. My car knows the way as if it's programmed. All the nights I slept over. All the nights we did homework after school. All the nights we partied in his basement or on the back lawn. His parents spent most of their time at their second home in Beaufort, South Carolina, playing golf.

It's just after 11 p.m. and I hold my breath as I type in the code to his gate and sail right into his neighborhood. Jase's house is swarming with people. It's in one of those old-money estate areas, all sprawling lots with woods between them.

His house sits at the very back. The biggest. Nestled in an almost forest. All my classmates' expensive cars line the long driveway and are lined up in the grass.

I watch as more and more people stream into his house. All the usual suspects. Some new faces from other private schools. Some people who graduated last year and are back for the holidays. I used to plan these with him. I'd come up with amazing themes and go to the party stores, gathering supplies and decorations. Always making sure there was some fun surprise. My heart pounds at the thought of Sasha taking over. Is she doing the same things I used to do?

I shake my head. Who cares? That's over.

I turn off the headlights and take a deep breath before getting out of the car. My therapist would tell me this is a very bad, very destructive idea . . . all the things I've done since the accident probably fit in that category. But I've got to try to fix this regardless.

I tuck my hair into my hoodie and pull it up as I disappear into a crowd headed up the long, snaking driveway and to the back of the house. People pour in and out of the side doors.

I slip in. The walls hum. The music pounds through me. The whole ceiling is full of balloons, and pictures of Jase have been blown up and placed everywhere. People leave Sharpie birthday messages on them. My fingers itch to write something rude and nasty.

But someone sideswipes me, bringing me back to my mission—*find Cora*. I ease in and out of familiar rooms. The three living rooms Jase's mom has decked out like they're straight out of Versailles. My mom would call it tacky.

The crowd is thick, and I try my best to scan it. The windows are blacked out, and there's a weird light making everyone glow.

All the faces look strange and distorted. I start to panic. What if I can't find them?

I duck into another room. Couches are filled with drunk and passed-out bodies. I text Cora and ask where she is. I wait for a response. Nothing. *Ugh!* I keep searching and combing through the crowd.

"I see you," comes a voice from the couch.

I whip around. Chance is all sprawled out, his mouth sticky and covered with brownies. He's got crumbs even in his dark hair. Three empty cups beside his camera.

I try to turn back around.

"Bryyyyyn!" he starts to shout, then cracks up with laughter.

"What's wrong with you?" I say.

His eyes are glassy. "What's wrong with *you*? You're not even supposed to beeeeeee heeeeeere. Everybody hates you."

"You're a drunk."

He laughs.

"I might have hit the world record for number of pot brownies you can eat. I'm up to ten now." He bursts out laughing, tears streaking down his cheeks.

"Where's Cora?" I ask.

"Whyyyy? Going to tell her your secret?"

"Shut up. I need to talk to her."

He shoves another brownie in his mouth and downs it with more punch. He slurs out incomprehensible words. His eyelids droop, then close.

I look down at his beloved camera. It's probably full of footage. Maybe ammunition he's planning to use on me. Ammunition he can't use if he doesn't have it. Wonder what's in there that *I* could use? I start to pick it up, but Sasha catches me.

"What the fuck are you doing here?" Sasha walks up to me.

I bolt deeper into Jase's house. I will hide out and wait so I can get that camera. I won't let Chance spin his narrative.

I'll take control of this story.

GEORGIE

SATURDAY, NOVEMBER 16
11:35 P.M.

I IGNORE ALL THE PEOPLE STARING AT ME, WONDERING what I'm doing at Jase's party now that Cora has thrown me off the cheerleading team, now that everyone hates me for breaking her and Baez up.

This is part of the plan.

Monica and I stand near a table covered with different punch bowls, pretending nothing is wrong. I check my phone and wait for Riley to show up while Monica tells me how different the squad feels without me on it. She's the only one still talking to me. Besides Cora, of course. But no one else knows that.

Stress pulses through me, and I can feel people staring, so I grab a brownie from the snack spread. It's not great, but chocolate soothes my nerves, even if these do probably clock in at at least 250 calories a pop. I'll have to make up the difference tomorrow. I'll have a protein smoothie for breakfast and run an extra mile. It'll be fine. I shovel it into my mouth and take another while meeting every stare and glare and scowl head-on, refusing to cower. I grab a third, and Monica gives me that look. She knows better than anyone that people are watching, judging. But as soon as we find out who SykeWard is, it'll all be over, and I can, like, actually relax. That's what I've been telling myself since I agreed to Cora's plan.

Being hated is worse than being invisible. My phone buzzes with a million texts from Bryn. I can't keep up. It's annoying.

"You good?" Monica asks, searching my face.

"Yeah," I reply quickly. "Why?"

"'Cause you're looking around the room like some sort of monster is about to get you."

That's what it feels like. The lie Cora and I are letting people believe feels like a giant, raging thing, ready to attack.

"And you keep pounding those horrible brownies," she adds. "Relax." She hands me a punch cup. "So you made a mistake. You *both* did. It's not fair the girl always takes all the heat when stuff like this happens."

Guilt wraps around me like a too-tight sweater. Monica might be the only real friend I have right now, and I keep lying to her. But there's too much at stake.

"Easy for you to say." I wave the cup away. I'm done with drinking after the Marilyn Monroe incident. "You didn't get kicked off the squad." The lies feel clumsy in my mouth. But I've been lying so long about so much—Riley, food, Vivek—that I should be an expert.

Monica puts a hand on my shoulder. "It'll blow over. I've been talking to Cora. It's only been a few days. Sometimes she seems super upset about it, and others like it doesn't actually bother her. I think she's a hothead—" She swallows the rest of her sentence as Cora approaches, Ruthie and Christine by her side.

Christine and Ruthie glare at me while Cora slowly and methodically fills her cup with an electric-blue liquid. She doesn't so much as glance my way. Invisible again.

"Monica?" Christine says. She's got the hiccups and is already slurring, but it's cute on her, since she's so small and unassuming. Like a drunk toddler, if toddlers were allowed to get drunk. "You shouldn't stand near trash cans. You might end up smelling like one."

Her cold blue eyes find me, and she smiles.

Monica steps forward, about to say something.

I stop her. "It's okay."

"She doesn't need your permission," Ruthie adds, downing another whole cup of punch.

I refuse to back down or break eye contact. Strong and steady.

But Monica shuffles away from me, and Christine yanks her close, draping a floppy arm around her neck. "Much better. She's no longer one of us. Should've never been to begin with. You've got her spot now. You're such a better jumper."

Monica's eyebrows lift with surprise and she looks stunned.

I shrug. Whatever. I'll fix it later.

Cora still says nothing.

The others fill their cups with different punch. The sloshing makes me nauseous.

"Cheers, babes." Ruthie lifts her cup, glaring at me. "To ride-or-die bitches. Only loyal ones."

I roll my eyes and fuss with my phone, waiting for Riley. I watch them guzzle Day-Glo liquid and think about the old family parties. How everyone would shout "Chak le, Chak le" before drinking up. Even louder if it was a Sunday and my dad and uncle were watching cricket matches. In India. Before Vivek and the accusations and the mess. Before we stopped talking to my uncle and my dadi and everyone in Delhi. Before we were the only Khalras we knew.

I wonder who my dad drinks with now. He never does it at home anymore. Or watches cricket. Guess he goes to Asha's house for that stuff. Mum never liked cricket, anyway.

Graham Williams rushes up to Cora, towering over us all. I only catch a handful of his urgent whispers. Baez. Drunk. Migraines. Vomiting in the bathroom. Asking for her.

They saunter away, but Cora glances back at me and winks. I nod, then grab another brownie from the table platter. Then another. Somewhere along the line, they got delicious, and now my head is airy. Almost worth the calories—until I start doing the math in my head. *Ugh. Maybe eight hundred? Shit.*

Warm hands slide around my waist. I jump.

"It's just me," Riley says, pulling me tight to him.

I try to sink into his arms, but his hands travel down my body and I shift a little.

"What's up?" he asks.

"Nothing," I say, still chewing the brownie. I'm jumpy tonight. Or maybe still getting used to hands on my body. Guess this is what it means to have a boyfriend. I still can't believe he's my boyfriend. I lean up and kiss his cheek, all red and cold from the November night. "What took you so long?"

"Saturday-night breakfast-for-dinner. It's tradition. My dads wouldn't let me out of it. One of my sisters made French toast." He grins, kissing my nose. I love how much he loves and talks about his family. Makes me wish I wasn't an only child. And that my parents actually liked each other.

He reaches for a brownie while I use my compact to check that I don't have any in my teeth.

"They're terrible. Kind of dry, almost grainy."

He stuffs it in his mouth and chews like he's some food critic about to deliver his review. He flashes a chocolaty grin. "These are full of weed."

"What?"

"Marijuana. Pot. You know?" He's smiling.

I touch my stomach. "I've never had that."

"Oh, then it's going to be a good night." He pulls me forward and gives me a chocolaty kiss.

"What's going to happen? Should I go throw it up?" Panic settles into me. I had, what, five? How much weed is in each one?

"No. You'll be super relaxed and laugh a lot." He kisses my cheek. "Let's dance."

He drags me to the living room, where everyone has squeezed in, dancing in front of a DJ. There's a bass backbeat thumping loud and fast, though it might just be my heart. I can't even hear my own thoughts racing. The windows are blacked out. A black light makes everything shift and pop, the liquid in everyone's cups glowing.

I try to dance without stepping on his feet or knocking into other people. I've never really danced with a boy before, and I feel all stupid, like my body doesn't know what to do with itself. It's making me dizzy. But the good kind. My limbs start to feel all buzzy and heavy, like they're made of quicksand.

Riley grins, his teeth bright pink from the light. My thoughts and worries stretch out, and I almost forget them all. I reach up and touch his face. "You have a beautiful smile. A beautiful face." I kiss him. As he pulls me closer, the heat starts low in my belly. But I don't know if I actually want to kiss him here, with all those eyes on us, or if it's just the brownies. I should have eaten more of the grilled chicken Mum left out for me. My head rests against Riley's chest, and I can feel this odd sort of rhythm beneath me, his heart maybe, going tharump, tharump, tharump, hard and fast. Because of me? Or because that's just how hearts beat?

My head is a mess. I don't know whether I want to laugh or cry, dance all night or sleep forever, kiss him or push him away. I plop onto the nearest couch.

"Water?" he asks. "You coming?"

"I can't get up," I say, and burst out laughing, knowing it makes no sense.

"Be right back." Riley disappears into the crowd.

The room swirls around me and it feels like it's been a thousand hours since Riley left to get water.

I stare into the dancing crowd. I spot Bryn coming straight toward me. It feels like a mirage. I can't tell if it's actually her. I wave and shout her name into the roar of music. I reach out my hand to yank her down on the couch with me, then a tall body cuts her off. Jase.

"Get the fuck out of here before I call the cops," he barks at her.

I can't get any words out. Everything feels delayed.

She tries to argue with him and I can't make out anything they're saying. Their voices feel a thousand miles away.

She retreats, disappearing into all of the bodies.

Jase towers above me.

My heart skips. I look around. Where's Riley? Where did Bryn go?

Jase takes my hand and pulls me up, one-handed, like I'm light as a feather. I overshoot, landing firmly in his grasp, his arms around my waist, his nose level with the top of my chin. "You smell good," he says in a whisper that sends shivers up my spine. "Do you taste good, too? Like last time?" He leans down and I push away, but his grip is firm. "Oh, you need more punch. Your teeth aren't glowing." He tries to yank me forward.

"I'm good." My words sound murky, far away. Like maybe I haven't said them at all. "Riley's grabbing me some water."

"You look like a girl who likes her champagne," he says, but the words are scrambled in my head. "We have a whole fridge full."

"Nope, I'm good," I say, clearer this time. "I already had too many of your terrible brownies."

"Special brownies. They're like magic." His smile consumes his whole face. Bright red lips and pale white skin. Like a clown. "I spent big money on those. Five milligrams of THC each. Plus some extra."

I don't even know what that means. Just that I've probably had one too many.

I try to sit back down, but the couch feels farther away than it was before. I almost stumble, and Jase catches me. "Whoa, whoa, whoa."

Everything spins. The room is fuzzy and dim, and I feel like I'm swimming in the dark. The edges all blurry, my mind playing tricks on me. I see Riley's face, then Jase's face, then Riley's again.

"You need to lie down," Jase says.

I let him take my hand and lead me forward. We pass by bodies. So many bodies. I stumble down some stairs and into a bedroom. I can rest, maybe, for a minute, figure myself out.

I crash onto the covers, like a bed of clouds. My whole body floats.

His hands are soft. That's what I keep thinking when he touches me again, when he finds me on the bed in the room that appeared out of nowhere. That's what I'm thinking when he pushes me down onto it, and climbs on top of me, and kisses and kisses and kisses me until I can't think anymore or breathe anymore or say anything anymore, let alone no. That's what I'm thinking when I hear the door open and close, and those soft hands slip up my dress and unzip the back.

Lights flash and I can't seem to move, my limbs too heavy, my head too cloudy.

Soft. That's what I think, happy, for once, to not have to care anymore.

CORABAE526

Saturday, November 16 11:45 am
♡ 301

A List of Things About Georgie Khalra:

1. She's a slut.
2. She should've never hooked up with other people's boyfriends.
3. She broke the girl code.
4. She should be afraid of me.
5. She should have her ass beat.
6. She wants my life.
7. She's miserable.
8 She's gonna pay.

Bryn:

Come over when you leave the party. I actually just left.

Cora:

WHAT??? You know you shouldn't have been there.

Bryn:

I know, I know, but I was looking for you. I have to tell you something.

Cora:

What's up?

Bryn:

Tell you when you get here.

Cora:

I gotta tell you about tonight. It's been a whole mess.

I'll stop by.

Can't sleep over cause Millie went home early and she's covering for me with my mom.

Bryn:

Cool.

CORA

SUNDAY, NOVEMBER 17
1:25 A.M.

"ARE YOU JUST GOING TO LEAVE HIM?" ADELE SAYS AS WE cross Jase's lawn toward my car. My stomach's all tight and anxious after the fake fight Baez and I had during the party. Even though we planned it, even though we talked through exactly what to say and do. The whole thing sucked. We don't scream in each other's faces. We don't talk to each other like that. We don't insult each other.

The argument rings in my head, our words playing on a loop:

"You barely let me out of your sight anyway. Dammit, Cora. You got handcuffs there?"

"You're a fucking liar, Baez. You know that. You pretended this whole time that nothing happened."

"Maybe you made me do this. All the complaining. All the insecurity."

"You're an asshole. Foxham's next great lacrosse star, all about the groupies."

Even though each word is a lie, they burn; the heat of them lingers long after.

"He can clean up his own mess," I say, trying not to let the full pinch of leaving a drunk Baez overwhelm me. I can see him in my head: hovered over the toilet in the downstairs bathroom, vomit all over his lacrosse jersey. I sent Graham down there with aspirin. He'll be okay. I add more mock upset to my voice. "He shouldn't have had so much to drink. I'm over him." The drinking part is true. I know why he did it, though. Made it easier to play the part.

Adele's eyes narrow as she inspects my face. She knows me too well. "He'll sleep it off. Jase can worry about him—and the mess he's making on the floor."

"Exactly," I reply. "But he'll be really pissed when he finds out I swiped this." I hold up Baez's phone. "Now I can post on his social."

"Brutal. He deserves it," she replies as I press on the gas and zip out of the neighborhood as fast as I can. "He swore he didn't do it. Why all of a sudden admit to it?" She clicks her fluorescent nails on the armrest.

"I don't know. Why don't you ask them? They're the ones that did it." I speed down the block. I need to drop Adele off fast, give my brain some quiet. Her question set my nerves on edge.

"I just think something is off. Like—"

"Stop with the questions, okay? Damn." My hands squeeze the steering wheel. My pulse races and I can't relax.

Adele looks super sad for a second, her cheeks pink. Then she sort of shrugs and nods. "What's up with you? You've been a mess all week."

"Uh, try going through a breakup."

"It's more than that." Her eyes examine me.

I stare ahead at the red light until my vision blurs.

My life as a six-word memoir: *Everything is going to be fine.*

We ride the rest of the way in silence. I try to ask her about Leilani. But she gives clipped one-word answers. She doesn't even say bye when she gets out of my car. My stomach is a tangle of nerves. I want to just tell her the truth. Tell everyone the truth. My legs tremble as I watch her walk to her front door. She doesn't look back and wave like she usually does.

I text Graham to check on him before I pull out of the driveway. I wait for the little dots. "C'mon, c'mon," I say to my phone, but there's no answer. I send four more texts. Nothing. I back down the driveway and call Graham. No one picks up. Maybe I shouldn't have taken Baez's phone.

I think about driving back to Jase's, but a text comes in from Bryn. An urgent follow-up to her earlier text: *Come now.* Shit! I forgot I promised her I'd stop by before going home. It'll be a good distraction, something to keep me from turning around and heading back to Jase's house to get Baez. We have to push through.

One more week of this. Right after Thanksgiving. We'll catch Chance in his lies and put an end to all of this. I'll out him as SykeWard. It'll all be over.

I park on the street, then tiptoe to the back gate. I punch the key code. It's my birthday, which always makes me smile. The motion sensors near the pool don't beam on as I leap over them and make my way to the little house. The windows glow and the red door is cracked open, waiting for me.

I used to be jealous of her pool house, wanting a little space all to myself. After Millie skipped grades, I wanted to be somewhere far away from my parents' excitement about their genius daughter. I glance up at Georgie's house, the teal shutters in the darkness, and wonder if she's home and asleep already. I wonder if she's okay. Everyone was so cruel tonight on my behalf. I'm sure it hurt. I'll text her later, too.

"Cora," a whisper comes in the dark. Bryn's pale white face peeks out. "What took you so long?"

I rush into her warm little space. A fake fireplace crackles, and she's got books and papers everywhere. The table is littered with half-eaten bags of chips and cookies and pretzels. I find the one empty spot on the couch and crash into it. "Jase's party was a mess. Baez and I had another fight."

"Oh."

"He got all drunk again. And you know how the headaches come."

She nods. "He's not your problem anymore."

Those words feel familiar. She never liked him. "What's up?" I check the time on my phone. "I can't stay long. Millie's covering for me." If this was last year, we would've stayed at Jase's together until at least 3:00 a.m., then crashed here. She'd make breakfast in the morning, fancy eggs from one of her mom's recipes. The thought makes me nauseous.

"About that fight—" She picks up a notebook, holding it to her chest like it's some sort of shield. She's pacing, making me dizzy. Her lips are all red and swollen like she's been biting them.

"What's wrong? I told you I'd help you with the Thanksgiving can drive tomorrow. I can come back over. Millie said she'd help, too."

"It's not that." She's all shaky. "I have to tell you something."

I stare at her. "What?"

"Baez didn't—" Her phone pings. Then mine.

We both look down.

Our screens fill. The blare of sirens consumes the space, red and blue light flooding the windows.

"What's going on?" she says, racing to her door.

My eyes can't decode the information fast enough. They catch

fragments. There are naked pictures of Georgie. There are jokes. There
is upset. A flurry of comments and captions.

COPS CALLED TO JASE'S HOUSE

PARTY BUSTED

GEORGIE A MESS

My heart drops. *What happened?*

Cora:

OMG, you okay?

Georgie?

From: Principal Rollins
Attn: Jashan "Georgie" Khalra
Sent: Monday, November 18, 7:29 AM
Subject: Meeting

Dear Jashan,

I'd like to speak with you about an important matter. Please come see me after second period. I'll send a pass for you.

Best,
Principal Rollins

MORE DRAMA AND TRAUMA AT FOXHAM PREP?
ANOTHER SEX SCANDAL FOR THE TEEN ELITES

CHILD PORN RING BUSTED
IN POSH DC SUBURB

COPS COVER UP SEX SCANDAL
INVOLVING CONGRESSMAN'S SON

TateNotTotBro1289

Monday, November 18, 8:01 a.m.

♡ 21   ◌ 5999

Jase's party made the news.

FrankieLikeTheBull: Damn.
48 mins   ♡ 52

KeishaSoFly: They're saying bad shit went down at that party.
35 mins   ♡ 12

DeeSquared228Squad: Georgie's been hooking up with
everyone now that she's lost all that weight.
33 mins   ♡ 143

AlltheLoveleen213: This isn't good.
32 mins   ♡ 186

AhMADManKhan: Looks like both Baez and Jase scored big that
night.
29 mins   ♡ 13

KayBae215: There's more photos, too. They're bad.
28 mins ·   ♡ 100

RayRay526: Somebody send me a link. Riley bout to be mad as
shit.
24 mins   ♡ 14

MantzMadness22: That's child pornography. Technically. She's
under 18.
22 mins   ♡ 131

Maura345: R.I.P. Georgie. Somebody write her eulogy. Cora is really gonna kill her now. Sasha too. She is dead.

21 mins　　♡ 283

VibsterMD: I don't even know who this girl is anymore.

17 mins　　♡ 3

DialloNotDiablo: Guess Baez had nothing to lose after Cora broke up with him.

15 mins　　♡ 134

ChaseTheGirls: Oof.

13 mins　　♡ 213

Comments Loading

BAEZ AND GEORGIE WERE COZYING UP SOLO AT CORA'S PARTY.

BAEZ AND GEORGIE DEFINITELY MADE OUT UPSTAIRS IN CORA'S BEDROOM.

COMPLETE AND TOTAL YOU-KNOW-WHAT AT JASE'S PARTY.

GEORGIE AND BAEZ HAVE BEEN FOOLING AROUND FOR MONTHS BEHIND CORA'S BACK.

CORA PUT GEORGIE ON THE CHEERLEADING TEAM TO KEEP AN EYE ON HER.

GEORGIE AND JASE HOOKED UP IN THE PHOTO BOOTH AT SCHOOL.

BAEZ AND GEORGIE HAD SEX AT HIS BIRTHDAY PARTY.

CORA AND BAEZ HAD A MASSIVE FIGHT. IT'S OVER.

GEORGIE IS HOOKING UP WITH RILEY NOW TO MAKE BAEZ JEALOUS.

CORA THREW GEORGIE OFF THE CHEERLEADING TEAM BECAUSE IT WAS CONFIRMED. GEORGIE AND BAEZ TOTALLY HOOKED UP BEHIND CORA'S BACK.

CORA'S MOVED ON QUICK-HOOKING UP WITH EX-GIRLFRIEND JUJU OLIVIERI-ORTIZ, CHANCE'S FAMOUS COUSIN AND OLD FOXHAM STUDENT.

BAEZ, GEORGIE, AND JASE HAD A THREESOME. AND THERE ARE PHOTOS.

PART FOUR

THE TRUTH

truth [trüth] *noun*

1) the quality or state of being true

2) reality

3) facts

4) believed

5) always different depending on who's telling it

BRYN

MONDAY, NOVEMBER 18
7:05 A.M.

I KNOCK ON GEORGIE'S HOUSE DOOR TO PICK HER UP FOR carpool, to see if she's coming to school after everything that's happened, to see if she's okay since she isn't answering her phone or texts. The woman who isn't her mother opens the door.

"Is Georgie ready?" I ask.

She frowns. "She's not going to school today."

"Is she okay?"

"Bye-bye." The woman closes the door in my face.

I text Georgie over and over again. No luck. I leave her a voice message. I have to make sure she's okay after I read about everything that happened. I call Cora. She's a mess, too, rattling off all the things she's hearing about what happened that night, but nothing seems certain. She tells me to meet her before first period in our spot. I speed to school, but before I can get to my locker, Mrs. Nguyen, one of the school administrators, sweeps all of us into the media center.

Everyone peers around, anxiety skyrocketing.

Melissa blurts out, "Why do we have to come in here?"

"Ms. Rauch, please raise your hand next time you have a question."

Melissa holds up her hand.

Mrs. Nguyen sighs. "Yes, Melissa?"

"Why do we have to meet?" she asks.

"If I knew the details, I would've told you." She clicks her tongue and leads us forward. All the senior girls head in the same direction, a herd of perplexed goats. Whispers and gossip crackle like tiny firecrackers.

Cora and I see each other. She flashes me a confused look.

We all file into the small theater at the back of the media center. Cora saves me a seat beside her. I plop down.

"Any idea what's happened?"

"No, I'm still hearing the same things you are, but the details get wilder every time I hear them. I have no idea what's true."

I gulp and hold her hand.

Our guidance counselor, Mrs. Ramirez, and the senior-class adviser, Ms. Yu, march into the front of the room, their bodies illuminated by the screen behind them.

The whispers cease, and the immediate silence of the space is charged with questions.

"Good morning, senior girls," Mrs. Ramirez says.

"Good morning, Mrs. Ramirez," we reply in unison, like this is still third grade.

"I know this meeting throws off our morning schedule, but it is of the utmost importance that we confer with you all about some recent happenings. We are having school-wide meetings today with each class about what constitutes consensual sex."

The last two words pop in the room.

"Consensual sex means asking for and getting permission before you go any further. It means setting and respecting boundaries. And that applies to every sexual activity, whether penetrative sex or kissing or taking and sharing photos of someone else's body. Raise your hand if you understand the definition."

My stomach feels like it's being squeezed by a vise.

"We're going to watch a short video that reviews some scenarios to illustrate what is and what is not consensual sexual activity."

The lights dim.

Whispers explode.

A girl near me says, "It's about the rumors."

Another replies, "I heard Georgie had a threesome."

A third adds: "No, it's way worse. Georgie accused someone of forcing her."

"I heard that, too," a fourth chimes in. "There are photos."

"She had Baez's jersey on when she woke up. That's what Becca said."

Cora's face registers shock, then panic, but she doesn't say a word, just stares at her hands.

"Girls!" Mrs. Ramirez barks. "Silence!"

My stomach flips. The thought of any of this being real sends a chill up my spine.

Ms. Yu shushes the room, and the video starts.

A woman sits in a nurse's office and holds a pamphlet. Her voice drones on about what healthy sex looks like. Several couples demonstrate the principle of *No means no!*

The room chuckles at the terrible acting.

Ms. Yu shushes everyone again.

Girls look around for Georgie. Thank god she's not in this room right now. I think about this morning, the housekeeper's face. I text her again, but there's no response. I chew on the inside of my cheek until it's raw, and my mouth fills with the silvery taste of blood. I have to do something. To fix it somehow.

This has gone too far.

● ● ●

Everyone watches as Baez is led into the principal's office. I hold my breath until his back disappears inside. One of the hall monitors tries to rush everyone along, as if there's nothing to see. There's so much to see. Nothing else matters today.

I drop down and pretend to fix my shoe, keeping an eye on everything. Some slip out their phones and take pictures of Principal Rollins's door shutting as Baez goes in.

I wait for the hallway to clear and find a corner to crouch in. The whispers float above my head. The tremors ripple through me. This whole thing has spilled out, and now all the adults are "concerned." What will this all mean? What actually happened? Can he get in trouble for this? Can the stuff people say about you take things away—even if they're not true?

I skip AP Psychology and wait.

I skip lunch and wait.

People gaze at me. A few teachers try to tell me to get to class. I nod and say I am going, but I stay put. Adrenaline and worry are still erasing my appetite.

I can't take my eyes off that door. Away from that office.

I hear the rumors repeated as everyone changes classes again.

"Nasty photos. Someone took them of her naked body. They're everywhere." Freshmen whisper to freshmen, sophomores to juniors, the ripples getting bigger until they become a roaring tidal wave, ready to take down everything in its path.

"I bet she wanted it."

"Can you blame her?"

"Do you think she was trying to be sexy or something?"

"They're going to make an example out of him."

"Are the parents pressing charges?"

It's endless, a cycle, a dog chasing its own tail like a fool, never to catch it.

"Stop talking about it," I bark at them, and the whole hall goes silent.

They look startled. And if I'm honest, afraid.

A teacher asks me to cool off and leave the hall, but I ignore her. She threatens to call my parents—because she doesn't know how ridiculous my dad is—and I tell her to go ahead and do it. I don't even care if I get detention at this point. Even though I never have, in my twelve years at Foxham.

I'm frozen in place.

I'm in a bubble that might never burst.

The office doors swing open. Baez shuffles out. Shoulders sagged. Feet dragging. His parents follow. He's headed for the entrance foyer and out the front doors.

What happened that night?

BAEZ AND GEORGIE WERE COZYING UP SOLO AT CORA'S PARTY.

BAEZ AND GEORGIE DEFINITELY MADE OUT UPSTAIRS IN CORA'S BEDROOM.

COMPLETE AND TOTAL YOU-KNOW-WHAT AT JASE'S PARTY.

GEORGIE AND BAEZ HAVE BEEN FOOLING AROUND FOR MONTHS BEHIND CORA'S BACK.

CORA PUT GEORGIE ON THE CHEERLEADING TEAM TO KEEP AN EYE ON HER.

GEORGIE AND JASE HOOKED UP IN THE PHOTO BOOTH AT SCHOOL.

BAEZ AND GEORGIE HAD SEX AT HIS BIRTHDAY PARTY.

CORA AND BAEZ HAD A MASSIVE FIGHT. IT'S OVER.

GEORGIE IS HOOKING UP WITH RILEY NOW TO MAKE BAEZ JEALOUS.

CORA THREW GEORGIE OFF THE CHEERLEADING TEAM BECAUSE IT WAS CONFIRMED. GEORGIE AND BAEZ TOTALLY HOOKED UP BEHIND CORA'S BACK.

CORA'S MOVED ON QUICK-HOOKING UP WITH EX-GIRLFRIEND JUJU OLIVIERI-ORTIZ, CHANCE'S FAMOUS COUSIN AND OLD FOXHAM STUDENT.

BAEZ, GEORGIE, AND JASE HAD A THREESOME. AND THERE ARE PHOTOS.

IT WASN'T A THREESOME. IT WAS A DIRTY PHOTO SHOOT.

From: Principal Rollins
Attn: Foxham Listserv
Sent: November 18, 3:25 PM
Subject: A Message from Foxham Prep

Dear Foxham Community,

As parents may have heard from their Foxham Prep students, police were on campus today to interview two seniors, both of whom have been accused of inappropriate behavior with a fellow student.

We are investigating the situation, and the faculty and staff at Foxham are cooperating however necessary with the authorities.

We also addressed student concerns today in a mandatory session to prepare students for further discussion around sexual assault, abuse, the rules of consent in sexual interactions, and putting lewd photos on the internet. Our counselors will be standing by for questions, concerns, and support.

If you have questions or concerns regarding this matter, please reach out to counselor Mrs. Ramirez or myself; we would be happy to further discuss our approach and further actions.

Thank you, as always, for entrusting us with the care and education of your children.

Sincerely,
Principal Rollins

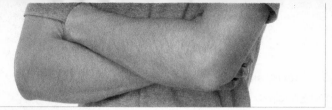

JaseThaGod202

Monday, November 18, 7:56 p.m.

♡ 4769 ⬓ 9345

Didn't hook up with Georgie. Not my type. I'm all about blonds
. . . plus, I'm allergic to curry.

FilmmakerChance: You're a douche.
57 mins   ♡ 236

LaLaLeahJenkins42: All girls are your type. You're a liar.
55 mins   ♡ 15

AmirNotKhan007: Racist!
53 mins   ♡ 34

FilmmakerChance: I've seen you with other girls.
53 mins   ♡ 62

NicoMuyRico020304: Fucking player dude.
52 mins   ♡ 100

AhMADManKhan: You're an ass, but like still my boy. Cool it on
the racist shit.
52 mins   ♡ 28

AJRiveriaTodelo301: You were all about that chick tho. I saw you
talking to her. All in her hair and shit.
49 mins   ♡ 28

BrynChildDC: You're a liar. Soon everyone will know it.
48 mins   ♡ 82

DeeSquared228Squad: You're trash. I don't know why anyone
hooks up with you.
43 mins   ♡ 140

PrincessChristine4578: I saw you go in the basement.
42 mins   ♡ 138

EstradaNada: Bro . . . this is shitty.
39 min   ♡ ·205

KatNotKateLee: You're a dick. Sasha should break up with you.
37 mins   ♡ 215

VibsterMD: Fuck you for the curry comment. There are so many cultures who eat curry, you fucking dick.
35 mins   ♡ 92

DialloNotDiablo: Not cool.
32 mins   ♡ 38

AdeleBelleParis1231: Take this down, Jase.
21 mins   ♡ 13

Comments Loading

Monday 9:26 PM

Bryn:

You okay?

Monday 9:28 PM

Bryn:

I called you a hundred times. Pick up.

I called your house.

Monday 9:41 PM

Bryn:

G, call me back please.

G? Please.

Monday 10:16 PM

Cora:

OMG! Are you okay, G?
I'm hearing so much shit.

Monday 10:27 PM

Cora:

This was all my fucking fault.

I'll tell the cops everything. I'm so so
sorry.

Monday 10:50 PM

Cora:

Can you please tell me what
happened? They're questioning Baez
and Jase.

????

The *Hill Tattler*

EXCLUSIVE

The *Tattler* can report exclusively that there's major drama unfolding at the posh Foxham Prep Academy, an $80,000-a-year private school that turns out future senators and lobbyists, educating the children of the elite among the DC political set. They're always having some sort of mess, though.

The misfit on campus has always been one Abaeze Onyekachi. Baez, as he's called at school, is a star player on the champion Foxham Prep lacrosse team, with strong college sport prospects. He's also the longtime love of Cora Davidson, daughter of esteemed White House counsel Edward Davidson.

But the two reportedly split, as Onyekachi was accused of hooking up with a fellow student. With a B average and a police record—for multiple traffic stops in the Foxham Prep neighborhood—Onyekachi's bright star is dulling fast. Neighbors say he's courteous and helpful. His father also has some questionable ties in their native Nigeria, which they visit "all too often," says a neighbor, who calls the boy a thug. "Knocked over my trash cans the other day. Didn't even say sorry. You're American now. Stick to America or go home."

GEORGIE

MONDAY, NOVEMBER 18
11:04 A.M.

"NOW, BETA, TELL US, WHAT IS HAPPENING?" MUM ASKS, and I'm surprised her voice isn't full of anger. "What is going on? You wouldn't talk to the police. But you must talk to us."

She and Papa are sitting on opposite sides of me at the kitchen table. The first time we've all been in the same room in months.

Papa stares at me like I'm a broken doll, the porcelain bits in scattered pieces all over the floor. My heart drops, each beat sending waves of heat and shame to every part of my body.

Nita Masi brings me a cup of water, warm with honey and lemon, and nods toward the stove, where she's already put the chai on. She sets out a plate of aloo parathas for breakfast. The warm bread oozes with butter. I haven't been allowed to touch them in months. Mum fusses for a second but then nods. I can't bring myself to reach for one, though. My stomach is a mess of nerves as I prepare to tell my parents everything that's been happening, everything I can remember about Saturday night, to unravel all the lies I've told. And my head is floating from the weed still in my system.

"What is going on?" Mum presses. "What happened that night?"

"Be patient," Papa interjects. "You heard what the doctor just said. He hasn't been out the door but five minutes. She still has so much THC in her system."

Mum scoffs at him.

I take a deep breath. "I can't remember everything . . . but I do know that something bad happened to me," I say.

Mum gasps.

My whole body still feels strange and floaty. "I went to a party on Saturday night."

"A party?" Mum replies.

"Yes, a party. I have new friends. Well, *had,* briefly. My life's changed."

"It seems so," Mum snaps back. "All the Aunties can talk about is you right now. How different Jashan is. How Jashan is not the same girl they knew. The things they're saying."

"Enough." Papa puts his hand up. "Let her speak."

Mum doesn't even look at Papa. It's the first time he's been home in weeks.

"I made so many mistakes." I take a deep breath and let the truth pour out. How I wanted a new life after coming home from weight loss camp. How I wanted to try on a new personality. Be less like me and more like Mum. How I wanted to know how to chitchat and to have friends and to have people want to be around me. Social. Well liked. I skip the gory details—the rumors, cheerleading, Riley. And then I'm there again, at the party. The thrum of the music, the flash of pink lights. How I ate a lot of brownies, not knowing that they had weed in them, and all I can remember is dancing and then needing to lie down. How I woke up naked and covered with a dirty jersey. How all I could remember was a flashing light. How all I heard was laughter and the sound of vomiting. How I know something bad happened to me.

The sobs feel like they start way down in my toes, working their way up through every inch of muscle, through my calves, into my thighs, up through my stomach and chest and arms. I'm shaking with the force of them. Mum rubs my back, making small circles at the center of it like she did when I was a small child and couldn't sleep. "Shhhh," she says, wrapping her arms around me. "Shhhhhh, beta, it'll be okay."

Her voice breaks, the usual strength filling with hiccups.

"I just want you to be happy, beta," Mum says. "That's all I ever wanted."

"But you wanted me to do what made *you* happy and not what made *me* happy."

Her voice wobbles. "I was trying to do what I thought was best for you. Teach you how to be successful." She looks away from me. "All that weight felt like you were carrying around what happened to you back home."

"I was. But it wasn't in my body, Mum." The realizations hit me in waves along with the sobs. One after the other, a tsunami of truths. "There was nothing wrong with my body. There was nothing wrong with the way I looked. There was something wrong with what happened to me. But we never talked about it. We never talk about anything out-side of suitable grades, suitable activities, suitable boys, and how suitable Indian girls are supposed to represent their mothers."

Mum puts a hand to her mouth. She's trying to keep her lip from trembling, to bite back the tears. "Maybe I was wrong, beta. Maybe you should blame me. But I tried my best."

"Boarding school. That's what we need to do," Papa says, his voice firm. "We should've done it to start."

"*You* said no when I brought that up," Mum reminds him.

They argue in a flurry of Punjabi and English.

"Enough!" I shout, standing, towering over them even though it feels like I might topple us all. "Ever since we left India, you've been talking over me. Talking *about* me. Deciding who I was going to be. What I'm supposed to do. As if all of these plots and plans could erase what happened to me. To us. Back home. But it happened. We need to stop pretending it didn't."

Mum jumps up. She raises her palm, trying to silence the truth again. To bury it, and me, alive.

"No!" I yell even louder. "You turned me into a victim. I didn't know how to say it out loud. I didn't know how to learn to remember what happened, to process it, to move through it. You made me hide, erase it. But it happened. And now something bad happened again."

A hot tear slowly rolls down Papa's cheek. "Who did it? Who took those photos of you? I will make them pay. Rajesh Uncle is getting them all taken down as we speak. We will sue!"

"I don't know. . . . I can't remember. . . . But I *will* figure it out!" I shout, my words silencing theirs for the first time in my entire life. "I made a mistake. I let people believe things about me, thinking I could control it. I have to tell everyone the truth. I have to piece together who did this to me. I will cooperate. I need you to trust me for once."

The November-evening sky is dark and mean, shot through with gray and streaks of thunder. The warning is clear: *Stay home. Do what you're told.*

I stare out at the soft snow that's turned into black ice lining the streets as I wait. Principal Rollins, Mrs. Ramirez, and the police are on their way. Better these conversations take place in private spaces, Mum said when she called. Where they might still be swept away, or denied altogether.

My stomach roils, empty and acidic. But this time I will have my say. I need to figure out my truth, no matter what the cost.

Mum shifts in her seat, fussing with her cardigan and releasing a series of upset hums. Papa paces back and forth.

"Are you sure?" he asks again and again, the worry heavy on his brow and in his voice. "We can switch you right now. No meeting. Nothing. There are other options. Your pupils are still dilated. Those drugs are still in your system." Worry lines his face now, making him look so much older. "You don't have to go back to the school," he says again. "We don't even have to have this meeting. We can change our minds. They can turn around and leave."

"I want to."

"We can look at other schools. I spoke to the principal at Fairfax Academy in Northern Virginia, and he said he'd be happy—"

"Papa, I don't want to move."

"You can do independent study. Or even get your GED."

"I want to graduate from Foxham. I think I've earned that."

"We can even look at a boarding school, maybe in Switzerland."

"No."

I start climbing out of the chair, but Papa grabs my hand. "Beta, I just want the best for you. I'm worried about you. And I don't know how to fix this. I don't know how to make you better."

Mum barks at him in Punjabi—that it's his fault. That he disappeared into the arms of his mistress, leaving her to clean up the mess. That maybe, together, they could have figured it out.

"There's nothing you can do to fix it, Papa," I say. There's nothing anyone can do.

I have to handle this myself.

My phone buzzes in my lap. All the messages toppling my social media. The whispers and comments swarm and sting like wasps. Cora said not to look. That it might just kill me. She was probably right.

"She's ruining their lives."

"Baez is going to quit school because of her."

"Jase's family is gearing up to sue. He's denying anything."

"So much potential. She killed it all."

"She was wearing Baez's jersey. Clearly, they're still messing around and she panicked."

"Slut."

"Bitch."

"Whore."

"She shouldn't have worn that skirt if she didn't want people looking."

"I bet she staged those photos herself. Trying to show off."

I didn't do anything wrong. That's what I tell myself, over and over again, squeezing my eyes shut, desperate to remember something, anything, about what happened. About who took those photos. I look straight ahead, trying to focus on my reality here in this room, instead of letting all those amorphous voices into my head.

I take a deep breath, try to stop my brain from spiraling with all the things Rollins will no doubt reveal in this meeting that will make me look like I asked for it, or that it was my fault, or that if only I'd done something differently . . . I try to stop the shakes and the sobs that rise up in my throat. I have to stay composed. But I can just imagine what they'll think of me when they hear.

That I would put myself in that situation.

That I wanted to be seen. By these boys.

Strangers to them and celebrities to those in Foxham's halls.

But I didn't ask for this. I didn't do anything to deserve it.

I wanted to dance with Riley all night.

I wanted to laugh at his corny jokes.

I wanted to stick to Cora's plan, to figure out how to end the torture.

The past has come back to haunt me, to swallow me whole.

But this time, I won't be silent.

The doorbell rings.

Principal Rollins is pleasant, but his face is grim as he enters my home. Mrs. Ramirez's eyes are bloodshot and droopy, and it seems like she's been crying as much as I have. Three police officers, two women and one man, follow close behind. I scan their name tags: Officer Woolsworth, Officer Rodriguez, and Officer Sherman. Each one nods at me, eyes full of pity and concern.

Rollins clears his throat a few times, looking at my parents. Nita Masi offers chai and snacks. Everyone politely declines. One of the officers turns down the volume on her walkie-talkie.

"What shall we do about this, officers?" Mum says, her voice squeaking like a young child's. This is not the Mum I know. The panic is growing; I can see it in the way she clenches the arm of the chair, the way the veins on her thin brown hands leap out. "Please. We're very concerned."

"I want you to be prepared—especially you, Georgie—for what they're about to show you. I don't know if you actually want to see it."

"I want to see everything," I say. "It's all so fuzzy."

My papa puts his hand on mine, and his voice is firm when he finally speaks. "We are prepared, Principal Rollins. We want to know exactly what's going on, officers."

Officer Woolsworth pulls out an overstuffed file. It's marked with my name, alongside Baez's name. There are endless sheaves of paper inside of it, and at the top, some printouts of photographs. My mother cranes to see what they show, but Rollins clears his throat again.

"I should warn you, these are quite graphic," he says, but my mother snatches the file out of the officer's hands before he can say more.

She spreads the images out in her lap.

It's worse than I thought. Way worse.

The tears are already streaming, unstoppable now, as I look at the images. The night rushes back to me in waves.

I recognize Jase's house, the living room. Pictures of kids dancing, including me and Riley. I'm clearly high, laughing. Though I didn't mean to take anything. The pink of his teeth. And then I remember. The basement room. Baez, throwing up in the bathroom. How out of it he was. Head in the toilet bowl.

And then the cold. Waking up alone in that room, in that bed, the way my skin rose with goose bumps, the way my body shook with chills. Then Riley finding me. Him calling the cops.

But that's not even the worst of it.

The evidence they show us is far more horrifying. I can't even begin to process it. The room, lit bright.

My body, naked, my dress gone. I look way past high. I look dead.

But there's more. The jersey. Baez's jersey. Thiry-three. Baez passed out, his legs poking out from the bathroom door. I lay facedown, passed out cold. These images feel seared into my flesh like brands.

My parents are frozen in place, my papa's face flushed red with rage and defeat. My mum shakes in her chair, unable to speak or do anything except sob.

"Riley Wong called the police that night after finding you in the bed," Officer Rodriguez says. He turns to my parents. "We are gathering student statements, and we are awaiting additional reports. Since Georgie is a minor, posting naked photos of her constitutes child pornography, and thus, a felony. Lawyers are involved, but charges can't be pressed without your—and Georgie's—consent."

"Absolutely not," Mum says immediately, falling back into that mode she did the first time back in India. "These images might be photoshopped. That doesn't look like my daughter's body at all." And she would know, right? She's only been policing it forever. "We don't want any trouble or any press."

Papa looks weary, worried, tired. He's not sure what to do, and I can see the exhaustion—and fear—all over his face. He still blames himself for last time. But Mum was in charge then, and it seems she still is now.

Officer Sherman purses her lips. "We'll need a statement."

Principal Rollins leans forward. "Georgie, I urge you to think long and hard. And I want you to know this: I'm on Team Georgie, no matter what. If you decide to move forward and press charges, Foxham Prep is behind you. If you want to keep this quiet, that is your choice, and we will honor that choice. But either way, we cannot allow this sort of thing to happen here. Do you understand? We must not allow this to be part of the culture of our school."

"She won't be—" Mum starts to say.

"I will decide," I reply, cutting her off.

As Rollins rises to leave, Mrs. Ramirez does, too. She gives my parents her card and turns to me. "Georgie, I'm here if you need me. If you want to talk, my door is always open—and I'm happy to come to you, too, or refer you to someone who has strategies and techniques for approaching a situation like this."

I nod again, exhausted by the pity, and my mother looks down at the card, a sneer in her smile. "Thank you, dear," she says, "but Georgie has a trusted family therapist we'll take this to. She's had some, uh, issues, in the past, and the therapist knows the history well." She holds out her hand to shake Mrs. Ramirez's and then turns to Principal Rollins. "We'll be in touch." She ushers them all, including the police officers, out of the room.

I help Nita Masi clean up while my parents continue to argue. The sound of their screams make me drop a teacup, splattering chai all over my T-shirt and the floor.

Nita Masi *tsk*s and tells me not to touch the broken shards. I fuss with my T-shirt, trying to control the fresh wave of tears, as I bend down to gather the glass anyway.

"Beta," Nita Masi says, stepping closer, ready to shoo me away. Her expression turns strange, confused. "What's on your back?"

"What?" I crane to look. "Is it chai?"

Her warm fingers lift the back of my T-shirt, tugging down my pants a little.

"Words here." Her touch lands on the small of my back, and I flinch.

"What?" I stretch even harder to try to see. "What does it say?"

"White boys do it better," she reads in her thick accent, then steps away, horrified.

My heart drops into my stomach.

"What does that mean?" The tears cloud her voice. "Who would mark your skin like this?"

Jase.

Monday 11:32 PM

UNKNOWN:

Watch yourself, Georgie. Wouldn't want to have to hurt you for telling lies.

Georgie:

Who is this?

Who are you?

Monica:

G, you okay?

Georgie:

Not really.

Monica:

Here if you need me or want to talk.

STUDENT STATEMENTS:

Ruthie Alvarez: "Oh yeah, I saw her go in the room with Jase, and Baez was in the bathroom. He was a mess after fighting with Cora. He was so trashed. I thought Georgie was into it. She has a, uh, history with both of them. But we were all pretty trashed that night, and I passed out. I wish I could have done something to help."

Sasha Lucas: "Jase was with me for most of the night, but I left around one a.m. Like Ruthie, I was kind of drunk, and my leg gives me trouble ever since the accident. I've seen her flirt with both of them before. I don't think either of them actually *need* to take naked photos of anyone. I mean, they're with two of the most beautiful girls at Foxham Prep. I think Georgie's making up lies for attention. I heard it wouldn't be the first time. She's just trying to show off."

Vibha Srinivasan: "I mean, this explains so much. Jashan really hasn't been herself this whole semester, and I—we all—treated her terribly. I just want to say, I'm here if she needs someone. I know her parents will be devastated. Have you called them yet? Oh god, I can't even imagine. Poor Jashan. Maybe I should talk to her? Do you know where she is now?"

Anthony Richards: "I don't know what that girl's claiming, but my boys didn't leave my sight that night—there was no foul play. Jase and Baez were with me. They had mad shit to clean up during the party. But if there was a photo shoot, and I'm not saying there wasn't some sexual activity, it was definitely consensual. That girl's been asking for it for months, wearing all those tight-ass sweaters and short skirts and shit."

Frankie Russo: "Georgie was all about taking pictures before. Her whole social media is full of selfies. I saw her taking pictures with Riley. She's super vain and thinks she's better than everyone else. I bet she took those photos herself. I bet she wanted everyone to see her new body. So many people do that."

CORA

TUESDAY, NOVEMBER 19
9:05 A.M.

I SKIP SCHOOL AFTER TEXTING MOMMA THAT I JUST GOT MY period and have terrible cramps. In the hall, I hear her on the phone with Mr. Yonas, the school secretary, as I scoot through the bathroom and into Millie's room.

"Wake up," I say, rustling her covers. "Please, *please*."

Millie grumbles and turns over. "Ugh, I was up late finishing a paper. Go away."

"C'mon, Millie. I need you." I get in bed with her and shake her. She pulls away and protests.

"Okay!" She snatches off her eye mask and reluctantly sits up. "I'm up . . . I'm up." Her pink scarf slides off and her hair is a mess.

I hand her my phone, the article about Baez being interrogated by police and Jase refusing to cooperate. "There are so many of these. Ones about Foxham, too. They're already saying Baez is guilty. That he took those photos and uploaded them." I start to pace in front of her bed. I don't know what to do with my body. "But he couldn't have. I still have his phone. Should I call the police and tell them?"

"Shit, maybe we should've outed Chance right away," Millie says.

"Yeah, but you know that doesn't erase what people have already decided to believe."

"Slow down. Let me think." Millie clicks through everything. "None of this shit is true. Where do they get their sources? *'Abaeze Onyekachi seen bragging about his exploits. Abaeze Onyekachi, a known playboy according to student sources.'*"

"I set up an alert. That way I can see them all." My empty stomach bubbles up. The statements clawing at my skin. "It's all lies. This is so, so, so bad."

She gets up and goes to her computer. "We were both there. What happened after I left?" Her eyes narrow and her brow furrows, a sign that her super-logical brain is chewing on this puzzle. "Go through it."

I smash my shaky hands on top of my head, trying to give them something to do, so they'll stop shaking. "Baez and I had our fake fight. He had had too much to drink. Was on the edge of a migraine again. You were there beside me."

"I know, I know. But I left right after. Those brownies made me all sick."

"Yeah, 'cause Jase put weed and who knows what else in them."

"What the hell? Who does that? Isn't that illegal? He basically drugged everyone without telling anyone."

"It's Jase. He always does what he wants."

My phone pings with more alerts and notifications. I'm afraid to ask her what they say.

"Keep going," Millie presses.

"Okay, so we fought. Baez threw up. It was terrible. Graham took him to the basement bathroom to clean up. That's the last time I saw him."

"Wait . . . wait!" Millie looks up at me. "Graham said he took him home when he left the party to get ready for his family's flight." She puts down my phone and picks up hers. She calls Graham. "C'mon, c'mon, pick up."

I'm sweating. I go to her window and crack it. The cold November air pushes inside.

"What time is it?" she asks.

"Nine thirty."

"Then it's three thirty in the morning in Hawaii. He's knocked out."

"Shit, shit, shit." I feel like I might vomit all over her windowsill.

Millie gets up and puts her cool hands on the back of my neck. "Calm down. He'll be awake soon. He'll tell us what happened. Everything will be cleared up. Baez wasn't in that room with Georgie. He didn't do this. We know that."

"How is he going to explain that jersey?" I ask, a pit burning inside me.

"He threw up all over it. He probably took it off. Stop stressing. Stop worrying."

"I can't." I pull away from her. Two seconds from a meltdown.

My phone goes off again. It's the tone I set for Georgie. I almost fall trying to get to it. She's texting me, one after the other. I fumble with my password and click them open.

It's a picture of brown skin with the words *White boys do it better*. Millie looks over my shoulder.

"What is that?" she asks.

"I don't know." I quickly text Georgie back.

She writes: Jase. He wrote it on me.

I call her. She clicks me to voicemail and writes that she can't talk because of her parents and the lawyers.

"What's happening?" Millie asks.

"I don't know." A headache punches its way into my temples.

Her final text: Jase's family refuses to cooperate and is threatening to sue. I have to give my phone back to my mom. I'll text you later.

"What are we going to do?" I say.

"Clear Baez's name *and* confront Chance about those rumors. It all led to this," she says. "Let's get to work. Momma and Daddy leave after brunch."

We make eye contact and touch foreheads.

We're going to fix this.

We have to.

I hide in the basement while Momma, Daddy, and Millie cook brunch. Their laughter drifts through the vents. Each piercing chuckle grates over my skin. I can't bring myself to join them, even though it would be the distraction I need and take me away from social media and all the notifications about what's happening. I just can't wait for them to go on their little anniversary vacation so Millie and I can stay behind and get to work.

My heart somersaults. Graham hasn't called Millie back yet. It's been three hours. Baez hasn't answered. Georgie hasn't had her phone again. My head is a storm—a sadness raining down, drowning me, and anger hot as lightning.

I throw my phone, then pick it up, then throw it again.

I wipe away tears I can't keep from falling. I don't want Momma or Daddy asking me a million questions. But I can't stop looking every few minutes.

There's a tap on the basement door.

"What?" I holler.

Millie's face appears, but then I hear Momma's voice drift down. "I know Coraline Emma Davidson is not yelling in my house."

"It's time to eat," Millie says with a shrug.

I drag myself upstairs. My stomach growls; the scents of honey biscuits and waffles and fried chicken wrap around me. But I don't think I can eat. The buzz of my phone is all I can think about.

I crash into my seat. Momma stares at me, a perfectly manicured eyebrow lifting with curiosity and annoyance. "Is something bothering you, Turtle? And on such a wonderful morning."

"Everything."

"Well, we won't be discussing all of that mess right now. Let's have one morning without stress," Daddy says.

"You can say the prayer," Momma says.

"Do I have to?"

Daddy clears his throat. "Your mother asked you to do something. When did we not do what we were told immediately? What's going on with both of my girls?"

Millie flashes me a look.

He opens his arms and flashes his palms upright. Momma slips one hand in his and one in mine. He closes his eyes. "Cora, if you would please bless the food."

I sigh. Tears swirl inside me, and I want to scream. "Dear Heavenly Father . . . we ask you to bless this food and the hands . . . that prepared it. . . ."

The doorbell rings.

I jump, then open my eyes.

Daddy stares at me. "Finish, please. Whomever that is will have to wait."

"For the nourishment of my body . . . and . . . Amen!"

I drop Momma's and Millie's hands.

"That left a lot to be desired," Momma replies. "Will you get the door, Millie? I don't know who that could possibly be."

Millie walks out of the room. Momma passes me a plate of fried chicken. I shake my head.

"Your appetite has been low. Please eat something." She takes my plate and makes it, piling it with waffles, chicken, bacon, and grits. "You not eating is not going to make everything with Baez and school any better."

"I'm fine," I lie.

She purses her lips. "You know I'm your mother, right? I'm in tune with you and know when something is wrong. You've been dragging your tail."

Millie returns with Baez at her side. He holds a bag of food from his restaurant. The liquid in my stomach bubbles up. A hot flash prickles my skin. His skin is a paler shade of brown, and his eyes are all blood-shot and puffy.

"Good morning, Mr. and Mrs. Davidson. I was wondering if I could speak to Cora for a minute or two." His hands and voice shake.

"Baez!" I rush over to him. "Are you okay?" I almost burst into tears.

"Cora, did you invite company over?" Daddy asks.

"Oh, no, sir. She didn't know I was—" But I tackle him and knock the words out of him.

"Can I have a few minutes?" I ask, barely able to keep my voice from breaking.

Momma and Daddy exchange a concerned look.

"Five minutes," he says, his tone a warning.

I slip into the hall. But I can feel their unease lingering. I close the dining room doors behind me.

"My parents pulled me out of Foxham." His shoulders slump forward, and big tears race down his cheeks.

I close the gap between us.

"I swear to you, I didn't do anything." He dissolves into a heap of tears.

I wrap my arms around him. "I know. I know. I'm going to prove it. I'm so sorry I dragged you into this." Tears rush down my cheeks as I watch him cry.

"I didn't do it. I would never do anything like that. Not to you, and not to her." His shoulders jump up and down. "Graham dropped me off at home. I left my jersey behind. It was covered in puke."

"I know, I know," I say.

"Graham's going to come back from vacation in Hawaii and give a statement. He promised."

Relief surges through me. "And I have your phone." I take it from my pocket and hand it to him. "How could you even take pictures of someone with no phone—"

The dining room doors snap open, and Daddy walks into the foyer. He stares down at an inconsolable Baez. Daddy's brown skin is wrinkled with frustration and annoyance. "Son, it's time for you to leave. And I'm not comfortable with you seeing my daughter anymore. Not with all that you have going on. I don't know the details, but I'm not happy with the things I've read. All I know is that it's time for you both to take a break until it's all figured out."

"But, Daddy—"

Baez's still shaking as my father grabs his arm and leads him out, but he goes without a fuss, looking back at me as he does. His eyes are pleading, his body racked with stress. I just want to reach out and pull him into a hug, to lock the two of us away forever, to let the world and all its terrors fall away.

But he's gone before I can say a single word.

FilmmakerChance

Tuesday, November 19, 8:12 p.m.

♡ 599   🔍 6987

What really happened that night? Who was there? What did you see? Don't believe the fake news.

HarperSebastian612: Georgie had had so many brownies. So did I. We were all a mess. There wasn't just weed in them.
57 mins   ♡ 236

ABadassMelody: Georgie was assaulted. Even photographing someone against their will is a violation. Believe women.
55 mins   ♡ 15

RajLikeKing: I saw Georgie on the couch, then she was gone.
53 mins   ♡ 34

PrincessChristine4578: Take this down. It isn't cool to speculate.
52 mins   ♡ 100

Hugh67898: Something bad went down. Somebody needs to come clean.
52 mins   ♡ 28

AJRiveriaTodelo301: She's a liar, yo.
49 mins   ♡ 28

AhMADManKhan: Everybody was real fucked up that night. I can't even remember. Like, at all. Jase isn't so deranged that he'd roofie the brownies, would he?
48 mins   ♡ 82

DeeSquared228Squad: I feel bad for Georgie. Y'all are frying her.
43 mins   ♡ 140

KatNotKateLee: Georgie shouldn't have had the punch and all those brownies.
42 mins   ♡ 138

AdeleBelleParis1231: Stop victim-blaming.
39 mins   ♡ 205

KeishaSoFly: Believe her.
37 mins   ♡ 215

BrynChildDC: Don't talk about her like this.
35 mins   ♡ 92

ChaseTheGirls: I heard she wanted it.
32 mins   ♡ 38

AdeleBelleParis1231: Shut up ChaseTheGirls. You're trash.
21 mins   ♡ 13

TateNotTotBro1289: Somebody is lying tho. And Georgie's been a huge slut.
12 mins   ♡ 16

Comments Loading

ONLINE POLL

Is Georgie lying for attention?

| YES | NO |

Cora:

This is all my fault. Those fucking rumors lead to this shit . . . everything is a mess.

Please tell me you're ok or not ok . . . or just something.

I'm so angry and upset and I want to scream at everyone. I'm furious with it all.

Friday 9:45 PM

Georgie:

I'm not ok.

I'm fucking pissed.

I'm fucking sad.

I'm fucking angry.

Friday 9:46 PM

Cora:

They need to pay.

Georgie:

All of them.

Cora:

So should I still throw the party this weekend? Should we still do the plan? I'm not sure now. Like, I'm so freaking worried.

Georgie:

Yes. We have to.
They have to pay, Cora.

Cora:

You sure? Maybe we shouldn't do the whole thing.

Georgie:

We're going to out two people now.
Chance and Jase.

Cora:

Bet.

BRYN

THURSDAY, NOVEMBER 21
6:43 P.M.

MOM DOESN'T SAY ANYTHING ABOUT MY HAIR OR THE MESS in the pool house when she brings me dinner out here. Her first night back, but none of us can muster the strength to actually celebrate. So I'm holed up, combing through all of Chance's camera footage, loading it on my computer, and relishing how I went back and stole it right from under a passed out Chance at Jase's party.

Back before her latest stint in rehab, she'd poke her head in, say two or three words, but then leave me be. She's all about respecting boundaries and keeping safe spaces and all that. I don't know if it's freedom, or some kind of carefully metered punishment. Maybe a bit of both. I'm sure she has some textbook reason for it. But today, she's come in here twice already.

I feel her eyes flit over me, examining my hair, but she won't say anything even if she thinks it's a mess. If I asked for her opinion, she'd just deflect: *Do you like it? What do you think about it? Is it everything you wanted it to be?* and turn it into a therapy moment. Happens every time she returns from rehab. She always says that unnecessary parental commentary and criticism during adolescence can stunt one's sense of self. But then I just never really end up knowing how she feels about me. Or anything I do. Maybe if I tattooed a skull and crossbones on my forehead she'd say something.

"How is Georgie? I sent flowers after what I read in the papers. People can be so cruel, and your generation really misuses social media. It'll be so hard to wipe the internet clean of those pictures," Mom says. Her nails are painted burgundy and make her fingers look like sticks of chalk. I told her about those dark colors with her super-white skin. Not cute. But she says I have a need to control everything, and she won't be subjected to it. "I need to go over and see her mother. She's called me twice about getting together. Come sit here."

"Ugh, I'm busy," I say, not looking up from the camera.

"Your dad wishes you'd come inside and eat with us," she says. He's probably at the dinner table picking at the food Mom made and poring over White House briefs.

I ignore her comment. My head is a mess of guilt and worry about how I'm going to help Cora help Baez and also make sure no one finds out about the rumors and SykeWard and me.

"You fix what we talked about?" Mom uncovers what looks like a chunk of a green bean casserole and a slice of meat loaf.

My shoulders jump, like I've been hit in the back. "I don't want to talk about it. I'm trying." I scramble out of bed and sit at the desk. I am actually hungry today. Which is a first.

"Sorry," she says, retreating to sit on the bed.

"Are you going to sit and watch me eat?" I ask, mid-chew. It's making me nervous.

"Yes," she answers.

"Why?" I stare into the chunky bits of meat loaf, instead of at her blue eyes.

"I've missed you. Missed simple things like these."

A hot pit threatens to tear a hole in my stomach. I want to scream in her face . . . and Dad's, too. I can't deal with any of this right now. Everything is falling apart, and she's waltzed back in here after being gone expecting to be missed, expecting to pick up right where we left off. I don't have time for this.

I chew a little food and flash it to her in my mouth. "Maybe you should just feed me, too."

She changes the subject, which she often does when she feels uncomfortable. "How's school with the scandal happening? Are you planning something special as school president?"

"It's fine."

I stuff down any opportunity for a response with her too-dry meat loaf. She doles out advice I didn't ask for. "Don't bottle it up," she's saying again, for the gazillionth time since the whole thing happened. "Engage with people—even bring it up first to deflate the tension. Stay positive."

I spit the half-chewed wad of food into a napkin. "Mom! Leave me alone." The words are harsh and I hate them right after I say them, but I just can't with this shit right now.

Her face twists and she leaves.

I turn back to the camera. The footage files pop up. He's got a million clips on here.

The latest from Jase's party. His grinning face fills the frame. A memory pushes its way in no matter what I do. We met at this holiday brunch at the old folks' home that my mom was involved in planning; it was for some charity or other. My parents believe giving to charity is part of living a well-balanced life.

I was all dolled up, my hair a shock of bright red—holiday spirit, I kept telling Mom, who was livid—and I had this red-and-green pleated skirt on with my black leggings and a green sweater. Thinking back, I probably looked like an elf. A cute little elf. Mom should have been pleased. I even brought dreidels and chocolate gelt. It was the ultimate Chrismukkah situation. I looked festive. She is the first one to say that people who have had trauma happen to them should try to celebrate holidays and "rediscover" what's beautiful about the human community.

I always need to rediscover that, as if my mind's put it in a little box hidden away.

Jase was the only other person my age there—his aunt was on the board and insisted he come, too. We didn't speak for the first half of the brunch, but he kept catching my eye and making funny faces at the speeches the old people made, about community and charity and the holiday season. When they all finally sat down to eat their pancakes and eggs, he stole the seat right next to me.

"I'm Jase," he said. "Just moved here from South Carolina. And you? Imported from the North Pole?"

It wasn't funny. And I'll never forgive myself, but I giggled. Like one of those girls. I batted my lashes and flirted. It worked. Because by the time I got home, at 2:30, Jase had texted me five little words: *When can I see you?* I'll never forget them.

He came to the pool house later that night, and he stayed the night. And every night after that. For months. We talked about everything. The lazy parenting our generation received, vapid youth, white privilege, the war in Afghanistan, stem cell research. He had the most fascinating brain. He was the new kid in the tenth grade. I was his tour guide. We mapped out plans for the future, and the future was bright.

I look over a list of things we said we'd do. Looking at it now, I realize it doesn't even sound like me. The girl who made the list sounds idealistic, like a fool, a lovesick idiot with no real ambition of her own.

But I liked her. I liked being her. I could have been her forever. I thought we'd be together forever.

I move away from the computer and lie in my bed, staring at the ceiling. Glow-in-the-dark star stickers I put up there years ago jump around as I open and close each eye randomly. The accident threatens to wiggle its way back into my memory.

I remember following them. I remember seeing one girl kiss his cheek through the mirror. I remember the thrill of running the light. I remember the heavy noise his car made when it hit the other, and the sound of crunching and glass shattering and the hot burn of the airbags.

I jump out of bed to get away from the stars and the light and the memories. I grab an iced coffee from my fridge and pace a little. I try to think of anything and everything else.

I click play on the video. It's footage from the party night. Chance's stupid interviews. He's asking a thousand people about the rumors, speculating, getting their opinions, even expanding on them. Jase's recorded voice sends a shiver over my skin. He's talking about the rumors, Georgie, and how hot she is. Then it cuts to Christine, but in the background, I watch a replay of Jase catching me at his party and kicking me out. But then, I spot Jase leading Georgie through the basement door.

I click and rewind. I watch again. And again. And again. *Is this evidence?*

I flip open my notebook, my eyes combing through the clipped pages of scribbled details, notes fished from trash cans, sad photos of Baez and Cora's fight, screenshots of comments and pics that climb right off the page. The projector I connected to a second computer flashes a social media feed. The rumors feel alive, writhing along the wall, ready to explode with possibility. I play more video clips from Chance's camera. There's one of Cora and Baez's fight, and I let it repeat over and over again until I can recite it. I stare at it until my eyes cross and blur and the pages and pictures lift from the wall like tiny bees.

I have to calm down. I have to breathe.

Focus, Bryn. Find what you need to clear your name—and Baez's. Otherwise everything you worked so hard to get back . . . will be gone.

Bryn:

Cora—this is going to sound crazy, but I feel like Chance had something to do with those rumors.

Cora:

Not crazy. I've been thinking the same thing.

What you got?

Bryn:

Footage. Also, interesting stuff about Jase.

Cora:

•ᴗ•

Bryn:

Let's say I have footage that will help all of us.

Cora:

Spill.

Bryn:

Going thru it. Show you tmw?

Cora:

Come over early.

Bryn:

Cool.

Cora:

You ok?

Still ready for the plan?

Should we just not do this? It's ok if you've changed your mind.

Georgie:

I'm ready. We have to. We have to make them pay.

I need this.

Cora:

Bryn has something on Chance, too. She's going to show me. But at the party we will force the truth out of everyone. Millie is working on a video. Check your email.

Georgie:

Will do.

GEORGIE

FRIDAY, NOVEMBER 22
11:25 A.M.

"BETA, YOU HAVE TO EAT SOMETHING. ANYTHING." MUM TRIES to make her voice soothing. But it grates on me, making my stomach roil as I stare at the spread she's had Nita Masi lay out.

It's been three days since I've eaten anything solid. The thought pops into my head that this is the best diet Mum could've hoped for, because the very sight of food makes me violently ill. They've outdone themselves today: a saffron-streaked lamb biryani, cooling cucumber raita to offset the heat. Freshly made paneer pakora and Nita Masi's homemade mint chutney. Syrupy gulab jamun and a whole platter of sweet, crunchy jalebi, the once delightful Day-Glo orange now making me want to heave.

The things my body used to crave incessantly, things I'd sneak and steal, now cover the table as my mother begs me to eat. But I can't bring myself to take a single bite.

I don't know exactly who I'm punishing—her, for all the endless years of torture, all the pain and pinching she put me through. Or myself, for letting it happen.

Nita Masi steps close, trying to rub my back in that old, familiar way, and I leap out of the chair like she's burned me with fire. "Don't," I want to shriek, but it comes out a whisper. I don't know how to be in this body anymore. It took forever to figure it out last time, to reclaim it as much as I could. But I don't think I have it in me anymore.

The doorbell rings, and Nita Masi rushes off to answer it.

"Please eat, beta," Mum's voice begs. Some version of me, deep down inside, should be pleased with her pleading, a satisfactory turnaround given our history.

But I'm having a hard time finding that Georgie now. This one, all she knows is rage. And shame. Always shame.

"I can't." I stand. "I think I need to go lie down."

That's all I've done for the past few days. Lie in my bed, my pillow soaked with both angry and sad tears, and stare at the ceiling, trying to figure out how I let it all get this far, how I let it all happen. Just lying in the dark, letting the shame swallow me whole. Wishing I could just disappear.

But anger always wakes me up when I drift off. The desire for revenge, to hurt others like they've hurt me.

Nita Masi walks back in, a pained smile pasted on her face. "Babyji, you have company. A guest."

Vibha steps out from behind her. She's wearing khakis and a button-down, her backpack slung over her shoulder. Her little gold Model UN pin sits on the lapel of her blazer. For a minute, my heart lifts, happy to see her, familiar if nothing else. But then I deflate again. I can't take her scolding now.

"I was worried about you," she says, trying to keep her voice casual. "And I brought your homework and assignments from Mrs. Ramirez. Thought you might want them."

"Oh, I'm so glad," Mum says, clasping her hands excitedly, like she's just told me I got into Harvard or something. "Come, sit, I think Jashan can use some good company. Have a bite." She looks at Vibha meaningfully. A nudge. "Chat." She waves toward the food. "I'll go take care of some paperwork." She turns back to me. "I'll be in the study if you need me, okay, beta?"

I nod. Nita Masi fixes a few plates, exacting, careful, the chutney just so, a sliver of raw onion, just like I always have, and leaves them on the counter where the barstools are.

I stare at Vibha but don't move from my spot across the room.

She sits and pats the seat next to her. Like she would have done a long time ago, back when I was at her beck and call. I still don't move. She sighs. She picks at the plate. "I mean, I've been worried about you for a long time, as I've made clear. But, Jashan—" Her voice breaks a little, a rare show of emotion. "I had no idea. That it was this bad. I hope you're going to press charges. That Baez, I knew something was up with—"

"Baez didn't do anything," I say.

"Yes, he did. I read that—"

"And I was there. Remember? Playing the victim. The proper role in these situations, Vibs?"

Her eyebrows knit together. "Playing the victim? You *are* the victim. Right? Your mom told my mom—"

"Okay, so I think I get it now. If I actually, like, wanted to be with Baez—a Black boy—or Jase—a white boy—or even fucking Amir—"

She turns a livid red. Low blow.

"—then I'm disgusting." I take a deep breath, steeling myself. "But if I'm the *victim*, then oh, poor me, I need your support. At least to my face, right? When it's appropriate? Because I'm sure the Aunties will cross me right off their eligible-brides lists once they find out I've been ruined. My naked body splayed all over the internet."

Vibha stands and clasps my hand. The warmth of her touch is a shock. I snatch my hand away, taking a step back. "I should have told your mother when this first started," Vibha says. "I could have saved you from this, kept you from putting yourself in that situation. I mean, so many people have said that you deserve what you got, that you were asking for it—"

"That's what you think. Just like everyone else. I can see it all over your face. I *put myself* in that situation. I wore those clothes. I had a drink. I kissed a boy. I went to a party. I ate too many pot brownies that I didn't know had pot in them. Because I wanted to. And maybe I would have had sex, too, if I wanted to." Shock registers on her face. Tears are rolling down mine. "But I was never asking for it, Vibha. Not ever. Not before, not now. I never wanted to have my whole body on social media for everyone to comment on. So fuck off with your sanctimonious sympathy. I guess you've just proven what we knew all along. I really don't know you at all. And you never even began to know me. So, miss me with the protective didi act. You aren't my sister."

I'm crying, sobbing, the tears rippling through like a tidal wave, and I see them trickle, slow, soft, down her cheeks, too. I think she's going to pull her classic move, just turn on her heel and run, the way she's done so many times before.

But she steps closer, slowly, like I'm a deer about to bolt. She places a small palm on my shaking shoulder, runs gentle fingers through my hair. "I'm so sorry, Jashan. I really am. I didn't—I—I wasn't sure how to handle things, this new version of you, trying to take on everything and everyone all at once. The Jashan I knew—I didn't know how to let her go. I know I didn't help things; I know I hurt you. I'm sorry."

For a few moments, we just let the tears fall. She doesn't hug me or make me look at her, or push me to meet her eyes or expectations. Maybe for the first time since I've known her. And I don't say it's okay, or that it will ever be. But I'm grateful for the words, even if they might be too late.

She stands, abrupt. All business again. She opens her backpack, pulling out an endless stack of folders. "This is an important year. You haven't missed that much yet. You could still catch up, get back on track," she says in that familiar tone, like she's the mum and not a kid. Then she sighs. "Or let it go. Forget it. Either way. But I'll be here if you need anything. If I can help you." She zips up her bag, her mouth tight. "You know how to reach me."

I stare at the stack long after she's gone, then head back to my room, my bed, and darkness, letting an uneasy sleep take me.

My stomach growls. I left this afternoon's spread untouched again. If you could survive on sadness and rage, those would be my meals of choice right now. The house is dark, hushed, almost eerie.

I get out of bed. My brain needs something, anything, to soften the edges. I peer into Nanima's suite, and she's asleep again in the armchair, the glow of the TV bathing her in blue light. I tiptoe, quiet, into the room, settling at her feet the way I used to, resting my head soft in her lap, her pashmina shawl warm against my skin, reminding me not to cry. Not here.

I listen to her breath, feel her fingers stroke my cheek, far away and absentminded, and wonder if she sees this new version of me, if she realizes how much I've changed.

"I'm so angry, Nani," I whisper to her. Then the tears start again, thick and salty, and I know I have to pick myself up, to not ruin the one safe space. So I scramble up and toward the kitchen, and turn on only the light to the butler's pantry, just enough to see what's exactly in front of me.

Tea. That will do. Not the kettle, which could wake the dead with its whistle. Just the pot, a sprinkle of rose petals and fennel seeds, a small glob of honey. I watch it simmer, wishing it would boil over. Craving the burn.

A noise rustles. I stare at the pot, telling myself I'm imagining it. But my skin prickles. I peer out the back door and see the shadow there, and nearly jump.

A gentle rap at the kitchen door, light but insistent. Murderers don't knock and peek, right? Murderers plow through.

It happens again, the gentle *tap tap tap* on the outside gate as the shadow steps closer, takes shape.

Riley.

My heart leaps into my throat, happy and horrified, all at once. But he's still knocking, and Papa's probably asleep in the guest room, so I better answer it.

The door creaks as I open it and step back, my skin covered in gooseflesh.

He reaches for me immediately, the full force of his embrace envelops me, nearly knocking me over. "Thank god you're okay." He pulls back, looking down at me. "I'm so sorry. I didn't mean to scare you. I just had to see you."

My mouth hangs open, a tingle zips through me, along with a flash of heat. Guilt. Shame. Humiliation. How can he even look at me? How can he want to touch me? I pull away, the tears already a flood. I try to pay attention to what he's saying. But the secret whisper inside me gets louder and louder. All I keep thinking is, *This is my fault.*

I volley between anger and sadness every day . . . really every hour, and I can't seem to keep a grip on everything. I must have spoken out loud, because he steps closer again—making me flinch, even though I don't mean to—and whispers, "It's not." He shakes his head. "It's not your fault."

I swallow hard. His eyes are shiny, wet. Like he might cry. Kind of how I feel. "I reported all the pictures of you online," he says. "We shouldn't have been there at all. I shouldn't have left you alone. I was looking for you, upstairs, in the back, all through the house. The basement door was locked. I—" His voice cracks. "I should have known something was wrong. I'm sorry. I'm really sorry."

I shake my head. "It's not your fault. I shouldn't have—" I think about all the times I craved all the attention, the new Georgie. Should I be punished for it? *This is my fault.*

"We should—you should press charges on whoever put those photos up. I'll tell the police everything I know. I'll go with you, be right by your side."

I stare at him, the words not quite adding up.

"Do you understand?" He goes quiet, and I'd kind of give anything for him to just hold me. But the thought of him touching me at all makes me want to leap right out of my skin, and run away forever.

I take a deep breath. "I don't know if I can. I don't think I can deal with all of this—and so much worse—again. I don't think I can do that to my family again. And this time, all the questions, all the press, all the pictures. I don't think I'm strong enough."

"Again?" he asks.

I take a deep breath and tell him about Vivek's abuse and why my family left India.

Sadness floods his eyes. "I'm here. Whatever you choose to do. I'll be by your side—if you still want me to be."

I don't know when the tears started falling again. "You don't have to," I hear myself say, even though it pinches. "I get it if you don't want this. It's a lot. Too much. And I don't think I can do this, be with anyone, not really. Not for a long time."

He takes my hand, soft, careful, like I might break, entwining his fingers with mine. Watching to make sure I'm comfortable. "You don't have to be or do anything. I'll just be there when you need me, however you need me. Okay?"

I nod, stepping closer, allowing his arms to slip around me, allowing myself to be hugged. We stand there for what feels like forever, my breath slowing, my brain still racing.

A boom shatters the peace. A shriek of fire, like a series of Diwali patakas shooting in the air. Or gunshots. Loud, violent. They sound like they're coming from Nani's suite.

Riley darts to the window. "What is that?" he asks. "Is that—"

My father rushes into the kitchen then and stops cold, seeing Riley. A stranger in his house. "Who are you? What's—" The shout is drowned out by another series of shrieks.

Fireworks? Or something worse.

We race toward the back of the house. I stumble forward, a stench pushing inside. Embers shoot upward in the backyard, the doors to Nanima's bedroom porch cracked open.

Not fireworks, no.

Giant bags of shit, set ablaze.

As they start to burst, going up in flames.

And Nani sits asleep in the chair by the window, oblivious, lost to the world.

"Call 911—" Papa shouts to Riley, forgetting for a moment that he doesn't even know who he is. "Now!" He grabs an extinguisher from the utility room and runs out the door, aiming the hose at the porch.

Flames explode beside the house, too. I dart past, pulling at the door.

Mum races in, her face a mixture of shock and horror, as sirens scream in the distance.

"What's happening?" she shouts. Nita Masi stumbles in behind her, tears and confusion on her face.

"Who would do such a thing?" Papa asks.

My eyes look for Riley, and I know he's thinking exactly what I am, the answer obvious.

There are several more flaming bags of shit scattered across the porch. Enough to torch the whole house, if they were left out there too long. With all of us in it.

The sound of fire trucks echoes through the neighborhood.

All the trees are TPed, and there are eggs smashed against the windows and the siding. Firefighters cross the lawn and spill into the house, filling buckets and running the hoses, dousing the flames, one by one.

The fire is almost out by the time the cops arrive. They survey the perimeter as Mum sobs, her body shaking in a way I've never seen before.

"I just don't understand," Papa keeps saying. "I don't understand who would do this."

Riley looks grim as he pulls out his phone. Papa leans forward, his face devastated as he sees the messages filling the screen.

An anonymous poster takes full responsibility for the chaos. Photos and video of the flames and the mess with the caption: *Sluts like Georgie Khalra get just what they deserve—a pile of dogshit.*

Cora:

OMG! Your house!!! What's going on?

Georgie:

Toilet paper and dog shit and everything. They almost set it on fire.

Cora:

I'm so—I'm so sorry.

It's gotten out of control.

Georgie:

They could have killed someone.

I hate them all. They have to pay, Cora. We have to do something.

Cora:

And they deserve to pay.

The plan will work. I've got the party all set up. The video is almost done. Bryn is putting the finishing touches on the one for Chance. Just send us those last photos for the one for Jase.

Georgie:

I've added something else to the plan. Check your email.

Cora:

Okay.

Georgie:

Promise they'll pay.

Cora:

I promise.

THE *MUMBAI MIRROR*

May 7, 2015

Sexual Assault Scandal Rocks Khalra Corp.

Amid reports of a sexual assault scandal that rocked the esteemed Khalra family in Andheri last week, Khalra Corp., the multi-million-dollar cybersecurity company headed by Ranjit and Ravinder Khalra, has announced an expansion into the global market, a move some say will stabilize the company's recent stock offering, which flew into a freefall last week after the controversy broke.

Vivek Khalra, the older scion of the company, who is set to take over as the chief operating officer and inherit millions in two years when he turns 21, was reportedly accused of sexually assaulting a minor in the Khalra household—and the *Mumbai Mirror* has learned that the report was filed by the caretaker of Ravi Khalra's daughter, Jashan, 12, on behalf of the minor. However, since the initial police report was filed, the cases have gone missing, with some Andheri precinct representatives saying there was no case filed at all. Also, the ayah in question, Anushri Devi, has reportedly disappeared. *Mumbai Mirror* reporters reached out to the family for comment but got no response.

In any case, the expansion will mark a major move for the burgeoning tech brand, which till now was based primarily in India, with a focus on markets in East Asia and Russia. The US expansion will include the network on the East Coast, with a flagship branch set to launch in the DC area within the next year, as they've brokered a deal with the US government. No further comment from the Khalra khandan was available at the time this article went to press.

Come One, Come all to the Grandest Ball this Fall

A Masked Marquee Evening Event
Saturday, November 23
10 p.m. sharp
The Davidson Estate
Black-tie costumes
Great Gatsby–themed attire,
and masks required,
the grander the better
RSVP HERE

See You There!

EZ AND GEORGIE
ERE COZYING UP
OLO AT CORA'S
ARTY.

BAEZ AND GEORGIE
DEFINITELY MADE OUT
UPSTAIRS IN CORA'S
BEDROOM.

COMPLETE AND
TOTAL YOU-KNOW-
WHAT AT JASE'S
PARTY.

GEORGIE AND BAEZ
HAVE BEEN FOOLING
AROUND FOR MONTHS
BEHIND CORA'S BACK.

CORA PUT GEORGIE ON
THE CHEERLEADING
TEAM TO KEEP AN
EYE ON HER.

GEORGIE AND JASE
HOOKED UP IN THE
PHOTO BOOTH AT
SCHOOL.

BAEZ AND GEORGIE
HAD SEX AT HIS
BIRTHDAY PARTY.

CORA AND BAEZ
HAD A MASSIVE
FIGHT. IT'S OVER.

GEORGIE IS HOOKING
UP WITH RILEY NOW
TO MAKE BAEZ
JEALOUS.

RA THREW GEORGIE OFF
CHEERLEADING TEAM
AUSE IT WAS CONFIRMED.
ORGIE AND BAEZ TOTALLY
OKED UP BEHIND CORA'S
CK.

CORA'S MOVED ON
QUICK-HOOKING UP WITH
EX-GIRLFRIEND JUJU
OLIVIERI-ORTIZ, CHANCE'S
FAMOUS COUSIN AND OLD
FOXHAM STUDENT.

BAEZ, GEORGIE,
AND JASE HAD A
THREESOME. AND
THERE ARE PHOTOS.

IT WASN'T A
THREESOME. IT
WAS A DIRTY
PHOTO SHOOT.

GEORGIE HAS "CRIED
RAPE" BEFORE. IT'S
WHY SHE LEFT INDIA.

Saturday, November 23

Dear Mum and Papa,

First off, I love you. Even though I might not always do the right thing or say the right thing, I do try. I do want to make you proud.

I'm about to do something that I know I shouldn't do . . . and I don't want you to panic. I want you to trust me.

I have a plan.

Don't believe the phone call. You're not on social media, so you won't even see that.

I'm okay. I'll be back.

Love,
Georgie

CORA

SATURDAY, NOVEMBER 23
9:30 P.M.

BRYN WAS RIGHT ABOUT THROWING A COSTUME PARTY. She's always been good at this kind of thing. Making it a masquerade *Great Gatsby* theme couldn't have been more perfect. Jay Gatsby was a mysterious, wealthy liar, and knew how to throw an extravagant party. Only differences are I'm not a middle-aged white man and this should be called more of a revenge party.

Nobody would even think about missing it.

Nobody wants to *not* be at one of my parties.

Nobody wants to be left out, dismissed.

But by the time I'm done, Chance will regret messing with me. I'm going to take him down, bit by bit. Shatter him. Until there's nothing left.

I walk around my decked-out backyard. The party company has made luxurious tents filled with heat lanterns and small fake fire pits. You'd never know it was a freezing fall night.

There's the sparkling glass chandelier, which makes the lush gold fabric on the cocktail tables shimmer. The elegant tower of crystal flutes, waiting to be filled with chilled champagne. The hot-chocolate bar with all sorts of sweet toppings, plus vanilla vodka, peppermint schnapps, and bourbon for spiking. The lavish spread of desserts—petit fours, macarons, chocolate-covered strawberries, and fondue—all from the best bakery in northeast DC. The white flower-and-feather arrangements bursting from the tops of tall gold vases, with real strings of pearls dangling from the sides.

None of my other parties will ever compare to this. I feel like my momma, enchanting people, making them fall in love with her, and always making sure she threw a party everyone wanted to be invited to. Creating a beautiful trap.

I test each of the hidden cameras, making sure they're all pointed in the right directions, and the microphones work. The dozen cameras capture everything inside and outside of the tents at all angles. I won't want to miss a single thing.

I finish up and press my earpiece. "G, come in, come in."

Georgie's voice answers. "Here."

"How do you feel?" I ask.

"Ready to hurt them all." She's panting. "Are the videos done?"

I wait for her breathing to slow. "Bryn did the one for Chance. The footage from his stolen camera provided the extra shit we needed aside from SykeWard's social media posts. Millie made the one about Jase. Did you watch it?"

"No, I couldn't."

"I understand. Just know, we're going to get him. It's all going to be over tonight. The End."

"Okay," she says a few dozen times, her breath soft and slow, matching mine.

"I promise. Just stick to the plan."

Georgie takes a deep gulp.

"How's the sound on your end?" I put my hand to my ear to turn my microphone down.

"Loud and clear," she replies.

"Are you ready?"

"Yes. Are you okay with what I planned?"

I want to say no, but I don't. We are in too deep. "Of course. Whatever you want to do. I know we can expose Chance and Jase. I know we can get revenge—and justice."

"How's everything looking?" she asks.

I run her through the details—the crystal, the champagne, the lights, the technology, the flow of the night—as I walk back inside and up to my room. Twelve video screens take up an entire wall now, showing all angles of the party. I maxed out the emergency credit card my parents gave me. Daddy's going to be mad. No doubt. But while they've gone to Bermuda to celebrate their anniversary for the rest of the weekend, I'll fix all of this, and I can return it before they even notice. "This is going to work." The confidence surges through me.

"Chance will have to tell everyone the truth. Jase will have to tell everyone the truth. We will force it out," she says.

One of the staff members I've hired for the night peeks her head into the room. "Your guests are starting to arrive. The first car just pulled up."

"Okay, gotta go," I say. "It's going to be fine, right?" I try to swallow down the tiniest quiver of fear.

"More than fine," Georgie says. "It has to be."

I sit in front of my computer before going to do my hair and makeup, and within minutes, the first photos—black-and-white strips of four images—pop up on the screen. There's a photo booth right outside the tent entrance. Everyone who wants to enter the party must use it, take a quick picture identifying themselves and what mask they're wearing.

Entrance fee. Two of the party-staff members are there to make sure that happens. The guests will get a copy of their photo strips as souvenirs, and another copy will download to my computer.

I watch with delight as the pictures start to load, my facial recognition software matching the faces in the photo strips with the portraits in the Foxham Prep directory and yearbook.

I don't laugh as the photos come in rapid succession. Smooches, frowns, even a few naked asses flashing the camera. I guess if I need to recognize anyone by the way they stick out their tongues or asses, I'd be all set. Thankfully, everyone has at least one regular, smiley shot. Everyone is decked out in their fancy costumes. They all took my theme request seriously. No one wants to be turned away from a Cora Davidson event.

The tents fill. I watch my video screens for a few minutes as they look around and take in all the decorations and the music starts.

"You ready to go outside?" the staff person asks.

I jump out of my seat, practically buzzing.

In the hallway, I stop in front of a large mirror and give myself a once-over, making sure I fully fit the part. I barely recognize myself with this retro wig and fringe dress and T-strap heels, but I put on a decadent carnival mask to complete the look.

Millie peeks her head out of her bedroom door. "You ready?"

She's wearing an identical outfit to mine. We are indistinguishable from one another tonight.

"Your headset working?" I ask.

"Yep."

"Then let's do this."

Bryn's waiting for me downstairs. She's got a thumb drive in her hand, and she's wearing a sparkly silver flapper dress and strappy heels she stole from my closet last summer. "It's ready."

"Perfect." I kiss her cheek as she slips on her Venetian mask. "Now, let's get everything started."

She's made this so much easier, and I'm so happy she's back in my life. We're double trouble again.

I sit in front of the cameras.

I watch as Millie goes outside through the side door. She blends in with them as they walk along the path leading to the tents.

The spiked-hot-chocolate bar is swarmed. Others go straight for the champagne.

My phone is glowing with tags. The party's hashtag is steadily growing with photos and videos.

Good.

Millie makes her rounds, playing her part flawlessly, everyone telling her—*me*—how beautiful she looks and how awesome the party is. I catch snippets of conversations and start recording them. I don't want any part of this night missed.

"This is the best party I've ever been to," one girl I don't know says.

"Of course it is," a second girl says as she grabs a macaron. "It makes sense. Cora always throws the best parties."

"And she's got something to prove," a guy adds. "She's probably tired of everyone talking about the whole scandal and thing with Baez."

"If Cora wanted everyone to focus on something other than that, this party was a good idea," another girl adds. "People will be talking about this for months."

Millie smiles. But it's an angry one. Rage churns inside me, and I wish I could push a button and make mud or oil or dog shit fall from the ceiling on top of them.

My hands ball into fists.

Momma always said that anger grows like a weed in the soul. But I don't know how to pluck it out anymore, and now it threatens to stretch throughout my arms and legs and torso, consuming my entire body. Normally, the anger feels good. I've been curling up with it at night since all these rumors started.

It reminds me what I'm here to do tonight.

Chance barrels into the hot-chocolate tent. I know it's him immediately. He's boasting and going around with a fancy new camera, asking questions. I turn up the computer speakers so I can listen in.

One of the party servers opens the curtained-off section. It's got a select group of people. All our old friends. Christine, Ruthie, Ahmad. Jase is even there, hamming it up like nothing is happening right now. There's no pending case being investigated. There's no bad press. There's nothing he did wrong.

I check my phone a thousand times. Waiting for it to hit midnight. The numbers feel like they're changing over more slowly tonight.

Millie's whispered voice echoes in my earpiece, "It's time. Everyone is here."

"Coming," I reply, my heart hammering in my ears.

I race down the stairs and out the back door. I join my sister on a makeshift stage. I take a deep breath and try to keep myself from anxiously shivering. It's just like before a big game. I'm a ball of nerves, ready to perform.

Millie points a remote at a wall. A projector screen drops down.

I take the microphone, and the music turns into a whisper. I greet everyone and get them cheering and excited. They think it's just going to be one of my signature parties. They settle into the fun. "Time for part one of the festivities. A little welcome video." I remove my mask and wink at Bryn right below me. This is it. This is the big show.

Bryn's video plays. It's spliced-together clips of Chance talking about the rumors. Stoking them. Interviewing people under the guise of his documentary. My stomach twists as each minute passes. I try to watch his face, wait for the guilt to turn his white cheeks red.

"What's going on?" Chance yells out. "Who made this?" He climbs onstage and tries to take the projector remote from my hands.

Bryn jumps up and shoves him back. "Got something to hide, Chance? Or should I say SykeWard?"

"You're a fucking liar. *She's* the real SykeWard!" Chance shouts.

My heart jumps as he points at her.

Bryn crosses her arms over her chest and yells, "Just letting everyone know what you did and who you are. That's right, everybody. Chance is the reason for all those nasty rumors. He started them back in October and has been making a mess of people's lives. All so he'd have something to report on in his 'documentary.'"

Chance's face turns bright red. "I didn't do anything. I was asking questions for my documentary. This is all your doing, Bryn."

Bryn starts to laugh. "Clearly, we have the evidence. You've all seen it. Chance Olivieri is the one behind it all."

Everyone glares at him. I wait for him to come clean. My pulse races.

Someone calls him an asshole. Another throws a drink on him. He screams that it wasn't him.

"Why would you do that?" I ask him, anger hardening inside me. "Is this all because of JuJu? I still love her, you know. I didn't mean to hurt her."

"I didn't do this!" he yells. "Bryn's a fucking liar. She's the one who did it. It's based on where her mom is staying in rehab. Skye Ward Ranch. My mom's—"

Bryn's face turns tomato red. Hives spot her neck. She screams louder and louder, as if to drown out his words. My stomach twists. Something feels off. Why would he say this? My eyes volley back and forth between the two of them.

Millie motions at the bouncer I hired for the night. He picks

Chance up like a rag doll and escorts him out. Everyone hoots and hollers. Everyone who secretly hated him now chiming in and piling on.

Bryn crosses her arms over her chest and grins. "Pathetic." She waves at Chance and blows him a kiss as he continues to kick and scream and yell.

"What was that about?" I ask. "Why would he say that about your mom?"

"He's a liar." She takes the microphone. "My mom is at home watching movies with my dad. Chance has no idea what he's talking about."

A drunk Jase starts booing her while everyone else whispers.

Bryn's jaw clenches. "I fucking hate him."

The volume rises as everyone starts chattering, thinking that was our big reveal.

"Wait!" Millie calls out. "We're not quite through. One last video. This one we saved for last."

"Just wait until you see this." I press play, keeping my eyes fixed right on Jase. Ever since Georgie sent me the pictures of her body, the message he left on her back, I've been sick to my stomach. But now the evidence will be sent to the cops. He will pay.

The video starts. Footage from his party. The food spreads. The music. The crowds. He starts hooting and hollering and bragging. My voice-over starts: *"This was the party of the year. . . ."*

Georgie's face fills the screen. She recounts what happened to her. Beat by beat. The pictures from social media fill in one by one over her face. Horrifying images from the night for all to see.

Everyone gasps.

Georgie stands and turns around in front of the camera. The line—*White boys do it better*—scrawled across her brown skin. "This is what Jase did to me."

Phones start pinging. The social media notifications explode, choking my phone.

Everyone freezes.

It's Georgie's social media page: pictures of police cars outside of Georgie's house. A post saying that she ran away. The pictures of her letter.

I watch only one person's face. Jase's. His small eyes go from ecstatic glee to horror. Georgie's social media page has a picture of her back and a post explaining everything that happened, all the lies in a complete list. It ends with this: *I can't do this anymore.*

Everyone turns to look at him.

"You set Baez up," I say. "You put his jersey on her. There's no telling what else you did."

His mouth gapes open. "I don't know what you're talking about."

He snatches off his mask and stares at me from the crowd. Everyone parts, letting him get as close as possible to the stage. "I didn't do shit. They already searched my phone. You need to holler at Baez for that. He's been into that girl forever."

"That's a lie," I shout. "Baez didn't even have his phone that night. I had it. So how was he supposed to take photos?"

He gulps, then starts cursing at everyone. "Just turn the music back on."

"What did you do?" I repeat.

"I didn't do shit."

His words stir into my anger.

I nod at Millie. She plays another clip. This time of an interview between Christine and Chase, but in the background, you can see Jase lead a drunk and wobbly Georgie to the basement and disappear.

The crowd thickens around Jase and he gets agitated. The whole party holds up their phones, videoing him. "She was practically all over me!" he yells. "I just wanted to see what she looked like naked. You all did, too, be real."

The word *monster* flies around like fireworks.

As if on cue, Bryn takes back the mic for one last bombshell. "He SWATted a girl who refused to have sex with him."

Everyone gasps.

Jase turns bright red.

I didn't plan for her to drop this secret, but it works. He flips. She always knows just how to push him there. "Shut the fuck up!" he screams. "You don't know what you're talking about."

"There you have it. And if you don't know what SWATting is . . . it's when someone calls the FBI to your house, telling them that you're gonna blow up something or kill people. He did that. A real prince, Jase. You're a monster *and* a dick," Bryn says, taking over the whole thing. "I hope they charge your eighteen-year-old ass with child pornography, because Georgie is a minor."

The sound of Jase's voice and the police sirens and my anger all mix together, and I feel like I'm going to explode.

Bryn darts offstage, frantic, a response that makes the hair on my arms stand up. Something isn't right. And I need to find out what.

The *Washington Ledger*

Foxham Prep in Hot Water Again As Scandal Rages!

The once-esteemed Foxham Prep is again embroiled in drama as rumors fly about pornographic materials being distributed among the student body. Now eyewitnesses are saying that Jase Cunningham admitted to the crime after damning statements by fellow classmates.

Students allegedly witnessed Cunningham, the son of Congressman Jason Alan Cunningham Senior, accosting the victim of the crime at a party held at his home in celebration of his eighteenth birthday. While we're not allowed to name the students, who are underage, sources say all involved are prominent in the Washington, DC, community.

If prosecuted, Cunningham could face charges related to distributing child pornographic material, given that the alleged victim is underage.

Still, sources say, the victim here is also a young woman of color, which complicates matters further. Will justice reign in this case? More on this developing story as it unfolds.

Cora:

You ok?

Georgie:

Yes.

Cora:

I might've been wrong about SykeWard.

Georgie:

Wait what?

Who is it, then?

Cora:

I'm not sure. But I have a guess. Check your email.

BAEZ AND GEORGIE WERE COZYING UP SOLO AT CORA'S PARTY.

BAEZ AND GEORGIE DEFINITELY MADE OUT UPSTAIRS IN CORA'S BEDROOM.

COMPLETE AND TOTAL YOU-KNOW-WHAT AT JASE'S PARTY.

GEORGIE AND BAEZ HAVE BEEN FOOLING AROUND FOR MONTHS BEHIND CORA'S BACK.

CORA PUT GEORGIE ON THE CHEERLEADING TEAM TO KEEP AN EYE ON HER.

GEORGIE AND JASE HOOKED UP IN THE PHOTO BOOTH AT SCHOOL.

BAEZ AND GEORGIE HAD SEX AT HIS BIRTHDAY PARTY.

CORA AND BAEZ HAD A MASSIVE FIGHT. IT'S OVER.

GEORGIE IS HOOKING UP WITH RILEY NOW TO MAKE BAEZ JEALOUS.

CORA THREW GEORGIE OFF THE CHEERLEADING TEAM BECAUSE IT WAS CONFIRMED. GEORGIE AND BAEZ TOTALLY HOOKED UP BEHIND CORA'S BACK.

CORA'S MOVED ON QUICK-HOOKING UP WITH EX-GIRLFRIEND JUJU OLIVIERI-ORTIZ, CHANCE'S FAMOUS COUSIN AND OLD FOXHAM STUDENT.

BAEZ, GEORGIE, AND JASE HAD A THREESOME. AND THERE ARE PHOTOS.

IT WASN'T A THREESOME. IT WAS A DIRTY PHOTO SHOOT.

GEORGIE HAS "CRIED RAPE" BEFORE. IT'S WHY SHE LEFT INDIA.

GEORGIE RAN AWAY.....

"I'm a student at Foxham Prep and I know where you can find evidence linking Jase Cunningham to those photos of Georgie Khalra. He has two phones—one for friends and the other to buy drugs and keep dirty photos and videos. Be sure to search his room—it's under the third floor tile in the southeast corner."

BRYN

MONDAY, NOVEMBER 25
8:25 A.M.

I STAND IN THE STAGE WINGS WITH CORA BEFORE GOING IN front of the entire school. My perfect speech about Georgie and all that's happened is typed up neatly. I adjust my uniform and take a deep breath as Principal Rollins finishes up his morning announcements and presentation slides.

My hands quiver, the paper rustling in my hands. Georgie still isn't back yet, and she's not answering my texts or emails. The whole school, the whole neighborhood, the whole city is looking for her.

I don't know where she could've gone, what she could be doing right now.

The knot of guilt inside me tangles tighter and tighter by the day. All the horrible things I did piling up. The memory that I saw her at the party right before Jase took all of those horrible photos. I could've stopped it if I had stood up to him. I could've done something.

I feel Cora's stare, her beautiful eyes boring into me.

"They arrested Jase this morning," she says. "They found his other phone. It had everything still on there. Pictures, videos, etc."

"Good," I reply. "He's a monster."

The word feels heavy on my tongue. It was the wrong one to use, because I feel like one, too.

"I hear that Georgie's family is pressing charges. They're just waiting—and *hoping*—she'll come back home."

"I hope so, too." *I need her to come back.* It won't be so bad, and maybe I'll be able to live with myself and all the secrets if she does. I need to see that she's okay.

Cora pulls out her phone to text, and I'm wondering if it's Baez now that they've cleared his name. They'll be back together in no time. "Jase will pay for what he did."

"Chance was suspended this morning. I overheard them in Rollins's office when I went in to drop off stuff for Mrs. Ramirez. They should ship him off to a psych ward."

Cora bristles. "A *psych ward*?!" She looks at me for a second too long.

I catch myself. "Uh . . . I mean, like . . . maybe, like, just like rehab or something." I don't dare turn to glance at her, instead fixate on the principal's slide projection. The word *DEVIANCE* flashes, and he defines it.

I pretend to listen intently. She doesn't know anything. She won't even notice what I said. I repeat the mantra over and over again in my head.

"The entire school needs a reset after what's happened this year," Principal Rollins says. No one dares a word. He paces back and forth in front of the lectern in his green plaid shirt and scuffed-up boots and thick brown leather belt with a coppery buckle that is both ridiculous and amazing. "These rumors lead to destruction. They always do. They destroy friendships, trust, and faith. It is unacceptable. This isn't behavior we tolerate at Foxham. This sort of thing is beneath us. We might've lost a precious member of our school community due to this nonsense."

His blue eyes are muted, his face tight. Like it's hurting him to talk to us. Like he's above this, but he'll put up with us because he has to.

He clicks through one more slide and then invites me onstage.

I don't look back at Cora as I walk forward. I perk up, elongating my neck and holding the paper close. This will be the speech of a lifetime. The speech of my high school career.

I take a deep breath as I face the entire school. I feel a tiny tingle in my fingers, and that small, dangerous itch crops up inside me. The one that causes me to make bad decisions, back again.

I clear my throat, and it echoes. There's a shiver inside me. I get that fuzzy about-to-cry feeling.

Focus, Bryn.

"Good morning, Foxham students. I am your student body president, and I'm here to talk to you this morning about one of our own, Georgie Khalra." I describe all the wonderful things I know about Georgie. I try to talk about her in the present tense—a hope that she didn't do anything reckless. I remind everyone of my anti-bullying campaign and the consequences of it all. "Those rumors were a poison."

That's when it finally hits me, the magnitude of what I've done. Of the sick thing I accomplished. Of how my lie became truth and the spiral of it caused someone wonderful to possibly do something terrible.

"Our school is broken. We are broken." I want to say: *I am broken.* But the words get stuck.

People whisper about what's happened to Georgie. Adding more theories to the ever-growing list of rumors.

She ran away.

She went back to India.

She went into the woods and will never come back.

Tears stream down my cheeks. "Even if we knew the truth of what happened, it doesn't really matter. If it's out there, it's as good as facts, and now there's no stopping it." I recount how it felt after my accident, how much I can relate to her. My tongue feels heavy, as if wrapping what happened to her in what happened to me is somehow wrong. My body wholly rejecting it.

"Liar!" a voice shouts from the back.

Everyone turns to look, all those wooden benches squeaking at the same time.

The teachers gasp.

My heart gets lodged in my throat. Sweat pours down my face. My face is hot, and I can't stop swallowing, like there's something in my throat that just won't go down.

"G-Georgie!" I stutter.

She walks down the long aisle toward the stage. The sounds of her heavy footsteps echo one by one alongside the tinkle of bangles on her wrist. Her hair is big, shining beneath the light. She's not in uniform, instead wearing a beautiful dress.

"You're okay," I say, a surge of relief flooding me.

Tense seconds pass. Everyone looks around at each other before she marches onstage and shoves me away from the lectern. I hit the ground with a thud.

Cora starts to clap, and it sets off a wave throughout the room.

Georgie's face remains tight, zero smile. No warmth. She takes the microphone, glaring at me. "Bryn is the one who started all these rumors. She wanted to pull the attention away from what she did this summer. She set me up. All the things everyone said about me led to people treating me differently. Like I wasn't a *real* person. Like I didn't matter." She takes a deep breath. "Then Jase did the same."

I stare at the floor. The words hit me, one by one. The truth. The things my mom told me to fix. My heart thuds so loud I can't even hear my own thoughts, let alone the rest of her words. Maybe my own body is protecting me from coming face-to-face with what I did. I swear my heart might give out.

Cora shakes her head at me. The room bursts into chatter. Teachers try to get everyone to hush, and many flash disappointed frowns in my direction.

"Rumors have consequences!" Georgie yells before turning to me. Her eyes cold, her mouth a severe line, her cheeks reddened with anger. "And some of us have yet to pay."

GEORGIE

MONDAY, NOVEMBER 25
10:25 A.M.

THE EXHAUSTION—SADNESS?—ON DR. DIVYA'S FACE mirrors my own. We've been sitting in her office for the past forty minutes, mostly in silence, and she's doing that thing again, tapping her pen, drumming her fingers—her nails a light teal this time. The nervous energy creates a pattern that reminds me of some old Bollywood song, but I can't remember it.

I lean back onto the pretty cushioned couch and sigh. So much has happened since the last time I was here.

"So about running away," she starts for the fourth time. She can't wrap her head around it. "How do you feel about that?"

"I didn't actually do it. I was safe. We just—we needed people to believe that it happened. I would never run away for real." Even if I have to live through this. "I want to be right here."

"Do you understand the impact of what you did?" She leans forward and sighs. "That it caused those who love you immense pain and trauma?"

I look at my hands. She doesn't get it. Maybe it is deeply fucked up, in a way. But this whole situation has been, well, deeply fucked-up. And I'm still standing. I made it through. It has to get better now. #EternalOptimist. Or whatever.

Her eyes are full of concern. "It costs money for the police to look for you. There were Amber Alerts. The whole community was shocked."

"I know, I know. I'm so sorry. We had to find out who started the rumors and I had to expose Jase."

"But you did all this because of gossip . . . rumors."

"Yes, but—"

"There's what you do and what you don't do. You made a choice with catastrophic impact on people who care about you. You must've been navigating a lot in order for you to believe that lying and running away were the best options." She shakes her head. "Do you understand?"

"Do *you* understand?" My cheeks flush. "Do you know what it's like to be lied about? For people to think you're something you're not?"

"You told me you allowed it, though."

"Only for a little bit . . . and I was wrong. I should've never done any of this. I just didn't know how to fix it." The words sputter out of me, and I'm left breathless.

"You have a lot of healing ahead of you. You must've been scared and conflicted and angry."

I nod. A lot of baggage. To carry. Or shed.

"It's not deadweight you're still carrying around with you," she says, reading my mind, scribbling something down on her notepad. It has her name and address printed across the top, all official, and I know every word I say will go into my file, living on forever. "Not dead if it still bleeds when you poke at it." She scribbles down something else. "I know it's a lot." She pushes something across the table. "I understand it may be difficult to talk to me. This may be helpful to just put your thoughts into so they aren't lingering in your head. Sometimes, when we make our thoughts tangible, they don't pile up in our minds, and they're easier to process. Just a place to put your thoughts. To unravel what's happening in your head."

It's a notebook. Not a food journal or calorie counter, not a planner or record.

I nod.

"Whatever works for you. And I'll be here when you want to—when you're ready to talk more about it. But before we end this session, I do want to explain to you one more time why I think pretending to have run away—letting your parents, your friends, your neighbors, your classmates—believe you might've left was a very bad idea. You've been hurt. We need to focus on that." She takes a deep breath. "We may have to look at other solutions; talk therapy simply will not be enough. There are some medications we can explore, or in-patient options. But this is a very serious cry for help, Georgie. I'm worried about you. So are your parents. Your friends. Riley."

My stomach squeezes. I've been waiting to feel bad about working with Cora to expose Chance and Jase—and as it turned out Bryn—and waiting for the guilt of making the whole school believe that I ran away, waiting for the sadness to fill me up. I mean, I lost one of the only friends I had. But I keep thinking about how she wasn't really my friend at all. So it hasn't come yet. I don't know if it will. Which is a relief, because guilt is too heavy, too exhausting.

"I promise you, I didn't mean for it— I—" How do I explain? "We had to figure it out. We thought we had it, logical deductions, like math and magic. Millie helped. Cora's sister. But we were wrong. And then it worked anyway. I mean, it's possibly the *only* thing that worked."

She looks skeptical. "Your 'fake' runaway attempt?"

"I hid out in my neighbor's tree house. The one to the left. Bryn lives to the right." Even saying her name burns. "Yes. And it was fake. I planned the whole thing. Cora didn't even want to go along, but I made her. It was what I needed to get Jase to confess, to have something that would be bigger than his dad's money."

The rage still simmers inside me, and sometimes I feel like it'll seep out of my skin and it'll be hot to the touch. "Please believe me when I say I want to be here. Yes, I've been through a lot. And there's no way in hell I deserved it. I'll never say it was worth it or any of that 'made me stronger' bullshit. Because it broke me. All of it. But I want to live, to survive. I don't want to be a victim, okay?"

She nods, only half believing me, I think.

But I know my words are true. I let a size and a scale and a society tell me who I was for too long. I let my body be an object to be weighed and assessed, measured and controlled, by everyone and anyone besides me. I let my mind go right along with it. I'd like to believe I'm done with that. But I know I'll have to remind myself again on occasion. "I was wrong to do it. I feel shitty about it now."

"So what do you want to do, then?" she says. She's said this about five times this afternoon, as if I'll be able to somehow unravel the path my future takes within our one-hour session.

"I'll finish the semester remotely and fill out my college applications," I say. "And then I guess I'll have to figure out where I end up. And break the news to Vibha—and my parents—that it won't be Harvard or Yale." Maybe NYU, like Riley. Or maybe somewhere in California. A fresh start, no expectations.

"Georgie, that's great," she says. "I know you think you have to follow the plan, what they and others laid out for you. But even if this is the last time we talk"—she looks sad, like she knows it might be—"I want you to remember my words. You are good and strong and capable. You've always been good and strong and capable. You are your own person, and you get to make your own choices. About your body, about your mind, about your path. And if you need help, there is help."

I'm staring at my hands, afraid to ask, afraid of what the answer will be. "Even if I want to press charges?"

"Yes," she says. "You can. I'll help you if you need it. But you should talk to them, your parents. Tell them what *you* want. They need to start hearing it."

Riley's waiting for me outside the office, his headphones on, his sketchpad open. He's been working on portfolio pieces, and watching them unfold like magic makes me miss painting—the smell of the turpentine, the way the colors whirl and blend. I haven't picked up a brush in months. Maybe I'll take a class at the university, since I'll be homeschooling.

"How'd it go?" he asks, a little nervous as he takes my hand and plants a kiss on my head. Sometimes it's fine, sometimes it's great, sometimes I still pull away. He seems okay with it, though.

"I think I made a decision," I say, testing it out, trying to be firm. Not quite right. "I've made a decision."

He smiles down at me as we step into the elevator. "What's that?"

"I want to press charges," I say, wanting to suck the words back in as soon as they're out. But I need to let them breathe, to exist, to get stronger. "I'm going to press charges against Jase for taking those pictures of me."

He nods. "Okay. Then that's what you'll do."

My parents are downstairs in the parking lot, both of them leaning on Papa's car. The tensions between them have been worse lately, and if I'm the glue, well, then they're definitely going to unstick soon. Which might be better, healthier, for all of us.

"Good appointment?" Papa says, smiling as we walk over.

"Do you think—" Mum's face is lined with worry. "Perhaps that center in Massachusetts—did the doctor mention it?"

"I don't need another camp or center, Mum," I say, too harsh, but like Dr. Divya said, they need to start hearing me. "But I did tell her about my decision."

Mum looks wary, but Papa just looks curious. "What decision?" he asks.

"I want to press charges. Against Jase Cunningham. I want him to actually suffer consequences for his actions." Or at least think twice before he does it again. Riley flashes me an encouraging smile.

"He's a congressman's son. He'll humiliate you. It'll be all over the press. It's not worth it. He's not going to be punished anyway." Mum has a million reasons why it'll never work. "The whole family will suffer because of your—"

I don't care. "I'm doing it, Mum," I say. I've made up my mind. "With or without your support." She's glaring, waiting for my father to intervene, to throw down the final word and seal their united front.

But Papa steps between us and takes my hand. "I'll go with you, beta. I know it'll be a lot. But you need to make your voice heard. So I'll help however I can."

Mum doesn't say a word, just slips into the car, closing the door behind her. I can see her shoulders shaking through the window. She tries to wipe away the tears so we can't see them.

"Thank you, Papa." I stand straighter, swallowing the sob that's trying to claw up my throat. I need to learn how to be stoic. To stand up for myself.

"Well, let me go deal with your mum, then," he says with a deep sigh. "I'll call the lawyer and get started on paperwork. We have a long road ahead of us." Papa gives me a hug, strong and bearlike, and I can smell the sweetness of rose paan on his breath. "But take it easy today, beta. I think Riley said something about ice cream and stream something?"

"Movies and chill," Riley says, grinning. He turns to me, his eyes full of mischief. "You down?"

I nod, then punch his arm as we walk away, laughing. "Thank god Papa doesn't actually know what that means."

Georgie Khalra's Transcribed Statement

"It was just supposed to be a fun night. Jase Cunningham's birthday. At his house. My parents didn't know. My parents didn't know a lot of things. They thought I was next door at Bryn's, having a slumber party. She'd been over a few days earlier, they were happy that we were getting friendly.

I got there with my friend Monica, and I was waiting for Riley—Wong, my boyfriend. We've been, I don't know, dating a few weeks. No, my parents didn't know. They wouldn't approve. Yeah, they know now. They know everything. Mostly. Yeah, we were there, Monica and I, like ten thirty.

Bryn? Bryn Colburn, my neighbor. She wasn't invited to the party but I saw her there. She and Jase have some rough history. He's her ex-boyfriend. They don't get along.

I changed and Monica picked me up. When we got to the house, the party was already packed. A lot of the kids from Foxham. The cheerleaders, like Cora Davidson; Sasha, who's Jase's girlfriend; Christine Vaccaro; and Ruthie Alvarez. I remember seeing them with spiked punch. I didn't drink, no. I mean, I've had drinks before. But it didn't—it didn't go well, so no. I didn't drink at all that night. I was wary of what might end up in my cup. I was hanging out with Monica—she's also a cheerleader. We both had brownies, and I thought they tasted funny. I had at least five. Then Riley got there, finally, and he had a few, too. He said they were pot brownies. Which I didn't realize until I had too many. I was fine at first. Then we were dancing, Riley and I, and

I remember kissing him. Riley. Yes, I wanted to kiss him. He's my boyfriend. No. No, we didn't have sex.

I remember the lights made his teeth all pink. It was the black light, and our teeth were pink. Yeah, I was definitely high. I've never been high before. I don't think I'd try it again.

And then the brownies really kicked in, I guess, and I felt really woozy, so I sat on the couch. And he stepped away, like, for a minute, to get me some water. I saw Bryn in the crowd and remember her fighting with Jase, but then she ran off.

Then Jase kept talking, and I don't really remember what he said, but I was nervous. He's— I—I don't know how to explain it. He said sexual things, yes, in the past. And he kissed me once when I don't think I wanted him to? I don't think I—no, I didn't lead him on. Why would I? No, I was pretty clear I didn't. We were at school. In the photo booth. He cornered me. I literally said no. He didn't care. He took the pictures and posted them online. I asked him not to. To kiss me, or to do anything with the photo. At first I liked the attention. But he was kind of gross. Too touchy-feely, like leering. Made me feel weird. But he said those words. 'White boys do it better.' A few times. Because I told him I wasn't into white boys. Kind of to push his buttons. Yes. But also to make it clear I didn't like him. And he was Bryn's ex. I would never.

Baez? I don't really remember seeing him at all. Yes, there were rumors about us earlier. Yes, he said they were true. But they're not. It was all—it was all part of Cora's plan. To expose everything. To figure out who started the rumors. I don't know.

I guess he did implicate himself. But I don't remember seeing him. I remember Cora worrying about him. He was sick. In the bathroom throwing up because of the beer. No, I never kissed him. I never did anything. I never had sex with him, no. I told you. I don't even think I saw him that night. I just—I don't know where the jersey came from. I just remember Jase taking my hand, leading me through the house. I don't remember how I got to the basement.

I woke up with barely any clothes on, just Baez's jersey. Riley was asking me a million questions and then the cops came. He called them. Riley did.

I didn't know about the writing on my back until Nita Masi—my housekeeper—she found it. On my back.

Yes. I want to press charges. I told you, I don't remember seeing Baez there at all."

CORA

MONDAY, DECEMBER 2
3:45 P.M.

I RIDE IN THE CAR WITH DADDY, HIS EYES SULLEN AND FILLED with disappointment. There's more white and gray in his hair, and the lines near his eyes have deepened into the rich brown. There's no music, barely any conversation, and he hardly looks at me. Since everything happened and the school suspension began, neither of my parents have said much of anything to me.

He pulls into the circle in front of the school. Once he puts the car in park, he releases a deep sigh. "You need to go in there and get your things. In and out. You hear me?"

"Yes, sir," I reply. Since everything came out, I've been grounded. No cell phone. No car. No hanging out. Nothing. "I am sorry," I whisper.

"Are you?" His voice is ice. "You've been repeating that phrase over and over again, but I don't think you actually know the meaning."

A hot wave of shame hits me. I stare down at my uniform skirt. I hate letting him down. The way his voice drops low with upset. "I didn't know what to do."

"Did I teach you to make a mess?"

"No, sir."

"Did I teach you to play with people?

"Did I raise you to be a fool?

"Are you a god—manipulating very serious events?"

"No, sir." Tears well up in my eyes, and I can't stop them from falling.

"Then why didn't you act like the daughter I raised? The brilliant and kind one I love so much?" He shakes his head. "Why didn't you come to me?"

I stutter out an excuse, but it ends in tears.

"Baez could've faced serious consequences for the lie you made him tell. He was never with that young lady. Yet you pushed him to lie about it, and for what? A big game? Georgie made the whole community believe she'd run away. Disappeared. Maybe never to be heard from again. Do you know how serious that is? How her parents must have felt?"

I nod.

"You don't. Because if you did, you wouldn't have been part of something so *foolish*." He hits the steering wheel with his hand. "You don't know how afraid parents are. The idea of something happening to our most precious. You have no idea. If you did, you wouldn't have been so cavalier. So reckless."

"I wasn't thinking." I wipe my tears away. "I thought I could fix it."

"You can't control people, baby." He puts a hand on my shoulder, then lifts my chin. "You can only make sure you do the right thing in all cases . . . and this wasn't it."

"I know . . . I know now." I think about Baez and all he's gone through because I told him to tell the lie. Him at the police station being interrogated for hours. The bad press swarming his parents—and his mom's restaurant. All the hate online. The terrible comments. How you can't search his name—or Georgie's—and not find something racist and disgusting about them. How the news traveled back to Lagos, and the Nigerian newspapers reported about his family. How the Indian news outlets are depicting him. Calling him all kinds of names despite Jase getting arrested and charged.

I set off a fucked-up bomb.

"What can I do?"

He leans forward and kisses my forehead. The scent of his cologne slows my heart. "Clean this up with grace. The kind only you have."

I nod. "I will."

"I'll be waiting here."

I get out of the car and head for the school entrance. I probably should reapply my makeup before going inside to get books from my locker, because I feel like I look like shit.

"Are you okay?" Adele waits for me in the foyer. Her eyes comb over me, soaking in probably the circles ringing my eyes, and the puffiness of my cheeks. I haven't slept, and I know she can see all of it.

"I've been better," I reply.

She touches my arm.

"I still can't believe it."

"Neither can I."

Other students watch as we walk through the hall. It's only been a few days, and the energy is tense, like even the walls know what happened. There are whispers and stares and half smiles full of pity. Everyone knows what happened to me, to Baez, to Jase, to Georgie. Everyone knows that all involved have been suspended during the investigation.

And that Bryn started it all.

They know every sordid detail. There are videos. There are photos. There are comments. There are articles. Even an entire website has sprung up with a full timeline of everything that has happened and all the screenshots.

I can't even think of Bryn without bursting with rage. Her going to boarding school in New England doesn't seem like enough. Georgie's family suing them doesn't seem like enough. Everyone dragging her on social media doesn't seem like enough.

I'll never *not* be mad at her.

I'll never *not* want to hurt her as much as she hurt me.

I'll never *ever* speak to her again.

Adele and I walk to my locker. It's covered with notes and flowers. A shrine to me. Like I'm dead and people are remembering me. Like they're trying to erase all the things they said online. Like they're trying to take it all back.

I close my eyes. The party crashes into my mind. I might never be able to forget it.

I can see the look on everyone's faces.

I can hear the whispers and the shock.

I can feel the words Bryn shouted as if they were tiny ripples of an earthquake.

I feel the betrayal as if it's a hot poker skating across my skin.

"Have you spoken to Baez?" Adele asks.

"Not yet. A little texting when I could sneak my phone out of my mom's office. I tried, but his parents . . ." My voice breaks. The memory of Baez's mother's grimace when I showed up at their house fills my mind.

Tears brim in Adele's eyes, and she squeezes my hand. "It was just . . . so . . . I can't believe it." She wraps her arms around my neck and sobs. "The Georgie thing scared me. I know she didn't actually run away, but the thought of it shook me up."

"My dad grounded me for the rest of the year. He made me write essays about playing with people's lives," I say, and I can't even be upset about it. Georgie and I took the wildest risks. Each day I go to bed and think it was all a dream. My life is back to normal: Baez and I are still together, the rumor never happened, and things are the same. But then I wake up every day and the memories rush back in.

We stand in the foyer as other students move around us.

"I can't believe this all happened," I say.

Adele nods. "Over a lie."

"How can a lie be that big?"

Adele squeezes my hand. "The articles are still bad."

"They're not just bad. They're racist," I add.

"Yeah, of course. That's what I meant." Her cheeks go pink. "I'm just hoping they go away now that Jase has been arrested. I'm so glad Ahmad finally admitted what he saw. And fessed up about all the boys who took those photos. I also saw Graham's news interview."

"They better. I won't stop until they do—"

A series of gasps clip my words.

I pivot and spot Georgie.

She's wearing skinny jeans, an off-the-shoulder sweater, and a pair of flats. She's twisted her hair up into a high bun. She looks good. Beautiful, and like herself. Her old self.

The crowd parts as she walks through.

She goes to her locker without looking around. Her eyes straight ahead. She takes all the things out, packing them into a duffel bag. Monica approaches and kneels down to help her.

I take a deep breath. My heart flutters like it has magically grown tiny wings and might take off right out of my chest. I stretch out my neck and pull my shoulders back as if I'm about to step out on a runway. One with a thousand eyes on me. A buzzy feeling slides across my skin.

She really came through for me, and she's taking even more heat for it all.

I walk over to her. "You okay?"

She looks up.

I drop down beside her and help her pack her things. "I'm sorry."

"I'm sorry, too."

We finish filling her bag.

"Is Baez okay?" she asks.

"He will be," I say, and hope my own words sink in. "But what about you? What's happening?"

"Online school or maybe boarding school," she says.

"Oh" is all I can manage to reply. I take a deep breath, grab her hand. "But you'll be okay. We both will."

Her eyes meet mine, and she nods.

Together, we walk out, and I watch her get into the car with her mother, driving away. Not happy yet, maybe. But getting there.

---Original Message----
From: Baez Onyekachi
Attn: Cora Davidson
Sent: Sunday, December 8, 7:29 AM
Subject: I miss you!

I miss you. I got your email confirmation. I'll pick you up once you land in Lagos next week. Can't wait to see you.

Love, Baez

The *Washington Post*

NOVEMBER

Nearly a year after Jason "Jasc" Cunningham, son of South Carolina Congressman Jason Cunningham, was prosecuted for taking and distributing lewd photographs of a minor and fellow Foxham Prep student Jashan "Georgie" Khalra, the case is finally set to go in front of a judge. And not everyone on the Hill is pleased to hear it.

"You're ruining a stellar career, a real chance at something," says one courtside protestor, who refused to identify herself. "A congressman's son. He was going to make such a difference in the world. Creating change."

Cunningham Junior faces charges of the creation and intent to distribute child pornography, facing anywhere from several months to five years in prison if convicted, though a spokesperson for his law firm, Anderson, Dave, and Combs, says that with a plea deal for good behavior and no previous record, Cunningham could get off with a fine and community service. "He's obviously not guilty," said rep Dudley Combs, "but a plea means wrapping this up quickly. It's dragged on far too long already."

Cunningham's accuser, Jashan "Georgie" Khalra, an heiress to the famed Indian cybersecurity firm Khalra Corp, left Foxham after the incident, moving back to her native Delhi, India, with her family, and completing her high school career at the renowned Estate School in Geneva. She's now a college freshman in New York City, studying fine art and design. She could not be reached for comment on the case.

But a lawyer for the Khalra family did note specifically that no charges were pressed or expected against fellow Foxham student Abaeze Onyekachi, son of a famed Nigerian diplomatic and restaurateur family. He was cleared of all wrongdoing. Still, Baez, as his fellow students called him, returned to Nigeria to finish high school and presumably college. A representative for the family claimed no comment.

Bryn Colburn, former girlfriend of Cunningham, was sent to boarding school in Massachusetts for the final months of her senior year. She has not been seen or heard from after her father also resigned to focus on the family.

Coraline Davidson, the class's former cheer captain and daughter of White House senior counsel Edward Davidson, graduated at the top of her class and now attends Georgetown University, studying marketing and management. She and twin sister, Millicent, a sophomore at Harvard, are staples among the DC socialite and charity set alongside their mother, Norah Davidson.

Lists According to Georgie Khalra

Top Reasons Why People Believe Rumors in High School

1. People are dumb.

2. Rumors answer questions people want answered.

3. Too many sides to the same story.

4. Rumors give information even when false.

5. People are gullible. And they crave DRAMA.

6. The more you hear them, the easier they are to believe. And we talk a lot in high school.

7. They're usually only one or two steps away from the truth.

8. Fear makes the rumor better and more possible.

9. If you try to disprove them, it makes it worse.

10. It's easy to believe bad things about people you hate or envy.

ACKNOWLEDGMENTS

THIS BOOK TOOK A LOT OUT OF US, AND EVERY MEMBER OF our fabulous team deserves a shout-out for helping to get us to the finish line. It's been a long, strange trip, so we'll keep the thank-yous short and sweet.

To our families and friends, for all their love and support along the way, for being in our corner on every step of this journey.

To our fearless agent partners in crime: the powerhouse team at New Leaf Literary, especially Joanna Volpe, Meredith Barnes, and Kate Sullivan.

To Mary Pender at UTA, we're forever grateful for your insights and ambition on our behalf.

To Clay Morrell and the CAKE Team, you are the absolute best. You find every typo and make sure all cylinders are firing.

Thank you to our Hyperion family: our editors, publicist, the library and marketing teams, and all the people behind the scenes who make this magic happen.

And we can't forget the lovely early readers who helped us vet the manuscript through edits. Thank you so much for giving us your time to make sure we got things right.

And finally, last but certainly not least, our readers, who stuck around despite the cliffhangers and the antics. Thank you so much for reading and riding with us.

AUTHORS' NOTE

WHEN WE WERE IN HIGH SCHOOL, THE THINGS PEOPLE SAID about us felt enormous. Whispers. Passed notes. Cafeteria politics. Weekend party invites. Or dis-invites. The anxiety and heartache feel as fresh as yesterday.

But both of us went to high school before the birth of social media. The drama never managed to follow us home. (And if it did, our parents didn't allow landline phone calls after dinner!) Now the things people say about you can stalk you everywhere, online and IRL. Your smartphone is a permanent line to social media. And the trauma of it can be absolutely devastating.

This book is about the power of words and how the things you say can have *real* consequences in people's lives. It's about how lies can become truth to many if repeated enough times by the right people.

It's about the lies we sometimes start to believe about ourselves.

If you ever feel like you are in a situation like Georgie, Cora, or Bryn—where rumors and bullying are spiraling out of control; where you're being used, threatened, or sexually coerced; or where you simply feel uncomfortable about what's happening to you, please seek help right away. Tell your parents, a friend, a trusted teacher, or a relative. Reach out, get help, and trust that you will be okay. Don't wait until it's too late.

RESOURCES

National Sexual Violence Resource Center
www.nsvrc.org

RAINN
www.rainn.org
RAINN's National Sexual Assault Hotline:
1-800-656-HOPE (4673)
or hotline.rainn.org/online

The Body Is Not an Apology
www.thebodyisnotanapology.com